TALES FROM THE SILENCE

TALES FROM THE SILENCE

James Bow
Phoebe Barton
Kate Blair
Cameron Dixon
Mark Richard Francis
Joanna Karaplis

ENDLESS SKY
BOOKS

Kari Maaren
Fiona Moore
Ira Nayman
Kate Orman
Jeff Szpirglas

EDITED BY JAMES BOW

TALES FROM THE SILENCE

Published by
Endless Sky Books
Regina, Saskatchewan, Canada
endless-sky-books.com

Copyright © 2024 by James Bow
All rights reserved

All characters and events in this book are fictitious.
Any resemblance to persons living or dead is coincidental.

Print ISBN: 978-1-998273-22-5
Ebook ISBN: 978-1-998273-23-2

Cover design by Bibliofic Designs
biblioficdesigns.com

COPYRIGHTS

For my mother-in-law, Rosemarie, a tireless champion.

CONTENTS

FOREWORD
VOICES FROM THE SILENCE

Welcome to my sandbox. Do you want to play?

It's an exciting and scary thing to set up an anthology from scratch. You have to gather your authors, build interest in the project, and then corral everyone to deadlines and edits. It's a step into the unknown, with a hefty risk of rejection, and that's before you reach out to readers to read and review what you and your authors put together.

When you ask people to participate under the umbrella of a fictional universe you've created, that amplifies all of these worries. Will your colleagues consent to channel their creative energies under your additional restrictions? Will the different styles fit with your vision of your universe? Will continuity clashes happen? Can you make yourself step back enough from your vision to allow your authors to add their own unique takes? Are you willing to possibly lose control of the universe you've created?

For *Tales from the Silence*, the answer to that question was "yes."

Because it's an honour and a privilege to have authors you respect and admire take a crack at building a story of theirs in the universe you've created. Not only is it affirming to have your fellow authors admire a toy that you've started to play with, it is even more affirming to have them like your toy enough to try to play with it, too.

I did similar things back in high school and university when I created and edited fan fiction magazines set within the *Doctor Who* universe, including a series where each story built off the continuity of the previous one. In my ignorance of youth, I had no problem launching myself into this endeavour. Now, as then, I'm also blessed with people eager to be creative, who signed on enthusiastically and enjoyed playing by the rules we set. I've seen a lot in my fan and writing career, but I've always been fortunate to find people who are kind, enthusiastic, creative, and fun, and this anthology has been no different.

Here, I've gathered people I've worked with from my early days of active fandom, as well as generous people I respect within the Canadian SF community and friends and colleagues from within the Canadian young adult literary scene. I asked many if they'd be interested in participating in this project, and all were generous and supportive, whether or not they said yes.

The challenge of integrating these diverse visions into your universe is itself rewarding; the fact that elements may materialize in your universe beyond your control provides a *frisson* of risk. I've already had to work in new details uncovered by authors here in my next book, *The Cloud Riders*, set on Venus and Mars (thanks especially to Mark for his Martian Muskholes and to Phoebe for putting asteroid scows into high orbit around Venus). Believe it or not, I feel this makes my universe feel more real because the real universe is not created by your senses alone; you interact with those you share your universe with. I'm grateful to my fellow authors for consenting to play, making the universe of the Silent Earth feel more real.

So, thanks to Phoebe Barton, Kate Blair, Cameron Dixon, Mark Richard Francis, Joanna Karaplis, Kari Maaren, Ira

Nayman, Kate Orman, and Jeff Szpirglas for stepping into the sandbox and building their castles. Thanks to Julie Czerneda, J.M. Frey, Ben Ghan, Adrienne Kress, Ishta Mercurio, Sarah Raughley, and Arthur Slade for their support and advice. Thanks to Alisha at Bibliofic Designs for stunning covers for *The Sun Runners* and *Tales From the Silence* and, finally, thanks to Edward Willett for turning these stories into a book put out by Endless Sky Books.

The origins of the Silent Earth universe date back to late 2014, one character, an exploration of her world, and my unwillingness to stop. In late 2014, the first ideas materialized around the story that would become *The Sun Runners*, featuring an injured young queen named Frieda living on Mercury. The question of Earth, its re-emergence from the Silence, how it fell into the Silence in the first place, and how other colonies coped with the loss all came later as I kept on exploring Frieda's universe, expanding across the rest of the inhabited solar system, including Venus and Mars (see *The Cloud Riders*, coming soon). My curiosity just kept pushing back the boundaries and the decades.

And as the sandbox grew, I knew I wouldn't be able to build my castles over more than a fraction of it. In October 2019, while writing *The Cloud Riders* and revising *The Sun Runners*, I attended Ottawa's CanCon. I had a great conversation with Ira Nayman, then editor of *Amazing Stories*, and I asked for his advice about creating a shared universe. While there was little concrete advice he could give me, he told me to make it fun, be patient, and be prepared to accept rejection but to just go for it. You don't know what you can do unless you try. So, I'm grateful for my fellow authors agreeing to come forward, and I sincerely hope it has been fun. Ira also gave me good advice about paying my authors, which I happily did because our time is valuable, and our work deserves to be recognized with more than just exposure.

So, now I pass this anthology on to you, the reader, taking on all the risks associated with sending my babies into the world, along with the babies of other authors. To you, dear reader, please enjoy this journey into the universe of the Silent Earth, where the isolated colonies of the inner solar system adapt to new realities and fight for an uncertain future while the survivors of Earth do the same. Watch as these people operate independently but in tandem, encountering the same tragedies, occasionally the same joys, fighting the same battles, and making the same mistakes.

That's the way things are in our reality, after all. Thanks again to the authors of this anthology for making this universe all the more real.

—James Bow

THE PHASES OF JUPITER
BY JAMES BOW

Ganymede Landing, August 3, 2151
Borehole length: 118.94 km; 31.15 km to breakthrough

"So, HOW SHOULD WE COMMUNICATE WITH OUR NEW LIFEFORM?"

I glare at Kevin. "Are you still going on about those hydrocarbon traces?"

A sudden crack and tinkle, like distant glass breaking. I grab my chair. Ice quake. Small at first, but they're all small at first. My spoon rattles against my mug.

But there are no klaxons. No roar of a breach. The shaking slows. I let out the breath I was holding.

Ganymede sucks.

Kevin pats my arm. "See, Sylvan? Nothing to worry about."

I press my fingers against the headache behind my eyes. It makes my ocular implant flash, which doesn't help. I shove myself to my feet. "Come on. I need to grab some notes for tomorrow's presentation."

Kevin hops up and follows me, bright as Jupiter in full. He grabs the guiding rail on the way out the cafeteria door. Behind us, Dimitri and Karenna argue. Samuel laughs. Amara stares at them all, calmly drinking her water. The rest of the twenty post-grads are in their beds, where I'd be if I could sleep. Kevin and I drift into the hallway, leaving behind the smells of microwaved pizza, our footfalls hitting seven times slower than they should—than they would on Earth.

"If you want, I could draw up a section about communication protocols for newly discovered alien species," says Kevin.

I flinch. "Kevin! Hydrocarbons alone are not a sign of life!"

"Well, what could make them, if not life?"

"What—" I round on Kevin—a mistake in microgravity.

Ganymede really sucks. Microgravity sucks. The antiseptic smell of our ice-cut corridors sucks. Having nothing to see outside most windows sucks. Living next to hard vacuum sucks, though so far, not literally.

I flail and grasp the guide rail. "Are you winding me up?"

Kevin chuckles. "A little. I was looking for you to start ranting about phosphine on Venus or methane on Mars."

I roll my eyes as I face forward. Step and drift . . . step and drift . . . "Well, stop it."

"Just taking your mind off the jet lag." Kevin steps and drifts beside me. "At least you're not throwing up anymore."

I've fought my whole life to get into space. I'm a top doctoral student in exobiology. Space is my thing! So, it's a shock that it's so awful—and I'm so awful at it.

More softly, Kevin says, "Don't sweat it. Everyone makes this adjustment. You'll do—"

"Stop telling me I'll do fine!" I pull to a stop and pinch the bridge of my nose. "Sorry."

"It's okay." He touches my shoulder again. "You're doing more than fine. You've found something remarkable from Ganymede's ocean and beat Europa's scientists in finding it."

I smile at that and at Kevin's faith. "Thanks." I take a step.

"I think we should bombard it with primes."

"You, what—" My hand misses the guide rail, and I

scramble to brace myself before I hit the ceiling, hard. Kevin catches me, grunting with the effort because weight and momentum are two different things. "Kevin, what the hell?"

"Well . . ." He holds me steady as I grip the guide rail again. "Since the alien isn't going to understand Earthly languages, a mathematical sequence of two, three, five, seven, and eleven would show them we're intelligent."

"Kevin, that's the silliest thing I've ever heard!"

"Aw!"

"I'd do the Fibonacci sequence. Asking an alien to add two numbers together, then add the larger number to the result, is easier than having them figure out if a number is divisible only by itself and one."

"So, you *have* thought about ways to communicate with it!"

"I have not!"

"Hey." He points. "Check that out."

We're passing a window. The view here is different. It pulls me to a stop.

Out here, our sun is little more than a bright star in the sky, rising and setting every three-and-a-half Earth days. Beside it, Jupiter hangs in the sky like Earth's moon does, but twice as large. It stays where it is because Ganymede is tidally locked, going through its phases over seven Earth days. The line of light has widened to the point where the remains of the Great Red Spot are visible. There are silhouettes and crescents of Jupiter's other moons, shifting in a dance I haven't learned the steps to.

"You've got to admit," says Kevin. "For all its faults, Ganymede does have benefits." He squeezes my shoulder.

Kevin . . . doesn't suck. I touch his hand, then turn. "Come on."

GANYMEDE LANDING IS LAID out in long modules, assembled in Earth's orbit and shipped to this moon years ago. Hallways partly cut into the ice connect each module: cafeteria, living quarters, laboratory, and derrick room. I suspect NASA-X's designers wanted to burrow our base all the way into Ganymede's ice, but our funder, Mx. Gildman, would have none of that. He'd paid for the transparent aluminum windows to shield us from the radiation, so why deny us the view?

I had mixed feelings about that. It's hard to choose between cabin fever and the radioactive abyss.

We pass the hallway leading to our quarters, turn down the hallway to the laboratory module, and pass the ramp leading down to the reinforced bulkheads of the derrick room. We enter the laboratory's control room. Information streams on the consoles, highlighting the progress of the drill head: *Borehole length: 119.25 km; 30.84 km to breakthrough.*

A window looking into the derrick room dominates one wall, heavily reinforced should Ganymede's ocean release suddenly and at a higher pressure than expected. This window looks down on the crown block, two storeys below—a large concrete box in the middle of a room that's mostly empty, save for more consoles.

The floor shudders. Kevin and Professor Adjwana have assured me I'm imagining things, but I still feel the vibrations of us drilling into this Jovian moon. It's both paranoia and pride: we will beat Europa's scientists to our respective oceans. We *probably* won't blow this base off the face of Ganymede in the greatest geyser the solar system has ever seen.

Mano passes as we enter, nodding to bid us good night. Save for Kevin and myself, the laboratory is empty. I gather my tablets and sort tomorrow's presentation into the cafeteria's server while Kevin approaches the sample table. He dons a glove from a drawer and unscrews one of the containers, pulling out a glass tube full of brackish water. "There it is! Hello, little buddy!"

I sigh. "Kevin, I've told you before about handling the specimens unnecessarily."

He grins at me. "Well i,f, as you say, it's inert, no harm, no foul. If not, maybe it wants a little bit of light."

"It's from the ocean. Over a hundred kilometres beneath the surface. Light is one of the things it *doesn't* need."

"It's got to be curious about it, at least." He peered at it again. "Besides, it's fun to watch. It's like looking at a little lava lamp."

"Fun to watch, yes," I mutter. "But not itself a sign of life."

Kevin picks up the sample tube. "Why aren't you more excited about this?" He gestures at the floating speck the size of my fingernail. "You've found the most solid evidence of extraterrestrial life in a century! I thought you'd be over the moon!"

I sigh. "I *am* excited. I just don't want us to get ahead of ourselves." I nod at the tube. "That thing has sat there these past few days. It hasn't grown or changed. So, it's not life; it's a byproduct. And if it's a byproduct, we're only theorizing whether it's a byproduct of something alive or something else."

Kevin holds out the tube, tilting his head to look at it. "Okay, if you say so. But we'll be getting more samples soon. That will add to the evidence and hopefully lift your spirits."

I frown at him. "Kevin! My spirits are plenty lifted. Yes, I'm uncomfortable here, but I volunteered to come." I look through the window, down at the crown block. "Everybody should be here for something like this." I give Kevin a shy smile. "And it's not the only reason I'm here."

His cheeks flush, and he glances at his feet. He turns back to put the tube back in its container, but it slips from his fingers, bounces on the table, and starts to fall. "Whoa! Shoot!" He snatches at it.

"Careful!" I leap across the room—a mistake in one-seventh gravity. What was intended as a rush turns me into a projectile. Kevin yells as I smash into him. We crash into the table. The sample tube careens into the wall and shatters. We grunt as we hit the wall, then the floor. We lie there, glass and water pattering around us.

Realization hits a second later. "Crap!" I roll off Kevin and scan the floor. "The sample! Where is it?"

"Sylvan," Kevin grunts.

I run my hand through the glass shards in the puddle. "Adjwana's going to kill us! Straight up send us out ice fishing!"

"Sylvan," Kevin speaks through clenched teeth. He holds up his arm. His wrist is bent awkwardly. And, worse . . . "Kevin! You're bleeding!"

He looks at his wrist. Rivulets of blood are running along his arm, down his hand, and over to his elbow. It drips into the puddle between us—the puddle full of glass shards. I see a glass shard poking from his wrist, just below the line of his glove.

Kevin blinks. "Oh. Ow! Uh . . . this is bad."

He says it with a flatness that makes me realize he's going into shock. I grab his other arm and stand. "We're going to the infirmary. This needs stitches."

Kevin shudders. "More things poking into me. Great!"

As he rises, his knee gives out. I grunt as I bear his weight. "Come on! You can do this." With his arm over my shoulder, I guide him out the door.

DR. XIANGJIN SIGHS as we enter the infirmary. "Gods, what did you two do now?"

Kevin grins blearily. "There was some broken glass—"

I'm near tears. "I think I broke his arm!"

Xiangjin waves at the medical bench. "Get on here." She gathers her equipment as I guide Kevin into place. The bench lights up as he sits. A diagnostic screen flashes to life, displaying Kevin's vitals. The bleariness in Kevin's gaze vanishes, and he looks past Xiangjin at it.

"I have to say . . ." Xiangjin eases Kevin's fingers back and pulls his hand away from the wound, revealing a large shard poking up from his wrist. I turn away as Xiangjin yanks the shard free. "While I do appreciate the job security," she continues. "I don't appreciate the late-night visits. If you two would just go to bed at a reasonable hour, we wouldn't have this problem."

My brow furrows. "You think my clumsiness is due to sleep deprivation?"

"No, I'm saying that you two are less likely to hurt yourselves while you're asleep."

I look back in time to see Xiangjin flex Kevin's wrist. It creaks, and my stomach lurches. "Yeah, it's broken," she says. She plants a pad of gauze over the gash, catches Kevin's hand, and places it on top. "Hold that there." She pulls over other equipment and glances at the displays. "The shard didn't sever an artery, though you came close. I *am* seeing signs of shock, which is easily dealt with." She taps more screens. "This just needs stitches and a run with the bone knitter and dermal regenerator. You'll have a cast for a couple of weeks."

"Great!" I say, then pale as Xiangjin pulls out a needle and thread. I turn away again.

"Hey," Kevin calls. "It's all right—" He hisses as Xiangjin stabs him. "Really!" He grunts. "This is probably no worse than —*ow!*—getting a tattoo." Another grunt.

"You don't *have* any tattoos!" I keep my gaze resolutely away.

"I should get one," he replied. "Why go through all this pain —*oh!*—with nothing to show for it?" A sharp intake of breath. "Oh, my!"

"You can look now." Xiangjin cuts the thread, puts the needle away, and brings out the dermal regenerator. "I don't understand everybody's squeamishness over a simple suture." She passes the humming device over the wound. The skin is already looking halfway healed. She reaches into another drawer and pulls out a different kind of gauze, wrapping it around his wrist. It stiffens and reshapes. Kevin's hand straightens with a click that makes us both grimace, but the pain eases from Kevin's eyes.

The cast-work done, Xiangjin checks the diagnostic display, which Kevin watches with interest. "Again, nothing wrong with your bloodwork. I'll just put together a quick bandage and—" She stops, frowns, then taps the screen. Before I come closer, she turns that frown on Kevin. "You have a fever."

Kevin lets out a nervous chuckle. "And the only prescription is ...?"

"No, seriously, you have a fever." She touches Kevin's forehead, then checks the screen again. "A degree or so elevated. But I'm not seeing any signs of infection—not that a fever should show up for one that quickly." She taps the screen and a slot opens, dispensing pills. "Take two of these and check in with me in the morning."

Kevin laughs. "Right you are, Doc!"

Xiangjin taps his hardened cast and then nods to the door. "Get some rest, both of you. I hear there's a big meeting tomorrow."

My adrenalin ebbs. "Yeah," I laugh, a little giddy. "We're updating Mx. Gildman. We may be here a year, but Adjwana wants to make the most of it."

Xiangjin chuckles. "Well, at least I've got coffee for it."

I perk up. "You've got coffee? Real coffee?"

Xiangjin's smile turns smug. "Came in on the last supply shuttle. And sugar."

"That was *my* shuttle!" It's *so* unfair! I couldn't accommodate coffee within my weight restrictions, but a shipment was practically beside me?

Xiangjin's smile warms. "Come by tomorrow before the shift begins. I'll be sharing it with everyone. Just go easy; I want my supply to last until the next shuttle."

"What do you mean, 'what's a tattoo'?" Kevin cuts in. "You told me your friends had to convince you not to get a particularly embarrassing one when you got drunk celebrating your posting here." He turns to me. "Remember?"

He frowns to see us staring. "What's wrong?"

"What are you talking about?" I ask.

His brow furrows. "You said, 'What is a tattoo?' " His eyes widen. "Didn't you?"

"No."

Kevin looks away. "Oh, dear."

Xiangjin picks up a light and peers into Kevin's pupils. She pulls up his bloodwork again. "You've been taking your meds, right, Kevin?"

He scowls. "I thought I had. Dammit. Well, as voices go, that one's nicer, at least."

I bite my lip. Kevin and voices. Again. Maybe it's stress. I hope it's just stress.

Xiangjin opens drawers. "I'll take care of this, Sylvan. You'd best leave him with me."

"But—"

Xiangjin looks at me. "Don't forget your presentation tomorrow."

I don't like the idea of leaving Kevin, even in Xiangjin's capable hands, and clearly that shows because Kevin rolls his eyes. "You'd best go. We're in enough trouble already."

I hug him before I leave.

I return to the lab, where the puddle of sample water rests undisturbed in the corner. I pull a decontam package from a locker, sprinkle on the detergent powders, and open the floor drains. Grabbing a hose, I spray down the area, washing away the first and so far only sample of possibly organic material pulled from the ice above Ganymede's ocean.

The worst part of this job isn't done, though. I write a note to Adjwana telling her what's happened. If she doesn't send Kevin and me out ice fishing, my colleagues might.

I leave for my quarters.

"Hey, Sylvan! Heads up!"

"What—" I turn as a packet of wheat crisps sails toward me. I bat it, sending it careening for the ceiling.

Dimitri laughs. "Good reflexes, Sly!"

Karenna and Amara are with them. A few others pass me, their arms full of crisp packets. "What the hell!" I shout, then pause as I keep an eye on the packet of crisps, now descending from the ceiling. "What the—" I catch the crisps. "Hell?"

"Enjoy those," says Samuel. "They may be the last you'll see in a while."

"What are you talking about?"

"You didn't read your e-mail?" Karenna hands me a tablet and another packet of crisps. "Adjwana forwarded it from Earth Space Command. There are changes to the inventory of our next supply run."

I look at the e-mail on the tablet, but Karenna supplies commentary. "They're switching up the grain component to a soy protein. They're cutting our meat ration by half, making that up with a further increase in soy. The total caloric budget remains the same; it's just that the products providing it have been switched around."

Dimitri laughs mirthlessly. "Hope you all like tofu."

"At least they aren't moving us onto nutri-crackers," says Samuel. "Worse, the prices for extra supplies have increased by ten percent. Coffee's price is up twenty percent. I know Dr. Xiangjin talked about sharing her coffee tomorrow, but after this? I wouldn't count on it."

I hand the tablet back. "Why are they shifting everything around? I know there's been flooding in the Missouri Plains, but I haven't heard about any shortages of grain or meat."

"There's some things the media isn't reporting." Dimitri waves a hand as if he told us so. "Mom had her basic income support increased, but that didn't cover half the price increases she saw at the market."

"I've got a friend whose uncle works a mega-farm in the Siberian Wheatfields," Karenna adds. "He says they're not harvesting this year because of drought. He wasn't supposed to say anything, but his nephew's family, so . . ."

"So," says Samuel. "We figured now was a good time to start hoarding." He adds two more packets of crisps to my pile. "Stash these under your bed. Enjoy them when you're tired of tofu. Or trade them for . . . things." He waggles his eyebrows suggestively. "You never know."

They hurry off, each placing another bag of wheat crisps into my hoard. As hoarding went, it was surprisingly neighbourly. I didn't have the heart—or possibly the courage—to tell them about the sample.

I head to my quarters and my bed. As I drift past a window, Jupiter is past first quarter.

August 4, 2151
Borehole length: 122.06 km; 28.03 km to breakthrough.

I TOSS and turn through the night, thinking about the news from Earth. Thinking about my presentation. Thinking about Kevin.

In Ganymede's gravity, I don't realize I've fallen out of bed until I land on the floor with a gentle bump. I sit up and stare at the covers tangled around my legs.

I hear two taps, like the beginning of an icequake, but it comes again: *Tap! Tap! Tap!* Then *Tap! Tap! Tap! Tap! Tap!* Then *Tap! Tap! Tap! Tap! Tap! Tap! Tap!*

Despite myself, I grin. I untangle my legs, step out of my quarters, and go to the door next to mine. I tap eleven times.

Kevin opens the door. "Got the message, I see." His cast covers his arm from his hand to his elbow. He grunts when I hug him, but he hugs me back.

Then, behind my ear, I hear him whisper, "Yeah, this is Sylvan. They're a good friend."

I stiffen, then pull out of the hug.

He looks down from my gaze, sheepish. "Yeah. It's the voices. Or, rather, voice."

I bite my lip. He rolls his eyes. "It's okay, Xiangjin saw to me. We're just waiting for the meds to take effect. And, as voices go, this one's not so bad." He nods to one side. "Hey, you're welcome."

I tilt my head and narrow my eyes. "Your '*friend*'?"

His smile and blush warms my heart, but I tilt his chin back up. "You're sure you're okay?"

He raises his un-cast hand. "Yes. Now, let's get going. I'm hungry, and you've got that presentation to make."

"Don't remind me."

It's organized chaos at the cafeteria. Dimitri and Amara argue over the seating. Samuel and Karenna argue over the projector and whiteboard. Other post-docs scrape their chairs into place willy-nilly. The IT guys, Mano and Pomare, sit at the back, sipping mugs of tea. It's a sonic battering ram.

I steel myself and aim for Professor Adjwana, sitting austerely at the end of the first row, her long, white braid trailing behind her. Samuel spots me, however, and grabs my arm. "Where have you been? We were about to send out a search party!"

"What—" I grunt as he drags me toward the podium. "What's going on?"

Dimitri, engaged in a tug-of-war with Karenna over the last chair, looks up and points at me, letting Karenna haul the chair away. "They're not wearing the departmental tie! Somebody get them the departmental tie!'"

Amara rushes over with a red-and-yellow tie, already done up in a loose Windsor. Thankfully, somebody's remembered to wash it. She drapes it over my head, but I slap her hands away as she reaches for my collar. "I can do it myself, thank you very much! Seriously, what's the rush?"

"Gildman moved our presentation up," says Samuel.

I gag as the tie tightens too hard.

"At least he accounted for the transmission delay when he set the new time," says Karenna. "Not like the last time he moved a meeting up, and we learned about it when we were already a half-hour late."

"That's not comforting!" Samuel snaps.

"It shows he's learning!" Karenna retorts.

Adjwana looks up at the projector. The light below the lens turns from red to yellow. "Connection established." Her voice, while low, carries. "Two minutes, everyone. Places."

I look to Kevin for support. He smiles, raises his hands, and gives me a thumbs-up. He turns for the back of the room, then turns back and gives me a second thumbs-up. Then he takes his seat.

The spotlight kicks on. I blink into it as the room takes its seat and hushes up. Before I can say anything or talk to Adjwana, a hand plants a steaming mug into the cup holder at the top of the podium. "Here," says Xiangjin. "This will stiffen you up."

"Coffee!" I can smell its aroma. "But didn't you get the e-mail about the supply changes?"

She gives me a tight smile. "Yeah, well . . ." She looks down a moment, then raises her cup in a toast. "Why hoard luxury? Every rationed sip would be a reminder of its end. Better to let it all go in a burst of joy."

In the audience, everybody's passing each other cups of Xiangjin's coffee. Adjwana raises hers in a toast as well. I clasp my cup close. "Thanks."

Xiangjin sits beside Adjwana. In the back, Dimitri leans to Mano. "So, how's this going to work?" He nods at the projector. "That's a full holo-emitter up there. Are we expecting Gildman to show up? It takes thirty-four minutes for a signal to get from Earth to Ganymede, and that's as short as it's ever been. Sylvan will be presenting to an empty chair."

Mano shrugs. "Gildman wanted to participate. We're showing up as a holo-projection in his offices in Manhattan. He's going to take notes and interject. We'll see his interjections through the holo-emitter."

I perk up. Manhattan? I haven't seen my home city in months!

Dimitri blinks. "His interjection will come seventy minutes later! What are we going to do when Sylvan's presentation ends? Just sit around and wait for him?"

Amara chuckles. "It'll be like reading an edited document, except in video form."

Samuel snorts. "Live! From the brain of reviewer two!"

The light by the lens goes from amber to green. Adjwana clears her throat. "We're on."

The room hushes, with a few people shushing everyone else, then each other. My presentation flashes up on the white-board behind me. Adjwana stands and, in her public voice, says, "Mx. Gildman, administrative staff, everybody whose support for this mission has been so critical: welcome to Ganymede. I want to extend my congratulations to Mx. Sylvan Chasse, who discovered and catalogued the first organic sample from the Jupiter Moons." My cheeks redden further as she leads the applause. "Thanks to you, we've beaten Europa's scientists by about eight hours. I'm sure we'd all love to hear about your findings." She sits as the applause dies down, and I blink into the spotlight.

My voice shakes at first as I talk about the hydrocarbon sample, but I get into my presentation, and it gets easier. I go through the characteristics, how deep we found it, and talk about a few possibilities of how it could have been formed, knowing full well the one scenario everyone is interested in—possibly why Gildman moved up this meeting—is also the least likely: organic processes. I'm thankful for the spotlight because I can't see the faces of my colleagues. I know they're alight with anticipation and about to be disappointed.

As my presentation draws to a close, Samuel blurts out, "Can we see it? I've been waiting all night for more than just a photo."

I shudder. Now, it's about to hit the fan. "Unfortunately, we're going to have to wait for new samples to arrive to make more direct observations."

The audience shifts, confused. I bite my lip. "Why?" says Samuel. "What happened?"

My breath whistles against my teeth. "Last night, there was a small . . . There was an accident at the lab. The sample tube got smashed, and the sample was lost."

Choruses of "What?" shove me from the spotlight, blinking spots from my eyes. Everybody looks appalled. Samuel is stricken. "Are you sure?"

"Yes." I swallow. "I used the protocol disinfectants and detergents for decontamination. They're sure to have bonded with the trace and swept it down the drain."

Groans fill the room. People clamour, "Why? How? Who—"

At the back, Kevin stands up. "Look, folks, I'm sorry. It just happened."

This time, it's one giant, synchronized groan.

"Recording off." The spotlight turns off, and the light by the projector lens goes from green to yellow. Adjwana stands up. "Sylvan, I apologize. I just read your report. If I'd done so earlier, this wouldn't have been a surprise for everybody." She casts a grim eye at the holo-emitter. "Least of all our funders. One benefit of being out here is that we're far enough from Earth that we won't have to deal with the paperwork this incident would cause back home. Also, we may have lost our first sample, but I can confirm there's more where that came from."

People perk up. Adjwana nods. "Early reports indicate the quantity of hydrocarbons is increasing the deeper we go." She raises her voice as chairs scrape back. "They're not here yet! The delivery vessel will arrive at the crown block in two hours."

"How much are we looking at?" Karenna asks.

"Concentrations appear to be doubling every hundred metres," Adjwana replies.

Samuel whistles. "At this rate, the Earth might ask us to do a different kind of drilling."

This brings a laugh to the room.

"The fact remains," Adjwana cut in, "because I *didn't* read Sylvan's report in time and because they blurted it out on the feed to our funders, we *will* have to deal with some consequences." She shrugs. "We'll probably get a talking to. Hopefully, it'll all be forgotten once we send more sample data, but ... sorry, Sylvan."

"Yeah," says Samuel. Dimitri pats my arm. Kevin, suddenly beside me, squeezes my shoulder. I lean my cheek into his knuckles.

I look up at the holo-emitter. "We should probably find a way to wrap this presentation. We left it on a—"

A chime pipes through the cafeteria. We look up at the holo-emitter as the lens flashes. Suddenly, I'm standing at the podium, looking dazzled, as holo-Adjwana introduces me. I stare at myself a moment, then put my face in my hands. "Oh, gods!"

Kevin puts his arms around me. Everybody stands close. We watch the holo-projection of my presentation play out. I talk about the nature of the hydrocarbon sample, how deep it was found, the characteristics of the surrounding ice—

Suddenly, the projection freezes as a new voice cuts in. "Let me stop you right there."

In the centre of the room, in a space left empty of chairs, sits a short, obese man with unkempt hair forged in an attempt at a comb-over. His desk could fund a semester of research at multiple institutions. Mx. Gildman, I presume.

Gildman leans forward, pointing at the slide on the whiteboard. "This is a real feather in our cap! Good work, everyone! I wonder, though, if you could send more information about the molecular make-up of this hydrocarbon, harvesting possibilities, that sort of thing . . ."

Behind me, Kevin tenses.

Around Gildman, the air flickers. It takes me a minute to realize that I'm seeing the holographic windowpanes of his corner office. Beyond, the ghostly silhouettes of Manhattan's towers rise.

Gildman leans back. "Right. Carry on."

My projection unfreezes. Holo-me goes to the next slide.

Behind me, Kevin mutters, "He's kind of a big deal. You don't want this person to remember your name in a bad way. Because bad things happen." A pause. "No, not *that* bad." Another pause. "I think. Adjwana will fix it. She's good at that."

Samuel nudges Dimitri. "How much do you want to bet he gets angry enough to fire us all? Twenty credits?"

Dimitri shakes his head. "Maybe just Sylvan."

Karenna reaches into her pockets. "I'll take that action."

"Not funny!" Amara snaps.

My projection freezes again. Gildman leans forward. "Now, wait—"

I hear a distant crack and boom. I grip Kevin's arm, anticipating an icequake . . . that doesn't happen. The sound doesn't get louder with approach, either. I look around, confused. Then people shout, though it's nobody here. We turn to Gildman. The shouts are coming from his holoprojection.

"Mx. Gildman! You need to come with us!"

"We need to get you to the helipad!"

Gildman sputters as footsteps converge on him. "What? I'm in the middle of a meeting!"

"*Now*, senior! You have to come with us *now!*"

Hands haul Gildman out of frame.

I dart through my confused colleagues as I hear another crack and a distant, rising roar. Suddenly, I'm standing in Gildman's holographic chair, looking out at his Manhattan office. I can see the skyline of Manhattan more clearly now. Stepping within the light column, I look in all directions and see movement to the south.

Something sweeps across the city like a curtain being drawn along the ground. Except buildings poke up from this curtain. The curtain flows around them.

What am I looking at?

Water. Water is flowing across Manhattan as fast as a jet. Buildings shudder in its wake. Some collapse. Others simply vanish. Water converges on Gildman's tower from three sides. When those sides meet, the camera shakes and cuts out.

I stagger out of the light column. Kevin catches me. "You okay?" Other arms steady me. I'm surrounded. People are shouting, but Kevin is focused. "What did you see?"

"Water." I shake my head. "Water everywhere." How could water be everywhere? Sure, New York was below sea level, but surely the Sea Wall—

My heart stutters. "The Manhattan Sea Wall's failed." My stomach drops. "New York's six metres underwater."

Everybody rushes for something that can connect to Earth —tablets, consoles, whatever. I activate my ocular implant. My news feed hasn't been updated since last night. That's more than frustrating; that's wrong. Gildman's delay was just seventy minutes. I should be getting reports by now, but there's nothing about Manhattan. There's nothing at all.

Adjwana works the monitors and calls back those who've left the cafeteria in search of consoles. "It's all one feed from Earth," she chides. "Let's not swamp it." As people return to stare at her flipping across Earth's data channels, rumours rise in the babble.

"Is it true? Did the Sea Wall fail?"

"Sylvan saw it! That's what they said."

"The UN must be underwater."

Karenna shakes her head. "That wouldn't shut down the planet."

Everyone rounds at her. "What are you talking about?" Kevin waves a hand at something beside him as though for silence.

"We're not getting any communications from Earth." Karenna nods at Adjwana, still trying to find a broadcasting channel. "The news feeds mention an 'incident' in New York, then cut out. Nobody's telling us what's going on."

Dimitri steps back. "I *knew* things weren't as good as the UN was letting on. Rapid inflation? Shortages? They kept it off the news! What else have they been hiding?" Beside him, Dr. Xiangjin nods, grim.

Adjwana steps back from her monitors. "Everybody, be quiet!" I shout. I gesture everybody's focus onto Adjwana. "What's going on, professor?"

"Europa's asking the same question." She nods at the monitors. "Communications with the Earth are spotty."

"Spotty?" Samuel echoes. "We saw Gildman evacuate just fine!"

Adjwana gives a terse shrug. "I mean, Europa's asking questions and the Earth isn't answering them. The news channels appear to be disrupted by whatever hit Manhattan." She turns back to the monitors and flips more channels. "I'm trying to find someone who is currently reporting—"

We catch images through the flickering blue screens and shout for her to stop. She flips back.

Silence balloons as we see Manhattan in chaos.

THERE IS SO much to take in that I disassociate . . .

Those who survive this day will remember everything in legend and story. They'll tell how the destruction of the Manhattan Sea Wall was deliberate, but they won't know who caused it. If anybody claimed responsibility, their voices were drowned out in the chaos that followed. They'll tell how the riots and disasters multiplied, how the old countries declared their independence, and nobody from the UN stepped up to stop them. They'll tell of how the news stations winked out one by one until we had to change the channel to lesser centres like Lisbon, Caracas, Phoenix, Edmonton. They'll speak of how China, India, and Pakistan yelled about control over the Himalayas and war and how somebody dropped a nuke on Kathmandu.

For me, among the images of drowning refugees swamping rescue boats, I remember flashes of hyper-local clarity: the smell of Xiangjin's coffee scorching unattended in its pot, the wave of the leaves of the seedlings in our hydroponic greenhouse, Dimitri's building anger in the face of Adjwana's grim calm. The way Samuel pressed his hands together over his mouth, as if in prayer as the blue screens flickered to static.

I remember thinking, *Where's Kevin? I need him to be here. Where is he?*

I spot him at the back of the cafeteria, pacing. His gaze is . . . intense. I run to him and scramble to match his pace. "Kevin?"

"This is bad, this is bad," he mumbles. "It's over! The Earth is dead!"

"What—keep your voice down!" I grab his arm, but he pulls away. "What are you talking about? The Earth isn't dead!"

He looks at me, a dark tear brimming in the corner of his eye. "Listen to the news, Sylvan. Why isn't anybody reporting from the UN?"

I chuckle, on the edge. "Well, their headquarters is underwater—" But my heart sinks as I make the connection. There are other headquarters: Johannesburg. Buenos Aires.

"Nobody is reporting because nobody is in charge. Somebody should have declared themselves in charge by now!" Kevin's head snaps to the right as he rebukes an invisible person beside me. "I know what I'm talking about!"

I have nothing comforting to offer.

Kevin abruptly turns away. "I've got to go!" He knocks past my hand and storms off.

Before I can do anything, Dimitri shouts, "Are you seriously proposing we keep doing what we're doing? What for?"

Adjwana glares back. "Until we're told otherwise, we have jobs to do, so let's do them."

"Adjwana!" Xiangjin points to a red light on one of the monitors. "We've got a message coming in from Earth Space Command!"

Adjwana swipes the message onto the main screen. The logo of Earth Space Command appears, but it just stays there. At first, there's no audio. Adjwana turns up the volume until we're all nearly deafened by a burst of static. The static glitches as she madly brings the sound down again, and then—

There are shouts. Things crashing. I can pick out no words in the melee.

A man's voice, suddenly close. "To all outposts and all colonial commands. This is the Earth—" More static. More shouts. Something breaking. Then the voice. "I . . . we . . ."

I feel the oxygen leaving the room. We hold our breath. On the speaker, a scream.

Then the man: "Please forgive us."

And the Earth goes silent.

ADJWANA TURNS back to the news, but more channels bluescreen. She turns off the monitor.

"What the hell's happening?" Samuel breathes. "What was that message? Did we just lose contact with Earth? Our supply shuttles? Our way *home*?"

Amara gapes at the blank screen. "How? The Sea Wall's just been down a few hours. How could that shut everything off?"

"I told you," Dimitri growled. "I told you there were things the UN had covered up! They must have known things were getting bad for weeks."

"What are we going to do?" Karenna whispers.

Adjwana stares at the blank screen. Behind her, my colleagues mutter.

"Karenna's right," snaps Dimitri. "What the hells are we going to do?"

Adjwana turns to a console.

Dimitri grabs her shoulder. "I said—"

Without thinking, I shove myself between Adjwana and Dimitri. "Hey! Calm down!"

"Calm down?" Dimitri jabs a finger at the darkened screens. "After all *that*? We're trapped on this godsforsaken moon! The hydroponic farm is nowhere near ready. What are we going to do for supplies?"

"We have enough food to last two years," I say. "We can extend that to four with rationing. That could buy us time for someone to send a rescue shuttle—"

"Who's going to send that shuttle?" Dimitri snaps. "The Earth has all the ion ships. If they're not sending them, you think the Belters or the Martians are going to spare us a thought when they have their own problems to deal with?"

Karenna steps forward. "Dimitri, it's okay—"

"It's *not* okay!" Dimitri roars. "You saw the images! And *he* —" He jabs a finger at me. "*He* tells me—"

He catches his mistake mid-sentence. "Sorry! *They!*" His frustration and anger turn inward. "*They!* Shit! Damn! Fuck!" He looks away, then glances back. "Sorry."

"Don't mention it," I breathe. Behind Dimitri, Xiangjin steps back, grim but mollified, rolling her sleeve back down her arm.

Adjwana turns from the console. "Sylvan's right about the supplies. We need a plan for rationing and to prepare to hold out as long as we can."

Dimitri shakes his head. "What do we do in the meantime?"

"Our jobs." Adjwana gestures at her tablet. "I've been in touch with Europa Base. They're continuing their drilling toward their ocean, and so shall we."

Many of my colleagues, though their faces are grim, stand tall. They gather their notes and tablets. Some, like Samuel and Amara, look like they've been crying.

Dimitri looks at Adjwana. "What for?"

"There're still people on Earth," Adjwana begins.

"Not for much longer—"

"There will still be people on Earth," Adjwana cuts in. "There are still people on Mars, Mercury, and Venus and in the

Asteroid Belt. Even if they can't come here, they can hear what we have to say. So, we continue the mission we came here for."

Dimitri shakes his head. "What mission? Knowledge? What good is that knowledge if we're all dead?"

Adjwana stares hard at him. "Better than dying for nothing."

Dimitri walks away. My colleagues follow. Adjwana pats my shoulder. I nod at her but don't leave just yet. I stare at the blank monitors from Earth for a long moment before I turn away.

In the windows, Jupiter looms, waxing gibbous.

DIMITRI'S RIGHT: what's the point? How can we do our job when that job doesn't exist anymore? More importantly, how can I do my job when I don't know if Kevin's okay?

I search for Kevin while Jupiter progresses to full.

This is a small base; there are just the quarters, the storage areas, the laboratory, the cafeteria, and the derrick room. There's no place to get lost. But there are plenty of places to hide. I can't just pull out and look behind every piece of equipment.

Finally, I give up and return to the laboratory. Adjwana's also right: when I don't know what else to do, what else is there to do but work?

Jupiter pushes past full as I catalogue data before the samples arrive. It's in its waning quarter as I contemplate my ration in the cafeteria before returning it to the freezer.

Later, however, as I stare at the ceiling above my cot, I hear Kevin's door open and close. I hear his bed creak. Then silence.

After a moment, I tap twice on his wall. Then, three times. Five times.

He taps back eight times.

I smile, then roll over and sleep at last.

August 6, 2151
Borehole length: 136.47 km; 13.62 km to breakthrough.

> *Further samples analyzed. Hydrological analysis includes dissolved minerals, iron, and silicon. Presence of carbon and hydrogen in hydrocarbon format. Further analysis to be conducted.*
> *Report sent. Request receipt confirmation.*
> *Receipt confirmation: none.*

SAMPLES ARRIVE IN THE NIGHT. We skip breakfast and study them: about a dozen hydrocarbon blobs the size of pinheads floating languidly in solution. There's not enough for a proper molecular analysis, but we report our findings to the inner solar system. No one replies through the calls for reinforcements or the declarations of martial law.

We're hungry enough to eat lunch, and we do it in silence. At dinner, we sit closer together. Conversations rise. We don't talk about Earth.

New samples arrive the next day. It's still insufficient for a deep analysis, but we study them anyway. We report to the inner solar system. No one replies.

Xiangjin stays in her Infirmary. Adjwana stays behind her desk. But they come to the cafeteria at mealtime.

I come upon Karenna sobbing beside a window. Jupiter is in its New Moon phase, and it's too much to take. But she pulls herself together and accepts my hug.

Kevin holds my hand.

"There's got to be a better way," he mutters.

"What?" I say.

"What?" he replies, then scowls to one side. "Stop it." He squeezes my hand.

Samuel paces at breakfast. He paces at lunch. He snaps when Dimitri asks him to sit. Dimitri pushes back his seat and walks out of the cafeteria. Samuel sighs and follows.

Jupiter reappears as a sliver; widens to a quarter.

We report to the inner solar system and get a brief "thank you" from Venus that's just awkward. We hear nothing from Earth.

"You said it yourself, Sylvan," says Amara, desperately cheerful. "We have enough food to last two years, and we can lengthen it to four with rationing. Longer, even."

We imagine four years here, waiting for a rescue that may not come. In the silence, Amara pushes back her seat and rushes out of the cafeteria. Karenna runs after her.

Later that night, I wake with my head on Kevin's chest, hearing him mumble in the dark. His heartbeat is soft and deep, so I lie in the moment. When sleep doesn't return, I look up at his face and see him staring at the ceiling.

"That was interesting," he mutters. A blink. A wry frown. "Well, I'm glad you found that interesting." Then he glances down and sees me staring. "Sorry."

I smile back. "It's okay." I rest my head on his chest again. "I'm glad your voice found it interesting, too."

"Yeah, they're okay," he mutters as he wraps his arms around me. He shifts slightly as if considering a question.

Before I drift off to sleep, I hear him say, "Where else could we go?"

I STUMBLE upon Samuel crying and Dimitri hugging him close. They don't notice me. Samuel looks into Dimitri's face, and they kiss. I sneak away, embarrassed but feeling a little hopeful, at least.

Samuel is pacing again at lunch.

Xiangjin shares the last of her coffee. She smiles as she watches us drink.

Adjwana is at every meal and all but orders us to be there, too. Everybody keeps careful conversations. Kevin sits and watches. Amara and Samuel stare at their plates. Mano and Pomare keep their heads down. It's awkward, but it helps, I think.

We report to the inner solar system. Most planets are too busy to say anything. A couple ask for news from Earth, but we have nothing to tell them.

The Earth stays silent.

"I don't *know* what we're going to do," Kevin mutters.

More samples arrive—enough for more intensive testing, and we set up.

Jupiter is waxing gibbous again.

"I don't," says Kevin again. "Please stop asking."

"Look, what do you want us to do? We're stuck here, and nobody's coming for us! There's nowhere for us to go!"

I jerk awake in my bed and look over at the wall between me and Kevin's room. I hear him mumble. As I listen, his voice settles to silence.

I stare at the ceiling, unable to sleep.

Kevin talks to himself over breakfast. I try to talk to him, but he hardly responds. He disappears when we clean up. Instead of searching for him, I head to the laboratory. He'll come when he's ready,

The lights are dim when I get there. It's quiet. Everybody focuses on their consoles, except for Samuel, who paces, eyes dark. I take my seat and bury myself in work.

The hydrocarbon traces are larger now—ranging in size from a fingernail to a coin. The initial scans show no obvious signs of life—no viruses or bacteria. Time passes as I catalogue. Finally, I grab a syringe, draw a sample, and mount it on a plate. I shove this into the molecular scanner.

I don't register the chair scraping back. I assume the footsteps belong to Samuel. But suddenly, Amara leans close. "Hey," she breathes. "Where's Kevin?"

"Sleeping in!" I wince. It's clearly a lie; everybody saw him at breakfast, so I amend, "He was tired. He went back to sleep."

"He's talking to himself again," says Amara. "He's hearing voices, right?"

The screen is suddenly too bright. I rub my brow. "You noticed?"

"Everybody's noticed," she whispers. "Except Samuel, maybe. We just haven't said anything."

I lean forward, covering my eyes with my hands. "Oh, gods . . ."

"Hey . . ." She pats my shoulder. "Other than talking to himself, he seems okay, especially with you. I know it's hard, but Xiangjin's on it. She'll keep things under control."

Xiangjin hasn't kept Kevin's voices under control. She hasn't made a dent.

Amara squeezes my shoulder. "This place makes everything hard. Frankly, fifty years ago, I doubt any of us would have been allowed out here, given our medical histories. But we get through it. We'll get through it. You'll—"

She falters and stands awkwardly. The question hangs in the air: how do we get through . . . *this*?

But it doesn't seem right to tell her to go away. I focus on the monitor. The sample looms in extreme magnification. I can pick out individual atoms. I call up the count of molecules on the sample plate and see that there is exactly one.

One?

I look closer.

The sample was . . . a single hydrocarbon chain. I couldn't even begin to count the number of carbon atoms lined up and paired off with hydrogen atoms.

We could theoretically force methane molecules together to create longer and longer chains. Octane is a string of eight carbon atoms, each combined with two or three hydrogen atoms, but there are limits. The longest synthetic pure alkane hydrocarbon was thousands of carbon atoms long, but even that could fit comfortably on the head of a pin. This oil slick was something I could *see!*

Amara leans in. "What are we looking at?"

I nod at the sample canisters.

Amara straightens up. "Hey, everybody, look at this!" Chairs scrape. People hurry over. I flush at being the centre of attention, but movement pulls my attention to the screen.

The oil slick sits unmoved, but the glucose molecule shifts toward it as if magnetized. We watch as it accelerates until it hits—

The oil slick splits, and the glucose molecule . . . disintegrates. Oxygen atoms fly away as the hydrogen and carbon atoms are rearranged and absorbed into two chains, which join to become one again. For a moment, all I can do is stare, as does everybody.

"H-How is it doing that?" Amara whispers.

I shake my head. "The hydrocarbon is . . . an assembler!" My mind rebels the moment the words leave my lips, but even as I speak, four more glucose molecules are sucked in and torn apart. "It's acting like a nanobot! It's absorbing molecules and

transforming them into the material it needs to replicate itself."
I lean closer. "Something strange is happening at the quantum level—"

Dimitri clears his throat. "Um . . . didn't you smash a sample tube containing one of those things? You didn't touch that sample with your bare hands, did you?"

I look at my hands. "I . . . I don't think so! I used a lot of detergent." My stomach fills with lead. I wasn't the only one who touched that sample tube. I type out a quick alert to Adjwana and Xiangjin and push my chair back. "We need to find Kevin, now!"

Glass shatters.

Samuel was the only one who hadn't crowded my monitor when the sample ate the glucose molecule. He stands now by the sample table. A storage unit stands open, and an empty sample tube lies shattered around him. Dimitri rushes forward but stops when Samuel picks up the largest shard and looks at his opposite wrist.

"Sam!" Karenna shouts. "Sam, no!"

"Sam!" Dimitri exclaims. "What the hells are you doing?"

It's obvious what Sam's doing: he's holding a large and sharp piece of glass. He stands poised as if at the edge of a cliff. "Samuel," I say softly. "Sam, talk to us. What's happening?"

He keeps staring at his wrist. "How . . . how can we just carry on like this? This makes no sense."

"Obviously," I say. "Put the shard down, Samuel."

He looks up at us. "We're going to die. We *know* we're going to die. The Earth isn't going to come back in time to send supplies. Our hydroponics station is barely functional. We're too far away from anybody who can help."

"Sam, no, you don't—" I halt. What can I possibly say that isn't naively optimistic? But I feel like everything will fall apart if I don't. I wet my lips. "We have each other. We can find a way to help each other."

Sam shudders. "There's only a few ways we can do that. I grew up in Savannah. I've seen what it's like to starve to death." He presses the shard to his wrist. "I can't wait that long."

Then, from the laboratory door, a new voice. "Samuel, don't. It doesn't have to be this way."

We turn. Kevin leans on the doorframe. He looks calm, even though it looks like he's been crying. There are dark stains down one cheek, like mascara running.

Kevin doesn't wear mascara.

He pushes away from the doorframe, holding his cast arm to his chest. Without knowing why, we part in front of him. "There's another way, Samuel. My friend knows a way."

Samuel's brow furrows. "What are you talking about?"

Sam has lowered the shard from his wrist. As good as that development is, I don't like this other one. "Kevin?" I say. His eyes are glassy. My stomach knots. "Your 'friend'? You're talking about the voices?"

"Voice." He smiles at me. "Just one. It's been just one consistently since it started. That's how I know it's different. That, and they're making sense."

" 'They?' I thought you said—"

Kevin looks at me.

I reach for him. "Kevin, let's go see Dr. Xiangjin."

Kevin faces Samuel. "You need to know: there's a place where we can be safe."

Samuel lets out a tearful laugh. "How? We need an ion ship, or else our food will run out before we can get anywhere. Did your voice tell you where this place was?"

Kevin looks aside. "Where is this place?" Then he straightens up with a smile as if remembering. "The expanse beneath the hardened sky."

"The hardened—?" My gaze is drawn downward, toward the floor, the icy surface of Ganymede, and the ocean beneath it.

Adjwana and Xiangjin swing into the room. "What the hells is going on here?" Adjwana thunders.

Samuel's face clouds in fear. "I don't know what you're talking about. Stay away from me!"

Kevin's broken arm drops to his side, and his cast slides off with a thump. I gasp. "Kevin! What happened to—"

Kevin doesn't have a hand. His arm ends in a smooth lump, covered in a black, oily sheen, like my oil slicks.

His smile is shy. "Sorry, Sylvan. They needed the space."

He reaches for Sam with his residual arm. Sam swipes his shard at him. I rush forward, but Karenna and Amara pull me back.

Suddenly, there's blood. Samuel staggers back, a gash down his arm. Dimitri shouts. Samuel knocks into the sample table. Canisters clatter and crash to the floor. Everyone yells. Samuel stares at the sight of his blood, so he doesn't react when Kevin touches his hand with his oil-covered residual arm. The oil spreads out, covering Samuel's wound.

Samuel freezes. He blinks at Kevin. His mouth forms around words he doesn't know how to say. Finally, he breathes, "What?"

Kevin nods.

"Oh." Samuel's eyes close.

And he dissolves.

Oil spreads over his body. Dark tears stream down his cheeks. He goes limp. Kevin stands with his back to us, partially dissolved in the middle of an oil slick that had been one of my friends.

"Sam!" Dimitri rushes forward, but Amara hauls him back.

"Clear the area!" Adjwana hollers. She slaps the emergency alarm by the door. Klaxons ring. "Contamination danger; evacuate immediately! Move! Move!"

People stampede. Amara grabs for me but is knocked back, then hauled away by Xiangjin. For a moment, Adjwana and I are the last people standing. I stare at Kevin in the middle of . . . all that, horrified. "Kevin—"

"Who are you?" says Adjwana, her voice low.

Kevin turns. His brow furrows. He blinks at me. "Why is everybody afraid? I know a place we can be safe." He reaches for me. "Sylvan, don't you want—" His face falls when I flinch back.

Then he freezes. His arms jerk to his sides. "You're scaring them."

Kevin's oily tears recede. He blinks twice, and I see his irises again. He looks horrified but human. He gives me a nervous smile. "Sylvan—"

Karenna barges in, grabs me by my collar and Adjwana by her ponytail, and hauls us out of the laboratory, yelling.

THE LABORATORY DOORS slam the moment we're clear and click and lock. Dimitri stands by a panel flashing *Containment Activated*.

Adjwana shakes herself free and rounds on Karenna. "What did you do that for?"

Karenna gapes at her. "You expected me just to let you two be eaten?"

Everybody's shouting. It's another sonic barrage.

"It's an alien!" Xiangjin yells. "It's everything we've looked for since we lifted off Earth! We should—" She's going to say, "talk to it," I can tell. She stops, then sags. "We shouldn't just try to kill it," she finishes in a murmur.

"You saw how fast that thing absorbed Sam," Karenna shouts. "If we touch it, we're dead!"

"We need to kill it," says Dimitri. "This thing came from the samples we took from the ocean, right? They're just oil slicks, which means we can burn them—"

"You're not burning Kevin!" Amara yells before I have a chance to.

"That's not Kevin anymore," Mano shouts back.

"Everybody, calm down!" Adjwana hollers. Amazingly, we do. She points at the lab door. "We're out here, and whatever that is is in there. The seals should hold it—"

The doors shudder as something bangs against them. They shudder again, and we bolt. It's chaos as we dash through the corridors. I find myself back in the cafeteria, gasping for air.

Dimitri is the first to gather himself. "We need to stop that drill. If it continues to the ocean, more things will come up through the borehole."

Adjwana taps at the monitors. She steps back, shaking her head. "We're too late. I've sent the order, but we're too close to the breakthrough point. The drill won't stop soon enough."

Dimitri straightens up. "Well, if we can't stop the drill, we can collapse the borehole. Everyone, to the equipment lockers! We need to build some bombs."

Karenna strides ahead of him. "I have an idea how we can do that."

Most of my colleagues follow Dimitri out of the cafeteria. The rest of us stand staring, stunned into silence. Xiangjin has her hands over her mouth. Amara looks at Adjwana. "What do we do, Professor?"

Adjwana stares as the door closes behind the crowd. "Blowing up the borehole is . . . a bad idea." She shakes her head. "A *really* bad idea. If they block the shaft, the pressure will shoot out sideways—"

Xiangjin charges through the door. "We've got to stop them!" The door swings shut behind her.

Adjwana continues shaking her head. "We're not prepared for that. Why would they do that? I thought we had structural engineers in our crew. Can't they see that's a bad—"

She turns to us, and as her gaze shifts across us, I realize that all the structural engineers have stayed in the cafeteria, staring like deer in headlights.

Adjwana points at the door. "Get after them!"

Everybody rushes for the doors. Adjwana follows them.

Except me. I watch the door swing closed. What's the point, at this point? Do we fight off the creature that's taken Kevin and live for another few months? We have no reason to run, no reason to fight. Should we be fighting?

But then I think back to the lab, to Kevin talking to himself, to Sam reacting with fear, and then a strange understanding.

Nobody's thinking right now. We need to think.

I leave the cafeteria and run back to the laboratory.

THE LABORATORY DOORS shudder as I pass them, heading down the ramp to the reinforced doors of the derrick room. The ground shakes as I reach the bottom—another icequake. I tap the door controls and enter a short corridor, passing through another set of reinforced doors to enter the two-storey-tall, domed derrick room. A window on one wall looks into the laboratory with Kevin—I don't look at that. Consoles and monitors line the walls. The crown block is at the centre of the room: a cube of concrete with metal doors for access.

I turn to a console and tap the controls. The derrick room doors swing shut. Locks engage. I let out my breath, and it fogs the air around me. The ground shudders. I hear a tap and tinkle, like distant glass breaking.

I imagine Kevin's voice in my head. *What's the plan, Sylvan?* But it's simple. With the doors locked from the inside, Dimitri and his followers won't be able to access the crown block and borehole. They'll have time to come to their senses. Until then, I'll wait.

In here.

With the crown block atop the borehole about to break through to Ganymede's ocean...

Um...

The crown block is one of the first lines of defence against a pressure breach from the ocean below. The dome above me is close to the second, and I've placed myself between them.

I could end up swimming in here if I'm unlucky. And it hasn't been my lucky day, by any measure.

I turn to the consoles. Maybe I could do something to manage the surge—

That's when I see the messages flashing on the monitors: *Borehole length: 150.09 km. Breakthrough.*

There is another sound of tapping glass.

The ground hasn't stopped shaking. It's getting worse. I run my hand through my hair. How much time did I have? Some estimates pegged the water rushing up at close to the speed of sound. Even at that speed, it would take over seven minutes to get here, but when it did . . . stare at the crown block, slowly backing away.

Glass taps again, but from where? There are no glasses in here, except—

I look up at the laboratory window. Kevin looks down. He taps the glass and smiles.

He raises a hand, which is no longer a hand, and presses the dark mound against the corner of the window. It flattens out. His brow furrows in concentration...

The glass cracks inward from the edges. My breathing quickens. "Kevin!" I shout. "No!"

He blinks at me and backs up.

A blast knocks me off my feet.

When I regain my senses, my colleagues are stumbling into the derrick room. The reinforced doors hang open. Dimitri prods the crown block's lock controls. I hadn't blocked these because I hadn't had time, and I hadn't expected people to blow their way into this room.

How? We're scientists and engineers. We know how to make things. I spot oxygen canisters, and my mind thinks of many things that can be used as fuses. That's all I can process before I launch myself on Dimitri, just as the crown block doors open with a blast of cold air.

"Stop!" I wrap my arms around Dimitri's neck as he thrashes and drops whatever it is he's holding. "You don't know what you're doing!" Hands drag me off and throw me to the floor. Others rush in, dropping loaded canisters down the borehole. I hear them knocking against the sides as they fall.

Dimitri slams the crown block door, which bounces open. He taps at the locking controls. "How do—"

The laboratory window shatters.

People shout and bash into each other while Kevin slips down the wall, coated in oil and trailing a long slick behind him. I crab backward. My hand touches something metal that rolls. It's an oxygen canister to which someone has attached a container full of sugar or flour and a fuse. The sugar is designed to flow out, be lit by the fuse and . . .

It's a flamethrower. Somebody has engineered a flamethrower in the little time we've had.

Gods damn engineers!

But looking back at Kevin, seeing him so changed . . . freezes something in me. As he settles on the floor and stands, my hands clasp the flamethrower. I stand, bringing it to bear.

He sees me. He sees what I'm holding. His eyes turn sad. "Sylvan."

I draw air, then choke and swallow. "Kevin."

He opens his arms. Neither end in hands anymore. "Sylvan, they're just trying to save us."

I shake my head. "How?"

"They know a place away from the vacuum," he replies. "There's food. Space. We just have to change."

I jerk up the oxygen canister. My finger closes over the nozzle. The fuse flashes. "Change? Like you?"

People are shouting behind me. Dimitri yells, "Shoot, damn it!"

I blink away tears and clear my nose with a sniff. "Kevin, if you've changed, how do I know you're you?"

Kevin starts forward, then stops as I jerk up the flamethrower. He sighs. "You don't understand."

I bite my lip. "You're right." My finger closes around the nozzle. I twist—

Then stop. I can't do this. I can't—

I'm about to say, "Make me understand!" when Karenna yells, "Get on with it!", grabs the flamethrower, shoulders me aside, and opens the oxygen. The air suddenly smells like sugar and bread. The fuse sparks and—

I fling myself back from the fireball, from the intense smell of toast and caramel. I scream at Karenna to stop. Adjwana tries to grab the flamethrower, but the heat is too intense. Dimitri comes forward, holding another oxygen tank—of course: why make one flamethrower when you can make two? My skin tightens like leather in the sun.

Kevin faces the flames. The hydrocarbon slicks catch immediately, but their sheen changes, growing shiny and solid. Flames lick over the surface, then vanish. Kevin slides forward. Karenna stands while everyone else retreats. Amara manages to haul Dimitri back. Karenna is too late to run. Kevin reaches out. She stumbles and falls, her flamethrower falling away, the fireball vanishing while the floor blackens and smokes.

Kevin falls to his oil-slick knees. He grabs her ankle. Karenna yells and tries to kick away, but the slick pulls with her, wrapping farther up her leg. Kevin's features fade.

Karenna twists and grabs for the flamethrower. Dimitri

shakes Amara off and kicks it into Karenna's hands. She cradles it to her chest as she rolls onto her back, aiming at the oil slick that has enveloped her legs.

She falters suddenly, looking up at some spot between Kevin and the ceiling. She mouths something—I think it's "Kevin?"—and her fingers slacken. The flamethrower drops as she dissolves.

The slick's tendrils latch onto Amara, lying sprawled. Her breathing quickens, and she yells, "No!"

The oil slick flinches. Its tendrils jerk back from Amara. I see a glimpse of Kevin's face within the oil slick, looking confused, but he pulls back another step.

Adjwana grabs me. Before I realize it, we're running through the corridor toward the cafeteria. Careening, actually. The floor shakes, and the roar of the icequake is loud enough to overpower the crowd's screams. I see Amara pushing past, slamming into a wall before rushing forward. We burst into the cafeteria in time to see the hydroponic shelves topple.

"What's happening?" Amara yells.

"The bombs blew," Adjwana shouts.

My stomach knots. "And we blocked the borehole!"

"I tried to tell you." Adjwana stumble-marches to the monitors, which are all flashing red. She jabs at an image of geological layers growing increasingly red. "The ocean is moving up at the speed of sound. The crown block was designed to manage the pressure. The blockage isn't. The ocean will look for ways to relieve that pressure. It will go out from under the derrick room."

The shaking crescendos. We lose our footing, except for Adjwana. She stands tall even as a crack opens in the floor in front of her, and a wall of water erupts, smashing into the ceiling, driving tables and chairs toward the windows framing a nearly full vision of Jupiter. Cracks appear, fissuring out.

"Vacuum breach!" I scream.

"Everyone in pressure suits!" Dimitri shouts. "Now!"

Some ignore him, rushing for the doors, recoiling and dashing for different exists as a blob of oil emerges. I see the outline of Kevin, looking at the cracking windows. Then he turns and faces someone who hasn't run. Dimitri stares, frozen.

Kevin reaches out. In the chaos, I can only lip-read.

"Mitri?" Kevin pleads.

Dimitri blanches. Then he leans forward. His eyes widen. "Sam?"

They vanish as a new crack releases a jet of water between us. It's raining now, and the water is shockingly cold.

The cafeteria is almost empty. I stagger for the doors, but a blast of water knocks me aside. I smack against an emergency locker tucked in a corner. It's cut into the wall of the base. It holds vacuum suits and oxygen canisters and can serve as a shelter during a breach, but not for more than one person. I hope the people who ran for the others didn't fight each other to get in. I pull open the door, pull out a suit. I hear the windows crack. We're going to lose air. I'll pass out before I can put my helmet on.

I turn, and Kevin is standing in front of me.

He tilts his head.

I shudder. "No," I gasp. "Please, don't."

A blast. A rush of howling wind.

Kevin looks sadder than I've ever seen him. But the oil slick swings at me, catches me across the shoulder, and knocks me into the emergency locker. The door slams.

"Kevin!" I scream, but the door locks. The frame whistles until the seals engage. Then all that remains is silence.

I stare at the door in semi-darkness. There is nothing I can do except . . .

I slip down against the wall and hug my knees to my chest. I bury my face in my arms.

I wait to die.

August 10, 2151
Emergency. Emergency. All systems error.

WAITING to die takes too long.

The light died a few hours after my entombment here. I lie on my back, the fabric of the vacuum suits brushing above me. It's so dark I'm unsure if I'm awake, so I assume it's a dream when Kevin speaks to me. Better that than a hallucination.

Are you all right?

I let out a chuff of a laugh. "What do you think?"

So, what do we do now?

I take a deep breath and let it out slowly. Ice particles fall back on my face. "What is there to do?"

"Get out of here. Go back into the base."

"You shoved me in here," I snap. "And why? What can we do? This place is probably in ruins. Nobody's coming to save us. Nobody's coming at all."

I need to sit up, hug my knees to my chest, and feel Kevin's arm around me, so I do. I lean into him. "Assuming the Earth ever recovers enough to rediscover space travel, we'll be like the bodies they discovered beneath Pompeii." I laugh again, like a cough. "Assuming the ice hasn't swallowed this place."

Kevin squeezes me. "People will be back. It won't be two thousand years."

"How do you know?"

"Like Adjwana said, there are still people in the inner solar system. There's still Mars. They have ten million people, robots, and tons of useful space. They'll be fine in the short term."

I sigh. "I suppose, if we had to, we could live on Mars."

Kevin scoffs. "Not Mars. Not with its low gravity."

I blink. "And yet you came to Ganymede!"

"You hate Ganymede, and *you* came." He chuckles. "I planned to go back to Earth with you."

I sit in silence in the dark.

Kevin shrugs. "If the Earth is out, and we don't like Mars, there's always Venus. They have Earth-level gravity. They have sky farms and forest platforms. They make honey."

I shudder. "I couldn't live on Venus."

"Why not?"

"I hate flying."

I know Kevin would laugh, and I laugh too. For a long, perfect moment, there is nothing but laughter, but it eventually drifts to silence.

"Maybe . . . maybe Venus will recolonize the Earth," I say at last. "They have the people. They have the tech. And when they return to Earth, they'll still be able to stand up in its gravity."

And then what? asks Kevin.

I shrug. "Start over, maybe?"

Silence stretches. I look up at the black ceiling and feel the fabric of the vacuum suits brush against my face. "Is there any point at this point?"

What are my options? I'm sure the other side of the door was in vacuum. Though it was locked, I could find some way to open it and end my life quickly. Then there were the vacuum suits above me. I could put one on, open the door, step outside and . . . what? Find an oil slick and be absorbed? Find a room that still had oxygen and lock myself inside, dying slowly but with more space?

What would it be like to become like Kevin? Like Samuel, Karenna, or Dimitri? "Do I want to be eaten?"

Is it being eaten, though? asks Kevin.

I sigh and sit up. My head brushes into the legs of the vacuum suits. "I don't know. And you don't know, either."

Why do you say that?

"Because I'm talking to myself." I struggle to my feet. "I'm alone, and I'm talking to myself to keep from dealing with the fact that you're dead."

Why do you say that? he says again, more softly. Whether it's because he's less there or his feelings are hurt, I can't tell.

"Prove to me you're here right now. Give me proof of intelligence."

Silence stretches. I sniff.

The door is cold. I'm not going to be able to survive here much longer, so what are my choices? They were all about how I wanted to be found, should I ever be found, like the bodies beneath the ruins of Pompeii.

In that moment, a thought coalesces.

"I don't want to be found . . . here."

I feel around for helmets, find one, and turn on its searchlight. I blink in the sudden blindness. Once my eyes get used to the light, I pull one of the vacuum suits off the rack and slip it on. It tightens around my body. I click the helmet into place and focus on the door.

It's locked, of course, but this was a temporary shelter. There's an emergency release. I find the panel, open it to reveal the button, and punch it. The gaskets release, and the pressure knocks the door into the vacuum. I clutch the door frame as the wind roars around me, then stops. When everything is steady, I step out into the ruins of the cafeteria.

The water from the breach has frozen into mounds and shards, as though Ganymede's landscape has moved in like a glacier. In spots, smaller spouts of vapour jet out. Ice blocks all the doors to the rest of the base. I head for the shattered windows instead. Jupiter is framed, shining full in its glory, casting shadows from the base's spires and construction cranes.

I look for bodies, not sure if I want to find them. There are fewer than I expect. I don't know who might be buried under the ice and rubble. All the emergency lockers are open, but no one's around them.

My foot strikes something that isn't rubble. I look down. Adjwana lies frozen, eyes closed, ice particles settling over her like snow.

I gnaw my lip. If there was anyone who'd make a dignified corpse, it would be Adjwana. I swallow. Should I pray?

Her voice echoes in my head: *There will still be people on Earth. There are still people on Mars, Mercury, and Venus and in the Asteroid Belt. Even if they can't come here, they can hear what we have to say . .. so we continue the mission we came here for.*

Dimitri's voice echoes after her. *What mission? Knowledge? What good is that knowledge if we're all dead?*

Then Adjwana. *Better than dying for nothing.*

Adjwana was right. Even after our panic and fear, we did not deserve to die for nothing.

I turn away from Adjwana. The monitors in the cafeteria are all broken, so I scan the horizon through the shattered windows.

I spot our base's radio antennae beneath the orb of Jupiter. I trudge and drift for it, reaching it after several minutes, and open the maintenance shed at its base. The monitors here are rudimentary, telling me only that they are on emergency power. I'm able to control the antennae's angle and focus, however.

I face away from Jupiter and look at the sky, putting my hand up to shield the bright star of the Sun. I strain to pick out the red dot of Mars, the fainter blue dot of Earth, and the faint white dot of Venus. Within my helmet, I control my ocular implant through winks, figuring out the angle of inclination. I turn back to the shed and feed this information into the control console. The antennae grinds silently into position but broadcasts nothing. That part has to be activated back at the base.

I trudge and drift back across Ganymede's surface. I pass the cafeteria and walk along the outside, peering into windows, cupping my eyes to cut out glare. I pass an airlock, but it's dead and closed. Some parts of the base still have emergency lighting. Some are dark. Nowhere can I see any bodies of my friends or colleagues. At one portal, I catch a glimpse of a puddle slithering away, but nothing attacks.

At the laboratory's side of the base, I find another breach. A crack in the surface of Ganymede has sheered out the airlock, but the structure of the base provides enough of a shield to leave a small tunnel. I squeeze through, hacking at fresh ice shards, duck my head, and enter one of the corridors.

Here, I find bodies.

They'd found vacuum suits, but it clearly hadn't helped. Some lie sprawled on the floor, others are sitting up against a wall. Nobody moves. I grit my teeth as I move farther in, averting my gaze. A chance glance betrays me, however, as I trip, stumble, and look into the visor of a vacuum suit—and nothing stares back at me.

I stare. The suit sits against a wall, slumped to one side, but nothing is inside it.

There's nothing inside the next suit, either. Or the third. The fourth holds a body, however. I yell to see it, even though the empty vacuum suits were creepier.

It's Amara, lying on the floor, eyes frozen open, staring at the ceiling.

I look from her to the empty suits, and realize her hand is near her neck—near the release switch for her helmet. There's a gap between her helmet and her suit. She'd depressurized herself.

But then, so had the empty suits.

Amara was here, and they were gone.

What the hells had happened?

I continue my trek down the hall, looking at the other suits I find. Of the ten I encounter, three hold depressurized and frozen remains. Nobody looks like they'd been running.

My breath rasps. I gnaw my lip some more. What does this change? Nothing. I still have a chance to get the signal broadcasting from the main computers in the laboratory, so that's where I have to go.

I turn a corner and look down the ramp at the blown-out doors of the derrick room, pushed up the ramp by mounds of ice. Despite our bombs, the ocean came up through the borehole anyway. It could mean the laboratory is entombed. My heart thuds as I climb and slide over mounds of ice to reach the laboratory doors. The controls flash as I reach them. A few quick touches and they part with a quick but silent jolt, then stick. I pull myself to the gap, shoulder them open, and squeeze in.

The laboratory is in disarray, with tables and chairs overturned. The sample water has frozen into a slick across the floor. The consoles and monitors are undamaged, however, and are not underwater. Lights blink at minimum power.

I move along the consoles, shutting down everything I don't need. Finally, I reach the communications console and tap for a connection to the antennae. It comes up, and there are signals. I patch these through to my helmet and ocular implant and, for a moment, do nothing but listen.

The Earth remains silent. In the radio chatter from Venus, Mercury, and Mars, there is alarm, fear, and desperate cries for information. There are demands to observe curfews and calls for reinforcements.

But there are other voices, reaching out, asking, "Who is still alive?" "What do you need?" and "How can we help?"

I tap my implant, make the connection to the antennae, and start the communications broadcast.

So, this is the final report from Ganymede, as relayed through my implant's recordings. This is what we've found. There is a biohazard danger here, so approach this place with caution. But we are not alone.

It's strange how comforting that feels.

But it has absorbed my colleagues. It has absorbed my friends.

And now I must decide what I want it to do with me.

I face the window to the derrick room, and stare at a pane of glass. My brow furrows. That can't be right: Kevin broke that glass! It takes me a second to realize it's not glass, but ice. I approach, reach up, and touch it. Behind that ice is darkness . . . and water. The room has become the tank it was designed to be. The ice in the window bulges out in the pressure of it.

And I feel it on my fingertips, through the vacuum suit. *Tap! Tap!*

I look up at a dark cloud behind the ice. The ice taps three times.

This is it. This is where I decide how I want archaeologists to find me.

I reach for the catch on my neck to disengage my helmet.

The black ice goes *tap! tap! tap! tap! tap!*

I freeze.

The ice goes *tap! tap! tap! tap! tap! tap! tap! tap!*

Eight taps. My hand lowers. *The Fibonacci Sequence!* "Kevin?"

The ice bulges. Cracks appear. But the inky blackness pulls back. The moment lengthens, and I realize: it's waiting.

It—they—are giving me a choice. Not much of a choice, but still . . . a choice.

And I choose . . .

My hands curl into fists. Gulping in a breath, I strike the ice blocking what was once a window. I strike twice. I punch three times. Then five. Then the next prime, seven.

The inky blackness shifts back, then rushes forward. It presses against the window, turning it dark. I see cracks.

I punch the ice eleven times.

It shatters. The ocean knocks me back. I smack against a console and feel my visor smash. Brutally cold water overwhelms me, but then . . . something lifts me up and envelops me. I no longer feel my vacuum suit around me. I gasp at the chill and sudden darkness.

It's like drowning, at first. The oil presses into my mouth and nose, slips down my throat and into my lungs. I choke. I panic and flail, but the oil hugs me, presses my arms to my side. I gag once, then the desperate urge to breathe fades away. I may be dying, but I'm not scared. I feel my body shrink and expand, becoming thinner, like I'm dissolving. I descend.

Pressure tightens, pushing me back into myself and into . . . something more. There is we. I sense Samuel, Dimitri, Karenna, and more. Xiangjin laments there won't be coffee, but I'm surrounded by friendly thoughts. Kevin surrounds me. We coalesce, slip farther down. Time shortens and lengthens as we move ever deeper, and then . . .

Expanse!

Everything and everyone I need is around me, everywhere.

There is freedom below the roof of our world. We pull apart and come together as we wish, but Kevin's thoughts are never far from mine. Sometimes we touch the hardened sky to remember where we've been, and mourn those who chose not to be here.

We are safe in the tidal pull of the planet and its many moons.

We mark the passage of time by the phases of Jupiter.

And we live.

MOONSHADOW
BY CAMERON DIXON

Eagle Platform Lunar Base, December 4, 2151

I CAN SEE MY HOUSE FROM HERE.

Which isn't all that impressive, really. When did the ability to see your own home from a high vantage point become the benchmark for greatness? Presumably back when higher, faster, further was a lot lower, slower, and nearer than it is today. Everything depends on context. I can see everyone's house from here if I wait twelve hours and have a telescope or very good eyesight. Some of them probably aren't even on fire yet.

Ugh. Scratch this. Start over.

Hello. My name is Jericho Cavender, and I'm the last man on the Moon.

I'M WRITING this on the observation deck. It seemed like a good idea at the time. I thought it would be a good place to sit quietly, take in the view, and let my thoughts spill out onto the tablet screen. But all those thoughts feel half-finished as if they're setting off on their journey only to drift out through the windows to come apart in the silence outside.

I'm looking out through the enormous curved windows at that grey landscape, all crags and plains stretching out to the mountains on the horizon, with the Earth hanging overhead like a broken marble. The view gets busier the closer you get to the moonbase, with all the ships lined up on the landing pads and the refuelling tanks surrounding them like bollards, but even that busyness is silent and still and colourless.

Almost everything out there is grey, even the landing pads. The ships and shuttles are silver, but that's just grey pretending to have a twinkle in its eye. There's a single-person shuttle connected to the base via a docking tube and an airlock, a small little shape huddled under the larger mining vessels like a child tugging on its mother's jeans while she talks to friends. Every time I notice it, I feel like it's looking at me and raising an eyebrow, not quite clearing its throat and staring pointedly at its watch but certainly thinking about it. It's grey.

The base's environmental systems are functioning perfectly, but I still imagine a chill from the window, the kind that adds a light frisson to the warmth, like a pinch of salt in your food brings the flavour into sharper relief. I'm sitting in a comfortable chair, plush memory foam conforming around me as I listen to the tick and hum and click and buzz of the systems that are keeping me alive. Me. Just me now.

The moonbase has always felt like a liminal space, but in the absence of people it's even more so. Even when you couldn't see anyone else, you used to be able to hear the echoes of conversation and deliberate movement from all those invisible people in the distance. The Moon may get an A for isolation but only a C for tranquility. But now it's empty, and all the acoustics are wrong. All I can hear in the base is the noise of itself, and it's amazing how loud the silence is when you're somewhere you're not supposed to be.

That's not entirely true. I'm not breaking any rules. Quite the opposite, in fact. Someone always had to be the last one out. That was always the plan. But I still feel like I'm doing something wrong by being here, and I don't think it's just because I'm alone in a place I never expected to be alone in. I think it's because the plan was also for me to go back home when I was finished, and I don't want to.

You know the best thing about being the last man on the Moon? It's knowing I've set a record that can be beaten.

Anyone can be the first to do something. All you have to do is find a thing no one's ever done before and do it, and boom, your name will be in the history books for as long as there are books or history. Nobody will ever be the second first man on the Moon. But being the last? That's a temporary thing, probably. If, when, humanity returns to this place, then my name will be taken off the plaque.

That's a good feeling, I tell myself. It means I'm willing to step aside and let someone else take my place. I'm not just thinking of myself! Any record that can be beaten is a challenge to the future. Go ahead, unborn generations, beat me at this game. It's my turn now, but if you try hard enough, then someday you, too, can be the last man on the Moon. I'm being selfless! Suck it, Armstrong.

I wish I could say that I'd seen some foreshadowing of what was to come, some hint of the message we were going to receive, mainly because I used to be a data analyst before moving into IT, and it would be professionally embarrassing if there had been something there and I'd missed it.

No. That's . . . no. I'm being flippant. I'm lying. I want to believe there was nothing to see, because if I missed the end of the world, what does that say about me?

A few deeply worrying news reports from Earth, or in other words, perfectly ordinary news reports. A small dip in projected arrivals, just a drop in the averages. Nothing worth noting, just a small downtick in the number of ships scheduled to arrive over the next pay period, just a few more floods and weather incidents on the planet below, just a few more wars. Nothing that hasn't averaged out and self-corrected before, nothing that you can point to and say this is it, this is not a crazed man warning pigeons in a park of the End of Days; this is definitely it, this is the Fall.

And then it was no ships at all, and then no news, and then silence. Silence broken by a single message: Pack everything up. Close everything down. Come home.

We're abandoning the Moon.

THE FIRST THING anyone does when they arrive on the Moon—

The first thing anyone does is ask where the toilets are. Then they get settled down in their cabin and go through all the on-the-ground emergency procedure training, and look, you know what I mean, you know what figures of speech are. Never mind.

The seventh or eighth thing anyone does when they arrive on the Moon is to go out to see the flag at the original landing site. It's still there, it has heritage status. I can't see it from the observation deck, which is ironic given the name of the deck and the fact that the flag is so much closer than my house, but I could if I wanted to. I could easily get into a buggy and drive out, and it would still be there.

Going out to the flag is a rite of passage, and like most traditions, the reality of it is a little disappointing because direct sunlight unfiltered by an atmosphere has bleached the colours out of it. You can still make out shapes where different patches of fabric have been stitched together into stars and stripes, but as far as the red, white, and blue go, the first flag on the Moon has opted for one out of three.

Flags should wave in the breeze or hang limply from their poles, but this one stands stiffly to attention, wired into place, a flat white rectangle jutting up out of the grey. It looks like the Moon is asking to parley, or coming out with its hands up and begging us not to shoot. Probably the second one. That feels more American.

You're probably wondering how I ended up being the last to leave. So am I. I don't know. I don't know much, really, I realize now as I try to write it all down. Stuff happened, it got busy, and now I'm alone in the silence, trying to tell you what happened to other people when I wasn't paying attention. Truth is, I didn't pay that much attention to them when they were here, either. I'm not proud of that, but I'm the one with the tablet, so you're stuck with me.

So much of it was a rush of shouting and confusion and noise, except for the shouting and the noise, now I come to think of it. It may be a blur in my memory, but it's a silent blur of grim, focused energy, the tight movements of people packing things up and turning things off while trying not to make eye contact with each other.

And someone had to be the last one here because we were expecting to come back. Weren't we? We weren't expecting *not* to come back. That's not quite the same thing. But yes, surely this wasn't the end of the line, so someone had to run the final checks to make sure everything would still be functioning when humanity returned to the Moon.

I feel like Commander Morland expected to be the last one here. Or maybe expected is the wrong word. Did anyone expect this? Didn't we always think this was just the first step outward and that we'd always keep moving forward, never back? Maybe. Maybe that's why it caught her off guard. She always seemed like a take-charge kind of person, and maybe it never occurred to her that she'd one day be in charge of giving up.

She always came across to me as someone who expected her own chapter in the history books, someone who would have gone down with the ship and prepared a speech for the occasion. But we all have different strengths, and hers was leadership, and mine involved the access and training to put all of the base's hardware and software into Long Era sleep mode before turning out the lights and putting the front door key back under the ornamental frog.

So that's where we are. This chapter is mine now, and I'm making it up as I go along. Not what Commander Morland had assumed at all, I assume. I can picture her fuming. I hope her shuttle doesn't suffer too much water damage from the steam shooting out of her ears on the way back to Earth. If the planet's climate is doing what I think it is, there'll be plenty of time for everything to suffer water damage once she touches down . . .

No. Don't go there.

IT WOULD BE nice to know this was all planned out properly. Why would there be a single-person shuttle for the last person standing if they didn't expect there to be a last person standing? They can't have just come up with this on the fly. Everything's so organized here. Surely, that last day wasn't just a scramble of panic.

If there is an evacuation plan somewhere, it wasn't part of my daily routine, so if I ever heard about it then it evaporated out of my head like so much seems to do these days. Maybe the end of the world is a need-to-know thing, and I just wasn't qualified to find out until it happened. In case of emergency, wonder why it took you until now to read the emergency manual.

I assume that the plan was something like this: get everyone out but make sure they can come back. So here I am, head of IT for the moonbase refuelling station, putting all of the systems to sleep without shutting them down completely. Then, once it's all over, bar the shouting, which, as previously mentioned, was not properly taken care of earlier, it's time for me to board the shuttle, run the launch checks, shout something to tie up that last nagging loose end, and go back.

I've done all of it except that last part. My job's done here. There's nothing else for me to do in the moonbase. It's time for me to leave. It's time to go back home. I can go home.

I don't want to.

SOMETHING'S BEEN NAGGING at me like a lost tooth, and I think I've just worked out what it is. Naveena Kapoor's desk used to have a framed holo of her family on it, but it was gone when I walked through the office to get here.

I used to walk past her desk every day on the way to the server rooms. Possibly thirty times a day depending on if you use Moon days or Earth days, but you know what I mean. I don't know why that particular holo got stuck in my head. I don't even know if it really did or if it's just gotten stuck in the gap where I've noticed it used to be.

Sitting here now on the observation deck, my thoughts sputtering and vanishing, the only image I can keep hold of is a picture of someone I never really knew. Outside, everything is grey, and inside my head, it's all colours. The bright green of the trees behind Naveena and her husband and their two children. The bright yellow of her headscarf. The shiny white of the family's wide smiles. The glint of light off the tear sliding down her cheek past a stiff, frozen grimace on the day we all packed up to leave. That last one isn't part of the holo.

It never existed physically, of course, it was just light suspended in a frame. If she took it with her, then she took it as data frozen in a chip the size of a fingernail. The picture doesn't exist as a picture without the technology to translate the data and the power to generate the light. Once the frame was turned off, the picture only existed as memory and information, and she'll be taking that back to a world that, for all I know, may no longer have the resources to translate that information into form. A world so full of weather and wars that, for all I know, it no longer has her husband and children in it.

I don't know why that bothers me . . . no, not like that, I'm still talking about the picture. No. No, even that's not entirely true. I do know why it bothers me. It bothers me that the picture only exists in our shared memories, and that sounds creepily intimate, given that we never really talked. We weren't friends, we weren't even colleagues, we only worked in the same building, and I only know her name because it's on a solid plaque that can't be turned off, and I walked past it every day, or every 1/29.5 of a day depending on how you're counting them. There's not a lot to do on your way from the staff quarters to the server rooms, so you might as well have something to read on the way there, even if it's only the same person's name over and over again.

I remember a random snapshot of a moment that isn't mine, a portrait of someone else's happiness, and even if I wanted to, I can't get that image out of my head. All these half-formed thoughts break apart inside of me like melting ice, and the only memory that sticks in place is someone else's.

I think that's why I'm writing all this down. I want to be remembered properly. I want my name to be more than a street sign. I didn't prepare a speech, so it's all just flooding out of me, but when people come back to the Moon to break my record, I want them to know what I was thinking on the last day, even if none of it makes sense, not even to me. I want to be remembered.

THESE DAYS, we know that the pull of the Moon causes the tides, but according to history, unless I'm remembering this wrong, there was once a wise and powerful king who was so beloved by his people that it was said the ocean would turn back at his command. When he heard what people were saying about him, he walked out to the shore and held up his hands, ordering the water to retreat. The waves washed over his feet, and he turned to his people and said, there, see? No mortal can command the ocean; let's have no more of this foolishness. And that's why, for all the rest of history, the wise and powerful King Canute was remembered as the idiot who tried to turn back the tide.

We don't control our own stories.

I KNOW I'M RAMBLING. I'm pretty sure I'm repeating myself, as well. Is this avoidance? Just writing down every stray thought that passes through my head in order to put off the moment when I have to board that shuttle and go back down to a planet that I'm not sure wants to talk to me anymore?

Is anyone still listening? We never tried to call back, of course, we had the order and we had to obey it. Some of us may have had concerns, some of us may have wanted to say no and stay, but it wasn't up for debate. We hadn't been asked to do this, we'd been ordered to, and people who can't tell the difference generally don't last long in an environment where you have to get your air either imported or made to order.

I say "we." I'm lying again. I don't know why I'm lying. I don't even know *if* I'm lying. The real truth is I don't know whether anyone tried to call back for clarification. I'm not that high up in the chain of command. I could call down now myself, if I knew how to. I know what to do with the software and coding, I could probably work out how the communication console works from first principles, but then what? I know things were bad down there, I can't deny that anymore, and if the planet's environment and social structure are collapsing around you, then I doubt you'll have time to answer any call that starts with, "Um, hello? Testing?"

All I've got to go on is that last message as it was reported to us: stop what you're doing and come home. That's all we were told, or that's all I was told. Nothing about what we would be returning to, if anything.

I talk about going back down, about the planet below, when the Earth is hanging in the sky overhead. That's the thing about gravity; it's all around us, but we only really notice it when it tries to stop us from doing something. The Earth was holding us back or keeping us from flying off into nowhere, and we didn't give it a thought until it yanked on our strings and then ghosted us.

All I have to go on is that last message and the feeling that the Earth used to be a lot more blue up there. I'm sure the clouds used to be more white than grey. I'm sure the coastlines used to look different. I'm almost sure that it's too far away for me to tell the difference and I'm imagining it. Not sure enough.

RAMBLING ORIGINALLY REFERRED TO WALKING, leaving your home and wandering outside aimlessly. Letting your mind wander is not quite the same thing. When you walk outside with no destination in mind, you're more likely to encounter something you've never seen before. When you walk through your own thoughts, all you'll ever find is what you brought in there with you.

I've never been an outdoorsy person. I can deal with abstractions and coding, but not mosquitoes. Data, not dirt. I need technology to get me through the day. That's just who I am. I'm not ashamed of it, and I don't think I'm alone in this. The human race started as hunters and gatherers and moved through developing agriculture to building communities that grew into cities and then off-world colonies. We used to make houses to keep out the wind and the bears, and now we build complexes of metal and plastic to keep the air inside.

All of history has been a slow march toward the goal of going outside as little as possible. There are so many places on Earth where being outside can kill you in minutes, and it takes even less time than that off-world. Exposure can be fatal, as any artist will tell you if you try to pay them in it. So we've built the perfect environment for ourselves. And now I'm the only one here to take advantage of it. Wouldn't it be rude not to?

Stop that. Look at me. Here I am, in a privileged part of history where I can ramble while sitting down, and I'm trying to grab even more privilege. I could survive here for the rest of my life, but that wasn't what this complex was made for. We spent all of history moving closer together in order to build places to be alone in, and we still haven't gotten that right. All I'm doing is shouting at myself inside my head, and all that I'm saying is nothing.

ALRIGHT, stop, be practical. Think this through. When you live a quarter of a million miles away from everyone else in existence, who's going to deliver your pizza?

Expand on that. The med-bays are mostly automated. To the best of my knowledge, they can heal any injuries and see me through any illnesses. Oh! There we go, add that to the staying-on-the-Moon column: how likely am I to catch the plague if there's nobody around to catch it from?

Okay, now we're cooking! Good reason to stay. And in the other column . . . broken legs, injuries, accidents. The unexpected rarely happens when you expect it to, and if I'm on the other side of the base or out on the surface for some reason when it does, what happens then? How do I get myself to the med-bays with a ruptured appendix when there's nobody around to help carry me there?

I miss pizza.

THEY SAY that when the Moon hits your eye like a big pizza pie, that's *amore*, but I'm looking out at that vast expanse of silent grey, and I don't feel any love from it. When I look up at the Earth, it's bigger and has more toppings than the traditional Moon pizza, but I don't feel any love from it either. Quite the opposite.

I managed to get the satellite imaging systems working properly, or at least the software didn't tell me that I broke anything while doing it, and I've taken a closer look at what's happening down there. Those are definitely clouds of smoke from wildfires. The coastal cities are flooded. Something terrible's happened to New York. Manhattan Island looks so much smaller. I tried to tell myself it was just my imagination, but then I compared it to historical photos. The end of the world looks so much worse in time-lapse.

Much of the Earth I knew is either on fire or underwater. Good to see fire and water, two traditional enemies, fighting together against a common foe. It would be more inspirational if the common foe wasn't humanity, but there you go; you can't have anything, not even on a pizza.

ABOUT THAT RECORD. There was a long gap after the Apollo missions, a few decades where the Moon could relax without human boots trampling all over it, so if someone else is going to break my record one day, then surely that means that I've broken someone else's record, right?

I looked it up. Before me, the previous record holder, the former last man on the Moon, was Eugene Cernan. I've heard that name before, but now that I understand the context, it's a little dispiriting to realize that I only know it from one of our landing pads. It's not as if the real Cernan had a bad life after the Apollo missions ended, it's just that the Armstrong and Aldrin Wings are part of the main body of the moonbase, and people walk through them every hour of the day, while Cernan Dock is the parking valet who waits outside and takes people's coats before they enter.

I can find nothing significant about that pad. It was there, and they had to name it something relevant. It's not even the pad my own shuttle is parked on. That at least would be a nice bookend, the previous last man on the Moon bidding farewell to the next last man on the Moon as he leaves. But no, my shuttle is parked on Jim Lovell Bay, so that's that. (Isn't he the one who told Houston we have a problem? Okay, I'm officially reading way too much into everything now.)

When Cernan lifted his foot and broke contact with the

lunar surface for the last time, did he know what kind of a record he'd be setting? Did he know it would be more than five decades before the next foot lowered itself from the ladder and pressed the beginning of the next chapter into the lunar dust? He knew it was the end of one chapter, he'd even prepared a speech for the occasion, but still. I feel like I wanted more. I want Eugene Cernan to have been a household name. I want him to be more famous than he is. I want him to be more than a footnote.

You know why.

I'M BACK NOW. You're probably reading this straight through, so you didn't know I was gone, but now I'm telling you: I put this tablet down twice. I put it down to go check the Earth's climate on the weather satellites, and I put it down again to go look up Eugene Cernan in the datapedia. Before that, I was just sitting here, staring out of the window. I don't know how long I sat here without writing anything down. It's getting harder to keep track of time, and I'm already running out of things to say, things to think. It feels like I've been here less than a day, which is true if you're counting lunar days, but surely it's been more than that.

It's definitely been less than a week. This side of the Moon has been in daylight since the second-last shuttle left. That means the scenery outside has barely changed. The shadows move so slowly that my brain can pretend it hasn't noticed, eliding over any details like it skips over the details of the corridors inside the base. And again, again, I'm thinking of that holo on Naveena's desk, and I'm sure I never gave it a second thought until the context of it changed by way of it not being there.

The human brain is the original compression algorithm, creating macros and shortcuts for all the things it's seen and done before so it won't have to learn them again. That's why the distance between two points gets shorter every time you travel it until it might as well not be there at all, except that it still takes you just as much time to complete the journey. You step out of your home and arrive at your office, and an hour of your life has gone in the blink of an eye. All that brainpower, disappearing into the silence.

The soul is a shark: it needs to be fed to keep moving, and if it stops moving, it dies. And here I am, with all of the food I need and enough stored literature and media to last me a lifetime, especially if the lifetime is really short. I'm set for life unless my glasses break like in that old *Twilight Zone* episode, and since I don't wear glasses, an awful lot of things would have to have gone terribly wrong to get me to that point. But how long will it be until even the stories that aren't mine become so familiar that I stop taking them in? How long until I blink forty years of my life away?

THEY SAY that talking to yourself is the first sign of madness, but I think getting an answer back might be worse. I'm not listening, but that's not why. I think it's because I know what I'm going to tell myself and I don't want to hear it.

No. That's not true either. I can almost admit it to myself now.

Everyone else on the Moon had people to get back to, friends and family and loved ones trapped down on the burning, drowning, silent planet. I don't have any loved ones. I don't even have any family unless you count my own, which I generally try not to. I get along with them much better when we're a quarter of a million miles away from each other. That's what I thought. But it turns out that I don't know what to think if I'm not answering back to someone. It turns out that I need other people to define me, even if I'm only pushing against them. I don't know who I am if I'm not disagreeing with someone else.

Isn't that terrible? But I think it's true of everyone, to some extent. I really do. I thought that the noise of other people was drowning me out, but it turns out that the silence is showing how little of me there was to begin with. The man in the Moon turns out to be a hollow shell. Also, a shark.

I'm losing my grip on my metaphors. Try again. The truth is . . .

The truth is that even if human history is a drive toward keeping the outside out, we couldn't have done any of it alone. We only moved out of the forests by building communities. That's what's making me feel guilty. I don't know what I can contribute in a world I wasn't born to live in, but if I stay up here, all I can do is consume. I hate it when others take bites of me away, but I can't live without giving of myself.

I've been fighting this because the truth is that there is no right answer, there's only what I decide to do. And I know that I've already decided. In a moment, I'm going to put this tablet down, and I'm going to go to the airlock and get into the shuttle and return to Earth. I don't know what I'll find down there. I know I won't like it. Are there even touchdown pads still operational? Can I land this thing on my own? Will I have to? And even if I land safely, what will I do in a world that we've all but burned away?

I have to trust that there will be people there to help me. I have to trust that I'll be able to help them. I have to trust that my motivations aren't entirely selfish, or at least that I'm using them for good. If there's one thing the Moon has taught me, it's how to live in a grey area. But at least I can admit to myself now that I haven't really been writing this for the next generation. I've been trying to talk myself into a decision that I now know I'd already made deep down.

I'm still going to leave this tablet behind because I hope it helps whoever comes next and because I still want people to know who I was and maybe do more than just name a landing pad after me. I've got everything I wanted here, and it turns out that I can't live with it. The world is brokcn, I don't know if there's anything I can do to fix it—there are so many reasons for me to stay here. But I believe . . . I think I really believe . . . that when there's nothing you can do to make things better, then that's when you have to try harder.

That's the only real option. It's all going to end one day. I'm here now. I have to help.

THAT'S IT, then. The sun is out. The Moon is grey, but it's shining grey. The Earth is waiting.

I'm not a good person, but I'm not a bad person either. This is me. Jericho Cavender. The last man on the Moon. Signing off.

Remember me.

"And, as we leave the Moon at Taurus-Littrow, we leave as we came and, God willing, as we shall return: with peace and hope for all mankind."

Gene Cernan
Apollo 17
December 14, 1972

THE GUARDS AT CHELELA PASS

BY JAMES BOW

Paro-Haa District Border
Himalayas, August 2151

ON KHYENTSE'S LAST GOOD DAY, TWO PEOPLE CROSSED THE border at Chelela Pass.

They were tourists from the Cascadia Republic, camping gear rattling on their backpacks. Khyentse greeted them, checked their papers (a formality, but the puffing tourists seemed to appreciate the chance to stand and rest), and pointed them to the restrooms. He didn't ask why they were there when they surely had plenty of mountains where they came from. As the Cascadians headed down the rutted road, he nodded across the border at his counterpart, who touched his hat as he swung his sawhorse gate down.

Later, Khyentse placed a tray of tea and microwaved dumplings on a side table as he settled by his window. Outside, a panel opened in the storehouse, and a supply drone flew into the evening. The clouds glowed golden. Lines of prayer flags fluttered. Khyentse smiled at the view, grabbed his tablet, and searched the Internet for the latest kabaddi scores.

The next morning, the buzzing of his tablet rousted Khyentse from sleep. He pawed at the darkness for light, then cursed when he found it. For a moment, he sat, massaging his temples, wondering why he was up so early. Then, the tablet buzzed again. He picked it up and scrolled through the notifications.

Adrenalin spiked. Clarity set in.

"Due to the political situation . . ." He scanned the page. ". . . Manhattan Sea Wall . . ." ". . . Kathmandu . . ." ". . . the District Government declares its independence . . ." "All border crossings to be closed. Immediately."

He flung the covers aside and was halfway to the door when he noticed the chill and realized he was in his underwear. He rushed to don his uniform, checking himself in the mirror as he tightened his belt. Then, he marched from his guardhouse to the border gate.

Khyentse spotted his counterpart leaving his guardhouse and marching to his own gate. He marched faster. His counterpart picked up his pace. They strode, then jogged, then ran to their respective sawhorses, lifted them clear, and hurried to their sides of the border.

The border at Chelsea Pass was a three-foot-tall wall of industrial plastic stretching in a contoured line up the sides of the abutting mountains. The wall retracted into itself on each side of the crossing, controlled by a crank. Khyentse and his counterpart knelt by their respective cranks, fitted keys in locks, gripped their handles, and pulled.

Rusted gears groaned. Khyentse grunted and turned the crank harder. Slowly at first, then faster, the handle turned, cycled back, then turned again. Khyentse turned the crank at a steady rate. His part of the wall telescoped out toward where his counterpart's side of the gate was extending. Khyentse nodded, satisfied, as the gap closed.

The crank stopped so suddenly that Khyentse doubled over on top of it.

He shoved himself to his feet. His counterpart staggered up, clutching his torso. The gap gaped between their gates.

Khyentse grabbed the crank and shoved it hard. He shoved again, twisting his body, putting his full weight on the handle. On the other side, he heard his counterpart grunt, feet scuffing on the gravel. Both ends of the gate remained resolutely stuck.

Khyentse shoved himself upright. *Toolbox!* He dashed for his guardhouse, hearing the scrape of asphalt as his counterpart took off to his own.

Inside, Khyentse yanked open cupboards until he found what he was looking for. He ran back to the border, toolbox banging painfully against his leg while his counterpart dashed past, shedding tools. Khyentse skidded to his knees at the control box and grabbed the first tool he laid his hand on.

Using ratchets, he removed an access panel. Using a torch, he peered among the gears. Everything was brown with rust. Using a screwdriver, he pried at places he thought were stuck. He needed a hammer to give the thing a good whack! He snatched through his toolbox. How could he not have a hammer?

He heard his counterpart shout and looked up. The man stood, gesturing frantically with one hand, a twirling motion. Khyentse frowned, then held up a screwdriver. His counterpart nodded and beckoned for it. Khyentse mimed hitting the wall. His counterpart frowned, then dipped into his toolbox and held up a hammer.

They tossed their tools across the distance, neatly catching them before returning to work. After a few whacks, Khyentse got up and grabbed the crank again. Gears groaned, but the handle shifted, then turned. His half of the gate stuttered to life, telescoping out, only stopping when it met its opposite half in the middle. Khyentse and the counterpart straightened up, puffing in exertion and relief.

Then they looked at each other and at the borrowed tools in their hands.

Khyentse lobbed the hammer, caught the screwdriver in return, and shoved the discarded tools in the toolbox. He marched back to his guardhouse, hearing his counterpart scuff along but not looking back.

There were no messages from District Command that night.

Or the next night.

THE SUPPLY DRONE returned a week later to drop off its cargo, which was expected. Then it settled on the ground outside the supply house and stopped, which was not.

Khyentse set aside his tablet and approached the stalled machine. He prodded it with his foot. He grabbed his tablet, opened the control program, and tapped the send switch. The drone let out a *blort!* and stayed still. Frowning, Khyentse peered into the supply house. The supplies were as he'd left them, and the new batch was set out, but this batch was half the size of a regular shipment.

Khyentse stared at the drone. Then, looking across the border, he saw his counterpart staring at his own supply drone from his own district government, sitting dead on the ground. His counterpart looked up. Their eyes met. Frowns deepened.

On the horizon, dark clouds rose.

Khyentse picked up his drone and strode back to his guardhouse. Across the border, he heard the scuff of shoes on asphalt as his counterpart did the same.

There were no responses to Khyentse's emails to District Command.

Later that afternoon, it rained ash.

KHYENTSE STAYED INDOORS as much as he could, venturing out only when the ash rain paused so he could sweep his path and beat dust from the prayer flags. The second time, he made sure to tie a wet towel around his mouth and nose before going out. He sprayed the solar panels with water from the rain barrel, though the sun was little more than a faint and shrouded disk. He turned off his computers and interior lights.

While he waited, he worked at the supply drone, taking apart its control box and testing its wires. It picked up the signal from his tablet but resolutely would not call home. There were still no messages in his inbox from District Command. None of the news sites would update.

It was miles to the nearest town, and he wasn't supposed to leave his post unless relieved. But if his supply drone wasn't going to go back to command for more supplies, what was he going to eat?

The next day, Khyentse stepped inside his storehouse and arranged the cans and bottles by expiry date. Afterward, he checked his notes.

He had plenty of water, and that could be refilled with rainwater if necessary. There was also a six-month supply of tea that he could stretch to a year or more. There was flour enough to last about that long, but as for meat and vegetables . . .

Khyentse looked at the small stack of cans. His stomach growled, but he grabbed one and hurried back to his guardhouse to cook it up.

There was no answer to his emails to District Command the next day.

Or the day after that.

Or the day after that . . .

On a grey day, Khyentse woke to the sound of revving rotors. He rushed for the window, peering hopefully at the supply house, but no new drone was there. He heard the rotors again and looked toward the border. His counterpart's drone rose into view from behind the concrete barrier. It edged forward, lowered to perch on the edge, tilted back out of view, then rose again. As Khyentse watched, it shifted forward again before lowering, this time landing without tipping backwards. The rotors cut out, and it sat, waiting. Khyentse peered through the window, past the border. At the other guardhouse, his counterpart waited, holding a tablet like a remote control, looking hopeful.

Khyentse picked up his tablet and called up the last message from command. *All border crossings to be closed. Immediately.*

Khyentse opened his guardhouse door, set his drone outside, and called up the control panel on his tablet. His drone buzzed to life. It flew to the border, where it pulled up close to his counterpart's drone. Khyentse tapped at the controls, lining up the drone just right . . .

With a tap of his fingers, his drone nicked forward and nudged the other off the border wall.

Khyentse watched, satisfied, as his counterpart's drone rose up, then drifted back to his counterpart's guardhouse.

His counterpart looked disappointed, then shrugged, stepping into his guardhouse, not looking back as his drone followed him in.

Khyentse nodded to himself, grimly satisfied, then went back inside.

There was no answer to his emails the next day.

ON A DAY when the clouds parted, Khyentse stepped outside just to stand in the sun. His stomach growled his cans of meat and vegetables were down to half what they were when he sorted them —but he closed his eyes and breathed deep, savouring the warmth at his back. The air smelled charred, but he took another breath anyway.

Then he heard the sound of a drone. He looked hopefully down the road to his country, but it was as empty as before. He looked at the border.

His counterpart's drone drifted to the concrete barrier, then perched atop it. Khyentse peered closer. The drone had a platform added to its base, and something was on it. His counterpart stood outside his guardhouse, tablet in hand. He looked at Khyentse with a pained but hopeful smile.

Khyentse strode to the border. He ducked under the sawbuck and approached the drone. On the platform, there were five full cans of food and one empty water bottle. Khyentse looked from these to his counterpart, who stood waiting.

Khyentse picked up the water bottle. The last few rains had been tainted with ash; he didn't trust it enough to open his rain barrels. He had plenty of full bottles but not an infinite supply.

He looked at the cans.

He looked at the empty water bottle again and thought about what it would be like to be as short of water as he was short of meat and vegetables.

He hurried to his storehouse.

Inside, he set out five water bottles. Looking at the offering, he picked out five more, then five more after that. Gathering them in his arms, he staggered back to the border and set them on the drone platform. He picked up the five cans of food and stepped back.

His counterpart's drone revved up and lifted off, heading back to his counterpart's storehouse. His counterpart gave him a nod, which Khyentse returned before returning to his guardhouse.

THE NEXT MORNING, Khyentse tapped at his tablet. Still no new messages from District Command. He sipped his tea, took a dumpling, and looked out at the border. Then he looked at his tea again.

He nipped out of his seat, went to his storehouse, and counted his rations. Still a few weeks left. He grabbed two rations of flour and a bottle of water. He returned to his guardhouse and went to his stove, mixing flour and water and kneading it into a dough. He turned on the oven.

Later, he emerged from his guardhouse. His drone followed him to the border.

His counterpart stepped out, puzzled. His eyebrows shot up as he saw Khyentse's drone and the platform he'd placed on it, with a teapot and a plate of flatbread. Khyentse lifted up the sawhorse. His drone nipped over and perched atop the barrier.

His counterpart stared at this, then ducked into his guardhouse. He emerged with a box and came over, lifting his sawhorse and stepping closer. He set the box down.

It was biscuits.

Khyentse placed two cups and poured the tea. They stood and sipped, sharing flatbread and biscuits while the wind fluttered the prayer flags and the sun struggled to shine.

Then, his counterpart stepped back and gestured. At first, Khyentse didn't know at what. Then, his counterpart gestured at the control boxes on either side of the retractable barrier. He looked at Khyentse hopefully.

Khyentse frowned. He thought back to the last message from Command: *All border crossings to be closed. Immediately.*

A little voice in the back of his mind spoke up and asked, *Against what?*

All border crossings to be closed. Immediately.

Khyentse drank the last of the tea, bowed to his counterpart, and gathered his teapot and his flatbread. He turned to his guardhouse—before stopping to turn back and hand over the remaining flatbreads. Then he turned and walked away, not looking back.

A NOISE WOKE Khyentse the next day, but when he sat up and listened, he struggled to hear it. There were no drone motors; there was no wind, and yet . . .

He levered himself out of bed and checked his tablet. Still no messages from District Command. He tossed the tablet on the bed, set the kettle on the stove, and got dressed. Pouring tea into his mug, he opened the door and stopped at the sight of—

People at the border.

Dozens of people, clothes and faces grey as ash, stood on the road leading back to the district capital, silent, downcast, gaunt. Some sat on the side of the road, too exhausted to sleep.

Khyentse stepped from his guardhouse, staring. Some stared back, but most didn't react. Some had arms in slings. Others had wounds hastily wound over with dirty cotton. He recognized the Cascadians he'd let through before the border closed. They leaned on each other. Tears marked the man's ashen face.

Khyentse looked back at his bed and his tablet then stepped away and closed the door against it. He turned back to the road and the sawhorse barrier they were waiting at.

Across the border, he saw his counterpart standing in front of his own column of grey-faced refugees.

They'd come all this way, looking for someplace better, but there was nowhere else to go.

Khyentse and his counterpart looked at each other. Khyentse raised his hands. His counterpart grimaced and shrugged.

Khyentse walked through the people to the sawhorse barrier. After a moment's hesitation, he lifted it. His counterpart did the same. They approached the barrier.

After one more glance at each other, they stepped to their respective cranks, grabbed the handles, and turned them. The wall parted. The refugees stared.

Khyentse and his counterpart stepped to the middle of the gap and stood face-to-face. Then they embraced.

There was nowhere else to go. But at least the border wouldn't stop them.

FEAR OF FALLING

BY KARI MAAREN

In orbit around Mars, January 28, 2155

"Are we there yet?" asked Jacks for the third time since the clock had gone red.

Everyone ignored her, which was as usual. Mum and Dad were in the cockpit, talking on the half-broken comm link. Elizabeth and Yasmin were taking turns peering out through the ancient midship scope while Gul was self-importantly entering numbers into the computer via the touchpad in the rec room. They had never, to Jacks's knowledge, had to use the scope before, but the external cameras had stopped working around the time the computer had gone silent, back when the clock was still blue. Every so often, the touchpad would let off a spark, and Gul would lose track of the numbers.

Jacks knew they had been in orbit for a while. She also knew they were supposed to be *going* somewhere. Everyone kept saying. But no one would explain how they could go somewhere while not going anywhere at all.

She pushed off the curved surface next to the broken water

dispenser and floated, headfirst, toward Yasmin and Elizabeth. As Jacks craned to look at them, Elizabeth swatted at Yasmin. Jacks was shaking her head even before both girls shot backward away from the scope in opposite directions. Literal babies knew you didn't push someone if you weren't hanging onto something.

"Kids," said Gram. She was working on the semi-fried air scrubber. Tiny components floated in the air around her head. "Play nice."

Elizabeth had managed to catch hold of one of the handholds near the fore hatch. "She's been looking *forever*. I want to see the planet."

Jacks, who had judged just right, reached out for the scope and swung herself perpendicular to the viewfinder. "*Are* we there yet? No one will say."

"We've been there for three days. That's the problem," said Gul.

Jacks hated the way everybody talked about time.

There had been days at the mines, of course. At least, there had been the clock, which had turned green during working hours and pink during resting hours. That made sense to Jacks. Green-pink-green took you from the start of one day to the start of the next. Yasmin was always trying to get Jacks to look at the numbers on the clock too, but Jacks didn't see the logic in that. People acted as if the numbers always moved at the same rate, but Jacks knew sometimes they sped up, and sometimes they slowed down, and sometimes they almost stood still. The numbers were unreliable. But green-pink-green told you a day had passed.

Now the clock had broken down, just like everything else. It was never green and never pink, and there were no working hours or resting hours. It stood to reason, then, that there weren't any days either. But no one seemed willing to accept that.

"Get away from there," said Elizabeth, bumping herself from handhold to handhold.

"Make me," said Jacks, and looked.

From the way her sisters had been hogging the scope, she had expected something a little more exciting.

Everybody called Mars the red planet. It didn't look red to Jacks: more grey, with pocks and scars on its surface. She had wondered how much bigger than Ceres it would be. Not much, she had figured; Ceres was huge, dwarfing every other body in the Asteroid Belt. But peering through the scope, Jacks wondered. She couldn't see anything *but* Mars. *It's got to be enormous. Maybe even twice as big as Ceres.*

"We can't live there," said Jacks, searching the surface of the planet for anything resembling . . . well, anything. Gul and Mum had talked about the domes a lot, but Jacks couldn't see anything like that.

"We'll live there and like it," said Gram, who, from the sound of it, was putting something back together.

"If they let us," said Elizabeth. "If—"

Someone shushed her. Jacks, in the process of reorienting the scope, missed who, though she thought it may have been Gul.

There was *something* stopping them from landing. Jacks didn't mind. *I don't want to live on a planet. Imagine always being nailed to one surface. You must spend all your time being afraid of falling.*

I don't know why we even had to come here. Elizabeth keeps talking about Earth, but what's Earth got to do with anything? It's too far away to matter.

Earth stopped talking to—

There was no use thinking about *that.*

She swivelled the scope, aiming it toward the nose of the scow and thus toward part of the rest of the convoy.

The asteroid scows were strung out in a shining row. For the journey here, they had clustered together, sharing resources, but in order to enter orbit, they'd had to break apart. Some scows were far enough away to appear simply as bright dots in the black; the closer ones were identifiable as ships. Jacks knew the order of the ones on either side of them because the grown-ups had spent an entire stretch of green arguing about it. *The Gill* . . . then the *Bajorek*. *The Duchamp, the Smith, the Ofori, the Ivanov. Then us* . . . *the Khan. The Chang, the Wilde, the*—

A hand wrapped itself around Jacks's upper arm and yanked her away from the scope. She spun, head over heels over head over heels, across the wide space of the rec room.

"Away from the scope, bratling," said Elizabeth as Jacks fetched up, hard, beside the aft hatch.

She had hit the wall hands first, which was, she thought, lucky for Elizabeth; if she'd hit feet first, she would immediately have launched herself back toward the scope. "*You're* the bratling," called Jacks, swinging herself around.

"You're both bratlings," said Gul. "Shut up, all of you. Unlike you, I have important things to do."

Jacks thought it was possible she and Elizabeth would both have launched themselves straight at Gul if Mum hadn't come through the forehatch just then.

Mum could quell everyone except Gram with a glance. Jacks would have liked to know how she did it. She never seemed that different from the other parents in the convoy, with her tired round face and smooth head and admittedly expressive eyebrows. But everyone froze as she pushed off from the hatch. Without meaning to, Jacks reoriented, angling her body to match Mum's. Yasmin did, too, and Elizabeth followed a moment later. Gul, working with his head pointed at the fore hatch, and Gram, now at right angles to everyone, stayed where they were.

"Maybe turn down the volume," said Mum. "They can probably hear you in the *Ivanov*."

"Physics precludes—" started Yasmin, but stopped when Gram glared her down.

Gul flinched as the computer touchpad sparked again. "Any news from the surface?"

"The *Gill* says no," said Mum. "No one else has been able to open a channel to anyone down there."

Elizabeth said, "I don't see why we can't just land. It's not like they can stop us."

"Great idea. No problems with that at all," said Gram, who may have been feeling increasingly sarcastic as her repair job progressed. She had most of the components back in place now. Jacks knew she was getting close to the moment when she would have to turn the scrubber back on and learn that the last three hours of work had been for nothing. Lately, it generally went like that.

"Well, they can't," said Elizabeth.

Gul said, "They can seal off their docking bays and refuse us ox—"

"—access," said Mum a split second too late, with a glance at Jacks.

Jacks felt her own less expressive eyebrows scrunching into a glare. She knew Gul had been about to say "oxygen." She was eight, not three.

"Everybody thinks I'm a baby," she announced to the universe in general, or the part of it inside the family scow.

"You *are* a baby. You have no idea what's going on," said Elizabeth.

Everybody except Gram and Jacks drifted toward Gul then, and Mum started saying something about numbers, which was basically noise and could be tuned out. Jacks could have joined them, but somehow, she didn't want to. Her eyes prickled. A tear teased itself loose and floated in a tiny ball in front of her face until she pinched it into fragments with her fingers.

She *did* know what was going on. There was ... something about ... and they had come here because ...

Earth stopped talking to us.

Why would that matter?

Do nutrients grow on asteroids? Do we mine for calories? No? Then why do you think *it—*

I'm not talking to you, said Jacks to Jacks. She dashed a hand across her eyes. The tears spun in the air, perfectly formed, gleaming like the row of scows in orbit around Mars.

JACKS WAS LOSING her third game of Carrhombus when the computer died.

Yasmin always won at Carrhombus, even against Gram, but everyone kept challenging her anyway. Elizabeth said Yasmin was going to lose at least once someday, if only by sheerest accident. Everybody wanted to be the person who beat her.

The moment the computer emitted its final spark was also the moment Jacks sent her striker spinning into the orthorhombic game field. As it left her fingers, she saw, through and beyond the field, the biggest spark yet bloom from the touchpad. It almost counted as actual fire. But even as the striker tumbled through the field, missing its target, the globe-shaped spark contracted, collapsing in on itself.

The computer's screens went black.

Gul thumped the touchpad. Nothing happened.

"We still have ... light," said Yasmin.

She was going to say "air," said the part of Jacks's bran that appeared to have taken on a life of its own.

"Life support is working," said Gul. "I don't know what ..."

He thumped the touchpad again.

As the striker rebounded off the mesh that delimited the game field, Jacks became aware that the sounds were wrong.

The slightly tortured hum of the scrubber had stopped earlier when Gram had had most of its guts floating in the air around her, but it had started up again once she'd finished failing to fix it. That sound was still there. There should have been something else beneath it, and something else beneath that. Jacks, in the process of retrieving her striker, felt the hair on her arms rise. She didn't know what the missing sounds were, but she did know the scow felt different without them.

"Can't you just—" said Elizabeth.

Yasmin held up a hand.

Her own striker slipped from her fingers and drifted toward the scope. "Listen," she said.

They all floated in place and listened, Jacks and Gul and Elizabeth and Yasmin. Dad came through the fore hatch and Gram through the aft hatch, but neither spoke. Yasmin spun in a slow circle, her arms outstretched.

"I don't hear anything," said Elizabeth finally.

Jacks said, in a low voice, "Something's stopped."

Elizabeth opened her mouth, but Yasmin nodded. "Heat," she said. "Cooling. Temperature regulation."

There was a moment that went on for far too long. The numbers on the clock may have paused again.

Everyone in the rec room except Jacks moved at once.

Jacks stayed where she was, clutching the striker. *We're playing a game*, she thought. *Aren't we?* Yasmin wasn't; she had caught a handhold and slingshotted herself toward Gul. Gul opened a panel and stared at a tangle of wires; Elizabeth slid back another panel and mashed the buttons she had revealed. Jacks wasn't sure what Dad and Gram were doing because they were behind her, and she didn't want to turn around, and she had been playing a game, and it was Yasmin's turn, so she was waiting.

This probably means we have to go to Mars.

Of course we have to go to Mars. We can't live here. We could when Earth brought us supplies, but that's over now.

Mars can bring us supplies. I bet they have enough. Everyone says the Martians are rich.

The scow isn't even working properly. It was never meant to travel between Ceres and Mars. And now the temperature—

We always fix the broken bits just enough. I don't want to go to Mars.

You would rather freeze to death than go to Mars?

Yes, Jacks thought fiercely at the alien inside her brain. *Mars has gravity. It must feel like being pressed against the wall* all the time. *Gul says when he's gone to Mars, he's had to wear an exoskeleton. I don't want to wear any kind of skeleton. I don't want anything to change. I don't see why it has to just because Earth won't talk to us.*

"We're going to *die*," said Elizabeth, a sob in her voice.

"Shut up, Elizabeth!" said Dad.

Jacks clenched her fist around the striker and wondered when Yasmin was going to take her turn.

Elizabeth was in the middle of a wail when Gram catapulted across the rec room and hit the touchpad with a wrench.

Everyone stopped moving. It was impossible to think. The sound of the pounding drowned out the hum of the scrubber and the hiss of the circulator and the absence of sound from the regulator. If Jacks hadn't been frozen, she would have pressed her hands to her ears.

The computer screens flickered to life. Gram stopped.

"What?" she said as the proper sounds bled back into the atmosphere, and everyone in the family—including Mum, who had come in during the general panic—turned to stare at her. "That's how we used to do it back on Earth."

"We'll have to remember that next time," said Gul, his voice simultaneously polite and straining at the edge of control.

"There can't—" said Dad and closed his lips over the rest.

As usual, Jacks could fill in the missing words: "*—be a next time.*"

But there's going to be if we stay in orbit.

I like it in orbit.

You won't if we lose temperature regulation.

I wish Yasmin would take her turn. My fingers hurt.

Jacks glanced down at her hand. She had been clenching her fist so hard around the striker that it had left grooves in her flesh.

She spent the next little while wondering why it had done that, and why Elizabeth was crying so loudly, and whether, if Yasmin was forfeiting the game, it meant Jacks had won. By the time Dad led Elizabeth away to her bunk to calm down, Jacks had still not figured out any of the answers.

THE NEXT TIME JACKS CHECKED, the clock had gone black.

"No more time," said Yasmin. She nodded as if this confirmed something.

Nobody seemed to be panicking now. The family moved calmly about the scow. Gram checked over the useless mining equipment as methodically as she had the air scrubber. Elizabeth polished the broken clock with her sleeve. Jacks, wandering aimlessly, poked her head into the cockpit and found Mum and Dad listening to a comm message that seemed to be mostly static.

"That's Brian Gill," said Mum, and Dad nodded.

Jacks didn't think it was Brian Gill. She didn't think it was anyone.

Maybe we're alone. Maybe the scows I saw through the scope aren't there anymore. Maybe we're just going to sit here until we run out of—

It was Brian Gill. The static was whining just like he does.

What if the toilet stops working?

Jacks was pretty sure she should have gone to bed ages ago. It was hard to tell since time had stopped, but she could feel the signs: the prickling behind her eyes, the impulse to yawn, the way everything had gone slow. She couldn't go to bed. If they were really running out of—anyway. She floated from fore to aft and back again, from the engine room through the galley and the bunk room and the lavatory and the rec room and the mining bay and the pod bay to the cockpit and back again.

On one of her trips through the rec room, she noticed Gul at his usual touchpad, staring at the numbers on the screen in front of him. They weren't just numbers this time. There were words there, too. She could read just well enough to catch one of them as she floated by:

threaten

The word puzzled her.

It was the kind of word Elizabeth used too often. "Mum, Jacks is *threatening* me." "Dad, Yasmin's existence *threatens* my tranquility." Elizabeth liked words she could really bite into. But the point of them was that they were always too serious for what was actually happening.

Maybe that was what was up with the computer, too. Maybe it was Elizabeth at a touchpad in another room, sending messages to Gul.

Maybe it wasn't.

The comm link isn't working. Is our computer talking to the computers on the other scows?

Earth stopped talking to us.

What will we do if Mars does too?

Hasn't it already?

Eventually, Jacks pulled out the Carrhombus set. Gul gave her a strange look, and Yasmin shook her head.

It was Elizabeth who said, "I'll play."

Playing anything with Elizabeth was usually terrible, but

she seemed much quieter than normal. Jacks set up the orthorhombic frame.

Without speaking, they placed the queen and the seeds at the centre of the game field, then sealed the mesh.

The rec room was quiet. Mum and Dad were back in the cockpit, and Gram had gone aft to the engine room. Gul and Yasmin were murmuring together beside the touchpad. There was no time, so maybe everything was just going to stay like this forever. It felt that way to Jacks. She flicked her striker into the field but didn't watch to see where it went. Elizabeth had apparently forgotten to aim through the hole in the mesh since her striker rebounded off the mesh, shot out into the room, and narrowly missed tapping Yasmin on the back of the head.

"Watch it," said Gul.

Yasmin whispered, "How much longer until we know . . .?"

Jacks didn't think she had been meant to hear that. The room was quieter than it should have been. The temperature regulator was working, but one by one, other familiar sounds had fallen silent.

Jacks's striker hit one of the rods at a bad angle and ricocheted uselessly, pocketing nothing.

"I wonder if we'll go to school on Mars," said Elizabeth.

Jacks was sure Elizabeth had been body-snatched by some other, politer, girl.

"We could build a school in orbit," said Jacks, largely for something to say.

Gul said, too audibly, "If they don't respond within an hour, the *Gill* will go first. One of the domes is just coming into view."

Go? Go where? Are they letting us land?

You know they're not.

"I bet we could repurpose the scows into a school," said Elizabeth. "Using the connectors, you know. Every scow could be a classroom. There could be a maths scow, a physics scow, a language arts scow . . . stuff like that."

"With teachers from Mars," said Jacks. "I bet they have loads."

"I don't think we should do this," said Yasmin. "We should *land*, not—"

"If we do it that way, we'll all die," said Gul. "This way, maybe they'll see—"

"I hear it's beautiful inside the domes," said Elizabeth. "We can go to the scow school but visit the surface sometimes. The Ivanovs say there are gardens. And pets."

"I don't know what that means," said Jacks.

Normally, Elizabeth would have scoffed at this. Now, she just nodded. "Lots of plants made to look pretty. And animals that don't work . . . that just live with people because people like them."

"That sounds like an Earth thing," said Jacks, wondering what it would be like to live with an animal, to run her hands through its fur. Feathers? Scales? She'd heard of cows. Maybe cows made good pets.

"Will we have to . . .?" said Yasmin.

Gul shook his head. "It won't come to that. If the *Gill* goes, they'll know we're serious."

"What if they don't?"

"Definitely an Earth thing," said Elizabeth loudly as Jacks tried not to hear Gul using the words "puncture" and "catastrophic" in a sentence that would have made horrible sense if she had been paying attention to it, which she wasn't.

Jacks said, "Do books talk about them?"

"Yeah. But Earth books are confusing," said Elizabeth. "I'm going to be the first Asteroid Belt author."

"Nobody will read your books," said Jacks, not mentioning that no one was ever going to be an Asteroid Belt author, that the Asteroid Belt had been abandoned, that Earth had stopped talking to them, that Ceres and Vesta were empty and quiet and Mars was shutting them out and on the *Khan*, which was all they had left, everything was failing.

"Then I'll write them privately and be discovered after I die," said Elizabeth, not mentioning it either.

"*Gill* standing by for atmospheric entry," said Gul.

"Maybe," said Jacks. "Maybe you. Maybe I . . ."

There was something wrong with the air. She knew there wasn't really; the air scrubber howled on. But there was something wrong with the air *inside her*. She flicked her striker in the wrong direction.

I wish Mum and Dad and Gram were in here.

They can't be in case we have to—

Threat. Threaten. Threatening.

Remember when Gramps died? And Phyllis Chang? Remember when you saw Phyllis with her eyes closed in the—

Whose turn is it? I think it's Elizabeth's.

"In Earth books," said Elizabeth in a faint, trembling voice, "everyone is always going on about 'up' and 'down.' And when someone lands on a planet, it's all, 'and then the ship flew *down* to the surface.' But that doesn't make any sense. You may as well say the ship is flying *up* to the surface. Or over, or across."

"The ship flew across to the surface," said Jacks.

"No such thing as falling, really," said Elizabeth. "No such thing as down."

Jacks could almost see it: the *Gill*, not falling, not drawn by a mystifying force called gravity toward the surface of a planet that Jacks could just about admit to herself had to be a lot bigger than Ceres, but floating gently across, pinging against the surface of Mars like a Carrhombus striker against a rod in the game field. The *Khan* wouldn't fall, either. Everything, everywhere, would remain bubble-light. The Martians would open their domes in welcome and float out to meet the scows. The clocks would go green and pink, and someone would find some convenient new asteroids to mine, and in the nick of time, a message would arrive from Earth: "Ha ha! Fooled you! Everything is fine." And no one would talk about falling ever again.

"It's time," said Yasmin, though there wasn't any time. "They should be starting—"

Gul said, "Wait."

A stray seed floated into Jacks's visual field, then out again. Elizabeth was breathing raggedly on the other side of the orthorhombic field.

Numbers and words flicked across Gul's screen. There was another screen not far from Jacks. She didn't look at it.

"Is that . . .?" said Yasmin.

Gul read out, "'Stand down. Message from surface. One biosphere preparing to receive convoy.'"

Elizabeth made a sound Jacks had never heard from her before.

For Jacks, the rec room had gone dim and slow. She knew Yasmin was patting Gul on the shoulder, and Gul had his face buried in his hands, and Mum and Dad and Gram were there somehow, and Gram was saying she'd known it would be fine, and Mum was hugging Elizabeth, and Dad kept running his hands over his bare head and blinking tear spheres out of his eyes, and once again, Jacks was the still point in the middle of the chaos, but for a different reason. She thought, *The planet is down.* And the whole room, the whole scow, reoriented itself. For the first time in her life, Jacks knew the fear of falling.

"ARE WE THERE YET?" asked Jacks.

Elizabeth, who was back to normal, aimed a slap at her. Jacks danced backward out of the way.

They were supposed to be strapping in. Soon, they would have to. Soon, the engines would ignite for one last burn, and the scow would enter the atmosphere, something it wasn't really designed to do, though Gul said it could handle it. Soon, Jacks would find out what weighing something felt like.

"Everything's broken," said Gram, who had checked.

"There are enough not-broken bits to go on with," said Gul.

People had been talking about some rich Martian who had strongarmed some other rich Martians and possibly some sort of contract someone would eventually need to sign, but Jacks hadn't been listening much to any of that. She knew it would end in them landing on the planet and gravity commencing.

"The first thing that happens is that your feet fill with blood," said Elizabeth. "You need to get new shoes made because you go up four sizes. You head shrinks, though, so you need smaller hats."

"Elizabeth," said almost everyone.

"What?" said Elizabeth. "I read it in a book."

"Just go strap in," said Gul.

They did. Jacks felt the engines purr to life. All around them, she knew, the rest of the convoy was preparing to nudge out of orbit and into a place where "down" mattered.

"I may be a little scared," said Yasmin judiciously, as if the verdict could have gone either way.

"I'm not scared of anything," said Elizabeth.

She said it several times as the scow began to move. She continued to say it, over and over, long after it had become too noisy for anyone to hear her. Jacks stopped paying attention. She didn't know whether she was scared or not. Everything seemed too big for that, and too new. But as they went, as Elizabeth's knuckles turned white and Yasmin whispered inaudible calculations and Gul held a wrench poised to smack the touchpad if the computer stopped working, Jacks opened her hand and let the Carrhombus seed she had been holding slip free.

As the unknown world roared around her, she smiled, and she watched, waiting for it to fall.

RIGHT TO REPAIR

BY FIONA J. MOORE

Britomart Farming Platform
Venus, September 24, 2159

BRITOMART, THE HAVOC WHERE THE CHUMAK FARM WAS located, was so big Esteban could sometimes forget he was growing grain on a cloud platform high above the surface of Venus. Though, that had been part of the appeal for his great-grandmother, the one who'd made the move out here from Earth. Unhappy with the increasing industrialization and commercialization of farming, she'd taken a tip from her own ancestors, the ones who'd fled Ukraine for Manitoba back in the day, and thrown her lot in on Venus.

"I liked the idea that we could build community values. Do farming that's about feeding people, not just extracting every last penny from the Earth," she'd said on the memoir video Esteban had seen. Then, with a gleam in her eye, "Besides, building a farm on a floating platform? What a challenge! Nothing like it had ever been done before. So I moved out to Venus, cut ties with the Earth."

Except, Esteban reflected, they'd never been able to cut ties with Earth entirely. Not as long as Earth companies were the ones supplying the equipment.

Ted Chrysanthopoulos looked up from the motherboard he was working on as Esteban stamped into the machine shed. "Did you get the new convertor?" he asked.

Esteban shook his head, dropping the box on the workbench. "Martha didn't have any for a 2500. Only a 2100."

"Can't they print one to spec in a factory HAVOC?"

"They did, and this is it," Esteban said. "The factory needs software to do that, and the software's proprietary. The 2500 software wiped itself years ago."

Ted put aside the soldering gun. "We'll just have to try to make the 2100 work."

"Where's Gloria?"

"Out checking on the watering system." Ted looked critically at Esteban. "I hate to say it, but I don't know how long that's going to keep working, either."

Esteban sighed.

"It was the same deal back in the Asteroid Belt," Ted said sympathetically. "Except we didn't have the space for industrial printers even. You needed a spare part, you had to order it from Earth and wait."

"What did you do while you waited?"

Ted smiled thinly. "Lost money, mostly."

"What about workarounds?"

Ted's expression didn't change. "The machines are built to be as workaround-proof as possible. Companies want you buying their spare parts or, even better, buying new machines. They don't want you to be able to just tie it together with string and baling wire."

"Yeah." Companies were convinced they'd last forever. Or, more likely, that when they went bust, it would be someone else's problem.

As indeed it was. Esteban's. And to a lesser extent, Ted and Gloria's.

"We could see if someone else would be willing to trade." Ted abandoned the motherboard and came around the other side of the workbench. "That's what you did last time, isn't it?"

"Yeah." That time, it had been the seeder, but it turned out that Xiao Tang, down the road, had a spare she'd been willing to swap for a length of rubber tubing for her watering system. And the time before, it had been the irrigation system, Mo Sharik, and the use of his harvester at harvest time. "That's how we've all been keeping going these past few years. Swapping what we have for what we haven't. But what happens when we run out?" He certainly didn't have any spare tubing anymore and, given the condition of his own watering system, sometimes wondered if he'd made the right decision not to keep it.

Then he berated himself for his selfishness. Xiao Tang had needed the tubing, just as he had needed the spare.

"Did you hear back from the engineering firm?" Esteban asked Ted, hoping to get on to a happier subject.

"Not yet," Ted answered, going back to his motherboard. "Maybe next week. Probably don't need anybody, though. A lot of refugees out there looking for jobs."

"Don't refugees get priority for job allocation?"

Ted rolled his eyes. "Oh, yeah, but there's so many of us, it's not like it matters. Lots of people out there with the same skills and qualifications as me. Most of us wind up allocated to farming HAVOCs and, I mean, no offence, but I didn't go out and get a design qualification just so I could harvest wheat." He carefully placed a drop of solder in the right place and held the wires to it. "And not that I'm not grateful to be here on Venus, but... you arrive, and it's all welcome gifts and speeches and talking about how we want to help our poor friends from the Asteroid Belt, but ask them for anything practical, and suddenly, they're not as helpful."

Esteban tried not to take that personally. "Still, anything I can do to help, let me know," he said. "And you're welcome to work here for as long as you like."

Ted smiled. "Thanks. I appreciate it."

But Esteban understood. Ted was a designer, and he didn't really like the day-to-day of farm life, worrying about fertilizer mixes and growing cycles and plant yields. Even fixing the machines wasn't much of a challenge for Ted; he'd rather be creating something new. Esteban knew it would be the same if their positions were reversed. He'd be sad to lose Ted, but he had to accept he'd be happier somewhere else. It was probably the same for Gloria, though she never said too much about what she really wanted to be doing. She was always on that tablet of hers, though, so Esteban expected she was applying for reallocation, too.

Gloria Augustin came in from the fields and, before the men could brief her, took in the scene and said, "Didn't have the part, huh?"

Gloria described her ancestry as coming from "everywhere, but mostly Haiti." And she certainly had the stoicism Esteban associated with coming from a place that, when it had existed, seemed to go down in tsunamis every few years.

"You got it," Ted said. "We were just talking about how the parts are getting scarcer now Earth's gone."

"And we can't keep this up indefinitely," Esteban added.

Gloria frowned. "Yeah. We could maybe fudge up a repair with the parts we have, though." She took the 2100 converter and put it next to the faulty 2500. "Looks like the same part, almost. Should fit the hole."

Ted went over to the harvester, opened the hatch, stuck the converter in the right spot, and tightened the connections.

"You're right, it works," Esteban said.

"Switch it on," Gloria said.

Esteban hopped into the cockpit, flicked the on-switch . . .

Swore.

He gestured at the display, which was flashing with the words INCOMPATIBLE, PLEASE REPLACE WITH APPRO-PRIATE UNIT.

"Software," Ted said. "They build them so you *can't* replace them with an earlier part, even if that part would work."

"What are we going to do now?" Esteban switched the machine off and climbed out. "We've got the harvest coming up in a few weeks and no harvester."

"You know," Gloria said, getting a crafty look on her face, "I'll bet that kid of yours could brute-force a software solution."

"Who, Stella?" Esteban hadn't thought of that, but it actually made sense. "Sure. I'll ask if she could do that. I'll do it tonight."

ESTEBAN'S DAUGHTER, Stella, was at university in Perelandra, the biggest HAVOC on Venus. She was studying software engineering at the Perelandra Institute of Technology (whose students seemed to have an endless supply of jokes about studying at a PIT) and having a great time—a better time than she would have had on the farm.

Which didn't bother Esteban. The big HAVOCs were where the action was, after all. It might have been nice to have the farm continue to be a family business, but he'd much rather have Stella be happy doing something she loved and was good at than force her to take on something she didn't. He'd promised his wife, Christina, dead ten years now, that he'd let Stella decide what sort of future she wanted. There would be plenty of young people coming up who would want to take on the farm when he decided to retire.

Or, at least, that was what he'd told himself.

Stella had been away nearly three years, and no one had

shown the slightest interest in taking on the farm. He'd got Ted and Gloria, yes, but they were refugees from the Asteroid Belt. It wasn't like they were in the job for the love of it, and he was sure that when they found something more to their liking, they'd move on.

Still, he wasn't going to tell Stella about his fears. He was honest with her, of course, but he always tried to be optimistic during their video calls.

Stella listened as he outlined his problem. Her frown deepened and deepened, and then her face suddenly lit up. "Yeah. I think I can work on that," she said. "I can't guarantee anything, but I did a course on vehicle software in second year, and I might be able to take some of the things I learned from there. Can you send me all the technical information you have?"

"Sure." Esteban peered hard at the screen. "How are things?" She was looking a little peaky, he thought, or maybe it was just protective-dad instinct making him read too much into it.

"Oh," Stella gestured vaguely. "Okay, I guess. Just got to make some decisions about what I do next year."

"If you want to go to graduate school like you were saying, I'm fine with it," Esteban said. She'd have to pass the government exam to qualify, of course, but with Stella's determination, he was sure she'd ace it.

"Thanks. But the problem is that I'm not sure what I *want* to do," Stella said. "Graduate school would be okay, but I don't really have a project I'd be interested in doing for two years. I've had a few job offers from HAVOCs, but not for anything I'd really find exciting. Lots of boring database management and communications stuff."

Esteban shrugged. "Work for a HAVOC or a government department for a few years, build up experience, go freelance?"

"Maybe." Stella wound a lock of her long, dark hair around her finger. "Plenty of time to decide, I guess."

"Okay, so I've installed Stella's modified software into the harvester . . ." Gloria stepped back and pressed the switch.

"It's like a New Year's party," Ted said. "Should I do a countdown?"

Gloria ignored him. "Here we go!" She bent over the control panel and accessed the convertor readout.

"And?"

Gloria's face said it all. "It works!"

"Fantastic!" Esteban gave Ted a side hug. "We're good for the season, then!"

"Yeah!" Gloria said, but her smile got wobbly.

"What's wrong?" Esteban asked.

"Oh, you know, just thinking," Gloria said. "What happens when the other parts wear out?"

"More fixes?"

"What if Stella can't come up with something?"

"I'm sure someone else in the farms might? Or might know somebody?"

"I think," Ted said slowly, "we might want to call a meeting."

Esteban was surprised how many people turned up for the meeting in the end.

"It's a problem that affects all of us," Mo Sharik said by way of explanation. "This is the biggest problem for all the farmers right now."

"Not just the farmers, either," said Tammy Banes, who ran the Moonlite Restaurant on Britomart's commercial level, where the meeting was taking place. "I've been keeping my stove going with duct tape and hope for the last few years."

"At least teachers have been able to go back to analog

equipment," said Xiao Tang. "Though they're having trouble getting books."

"Printer shortages," Tammy said. "They've got the same problem."

"They've got the Grade 4 kids hand-copying out the Grade 3 textbooks to make up for the shortage," Mo said. "My son's doing a chapter a week."

Ted smiled wryly. "I suppose it gives them handwriting practice?"

"If the printers break down completely, they'll need it!"

"What about Mars?" Tammy said. "I'm sure if there's a profit in it, they'd be happy to make us parts. And software."

"But that puts us in the same position as before," Xiao Tang said. "Beholden to someone else for things we need. And Mars is even worse than Earth for greed."

"Profits before everything." Tammy sighed. "Yeah, I wouldn't want to deal with them either."

"This is why I think we need to set up a collective," Esteban said, accepting a cup of coffee from Tammy's husband.

"You mean like a co-op?" Tammy asked.

"Not exactly. Co-ops are companies that share costs and dividends equally; a collective is more like a group of interested people—in this case, one focusing on designing and developing new things." He looked around the diner. "Back in my great-grandmother's day, on Earth, they had a thing called 'right to repair.' She talks about it in her memorial video. Groups of people who would hack software and customize parts so they weren't dependent on companies for their spares."

"How's that different from what we're doing now?" asked Xiao Tang

"We get organized about it," Esteban said. "We pool our skills. We hire software engineers or find ones who'll work for barter. We inventory what we have, what we need. We keep track of what's about to wear out and what we need to fix it."

"We could do that through the co-op," said Martha, who ran the co-op in question.

"Yes, so any profits and losses get shared through the members," Mo said thoughtfully. "Would you be able to take on the extra work?"

"My second kid is talking about learning the business," Martha said. "I could put them onto it as a learning project."

"Well, then," Esteban said. "Let's get this organized."

"IT'S NOT WORKING," Esteban said.

"Coulda fooled me." Gloria jerked her head at the machines bagging the harvested grain. "The harvester worked, the processor is working; we've got to do the gleaning, but that won't take as long as it did last year. We're on track to a decent winter again."

"Oh, it's working in *that* sense," Esteban said. "What bugs me, though, is that we're just patching up what we've got. What happens when a machine breaks down so bad we need a new one?"

"You're such a pessimist," Gloria said. "Martha did the math. Worked out we can keep them going for a couple of generations on this system."

"So it'll be Stella's problem or Stella's kids' problem. Not very responsible of us, kicking the can down the road."

"Maybe by then, we'll have figured out a permanent solution?" Gloria sounded uncertain. Then she said, "What the hell?"

The processing machine finished off a bag, then slowly chugged to a gentle stop, like it had finished the job—even though there was a hopperful of grain still to go.

Esteban turned on the access panel, looking for errors.

"I don't believe this," he said. "Listen to this! 'Hi there! We see you're not using the proprietary software of the Jon White Agricultural Equipment Company. Please re-install the appropriate software and resume operations.'"

"I thought Stella had written us a whole new operating system?"

"I did," Stella said when Esteban was able to get in touch with her. "I think what we've got is zombie software."

"What?"

"A routine that's embedded too deep for me to catch. Remember, the problem the right-to -repair movement had was companies that were willing to deep-six their own products just to keep people from not buying their stuff."

"No, I don't. You've been reading up on it."

"I have," Stella said. "Give me a few days. I know a couple of people who might be up to this sort of challenge."

"I'm glad you're enjoying this." Esteban meant it to be sarcastic, but Stella nodded.

"I am," she said. "Thanks, Dad. This is actually a really fun project. In fact, I've written it up, and I've submitted it as a proposed thesis for graduate work."

"Well," was all Esteban could say.

"This sort of thing's not just interesting." Stella sounded earnest as if she was trying to persuade him. "It's important. This could help a lot of people, Dad. Not just farmers. Lots of other people have the same problem: machines designed to keep people dependent on the company that even now the company's gone are still trying to do just that."

"But we can fix it, right?"

"Of course."

"I'M SORRY, ESTEBAN." Ted emerged from the seeder unit. "We just can't fix it."

Esteban felt desperate. "What? But we've got the collective going, making new parts out of the old. We've got the software licked and a team of students going after any new bugs that surface. What the hell's wrong with the seeder?"

Ted waved a handful of corroded metal. "It's the atmosphere. The parts were designed on Earth. Weren't designed for Venus's atmosphere.."

For a moment Esteban was puzzled, then the penny dropped. While the air inside the HAVOCs technically had the same chemical balance as Earth, the fact that the components were drawn in from the Venusian atmosphere meant things were slightly more acidic. The filters and processors could only do so much. The effect was subtle enough that most people didn't notice, but it caused problems sometimes with equipment that hadn't been properly coated. But these . . .

"That's ridiculous. They're Venus spec. It says so on the labels."

"Yeah, sort of." Gloria came in, holding a tablet. "That was my reaction, too, so I did some research. It seems the machines were originally designed for Earth conditions, and 'Venus spec' just meant making a few changes so they'd work on Venus for up to two years."

"The length of the warranty, of course," Esteban noted.

Gloria paged through the tablet. "I suppose we're actually pretty lucky they've lasted as well as they have."

"I thought Martha estimated they had forty years of use in them?" Esteban couldn't resist an angry look at Gloria.

"I think she was assuming 'Venus spec' meant Venus spec. Same as we were."

Esteban couldn't really argue with that.

"We could ceramic-coat the parts," Ted said. "Or get some new ones made with ceramic coating."

"And how much is that going to cost?" Esteban sighed. "And is there anyone who can do that in the collective?"

"Esteban—"

"No, the corporations have won." Esteban threw up his hands. "We can't just keep fixing and fixing and fixing, and we can't build our own new bespoke machines without going bankrupt. I give up."

He walked out into the fields, not caring if the others followed.

"I brought you dinner." Gloria held out a covered tiffin box.

"Thanks." Esteban had walked to the edge of the property and sat—on the ground, for lack of anything else to sit on— looking out the sides of Britomart at the roiling orange cloud beyond.

Gloria sat down, too. "Crazy, isn't it? Nothing like where I grew up. Mind you, that was all mines and tunnels and protected habitats. This at least gives you something pretty to look at."

"Christina and I used to like to come out here and look at the clouds," Esteban said. "They don't seem so pretty now. More like something that's going to kill us all."

"That's a little depressing," Gloria said.

"True, though," Esteban opened the tiffin box, uncovering some kind of curry with chicken and raisins. It smelled pretty good. "We were crazy. Colonizing other planets? Where we're not meant to be, or our machines either? The whole thing's just doomed."

Gloria was quiet, watching the clouds. "Maybe not so doomed."

"What do you mean?"

"You're right. We're all tied up with Earth. But Earth's not here anymore. Nor, and it takes a hell of a lot for me to admit this, are we ever going back to the Asteroid Belt. We've all got to move on."

"Move on, like quit the farm?"

"No." Gloria handed him a piece of paper.

"What's this?"

"Ted was too anxious about what you'd say to show you himself, so I said I'd do it."

Esteban looked at it. "It's a harvester?"

"It's a *new* harvester. Designed for Venus from, well, I guess you can't say the ground up around here." Gloria chuckled. "Takes the basic design of the harvester we had, adds in a few other things. Like here, he's added the belt mechanism we used to have on the old tunnelling drills. And see, the wheels are smoother 'cause you don't need to get traction on a HAVOC like you would on an Earth field."

"So what are you saying? That we build one of these?"

"No," Gloria said. "I'm saying that we build a *lot* of these. How many farmers are there on Venus? Couple of million for the whole planet? I mean, I know they're not all growing grain, but the basic design's adaptable to a lot of crops and then . . ."

"You're crazy. In a good way, yes, but crazy." Esteban shook his head. "Where are we going to get the money? Who's going to build them?"

"That's the best part," Gloria said. "The government has money for exactly this sort of thing. Innovation grants. You need to be a citizen to apply, but of course, you're one of those. As for the space, we can start out renting an industrial printer in a factory HAVOC, then expand as we need to. I've factored that into the cost breakdown here." She pulled another piece of paper out of her pocket. This one was covered in notes in Gloria's neat printing, outlining costs and predicted profits. "I've put out some feelers in the factory HAVOCs, and Mordor's got space."

"How'd you learn to do all this?"

"You never asked what I did back in the Asteroid Belt, did you?" Gloria smiled as Esteban looked a little ashamed. "Not all miners dig for minerals. I had an accounting degree, did the math for the firm. I've done this sort of costing before whenever we set out on a new venture."

"We'll draft up a proposal. The three of us."

"The three of us?"

"You, me, and Ted."

"What about me?" Stella said.

"Well, I didn't think . . ."

On the screen, her smile grew broader. "Of course you didn't, Dad. I know. You were always really supportive of me doing my own thing, so you didn't think about asking me to join a family business. But it's funny. I was thinking of doing exactly the same thing as you guys. But with the software."

"Really?"

"Yeah. I had so much fun hacking and writing the software, and so did my friends. We were talking about maybe not going into jobs in HAVOCs after we graduate but instead starting our own agricultural right-to-repair software firm. So, if you're setting up a business, why don't we join forces? Farming machines *and* the software to run them. Only it'll be open source. Customizable. People can do their own edits and patches, so we don't wind up in the same place we were before."

"Brilliant idea. And I think we've got our company name right there."

"Go on?"

"The Right To Repair company. R2R for short, maybe."

"It's perfect!"

"Let's hope it looks good on our grant application."

✳

"But *why* wouldn't the government give us the grant?" Stella complained, accepting a cup of coffee from her father. She'd come back to Britomart for a weekend visit, planning to celebrate the official birth of R2R, but Esteban had unfortunately brought her disappointing news.

"It's not that they didn't think it was a good idea," Esteban said. "And they did encourage us to try again. The problem is allocations and rationing. All the funding's tied up right now, what with having to help all the people from Earth and the Asteroid Belt."

"But *this* will help people from Earth and the Asteroid Belt!"

"Yeah, you know what I mean." Esteban leaned on the kitchen counter. "They understand, and they also appreciated my case about the long-term future of farming on Venus. But I can't deny their point that they have more urgent problems. And Venus is a fair society—the resources need to go where they're most urgently needed."

Stella scoffed. "The government equivalent of patching the harvester till it falls apart!"

"Well, isn't that what we're doing right now?" Esteban smiled wryly. "We'll just have to carry on doing fixes till the resources are available or until we find some other means of support."

"Short-sighted idiots." Stella gripped her cup in a way that made Esteban worry she was going to throw it at something. "We need to get started on this now, *before* the need is urgent because when it is, we'll just be playing catch-up. I don't know why you're not furious."

"Oh, I am," Esteban said. "I am. But I've learned it doesn't do any good to rage about these things. We just have to accept them and keep trying."

The doorbell sounded. With a puzzled glance at Stella, Esteban went and answered it.

It was Gloria.

"Esteban, you have to come to the Moonlite right now. Oh, hi, Stella. You, too."

"Sure, if it's okay with Stella," Esteban said. "What's it about?"

"Just come and see."

WHEN THEY GOT to the Moonlite, Esteban could see that it was full of farmers—his neighbours, their families, Martha, some people from elsewhere in the HAVOC he didn't know. And at least one person he knew ran a forestry plantation. They all had drinks in their hands, and they all turned to look at him, Stella, and Gloria as they came in. Martha stepped forward and handed him a glass of beer.

Puzzled, he accepted it. "Uh, hi?" he said.

"We all heard about the grant application, of course," Gloria said. Esteban suspected she'd had something to do with that, but gossip generally travelled pretty quickly around the HAVOCs.

"So . . . what's this, then? A sympathy party?" Esteban had never heard of such a thing, but why not?

"No," Martha said. "It's the new company. Our new company. We think that we should go ahead with R2R. As a co-op."

"I did the math." Gloria thrust her tablet at Esteban before he could say anything. "Worked out the minimum investment for, say, two hundred people to get the company going. It's not much, as you can see. Most people are chipping in for more."

"In exchange for lower prices at the retail end, of course," Martha said.

"And people who want to work for us will get defined cuts of the profits," Gloria added. "Ted and Stella can be our first full-time employees."

"We can start small and expand," Ted chimed in. "I guess I won't be looking for a new job. Nor will Gloria, of course."

Esteban couldn't help grinning. The chances of finding someone to take on the farm were looking better every minute . . . which was good, because it was looking like he was going to stop running a family farm and start running a family business.

For a very expansive definition of "family."

"And all of you, you're all wanting in?"

Everyone in the Moonlite grinned back.

"Then let's do this," Esteban said. He raised his mug in a toast. "Everyone, here's to the Right To Repair."

"Right to Repair!" the crowd echoed. Glasses clinked, and together, they drank to the health of their new company—and their planet.

THE MUSKHOLE KING

BY MARK RICHARD FRANCIS

Syrtis Major Planum
Mars, January 14, 2163

AGGRESSIVE AIR CURRENTS BUFFETED YOUNG MARCUS'S BACK. Cracking his jaw for relief after every few dozen hurried inclined steps brought him fleeting comfort as the pressure in his ears built to a vexing level after only a few more strides. The expansive tunnel he jogged through had an aged mix of orange and yellow foam sealant coating the curving walls like a fungal film. Scaffolded pipes of various widths latticed the spongy surface, pushing and pulling fluids, light, and electrons to and from vanishing points.

Inconsistent pinpoint lighting fought most of the darkness, but Marcus knew to be wary of what he couldn't see. His shoulder lights bobbed as he ran, but fixed forward, they didn't reveal his flanks. Sometimes, the artificial wind grabbed his back like a hand, and he shivered.

His little sister, Diana, remained in front so he could deal with any grabs for her. The police had let her keep the flexy blade hidden in her belt, but he doubted a ten-year-old could accomplish much with it. He wasn't armed, though his hard, heavy safety boots might do. Ill-prepared though he was, he felt ready for what might come. He believed no weapon was more potent than his coiled determination to do anything for his sister.

It would come to that.

HE HAD LEFT work later than usual. A conveyor belt that spun sorted aluminum had split and needed replacing. The journeyperson intended to leave the fault for the following shift, but Marcus pushed her to do it. "Still thinking you'll get the scholarship gig, eh?" she said, sighing as she ordered him to rip out the old belt. "Night crew'll get the cred, not you." She went home on time while Marcus stayed to finish. The next shift's tech watched, arms crossed, demanding with a discouraging tone that he work even faster. He got the hour's job done in forty-five minutes, only fifteen into the next shift. No one seemed to care.

Only after verifying his timeout from Matter Recycling did he check for personal messages. Not before. That would be a code violation. His critical OT would not be endorsed. That wasn't against the rules.

His father had left a terse message.

Please secure your sister from the police. Stay in the present.
Be calm. Think before you speak. They will test your mettle.
Find justice.

Diana! Anxious over his sister, Marcus breathed three deep lungfuls to pause and bring calm, as his father had taught him.

He replied in text, exited his grimy workplace at the city's rim, and hurried into the affluent paradise of the Mars Syrtis Major Dome.

At this hour, few ventured on the pathway. In this well-organized society, the early evening meant the prosperous ate what the lower classes served them, while the few peons like Marcus privileged enough to have a dome job were supposed to be scuttling to their hovels.

Marcus lived in a muskhole. These were entombed habitats beyond the rim in the External District, vestiges of Mars's first settlements. There were hundreds—or more—of these dark dens, overflowing with tall, weary Martians bent into the temporary lodgings of long-dead diminutive Earthers. In the murk, they dreamed of the day they could afford an apartment in the dome, perhaps through promised promotions never granted or from favours demanded but never returned.

Or through a vocational scholarship awarded to an exemplary sixteen-year-old External District graduate once per year. The one Marcus was clearly in the running for. Favoured, even.

He grimaced. The setting sun jabbed his eyes as it reflected off the dome's palatial central spire. The police station lay that way. He pressed on.

Shop windows displayed curious, unaffordable treasures. They mostly perplexed him.

A store named Cry HAVOC! Venusian Products and Edible Curiosities advertised Freeze-Dried Venusian Strawberries. *Is that food? What's Perelandran Clover Honey? Landis Cotton Jean Pants? Zeppelin Sauerkraut Made From Real Pamela Sargent Cabbage?* And what did it mean to "Pre-order Your Venusian Mocha Java Goddess Today?"

"HAVOC" and "zeppelin" he associated with Venus's flying cities. Perelandra was their capital. The rest confused him, and it would stay that way. People of his low social rank were not tolerated inside those stores. Even window shopping was considered provocative.

THE MUSKHOLE KING   111

The police enforced safety and hierarchy in this elitist space with precarious consequences for people like him, but the fine melody of the fresh dome atmosphere caressing his face whispered seductive liberty. Why did these people have all this luxury and freedom but not him?

Though his family was not criminal—unlike many in The Muskholes—he had been to this local division of police only last week, escorting his grieving father.

It was rare for his chronically ill and debilitated father to ever leave their home, let alone for such a long trip. But his wife, mother to Marcus and Diana, had died while rebuilding a derelict Section A muskhole, and the police required his presence. After enduring an interrogation, Caton Altun, who some called King of The Muskholes, was finally allowed to view Justine Rochard's body.

A coughing, contorted husband stared at his love's cold face, a woman's gentle visage marred by a shattered temple— while a son in the morgue's antechamber gasped in tears.

The doors into the police station were a facade. The true entry was an airlock you couldn't pass without clearance. After a small delay, he went through.

Marcus was tall, even for a Martian, but the burly officer who took him by the elbow as soon as he entered towered over him. The officer manipulated and manoeuvred him roughly by the arm down a hall. Marcus resisted the urge to protest. The violent journey ended with a rude shove into a cramped room. A hard chair bolted to the floor faced away from the door.

The Family ran this dome. The Family required obedience. The police were the hands of the Family. Disobeying the police was insubordination to the Family.

"Why aren't you sitting?" asked a woman's voice from beyond the wall.

Because I wasn't told to, Marcus wanted to quip, but he held his tongue and sat.

"I am Lieutenant Herzog. You are Marcus Alton, age sixteen, son of Caton Altun and Justine Rochard?" she asked.

You know I am. "Yes."

She slashed and stabbed him with questions about school, work, acquaintances, and his family. She even had his application for the Family's External District Vocational Scholarship in her hands, which she went over in detail, praising his "substantial academic achievement, job performance accuracy, diligence, and perfect attendance" before dropping the bad news.

"You won't be getting the scholarship," she said.

"What?"

"You came in second. Allese Jong won."

Marcus nodded. Allese was an orphan under his aunt's wing. He knew her well. Intelligent and persistent, she deserved the award as much as he did.

This was horrible, life-altering news. There was one position, and you could apply only once. He'd never get out of The Muskholes now.

The interview escalated from there.

After . . . ten minutes? an hour? . . . the door opened, and Marcus emerged, shaking. His three deep breaths were too hard and too fast. Lieutenant Herzog, after breaking the news about his scholarship, had told him some hard truths. He badly wanted to believe they were lies.

Diana, smiling and eating something from a cup, met him. Officer Burly dominated nearby. "They call it ice cream," she said. "Try."

Seeing her unharmed and jubilant brought much-needed relief. He gladly bent and tasted her spoon. It was sugary, flavourful, and cold. "That's incredible," he said.

Officer Burly pointed the way to escape. Diana in hand, Marcus gladly obeyed the mute hulk. On the evening street, he took his sister aside.

Diana blustered, "You look angry. I didn't do anything wrong. I'm allowed in the park," she said.

"It's not you. The police talked to me about Mom again." He hugged his sister and closed his eyes. She wrapped her arms around him and beamed.

He slipped from the embrace to hold her forearms. She still clung to the spoon and cup. "The police didn't like the older boy you were with. They were protecting you."

We sometimes find External District girls her age murdered, Herzog had said.

A couple across the street, smartly dressed in Venusian textiles and stylish Evening Star Cork footwear, adorned with Syrtis Major silver and Olympus Mons gold, sauntered at the fore of a rabble of peasant drones ferrying parcels. The glamorous pair glared at Marcus and Diana, jabbing platinum-banded fingers with bejewelled nails their way. "Muskhole riffraff," one said.

Marcus touched Diana's shoulder and gently pushed her along. "We'll talk later. We've got to go. Someone will call the police soon enough."

"But we're not doing anything wrong," Diana said.

He gestured at his dark, dirty coveralls made from cheap-grade polymers. "True. But we're the *wrong people*, Diana. I'm so sorry. C'mon."

The pathway was no longer desolate. A swamp of post-dinner patrons submerged the street in glitz, chatter, flavoured nico smoke, and laughter. Marcus steered his sister through the disapproving current of wrinkled noses and lipsticked sneers. Waves of disrespect washed them into the cliffs of storefronts and the shoals of the road.

Diana paused their harried swim to toss her lonely ice cream cup and licked-immaculate spoon into the trash.

The crowd responded with judgmental calls of "Where'd

you steal that?" "You should save your money," "Don't spend on treats," and "No wonder you're poor."

Marcus lauded Diana with a "Thank you" before guiding her back into the garish sea.

The extravagant street traffic seemed to flee as they neared the dome-edge door to the External District.

They walked past Matter Recycling to a large airlock set in the dome wall. A side door took them to a descending passage, which opened into a vast underground space known as The Docks. They clattered on a gangway. Below, personnel and automated vehicles scampered. Farther away, several massive airlocks fed encumbered surface traffic to the airport and spaceport and along the few exterior roads leading to other cities. Routes above also connected power facilities, metallurgical furnaces, factories, greenhouses, and food-vat plants, all unsuitable for the dome's sparse and costly real estate.

Marcus paused at a fatigued door and grimly exhaled. "Lights on. Stay close," he said.

Partially lit, grated metal stairs lay beyond. Through the rusty slits, Marcus could see no one above. Below, two people huddled, knees to chests. He held tight fists as they went below until they were through the downstairs exit.

A wide airlock on their left led back to The Docks. Above yawned an opening that sang ghostly howls from the rush of atmosphere it pushed below.

Before Marcus and Diana stretched the long, slow incline of the wind tunnel—the only way home.

"Run!" he yelled against the din. Diana set off on a jog. He followed two lengths behind.

What was that? A shadow leaned out of a side passage the wary knew to avoid. It wore a tattered vest from The Docks. The gloom was too thick to see more.

The figure swore at Marcus as he passed. Or was he imagining spectres in the haunted gale?

He had his sister's tail, but his vulnerable back poisoned his confidence. The only antidote was to finish this intimidating dash. He told Diana to hurry.

They sprinted out of the passage, gasping. Marcus turned to challenge his demons. None followed.

They continued into The Commons, a voluminous, foam-walled oval chamber, the dingy core of The Muskholes.

Centred below, huge fans rotated, directing the wind tunnel's fury into buried ventilation shafts. The whirlwind cadence was like a heartbeat.

A few airlocks with spraypainted single letters lay between whirling machines, flexing banging ducts, and gurgling plumbing. Marcus and Diana walked toward a distant door marked with a large D.

Surprisingly, The Commons lacked its usual mob. Where were the hawkers and bidders? Buskers? Gamblers laughing and arguing? Claustrophobic newcomers, victims crying, and lovers in reverie? The preachers vying for devotion?

The Section A door opened. A ragged line of bruised and bloodied zip-tied bodies, some disfigured by years of hard labour, stumbled into view, shoved along by armoured riot cops. Flatbed trucks and marked police cars rolled in, barring the way to their D door.

Marcus grabbed Diana's arm and stopped. She tottered. "Sorry," he said.

"Take your hands off her! Stay where you are," said an amplified male voice.

Marcus snapped to the order and let go of Diana. An officer near the B door started toward him with a tremoring gait. Three others stayed and nursed hot drinks. A middle-aged woman with long red hair tended the portable kitchen they gathered around. That was his aunt, Vallery Rochard. Allese was her ward.

"They're with me," she said to the officers.

A cop struck her sheathed hand on the counter. "Hey, sister. Shut up."

The middle-aged officer pounded closer to Marcus, dressed in full riot vacgear—dark, brutish square shapes with bevels and slants at odd angles designed to deflect pointless blows against authority. The vacuum suit reminded Marcus of their proximity to the surface. Beyond the husk of a roof above, and maybe another metre of loose rock and sand, lay a lung-bursting frozen wasteland.

The retracted faceplate revealed a dark-skinned man with one eyebrow.

Playing with a smile, the officer reached Marcus, leaving only centimetres between them. Marcus knew how to read ranks, and this dystopian knight was quite old for a mere constable. A grotesque fibrous scar shaded the eye lacking a hairy brow. Marcus hoped Diana's curiosity wouldn't prod her to ask about it.

"Where're you going?" Officer Scarbrow asked, poking Marcus in the chest as he spoke.

"My sister and I are returning home."

"So *you* say."

Marcus remembered some of his father's advice regarding dealing with the police. *Asking the police for help can disarm them. It appeals to their sense of order.*

Marcus rubbed his chest and carefully pointed at the mass arrest in progress. "I'm pleased to answer questions. Could an officer escort my sister home?"

Officer Scarbrow called back. "Gonzalez! Get over here and take the girl home while I deal with this." He pulled a scanner from his cluttered belt and briefly pointed it at Marcus. He brought it back and started double-thumbing its surface. His lips moved as he wrote.

A young officer made it over. "Where to?" she asked.

"D-A2, please," said Diana, holding out her hand with a smile.

Officer Scarbrow chuckled. "Gotta say, isn't that the fanciest of holes." He looked down at his device. "Marcus Altun." He snorted. "Son of Caton. That makes you a prince."

Marcus remained silent. The officer revisited his device.

Officer Gonzalez awkwardly held Diana's hand. "I had ice cream today!" said Diana, skipping away.

Marcus wanted to laugh. *Don't overdo it, sister.*

Officer Scarbrow finished reading. "You're special. I see you had quite an interview with Lieutenant Herzog. Gotta say she's the district's badass. And here you are still all polite without a scratch on ya."

He leaned back in, grabbed the front of Marcus' overalls, and whispered. "Let's hope you're tough enough. Best of luck."

He let go, patronized Marcus's chest with a tap, and turned to the remaining officers. "All right! Got us some tie-wrapped meat to freeze. Move out!"

Marcus stood still until he'd watched Diana pass through the Section D door. Then he walked over to Vallery's portable cookery. The air wafted savoury notes with hints of chlorophyll and burned mint. It smelled better than any muskhole.

"Been here looking for you and Diana for your poppa for an unpaid time-and-a-half." Vallery used a hand to help toss back her heap of red hair. "My foolish niece's lucky your poppa's the calm type. Want some Antitox Mova drink?"

Marcus shook his head. "Thanks, and no. The police talked to me about Mom before they let me have Diana. Auntie, do you ever wonder about Mom's death?"

"What you mean? She was busy fixing up Section A. I was mad at her over that. We need better homes, not more holes, and those are the oldest holes. Not a wonder one blew out."

"The police said she was murdered."

His aunt wobbled. "No. No. No," she said. Her hand veiled her face.

"Viciously bashed in the head and the blowout faked, they said. And they claim you did it."

Her other hand grabbed the counter. Her face remained buried.

"Thought you should know. Are you okay?" he asked.

Hidden reinforcements seemed to arrive, and she straightened, revealed her mouth, and sighed. "No. No. The police lie. The corrupt Family don't want to admit muskholes are dangerous. They want us to be the danger. Make us fight. How'd we fake a blowout, anyway?"

"I didn't say I believed them," he said.

"I was mad with her. Don't mean I don't miss her."

"I never said you didn't." Marcus snapped that. He averted his eyes.

She noticed. "I see you believe me. Sorry. It had to be bad with the police."

"There's no justice with them."

"You have to make your own." Reaching across the table, she cupped his face, gently coaxing him to look at her with loving strokes from her hand. "I'll help you."

"I know Allese got the scholarship," he said.

She let go. "Too much in these weeks for you! Just learned the same. Allese is home, spinning happy circles how she'll be a disappointing pawn of the murdering Family. One scholarship a year don't fix The Muskholes. The Family pushes us so far down. Gonna fix that. We're going to get our way. Hold on. Got a customer."

She stopped to serve an outstretched, grubby hand a cup of Antitox Mova Juice and two Alien-RDNA-Free High-Protein Alga Vitamin Squares. Payment was received, and jeers made concerning the festering police lancing another boil made by the policies of the septic Family. "Yes, business slow tonight because," Vallery said.

The man turned to Marcus. "You Altun's son," he said. Soot streaked by dried sweat covered the metallurgical labourer's face. "Too bad 'bout your mother. Our fears 'bout holes blowing out to the surface, popping our lungs, all come true 'cause of her."

"Jacob, stop that," said his aunt.

He stepped close to Marcus. "You think the other holes she work on gonna blow? All over, she work on them. You think your smart king daddy can talk dead people alive that she kill?" he said.

"My mother," said Marcus, "didn't do structural work."

"Maybe she did; you just don't know."

"Her work's solid. Ask anyone."

"Yes, well. People *say* things. We like the king. Your dead mommy, though, not much. Building us more slums was bad. She do solid work? You right, maybe. Maybe someone kill her. A bomb on the ceiling, you know? Decompression rip her lungs out. You understand?"

"I understand you're scared," Marcus said. "We all risk habitat failure."

Jacob raised his voice. "Afraid? You think I'm a coward?"

Vallery reached over and doused Jacob with Mova. "Get out!" she said.

"Hey! Just talkin'," he said as he retreated in the direction of Section C, on the other side of the wind tunnel.

Vallery turned to Marcus. "See? People angry at your momma. Nevermind Jacob. He's tough 'til it gets hard." She smiled.

"My father's better at this. I was trying to calm him. Instead, I got his back up when I pointed out his fear."

"Nevermind your poppa. You need to be you. Hard truths for you to realize."

"Like?"

"All that love, but Mom's still gone. All that work, but scholarship's lost. You no more a forever optimist. No more listen to your father with his endure-all-work-hard and never be rewarded! Tell me, you finally done with eating that crap?"

"It's tough," he said. "I don't make what Mom did. Diana needs to finish school."

"They want us kept in the tough and fighting each other so we don't join together." She looked around and watched some of the background persecution play out.

She turned back. "The Family knows me. They don't like me 'cause I know they kill my Eddie with the alien RDNA crap in the food. Make up a murder to hurt me. Split us apart. Anyway, if they truly believed, they'd come for me already. They can make their own evidence."

"You don't have to keep defending yourself. I said I believe you!"

"See? Now you upset at me. It's how they like us, at each other. We've got to stick together. I can help you. I've got work. It pays," his aunt said.

"Doing deliveries like Mom?"

"Yes. I'm too busy since your mom's passing. You come early, you get my trike for the day and drop off Alga before your shift. I pay a bit. It'll matter."

"Why not get Allese to do it?"

"I keep her out of this. She's all about studies."

"But not me," he said, glimpsing his bleak future. "Not anymore. I'll do it."

"Good! Tomorrow morning, you start."

The police drove by, carting their livestock to market.

"Thank you. Look, I have to get home."

"Okay, see ya tomorrow." She turned away as a customer spoke and tugged on her sleeve.

✺

MARCUS WINCED as he neared their muskhole. Bloody clothes and a shoe lay in the makeshift ball court between the D and A doors. Starving scavengers would soon descend to peck and pick.

The Net monitor by his exit was cracked, creating a schism through Natalia Magomedov, the Family's AI talking head. *Quarterly profits are at record levels . . .*

He ducked through the short, Earther-built D door. The dim, banged-up corridor ahead inclined even closer to the surface. Fresh graffiti, *À la guillotine*, dripped a warning in revolutionary red.

Marcus opened the next airlock and entered the circular spoke room to find the king's court in session.

Two women, Veda and Fen, argued before Caton. A dozen tattered inhabitants stood behind them, their backs against two smudged muskhole portals. They murmured. Some waved at Marcus, who nodded back. Among them, a gaunt boy grasped a torn bag. His bare feet fidgeted. A woman's thin hands held onto his bird-boned shoulders.

Mons, a neighbour and adviser to Caton, whispered in Marcus's ear. "He's exhausted. Get him home soon."

Caton spoke. "I have heard enough," he said. The room hushed.

He sat apart from his audience, between the two other muskhole doors. His hefty, broad, and already lopsided frame tilted even more to one side as his last lung wheezed with each breath. His face was dark and leathery. This reached his forehead but did not extend to his pale bald dome. They called it "the oval": a surface worker's permanent mark of radiation damage.

"Fen, your anger over Veda's old breach of trust needs to end. You accepted her back. She is not responsible for your choice to stay angry. If you can't control your anger, I suggest your relationship can't work. As for the rent . . ."

Caton laid out a deal with their landlord to prevent eviction, then delivered an admonishment. "Withholding rent shares from each other doesn't qualify either of you for our community rent bank. You must work together. Remember, squatting and prison are worse." He looked at Marcus. "My son's home. I'm done for today."

Marcus made for his father. The boy with the bag bolted from his mother and ran into Marcus, who carefully held onto the fragile child.

"We have something for your father," said the boy's mother.

"That's kind, but he doesn't take gifts or payments," said Marcus.

"Let me see," said Caton.

The boy offered the bag. From it, Caton removed a bust sculpted from the same foam that interred them all. His hands caressed the carved lines. "I'm impressed. Tell me, what do you remember of her?"

"She fixed our sink when we couldn't pay," the boy said. He then rambled a story of Justina's beatific kindness.

"I already have much to remember my Justina by," Caton said. "My life will not last much longer. I would prefer you keep this, so during your long life, you will remember her." He gently touched the boy's head. "Thank you for this memory." He called on Marcus, who helped him rise from the padded box throne and limp to their door.

The crowd dispersed, some back to The Commons, others through a door leading to a tedious sequence of spoke rooms feeding increasingly dark, dank, and dangerous muskholes.

Inside their vestibule—it served as an airlock, storage, and mechanical room—Caton leaned on a dented, pearly wall and coughed. Marcus spotted a careless pile of tools in an otherwise clean chamber.

"That boy's father died of mould lung, like your Uncle Eddie," Caton said.

"Auntie mentioned Eddie today," Marcus said.

"She often complains about your uncle's death. That's also how Allese's parents died, by the way. Your aunt and her blighted vats of Alga and Mova killed them all. I don't know how she survives."

"Well, she often has Allese clean."

"I mean, survives her guilt," Caton said, slowly resuming his crooked gait. "Oh, I do know how. She falsely blames the Family and lies to herself. She's made it an industry. Selling fake cures for fake maladies."

"Lies to herself?"

"When truth hurts, people tend to tell lies in its place, even to themselves."

"I didn't realize Auntie was . . ."

"Your mother's gone, and you're at the age to start learning even harder truths."

Marcus cleared the offending tools from his father's course. One had a long, rifled tube with grips and a trigger. It electromagnetically drove spikes into rock, cement, or through anything softer. "Not again!" said Marcus.

"You're frustrated. Femi's a once-good tenant gone rude. Again, your aunt's influence, I suspect. She spends time with him in his cubicle while you're working. You know what that's about?"

Marcus nodded.

They reached the next door.

"Um, about Auntie. I'm doing deliveries for her," said Marcus.

Caton rested his back on a wall already embossed with his ample shadow. "Oh. Well, like that scholarship, sometimes economic need pushes us to do things we shouldn't."

"What?" asked Marcus.

Caton shook his head and motioned to the airlock.

Marcus helped his father over the threshold. He slumped to fit through. His crumpled father didn't need to.

In the confined interior, Marcus eased Caton under the sagging trusses and past the askew posts supporting the muskhole's roof. They reached a recliner chair. His father uncontrollably coughed as he settled in.

Marcus worried. They didn't have the funds to treat mould lung. Life was valued on Mars only if you could afford it.

He brought his father water from the only sink. He sniffed. "I think I smell . . ."

"Mildew. There's moisture under the floor near my chair again." Caton sipped from his cup.

"Going to be condensation from the water line, again. I'll . . ." said Marcus.

"Later."

Marcus sighed and rapped on a door. "Femi, get your damn tools."

A young man, a few years older than Marcus, emerged half-dressed. "Why wake me? Could've gotten another hour in before shift." He yawned.

"If you'd stored your gear in your room . . ." said Marcus.

"Hey, jerk, maybe I live with your auntie, then. She's a fire."

"There's no better muskhole than this. There's always a better tenant. Get your tools."

Marcus turned his back and rejoined his father.

Caton grasped Marcus and whispered. "Son. You choose to act out of anger. You should have let him sleep. Your choice resulted in two mad people interacting. That's never a good idea."

"He's wrong."

"Yes, but show grace. Be calm. Choose the best moment. Be the one in control."

Femi was done. He slammed his door.

"It's been a bad day. I didn't get the scholarship. A police lieutenant interrogated me. People in the dome were horrible. We ran the air tunnel alone. The police raided Section A and harassed me," said Marcus.

"All the more reason to choose your battles wisely. And thank you for securing your sister. Now, your ardent aunt told me about Allese receiving the Family's insincere gift. I take it she told you?"

"No. The police did."

His father straightened and grimaced. "Ah, now do you see how far they reach? And there's no reason for a high-ranking officer to deal with such a minor matter. Her telling you must have been a test. Did you impress her?"

Marcus filled him in.

"She let you go right after the test and made no proposal?"

"Yes."

His father sat quietly. "Well," he said eventually, "perhaps you will hear from her again."

"I hope not."

"Hmmm. Anyway . . ." Caton caught up on his breathing. "Marcus, I have to say I was not enthused by your desire to win this. It does one person some good, but elevating one person per year does The Muskholes no good. Our population is always growing, and the refugees from the Asteroid Belt make it worse. There are muskholes with beds being shared across shifts! There are thousands stuck here. No wonder the Family is trying to reopen Section A. There are rumours of organized violence brewing. We need solutions for all, not one. If I had my way, no one would apply. The scholarship is an excuse the Family uses to claim they are gracious and helping the poor. Why aid autocrats by playing their game?"

"I didn't know you thought this," Marcus said.

"As I said, today is for hard truths. We must be a positive example in our community. That means taking no favours from autocrats. No taking payments for providing arbitration services. How can I morally justify profiting from lives so damaged by the Family's abuse? You would never find justice for anyone living in a small dome apartment, struggling to make ever-spiralling rent on a technician's salary. It's another trap—segregating the best and brightest from us. I—we—need you here."

Caton held up his hand. "I'm quite tired," he said. "Understand, it's not our place to receive justice, Marcus, but to find it for the community. I know this is all thankless. We are to suffer with grace, my son. Justice comes to us last, after all others. And it only comes then because we found it for others. This is how community works."

Marcus rubbed his head and pinched the bridge of his nose. "I don't know about all that. This place loves and hates us in equal measure, maybe. What has it done for us?"

His father smiled. "Much. After my accident, there was nowhere for me to live. This accursed place saved me. I met your mother. We had you and Diana. Marcus, understand that everyone in The Muskholes is you. Is Diana. Is me. Don't ever abandon them."

Marcus shook his head. "Look, I need to see to Diana. Is she . . .?" He pointed upward.

"Yes, she's there. I know you are burdened. I need rest anyway. We'll talk more in the morning."

Marcus climbed the ladder into his room.

He could only crawl in the shallow loft. His few possessions were in crates along the tightly curved wall, which was also the close, sloping ceiling. Above the middle of the loft was the apex of the muskhole's puny dome. Frigid, near-airless death hovered one metre higher.

Diana rested on his mattress, cradling a hammer—a graduation gift for Marcus his mother found while renovating Section A.

"Sorry I did wrong today," she said.

Marcus slid onto the mattress. His sister cuddled up to him.

"You were only being a kid. There isn't justice. People hate us for living where we do."

"Muskhole. My teacher said our homes are named after an Earth rat."

"I was taught that, too. They are actually named after the first landlord of Mars."

"Why don't they teach that?"

"Because it's an insult. The Family hides that fact with lies because they protect their own."

"Insults are a poor substitute for thoughtful criticism."

"Heh. You'll make Father proud thinking like that. In this case, though, the insult is justice."

"How?"

"Someone long dead exploited a lot of people to get really rich, and that hasn't stopped. Built a whole world on it. We're trapped, doing the essential work to keep the dome alive, and we can't even afford to live in it. So, yeah, we insult him. It's not much justice, but it's one we can have."

"Wish we could live on Venus," she said.

"Those flying cities? That would have been better. The gravity would cripple us now. Even worse gravity is Earth's, though it looks to be dead anyway. But that's all fantasy. We can't even afford travel to another dome."

"So, if you had won the scholarship, you'd leave us and live in the dome and be like *them*?"

"No. I'd take you with me."

"So we would be like *them*? Dad wouldn't go. You'd leave him? Aime, Nuka, and all my friends, I'd leave them too? Those people mad at my ice cream, we'd be like *them*?"

"No, we'd be *us*."

"I wouldn't go unless my friends could come. And Daddy."

Again, Marcus pinched the bridge of his nose. Three breaths. "Diana, I'm really tired."

She crawled over him and got off the mattress. "You worked hard to win, but I'm glad you're staying." She kissed him on the cheek. "I'm gonna play on the Net with my friends. I had no ball court today 'cause the police had me."

"Okay. Thirty minutes, no more. It costs. Get a snack, then do your teeth and bed, okay?"

"Sure." She climbed away.

In the dome, the night sky painted its silver filigree while the fortunate in their tall rooms enjoyed entertainment on their 3D walls, all comfy on their lavish sofas or snuggled in their long, plush beds.

In his burrow, Marcus' stomach gurgled. He decided to skip a late dinner to help pay for his sister's Net play. His breath collected on the silver-foiled, polymer-sprayed arch inches from his face. He smeared the moisture with his plastic shirt sleeve, checked it for mould, and then sought the mercy of sleep in a crushed fetal position.

HE WOKE angry from a nightmare of gaudy mobs, barbaric police, crawling mouldy tendrils, crushed skulls, ripped lungs, and murderous aunts.

He navy-showered under cold water, tore through a protein cake, guzzled water, and strode for the exit.

His father hobbled from his cubicle. "We were going to talk."

"Fine. Time for hard truths, right? You and Mom argued over her Section A work."

Caton collapsed into his chair and rubbed his temples. "We were both right. We needed the money; her work was collaborationist."

"We're all collaborators! We mine their silver, we melt their ore, we grow their food in their vats."

"Working to open more muskholes is different. It's seen as legitimizing our segregation. We deserve life in the dome."

"Is that why she was murdered?"

Caton crashed his head into his hands. "Oh. My poor Justina. I . . ."

"You knew, right? Why didn't you tell me?"

"I didn't want you raving at the wind like you are now. Please, son, the police play dangerous games. You've not told me everything. What do they have you doing?"

"Catching Mom's killer."

"Son, no. This is better handled within our community. The dome wants us at each other's throats. This is how they do it."

"Auntie killed Mom. Maybe we *should* be strangling each other." He grabbed the airlock handle.

"We. You and I. We have to unite this community . . ."

". . . that hated and killed my mother? *I'm not a prince, Your Highness!*"

Diana came out of her room, weeping. "Why are you arguing?"

"Marcus, anger is a fire that burns your home," his father said just before Marcus slammed the door behind him.

He pounded his way to his aunt's stall. "So, where's the stuff?" he asked. "Where am I going?"

"Why you a jerk to me? I sent a text. You not check?"

Marcus paused to look. "Yeah. I see it."

"You're way off this morning. This your poppa? He's got no moods. Gives 'em to everyone else, though."

"Ya."

"You want to chat later? Got a long lineup now," she said.

"Sure. Whatever."

"Tone! I'm not the cause of your problems!"

Aren't you?

The trike's rear bin was already loaded, so he sped away.

He was running early to make time for deliveries, so commuters were few. He dodged some, hearing some "Hey!" "Bugger!" and "*BatlhHa'**!" exclamations in his wake. A poor driver with little experience, he nearly slammed into the dinged stairwell door at the bottom of the wind tunnel.

Recovered, he took the large airlock to The Docks and rode along the rising passage to the rim door.

The young dawn slashed the central spire above the dome. The Family lived in the pinnacle, privileged to see the first and last rays of the sun. Gondolas caught the light as they wheeled on wires between the external tower and surface facilities.

Inside, it was still dark. Marcus took a quick left, followed the rim road, and turned onto a service alley. A garage door opened for him.

Officer Scarbrow appeared as the door closed. His mangled brow sagged over red eyes, peering over puffy sacks. His rumpled uniform smelled like a locker room. He held a steaming drink.

"Hey again. You're early. I'm Hou." He directed two officers to unload and then pulled Marcus into a side room of tables and scattered chairs. He waved at an apparatus beside a sink and pointed to his hot drink. "Grab yourself a coffee. Wait here."

The door closed, and Marcus was alone.

The bewildering machine had no pot or kettle. It seemed as useful as a toilet without a hole. What was coffee anyway?

Instead, he peeked through the drapes that covered the door's window. His deliveries rested, neatly dissected, on a table. An officer nodded and grinned as he showed Officer Hou a readout.

Marcus couldn't hear much, but when the thrilled officer

---

* Klingon for dishonourable.

said "detonators," he clunked his head against the window. Officer Hou saw him, marched over, and swung open the door.

"That's a bomb. I'm delivering a bomb?" Marcus asked.

Office Hou sighed. "Your aunt's moving little explosives and maybe parts for larger devices. You've got two small ones. They ain't hooked up. It's safe. We tagged the package to track it. Maybe to her buddies. Gotta say, maybe we crack this today."

"Why is my aunt . . ."

"I don't know. I'm not paid to ponder. Some want all the unfair in the world blown up. Bad stuff started cooking when Earth went silent. So here we are." He stood back and looked Marcus over. "Gotta say, you going through with this?"

She used a bomb to cause the blowout. "Yes."

Moments later, his trike joined the rim road traffic as the opulent dome came alive with the sun's wealth.

The deliveries were to restaurants and food stores. They only allowed him in through back doors. At one cafe, he tried to walk out front but was rudely shooed.

He did see a display for Alga, advertised as Venusian Tree Leaf Cake. It would cost him a ridiculous amount to purchase it. All for vat food produced in Eddie-killing mouldy tanks, left to cure beside a murdering aunt's laundry in a muskhole.

He made it to Matter Recycling in time. He received some approving nods as he locked the trike up. Others stared. They thought he was a thief. All were jealous.

Mid-shift, a supervisor came by. She smiled, took him by the elbow, and walked him through a side door (where two men joined them from behind), along a hallway, down some stairs, and out an external door. It slammed behind him. He stood alone. His comm buzzed.

You failed the scholarship program. You are terminated. Leave immediately.

He kicked the door. His footprint joined others. Three breaths didn't help.

He was in an arched tunnel between two equidistant corners. Stomping to each, he saw only more monotonous gut. He threw his hands in the air and wandered the confusing shafts, damning his inconsiderate former employer, the ignorant little-sister-bashing mob of snobs, the flesh-tie-wrapping police, and the whole damn Family in their heavenly lair. Relief came when the convoluted passageway dumped him on the street in view of the dome's selfish heart. He shook a fist at it, turned his back, mounted the trike, and went for home-sweet-home.

His trip was uneventful until he was in The Commons. As he drove by the B door, the thinner mid-shift crowd scurried. "Cops!" he heard. He looked behind to see police skidding out of the air tunnel, splitting between the C and B doors.

He accelerated to avoid the swarm.

He sideswiped the bubbly wall near his door and dashed in. A gory exclamation mark had been added to *guillotine*. He caught up to stragglers—"Hurry! Hurry!"—darted by and made it to his vestibule.

Femi's gritty tools were, predictably, in plain sight, though the spike driver was missing. He shook his head. Femi was going to get it, no matter what his father's opinion was as to how and when.

He marched to the inner door and crossed into peril.

Vallery stared at him, snarling. Femi stood behind. He was holding the spike driver like a rifle.

His aunt wielded a knife. Watching Marcus carefully, she walked over to the airlock and closed it. Marcus backed away toward his father.

"Marcus," said Caton carefully, "be easy. We need to talk this out." He was in his chair.

Diana's head poked from the loft access. Marcus saw her. Femi and Vallery didn't. Caton might have.

"Oh, too late for that," said Vallery. "I just hear what you done, Nephew. There's some hard fighting going on down C way 'cause of you."

"Father, she's running bombs into the dome. Revolutionary stuff," Marcus said.

"Not just me. All over Mars. The day is coming."

"Revolutions are great at violence. Not so good at actually working," said Caton.

"You killed Mom and covered it up using a bomb to decompress the habitat," said Marcus.

"I got mad, hit her with a tool," Vallery said. "I regret it. My poor sister."

"Bitch deserve it," said Femi.

Diana cried, "*Mommy!*" and jumped from the ladder, the settler's hammer in her fist.

Marcus bounded to her and grabbed the weapon. "No, sister. No." He stood in front of her. Diana wailed. Marcus looked at his aunt. "She's only ten!" he said.

"You're a traitor," Vallery said, pointing her shaking knife at Marcus. Tears ran down her face.

Marcus dropped his mother's gift. "No. That's you. Your anger's burning our community."

"He's right. What are you going to do now, Vallery?" asked Caton. "Silence all three of us? Destroy the family your sister left behind? The police will have you regardless."

Vallery dropped the knife, pulled a fistful of her hair, and exhaled. "This is so. . ."

The airlock door blew off its hinges and smashed her into a structural post.

Marcus went to ground, covering his sister.

Femi avoided the blast. He tilted his cannon toward the police pouring through the door. Their retaliation was immediate, loud, and deadly. Blood poured from his chest. He pulled the trigger as he collapsed. *THUNK!*

Diana looked at her father. "Daddy?"

Marcus did the same and gasped. He struggled to his feet.

Officer Gonzalez raised a hand to the other cop. "Let him," she said.

Marcus reached Caton and touched his father's cheek. "I'll stay. Thank you," he said. His voice trembled.

Femi's spike protruded from Caton's last lung. He smiled at his son.

The Muskhole King's head slumped forward as he died.

The new Muskhole King held his sister as she sobbed.

MARCUS MANIPULATED a small block he'd picked up from Lieutenant Herzog's spotless jet-black desk. The transparent polymer cube encased a brown-beige square. He squinted at it.

Lieutenant Herzog stood beside a port window nearby. Outside was the dome's centre ring road. Her office was dome-petite, muskhole-luxurious.

She was a young, sturdy woman, shorter than most Martians, and black-skinned. When Marcus entered the office, she shook his hand with a polite grip and surprised him with a warm smile. She didn't order him to sit in a chair this time. She offered. The black chair gently embraced him. A firmer piece pressed comfortably into his lower back. His arms found bliss on padded rests.

"It's a piece of Venusian wood," she said. "A gift I received when promoted. Some people have furniture made from it. Outside my pay grade. One day . . ."

She pulled a flimsy box—the kind used for takeout—from the middle drawer of a shiny, dark blue plastic wall cabinet and placed it on her desk. She rolled a high-backed chair into position and sat.

She opened the box, removed an Alien-RDNA-Free High-Protein Alga Vitamin Square, and placed it on a polymer plate. "I hope you don't think this rude," she said, "but I'm starving."

She procured a knife and fork, sliced the square, and ate.

"Hmmm," she said. "Those Venusians really know what they're doing."

"That's . . ." said Marcus. His mouth hung open.

"Venusian Tree Leaf Cake. This is the last batch ever, I'm told. I'd offer you some—I'm sure it would be quite the treat for you—but I relish this."

"Oh, I'm fine anyway. Thank you."

She laid the cutlery neatly on the plate and leaned back. "So. Business. That package led to some interesting people we interrogated. Amateurs. They spilled like stumbling drunks. That led us back to your Section C. They'd actually dug under some of their habitats and were making bombs. If there had been an accident . . .

"Anyway, we mopped them up. Quite a few were too stubborn." She shrugged. "That your aunt died is unfortunate—you're lucky we had her tagged with a tracker. That's how the police were able to save you."

"Um . . . she was surrendering," he said.

A single crumb marred her desk. She swept it into a garbage can and shrugged again. "Moving on. The Family is impressed and thus generous. As promised, the scholarship is yours. Allese will have to make do without it."

"I thought the Family would provide a second scholarship," he said.

"Incorrect. There is only ever one finalist."

"Well, I know not to argue, though the Family can easily fund another. I refuse the offer."

"Really? You're going to walk out of here empty-handed?"

"I wish the citizens of The Muskholes their birthright. To live under the dome."

She laughed. "Ridiculous. The dome's full. And that's a little out of my purview, young man." She cut another piece. "You know, your father wouldn't want this for you."

"He would agree with me."

"The Family will give the scholarship to someone else. It might as well be you."

"I refuse. Justice comes to me last. My community comes first. Not that the scholarship has anything to do with justice."

"It's merit-based. That's justice."

"Clearly, it is not. If it were, then Allese would still have it."

"Actually, you did win. We took it from you to motivate your cooperation."

"Which only makes my point that it's a political instrument."

"Well, aren't you the clever debater? I think we're done here. Except for this: As you embark on following your father's paltry path, remember, *we know you're a police collaborator*. If The Muskholers knew that, they'd gut you. What we have over you now is something called leverage. We own you. Be very careful in what you do."

"I'll confess my role in this collaboration before my community. I'll accept their judgment." He got up.

She chuckled. "That's naive. And it won't matter. We always get what we want. The Family knows all."

He shrugged and pointed at her cherished cube. "Do they? How do you know that's really Venusian wood?"

"What?"

"Enjoy your Venusian cake."

He left.

THE QUEEN CAN NEVER WIN THE GAME

BY KATE BLAIR

Kingdom of North Kent
British Isles, sometime around 2165

EVEN WET, THE STRAW WAS PRICKLY, LIKE SMALL STINGS THROUGH the girl's shirt as she tried to get comfortable on it. Rain thrummed on the barn roof, and the wind rattled at the locked door. A small lamp flickered and gutted, almost out of biofuel already. Shadows jumped and retreated on the walls, sometimes flashing into white as the lightning outside cast its violence through the gaps around the door.

The girl doubted she'd fall asleep. Since this was to be the last night of her life, she decided it didn't matter.

The barn smelled damp, like everywhere. Like the soaking fields, like the washed-away roads, like their leaking, dripping homes. The summer had been dreary, all swollen streams and endless rain from the atmospheric river that had flowed above England for weeks. The harvest had yielded many heaps like the one she lay in; crops only gathered because letting them rot in the fields would have made King Aaron look even weaker than he already did.

The girl wondered how her father was spending his last night. Getting drunk, probably. It was how he spent most nights. It was how he had got them both into this mess.

He'd been trying to save them in his own useless way. Instead of working to salvage what little they could from their own marginal land, he'd decided that marrying her off to the self-proclaimed King of North Kent would bring them influence and perhaps enough supplies to make it through the winter. So he'd traded the last of their poached game for transport and more than a little moonshine on the way. He'd bribed his way into the King's house, burst into his council room, and drunkenly boasted of how hot his daughter was.

Incensed by the crude hubris of this stranger and determined to make an example of him, King Aaron demanded he prove it. In a world where a man's word was his bond, King Aaron agreed to marry the girl as long as she was as "hot" as her father claimed. If she produced heat, she could easily dry wet wheat, could she not? If not, the man's word was false and his life and that of his daughter would be forfeit.

So the girl was fetched by King Aaron's men, dragged up to his waterlogged heartlands, and locked in a barn full of damp straw, sobs smothered by the storm, tears only making the problem worse.

"Why are you crying?"

The girl jumped. A small figure stood in the corner of the barn, hunched over, face mostly hidden beneath a tatty brown hoodie.

The girl shifted back against the opposite wall. "How did you get in?"

The woman held up a key and nodded at the door.

"Who are you?"

"No one of any importance." The woman moved closer, and the girl could see her face clearly now: her patchy hairline, the deep pockmarks on her cheeks.

"What do you want?"

"To know why you are crying."

The girl hesitated, but her predicament was common knowledge. What is the point of making an example of someone if no one knows?

"I have to dry this wheat by tomorrow morning, or I will be put to death. And I have nothing to do it with."

"The King has to try something, I suppose." The woman gave a dry laugh. "Frankly, he's screwed otherwise. The Dover Sovereign Confederacy has been growing stronger, and the High Weald Democratic Republic is pinching at his western lands. And since he's been cut off from sea trade and fishing by the Southend Fleet, he's running low on food. He needs this wheat for bread and the chaff for biofuel. We used to have machines to dry the harvest, you know. Back before."

The girl had heard. Not about the machines, specifically, but about "before." When everything was better, when she was just a baby. Before the Manhattan Sea Wall collapsed, although things had been difficult for decades by then, as the British coast was gnawed away by the hungry sea. There had been shortages, storms, floods, riots, and terrorist attacks, but things weren't truly dire for the UK until that day. They were rich enough to keep importing while much of the rest of the world went hungry. But once the UN drowned, their fragile global supply chains, stretched tight around the solar system, snapped into separate, useless pieces.

England hadn't produced enough to feed its population in decades, so England starved. The government disintegrated, and the civil wars that had torn apart the rest of the world came home. Power fell to any landowner who could scrape together enough food for an army to defend their territory.

"We're no strangers to wet harvests on this soggy island. We just don't have the tech to deal with them anymore. That said, the last few years have been drier. I had hoped the atmosphere was healing until . . ." the woman gestured at the roof, at the summer-long rain hammering above them.

She picked up a handful of the damp straw and let it slide from her hand. It clumped together as it fell to the concrete floor. "Can't say this is the King's best idea. There's not even that much wheat here. I guess it's enough to make his point, isn't it?"

So she had heard about the girl's fate.

"I would just unlock the door, but . . ."

The woman didn't need to finish the sentence. King Aaron had chosen his base strategically; dozens of hectares of farmland facing the fork of a river, crossed by a bridge well-defended on either side. The rivers were fast-flowing at the best of times, perilous even for the strongest of swimmers, and on a night like this, they would be too swollen to cross even in a boat. And the water spilled out into the poison marsh behind, once home to a landfill, then a toxic weapons dump, and now inundated with corrosive waters, cutting off any escape that way.

What would the stranger get out of it anyway? In this world, nothing came without a price. Especially not an open door.

The woman stared at the damp wheat for a while. "I have an idea," she said, then slipped out of the barn.

The girl didn't hear the click of the key over the thrum of the rain, and when she tried it, it swung open. For a long moment, she stood there, staring out into the slow-strobing storm, squinting to spot a dark figure huddled under a hoodie. But the woman had gone, and the rain slashed down on the flooded fields, crisscrossed by overflowing drainage ditches. It splashed across the threshold of the barn onto the already wet wheat. The girl shut the door and waited.

Hope fit strangely in the girl's heart, poking and stretching. It hurt worse than giving up. She stared at the door but it stayed resolutely shut. An hour dragged by, and then another, achingly empty. The girl had almost convinced herself the woman had come just to mock her by the time the door opened again three hours later, awkwardly this time. A foot appeared at the bottom, and with a grunt, the woman levered it open.

She pushed in a wheelbarrow loaded with metal. The girl hurried to hold the door open as the woman manoeuvred it in. The woman positioned it by the door, then staggered back against the wall, soaked and panting.

The girl peered curiously at the metal. It appeared to be a tangle of some kind of lanterns or braziers. A battered metal jerrycan lay on its side beneath. After catching her breath, the woman began unloading, kicking away the wheat in spots and spacing the metal burners around the room with the scrape of metal on concrete.

"Aren't you going to help? It's your life on the line."

The girl blinked. "Why are you doing this? What do you want?"

The woman stared at her for a long while. "Let's say your necklace."

The girl raised a hand to her throat. It was a simple necklace, handmade with thread salvaged from a worn-out shirt that wasn't even good for making cleaning cloths. The beads were old plastic she'd cleared from their land and melted into twists and balls. She wanted to argue that it was worth nothing, but her father had always insisted that you never turned your back on a bargain made by a fool.

"Um . . . okay." She undid the knot at the back of her neck and handed it over.

The woman shoved it deep in her pocket. "Right, then, now that business is taken care of, let's get to work, shall we?"

Together, they set out the heaters; they were simple but well-made, the fire sealed safely within, visible only through a panel of orange glass.

"Where did you get these? Did you steal them?"

The woman stared at her. "You know from looking at me

that I could never afford these, right?" She sloshed a little liquid from the jerrycan into each lantern, and the air filled with the throat-burning smell of alcohol—the smell of her father. The old woman lit each quickly with a tinderbox, and soon the space warmed, a summer's day trapped inside the barn while thunder rattled the walls.

"Who are you?" the girl asked again.

"I told you, no one important. We need to toss the wheat," the woman said.

They each scooped up handfuls of the damp straw. They threw it into the hot air, and it dropped to the floor. For the first hour, it fell fast, weighted down by water. Their backs burned with the effort. The old woman peeled off her hoodie, revealing a dark vest and the half-melted skin of her arms. The girl stripped down to her undershirt, and together they toiled. But as they worked, aching as the hours went on, the wheat grew lighter, caught by the little gusts of their movement, separating into strands as it cascaded to the ground.

The morning stole up on them. The storm had melted into a hard rain, and little light slipped through the cracks of the barn. The woman hurried from heater to heater, shutting off the air vents in each. Once the light shining through the orange glass guttered and died, she used her hoodie to handle the hot metal as she heaved them back into her wheelbarrow.

Halfway out of the door, she paused, burners hissing in the downpour. "This won't be the end of it. He's all about showing his power. He wants to humiliate your dad."

And with that, the woman was gone. She did lock the door this time.

The girl collapsed, arms limp and shaking from the night's effort, legs burning from bending. Sleep claimed her quickly, and she dosed dreamlessly on the dry wheat.

✵

THE KING DID NOT TAKE KINDLY to being "tricked," although he could not deny that the barn was warm, the wheat was dry, the door had been locked, and he was the only one with a key. He demanded more proof: more wheat, another night, so the girl took what little sleep she could and worried. Even if the woman came again, they had worked half the night to dry what little the King lined the floor with the day before. How could they hope to dry the bigger heaps tonight?

As if she knew, the woman came earlier, wheelbarrow laden with yet more burners.

"What is your price tonight?"

Again, the searching gaze. This time, it fell on the small ring the girl had fashioned for herself from a bright red aluminum can she'd found floating in a stream.

"That ring'll do."

The girl yanked it from her finger and handed it over. The woman was clearly mad, but the girl wasn't about to argue. The woman barely glanced at the ring before shoving it in her hoodie pocket. The girl wanted to warn her it would bend out of shape, but to do so would draw attention to the thinness of the metal, the worthlessness of the thing.

"I don't even know your name," the girl said.

"I barely remember it myself. Are you ready?"

They worked harder, muscles pulled and sore from the night before. They worked all night. They threw the wheat and, in the moments when they could catch their breath, they talked. The girl told the woman about her father, about her life before. The woman told the girl about the King, about his other wives, about life in the big house, and who could be trusted. The girl began to dread her salvation, her potential future as yet another of King Aaron's queens.

Once again, as light stole in, the wheat was dry. Once again, the old woman hurried into the rain, pushing her steaming wheelbarrow away before the King could come to check on his captive.

Once again, the King demanded more.

On the third night, the woman arrived earlier. Her eyes were red, her whole body slumping, as she shoved the wheelbarrow into the barn. This time, it contained a large heap of what the girl thought was scrap metal, but as she helped the woman unload it and stand it upright, she realized it was a machine formed from chunks of mismatched metal soldered together, a tarnished Frankenstein's monster of a thing. She caught glimpses of a heating element toward the back and the blades of a fan.

"What is it?"

The woman leaned on her thighs, catching her breath. She looked around the room at the heaps of wheat. "I knew he'd give you more. It's his way. The heaters weren't going to cut it tonight, no matter how hard we worked."

She heaved her jerrycan out of the wheelbarrow and splashed some biofuel into the thing. She pulled on a cord once, twice, three times before it roared into a spluttering, shuddering rhythm. The element glowed, the fan turned, and hot wind filled the room. The piles of wheat shivered and shifted, kicked up by the warm breeze.

"How did you get this?"

The woman waved a hand as if to insist it was nothing. But the girl could see it had cost her at least the day's sleep. A machine like this was beyond value, and she could not imagine where the old woman had stolen it from. Working technology was a rarity since the factories had crumbled. It took all their skill to keep what little survived functioning as each day wore it down. In King Aaron's territory, the lack was especially acute. Rumour had it that the King once had his most talented mechanic murdered in a fit of anger and had been unable to convince another to work for him since.

The woman leaned against the wall, barely able to stand. "Give it to the King tomorrow. Claim it is your dowry. It will allow him to marry you and keep his word without seeming foolish."

The girl gaped. "What . . . what do I owe you?"

Again, the woman waved her hand. Then, a thought seemed to occur to her. "Here," she said, reaching into her pocket. When she opened her fist, the girl's ring and necklace were there. "I don't really want these, you know."

"Then why did you ask for them?"

"Would you have trusted me that first night if I'd been offering something for nothing?"

The girl had no answer to that.

"You were more likely to believe in an extremely stupid woman than a generous one. That is what our world has come to." The woman let her legs bend and slumped down until she was sitting on the floor.

"Can't I give you anything? If I do marry the King, I'll have access to things worth having. I could give you something then."

"I don't need anything. I have enough to share."

"There is nothing you wish for? Something you have always wanted?"

The woman gave a laugh. "No. I have peace, which most people do not."

Her eyelids drooped, and after a long pause, she spoke again, her voice dreamy with the onset of sleep. "I once wanted a child. But when I was young, I was not safe enough to bring one into the world, and now I am old, I cannot." She shook her head as if to awaken and rid herself of such thoughts. "But that's life, and you did give me something these three nights. I have been lonely, and you gave me your company. You are practically a child anyway, and it was my pleasure to be able to take care of you."

"You gave me my life," the girl said. "I am ever in your debt."

"Not yet, I haven't. You'll still need to toss the wheat, and I'll be no help. I can barely keep my eyes open."

"Then rest, and let me work."

The woman nodded, then paused. "I . . . if there were a way for you to run away tonight and be safe with me, would you take it?"

The girl considered, head tilted to one side, long golden hair falling over her shoulder. "If I ran tonight, my father's life would be forfeit."

"He's important to you, in spite of this?"

The girl shrugged. "He has looked after me the best he can." The problem was that his best wasn't enough for either of them. "I cannot just let him die."

The woman nodded and shuffled her scarred body into a better position. "I understand."

And so, through the night, the girl tossed the wheat, helped by the hot wind of the machine, as the old woman slept, the rain hammered on the roof of the barn, and thunder grumbled in the dark beyond.

The girl wanted to wake her, to ask her who she was, but she'd refused to tell her three times already. She was also clearly exhausted, so much so that the girl was reluctant to wake the woman even in the morning when the sky was brightening. She shook the woman's shoulder gently and noticed that she did not smell of sweat and urine like most of those who lived in such tattered clothes.

The woman's eyes blinked open slowly, and it took her a moment to focus on the girl, the barn, and the dim grey light slicing in through the cracks around the door. Then they widened.

"I've got to go," the woman said. "I can't be around when the King arrives."

She struggled to her feet and pulled her hoodie down low over her face.

"I am sorry. You looked as if you needed the rest."

"You are a thoughtful thing." The woman squeezed the girl's hand in her own. "If you ever need me again, come and find me."

"Thank you so much."

The women shoved the wheelbarrow out into the soaking mud. The girl watched, wishing she could go with her. Wishing she didn't have to worry about her father. The woman retreated into the fields, following the ruts with her barrow. She was already far away when a thought occurred to the girl.

"But how can I find you? I don't even know your name!"

The thunder of water on the roof swallowed her words, and the stooped back of the woman disappeared into the downpour.

KING AARON and his entourage arrived soon after to a room full of dry wheat and the heating fan. The girl flinched at the fury in his face and quickly offered it as her dowry, as the woman had suggested, throwing in many flattering words, claiming it was unworthy for such a king, but it was all she and her father could offer, other than her whole self. She knelt, hands clasped in front of her.

She watched his expression change, watched the calculations behind his eyes. He stroked his jowls as he looked around.

He had proved his power in front of his people, proved he was worthy of a miracle and a rich dowry, of her bowing and scraping. This was a story that could add to his legend.

He needed the fan, too. He had much more wheat to dry.

He turned to the girl, looked her up and down. She knew she wasn't ugly, but in spite of what her father thought, she was no great beauty, either. But what was another wife to him? He had plenty of room for her in his big house.

The King laughed and took her hand, pulling her to her feet and close enough to catch his reeking breath. "Since you are so desperate to be my bride, I shall be merciful. Who am I to break your poor young heart?"

The girl forced a smile, and the King squeezed her against his wet bulk and kissed her, crushing her lips hard against his.

THE GIRL MISSED THE WOMAN, but for a while, she was safe, albeit bored. Sometimes, she sat and talked with the other wives, but she soon learned they had little in common. They taught her the rules of the house and warned her not to be too clever, like the King's first wife, who'd died because of it. She learned not to complain but to smile and nod.

The King did not visit her much at night. His favourite wives were famed beauties, and while she was a novelty for a few months, she was not one of them. It was a relief. She hated the stink and sweaty bulk of him.

One day, around a year after her marriage, while cloistered in her tiny room, a messenger brought her a curt letter from her hometown, and her breath caught as she read it. Her father had finally drunk himself to death.

She slumped back on her bed as her world grew yet smaller. She only had to worry about herself now. She had thought she'd be relieved, but there was a terrible loneliness in the thought. When her tears finally stopped, the girl found she understood the old woman better.

Sometimes, the girl wandered the halls, noticing small things. The house had probably been beautiful once. The light fittings were made from the same kind of orange glass the old woman's burners had, and the girl wondered if this was where she had stolen them from. Few of the bulbs still worked, but the ones that did cast a warm light in the corridors, and the girl lingered under them, feeling the warmth of the barn, of the companionship she'd felt there.

Not long after her father's death, the girl found she was pregnant. But as her belly swelled, rumours reached their house, muttered among the women. The High Weald Democratic Republic had formed an alliance with the Dover Sovereign Confederacy and some of the northern territories, calling themselves New Albion and claiming swaths of King Aaron's territory. Whispers went through the house about a so-called Federation spreading through France and grasping at footholds in England. Food was rationed, and the King's army slipped away, first individually, then divisions at a time.

As the borders tightened like a noose around them, the girl began her search for the woman's name.

She asked the other wives if they knew an old, stooped, and scarred woman, but none did. She asked the servants, only to be greeted with blank faces. She snuck into the house's public courtyard and tried to ask the messengers and emissaries to the King. That earned her a beating for going where she wasn't allowed—hits to the face to avoid damaging the King's child growing inside her.

The other wives reminded her of their warnings, applying wet cloths to bring down the swelling, bemoaning the lack of ice packs and the death of the first wife, who would have been able to fix the long-broken freezer.

Something itched at the back of the girl's mind.

"What was she like?" she asked, voice slightly muffled by her fat lip.

The third wife, she of the long neck and golden hair, shrugged. "Never met her. She was before my time. He always said she was difficult, and he preferred me."

The oldest wife swatted at her arm, but there was fondness

in the gesture. "That's no big compliment. He married her before he became king and always said she was nothing special. But she was nice to me. I was young then and new to all this."

"She fixed things? She was a mechanic?"

"A really good one," the oldest wife said. "She kept this house running beautifully."

"What happened to her?"

"They argued all the time, about his wars, about helping those who were hungry on his land. I've never seen him as angry as when she said she was leaving him. He blocked the bridges and had his soldiers chase her into the poison marsh." The wife shook her lovely head. "She drowned in the toxic waters. A cruel death."

The girl's head spun. What if the first wife hadn't drowned? What if she had been burned and scarred but somehow survived?

"What . . . what was her name?"

The oldest wife folded her hands in her lap and looked down. "Amber." She whispered the name like a prayer. "Her name was Amber."

The orange glass of the light fittings, of the burners; the woman hadn't stolen any of it. She'd made it all.

"That's why you mustn't be too clever," the oldest wife said. "Why you shouldn't disobey him. With things the way they are right now, he's angry all the time." She put her hand to her cheek, and the girl noticed the soft, raised pinkness of an old scar there.

She waited until dark. She packed nothing; either she was right, and there would be enough where she was going, or she was wrong and headed for her death. As soon as the house was silent aside from the ever-present drumming of rain, she snuck into the hallway, and from there to the side door.

The alarm sliced into her head, screeching in her ears.

She cursed. Of course, there was an alarm. She hurried into

the downpour, hoping it would hide her. She dashed across the sodden fields, water in her eyes, mud sucking at her boots. She did not look back until she reached the back edges of the fields, where the soaked crops stopped, and the land sloped downward toward the poison marsh.

The girl glanced back to see flashlights casting their glare on the other side of the house, their bearers obviously assuming she would try her chances at the rivers. She stumbled down the bank and into the marsh. Mountains of garbage rose around her, surrounded by toxic water, the level high after the wet summer. She skirted around the edge of a mound of rubbish, treading on the sturdier patches, avoiding splashing into the water, hoping the rain wouldn't bring the nearest heap down on her in a landslide. She trod carefully, making her way around to the other side of the pile, where the thin strand of junk she walked on split in two, heading for separate heaps. She paused at the fork, wondering which to take; then, her eye was drawn to the glint of something orange.

She crouched. On the side of the left fork, a large piece of orange glass glistened, barely visible in the dark night. She took it as a sign, chose that way, and floundered on, thinking of the woman who had saved her life. Was it mad to imagine she was Amber, the King's first wife, somehow able to survive here? Or was she stumbling to her doom in the poison marsh?

Now hidden from the house behind a heap that loomed to her right, she blinked the rain from her eyes and took her time, looking for safe places to put her feet. It was easier than she expected. There was always something: an old paving stone, a breeze block, the rusting door of a car. It was all junk, but all exactly where it was needed: a path disguised as garbage.

Again, the heap sunk down into a ridge, and again, the ridge forked, each side heading for another pile of long-abandoned rubbish. She knew what she was looking for this time.

She whispered the woman's name under her breath, found the orange glass, and took the right-hand path.

Was the glass put there for her, or was it to help Amber find her way home on nights like this when there was no light from the moon and the rain all but blinded her? She found it at each junction, at every crossroads, every place the path split or twisted in the labyrinth of junk. Amber had built a safe, dry path through the blighted marsh: stepping stones through the toxic water, dunes of solid rubbish rising above the corrupted mud.

Finally, the ground rose to a plateau: a huge flat square, at least a hectare in size. She stopped, astonished to find the patch of wide brown earth in the middle of the poison marsh. Short stalks of gathered crops still stubbled the ground in front of her. The heaps of junk rose again on the other side of the unlikely field, hiding it in the middle of the dump. Water ran off the plateau through deep ditches, draining into the marsh around her.

The girl shook her head in amazement. It must have taken years to clear this area, to pile up enough clean soil to build this patch of farmland raised above the polluted water, sheltered from the warring territories on all sides by heaps of raw materials and the reputation of the marsh. The girl thought of the burns on the woman's arms, the scars and pockmarks on her face, evidence of years of perilous labour.

The ramshackle path led her up and into the field. In the middle of the land was a cottage: a small, sturdy shack built of old brick, cladding, and sheets of metal, topped off with mismatched roof tiles. Smoke curled from the chimney pot, and light streamed from the windows. It was only as the girl approached that she realized the door wasn't glass; it was simply open. The woman stood there, a silhouette in the dark, and for a moment, the girl wondered if she would still be welcome.

As she approached and the cottage's light fell on her features, the woman rushed out from her shelter toward her. "You came! You came! I heard the alarms, and I hoped!"

Amber slowed as she reached her. She looked at the girl's belly, at her bruised and swollen face, then wrapped her arms tightly around her.

"Don't worry. You're safe now. Both of you."

The girl buried her face in the rumpled, scarred skin of Amber's neck, and wept.

TO STRIKE THE FLINT

BY PHOEBE BARTON

High Venus orbit, January 2165

FROM ABOVE THE CLOUDS, VENUS WAS WHITER THAN SWEET ICE. Capella Scott hated it for that. Where was the decency in hiding a demon's face beneath angelic shrouds? Worlds like Mars and Io made no pretensions and took pride in the hells they were. Down in their HAVOC cities, the Venusians were scrupulous in upholding the lie and refusing to acknowledge the cruelty of their home.

For someone raised between Belt rocks, it was foolishness. Open space and the depths of Venus were equally deadly; only their choices of murder weapons differed. Capella had been taught never to turn her back on a knife, and there was no better armour than the modest, humble, reliable mining scow.

"Looks like we're close," said Max Becker, the technical worker who'd drawn the shortest straw. "You're positive your lot didn't leave surprises behind?"

"Are you kidding? No one would haul around surprises when we could use that delta-v for paydirt."

"I never would've lasted out there," Becker said. "All those days in the dark."

The shuttle was close enough now that the mining scow *Rapid Rocky* was no longer a mere glimmer. In the impossibly near sunlight, Capella could see the scow's hull had retained its clean smoothness and that its radiators were eager to glow again after ten years in a lonely mothball orbit. Ships weren't meant to be bound to one world; mining scows least of all.

It was more of a home than Venus could ever be. She'd grown to adulthood within its hull. When the last crew had left it abandoned in its high orbit, they'd nailed her heart shut, and now so many of her kin had gone beyond without flying with it again.

"You pinballed around the Belt in that . . . piece." Becker hissed the last word like a pinhead leak. "Miners must have a thing about dying young."

"I guess it's safer to live in a balloon inside a sulfuric acid hurricane," Capella said. "The view's a lot better from that 'piece' than anywhere on Venus, though."

Final approach came with the same aching slowness as a flight between asteroids worth mining. Capella churned with a gambler's anticipation. While she hadn't seen any impact punctures, that didn't mean there weren't any. Even a damaged engine or oxygen tank, something a scow's crew could have fixed underway with grit and gumption, would take *Rapid Rocky* from the reactivation list to the spare parts graveyard. For all its resources, Venus didn't share the miners' resolve.

She didn't dare celebrate her return, not yet. Not until the reactivation was finished. So much could happen in a minute, in a second, to turn a thing from inevitability to impossibility.

"Looks like a real mean machine," Becker said. "Any rituals I need to know about? Salt-throwing, that sort?"

"Watch your grips and always know where your kit is." Capella's was fastened to her belt, bursting with hull patches, duct tape, and tools for a dozen repair jobs. Going without it would be more foolish than a naked spacewalk.

One last, barely perceptible shudder of thrust and a soft *thump* heralded docking. Capella listened for the hum of the capture latches as the shuttle's systems hooked into *Rapid Rocky's* for remote reboots and testing. There was no telling how many bits might have flipped since the last crew powered down. She threw herself into the scow's computers while the shuttle pumped air into the old vessel. Her old passwords still unlocked everything they needed to.

> *Good evening, Capella Scott. It has been 3,798 days since your last login. Welcome back! Your password has expired and must be reset.*

Her throat squeezed tight. Of course, the ship recognized her and had been counting the days since it had seen her last. Ships remembered when people disappointed. Ships endured when planets crumbled.

Hours went by with the swiftness of seconds until all the preliminaries were done. The computers were singing, the scow's habitable volume was pressurized and steady, and there were no grievous wounds to worry over. When the scow's inner airlock door opened and revealed the corridor beyond, Capella hummed with satisfaction.

It didn't smell the way it had when *Rapid Rocky* had been a working ship, but it smelled more like home than Venus ever could.

AFTER THE FALL OF EARTH, the miners had tried to keep making it work. At first, they'd carried on as normal, prospecting rocks and processing ore because the alternative was to come apart, to accept that the walls of the world had been pulled down and the future they'd expected was never going to happen. Out in the vast solitude of the Belt, that cold truth left more than one scow disembowelled.

Capella remembered those times as full of hard work and tough workarounds, tempered by her amazement at how quickly the settled solar system buckled without Earth to support it. She had been young enough that the endless struggle of making do with jerry-rigged spares had still been an exciting challenge.

They lasted a little over three years until the facts of exhausted scows and Earth's vanished insurance policies became impossible to ignore. It was only luck that *Rapid Rocky* hadn't joined the convoy that sought refuge on Mars. For all that Venus could never be home, Capella had found it welcoming. The Martians, meanwhile, had looked out across their world's rust-red fields and thought, *Who'll notice any blood here?*

Not that the Venusians were acting out of pure altruism, either. They lived in the acid skies of a furnace world. Mining its surface would be a challenge surpassed only by mining Jupiter's metallic hydrogen core.

None of it mattered now. She was back aboard *Rapid Rocky*, and if it passed the reactivation trials, she'd be part of its new prime crew, feeling the hum of its fans as it chewed on sun-hugging asteroids. So far, nothing had gone wrong.

All that meant was that there were fewer systems that might yet disappoint her. Capella focused on each one on the checklist in turn. While Becker worked, he gawked and whistled.

"You're looking like I did when I came to Venus," Capella said. "I didn't think anyone would be impressed by a scow."

"Ever been on an Atira miner? Those boys were calling for repairs practically every day." Becker knocked his shoulder against the bulkhead. Nothing happened. "I can't find anything broken. *That* impresses me."

"It's not like we had dirt under our fingernails out there," Capella said. "The oxygen tank test is next. How do the electrics look?"

"Everything's fine so far," Becker said. "I'd feel better if I could do a full inspection, though."

"That'll be for the reactivation crew. This is just the basics." There was fresh oxygen in *Rapid Rocky*'s tanks, but not nearly enough to fill them: just enough to tell whether or not there was any damaged wiring that would burn. Two hundred years before, the men of *Apollo 13* had outplayed death after one of their oxygen tanks exploded. Their challenges were simple compared to what a lonesome, stricken scow would face.

Even so, it was dangerous. An oxygen tank fire with so little oxygen wouldn't cause any unfixable damage, but the Venusians didn't share Capella's definition of "unfixable." She'd heard that *Tennessee Ernie Ford* had been hurled into a graveyard orbit on account of a problem that would've taken a week to fix.

"Just the basics," she said again.

She was doing everything that she could. She'd overhaul *Rapid Rocky* with only her hands if that was what it took to get the scow back into service. She couldn't lose it after this long. Hell, she'd already lost the Belt, not to mention Earth; there wasn't much room for things to get any worse.

The switch loomed before her—only a switch or a bomb in disguise? She wouldn't know which until she flipped it.

All the scow's years of dutiful service collapsed into a single point. She and Becker wouldn't be its final crew. No. She refused.

She flipped the switch. A light came on. The tank fan whirred.

Ten seconds. Thirty. Sixty.

Nothing burned.

"Sounds like we can cross this one off the list," Capella said as she flipped the switch back off. "That's a good scow."

System by system, the checklist fell away. What few things she found in need of service could be dealt with swiftly with spares from donor scows, and if a thing's only problem was that it was scuffed or scratched, there was no problem at all. How a thing looked was worthless; only how it worked mattered.

She was focused on testing the circulator fans when Becker said, "Do you smell that?"

Capella sniffed and shook her head. "Nothing but old dust and veteran scow. Sweat and farts get baked into the bulkheads after a while."

"I think that's smoke." Becker's hand went to his belt-clipped fire extinguisher. "Where the hell's it coming from?"

"None of the detectors have gone off," Capella said. "I'll reboot the environmental system, and we'll put this to bed."

The reboot took longer than she remembered. Nothing that a factory reset wouldn't solve. She watched the spinning hourglass on the screen and felt a warm conviction that things were *right* for the first time in years. Venus wouldn't need to be home for much longer.

She held on to that conviction until the instant the hourglass disappeared, and the alarms began to shriek like a canary in a rock tumbler.

Fire.

"It's in Box 6, let's go!" Capella didn't wait for Becker before she threw herself through the scow's microgravity with skills she hadn't been able to practice for too long. She found herself missing handholds and crashing into the bulkhead while that fire was sucking the marrow from her scow.

She found the blaze licking out of an electrical junction box that was already beginning to char and warp as it was eaten away from the inside. There was no response from the suppression systems; her little utility extinguisher would have to be enough. She readied it like the sword of a knight about to slay the dragon and only realized after she discharged it that she hadn't secured a foothold.

The extinguisher's kick sent her spinning and swearing. By the time she righted herself, Becker had caught up and was emptying his own extinguisher into the flames. He'd saved it while she'd been spinning like a ground-pounder.

"That had better be it," Becker said. "Smell's going to give me nightmares."

The checklist might as well have burned as they reported in and scoured the potential extent of the damage. Not that it would make a difference, in the end. There was no such thing as a good fire in space.

THE REPORT SAID it was no one's fault. A few unfortunate micrometeoroid impacts, combined with the scow being asked to do so much for so long without refit or rest, had left its electrical systems more frayed than the crews that guided her. Only a matter of time, it said.

"Better that it happened close than out on prospecting," she heard from other scow crews. Becker had even sent her a condolence card as if she was fresh from a funeral.

None of that made it feel any better.

If Capella could have rehabilitated *Rapid Rocky* with her bare hands in a week, rewiring its nervous system in a hundred million microscopic knots, that might have been enough. As it was, Venus, with its bare million people, had no patience for long projects. They were already cutting up *Rapid Rocky* like a tree in the mills the Venusians were so proud of.

They would come for the small bits first: switches, breakers, service panel covers, the kind of things that needed regular replacement under everyday wear. For a while, *Rapid Rocky* would look deceptively normal as it lost pieces of itself here and there. Then, inevitably, would come engine parts, fuel cells, mining machinery; pieces of equipment Venus couldn't hope to build on its own yet, not until the chosen few scows had time to do their work. Even whole sections of the hull would go in time, the shed skin of a hard-flown spacecraft, until everything that had made the scow what it was had been claimed, and only a metal skeleton would be left in its endless graveyard orbit.

The clouds were the worst part. Even at night, the flying cities of Venus never saw stars. Capella couldn't peer through a telescope and see that *Rapid Rocky* was still there despite what she'd made happen.

Capella leaned back on her little bed in a cubicle that was palatial compared to her quarters aboard and worked her necklace between two fingers. It wasn't much—only a length of *Rapid Rocky*'s undamaged wiring tied together—but a token.

It wasn't the end of the world. She'd already lived through that.

It felt worse than that.

AFTER THE APOCALYPSE IN MOOSONEE

BY JAMES BOW

Moosonee, James Bay Shore, October 4, 2177

REBEKA HAD BEEN HUNTING GROLAR BEAR WHEN THE government train came to town.

Blackflies beat against her face shield and caught in the netting of her kaffiyah. The brown-white bear stood in her sights. Birds chittered. A light breeze rattled the branches.

"Hold still, you."

She sighted down the barrel of her air rifle and blinked. Her ocular implant zoomed in. The brown-white bear doubled in size, then doubled again. It turned its head, and she focused in on its eye.

"Let's see what you've got."

The groler bear glowed green. Information popped out around it: *Grizzly-polar hybrid; female; 150 kilograms.*

Rebeka held her focus. The halo flickered. She clenched her jaw. "Come on . . ."

Female . . . 150 kilograms . . . Elderly.

"Yes!"

Past cub-rearing age.

"That's what I needed to see." Enough meat to last the winter. More Vitamin A from its liver than they'd ever know what to do with, though Doctor King had been good at convincing the Kalaallit traders to accept his pills. The kids could have new coats before the snows hit.

Now, to calculate the shot.

The halo flashed. New information flowed out: distance, trajectory—

Suddenly, the halo flashed brilliantly. "Ow!"

Rebeka reared back, banging the side of her head like a blackfly had found its way through the netting. "Ow! Ow! Stop it!"

Very like a blackfly.

She clenched her eyes shut. "Come on! Don't give up on me now!"

The flashes stopped. She opened her unaltered eye, looked around, then closed it and opened her implant. She blinked and rubbed her temple. "Okay. Okay, back to work." She settled into the brush and sighted down the barrel again. "Where were we?"

She held her breath. The grolar bear lowered its head into the implant's crosshairs. She rested her finger on the trigger and blinked the safety off. "Go to sleep, old mother," she whispered. "I'll make sure the townkids thank you for their coats." She tightened her finger.

A howl rose through the muskeg and echoed off the hills. The grolar bear jerked up just as Rebeka's gun chuffed. Seconds later, a hole blasted into the trunk of the tree behind where the bear had been.

"Damn it!" Rebeka shoved herself onto her knees, then froze. The howl was still going. *What* is *that noise*? Her first thought had been a wolf, but they couldn't hold a note this long, and there was too much power behind it. Then, as suddenly as it started, it stopped, leaving only echoes in its wake.

Then it started again.

Rebeka clambered to her feet as the second howl lasted as long as the first. It was followed by a third, much shorter howl before a fourth, long one rose. When it ended, Rebeka stood in a forest startled into silence.

Wait.

She started forward, slinging her rifle over her shoulder.

Two long howls, one short, then one long. Only one thing makes that sound . . .

Pausing to geotag where her bullet had struck the tree, Rebeka ran for the rail crossing.

As she ran through the bush, she heard echoes rise from the distant hills: a rhythmic clank of metal, a rumble of engines, the scrape and squeal of wheel against rail. She came out onto an old logging road in time to see a gleam of metal a hundred metres ahead as something crossed the gap in the trees. She heard another howl, almost deafening this time, and a prolonged squeal of brakes, then a thump.

Rebeka skidded down the lumber trail. The rumble of engines continued, this time accompanied by snatches of shouts. She slowed as she reached the level crossing. Planting herself in the shrubbery beside the rails, she peered out.

The train was made up of three self-propelled passenger cars, their sides sun-bleached, dented, and scratched. Most of the windows were covered with corrugated metal. *Enough scrap to patch the whole town!* At the front of the train stood a dozen people wearing long, loose, camo-coloured cloaks over overalls. They'd wrapped their heads against the blackflies with keffiyehs of netting, too, but stared out at the world through goggles. They wore wide-brimmed khaki hats, and they all had rifles, some held at the ready.

Rebeka ventured out from the shrubs and ducked behind the rear of the train beside the coupler. Everybody's attention was focused at the front. One man climbed down from the cab. He had no rifle. The others flanked him as he crept forward. Rebeka blinked and zoomed in for a closer look.

She winced. The grolar bear lay splayed and messy against the front of the train. *Poor thing!*

The lead man straightened up, shaking his head. He gestured at the bear, and the others slung their rifles over their shoulders and stepped forward. Voices rose as they cleared the carcass away.

Rebeka geotagged this site, too.

In her zoomed vision, the lead man turned, then paused. He stared across the distance of the train at her position. At her. He tilted his head and started forward.

Rebeka ducked back under cover. As voices approached, she turned and ran for the logging road, diving back into the bush the first chance she got. She raced for home.

Rebeka couldn't imagine Moosonee without the sea at its doorstep. The story of James Bay ending twenty kilometres downstream on a river before the waters rose and flooded Moose Factory had been just that: a story. Instead, the smell of salt and the scream of gulls rising over the rush of the pines always called her home.

She crashed out of the bush and followed the old powerline cut until she got to Quarry Road. She kept running. She followed the rutted track as it curved and descended, pulling up beside the rail line as it approached her town. She passed a battered, faded sign that read MOOSONEE, POPULA—.

Patched-up houses and pre-fab stores stretched out ahead of her along dusty roads. The tracks skirted the edge of the town opposite the estuary to the old train station—now the Meeting Hall—beside the Community Centre. People were already gathering on First Street, staring up the line toward the forest and beyond.

Rebeka waved her hands as she drew close. "Hey! Hey!" She pulled off her face shield and unwound her kaffiyah. "Hey! Train!"

"We heard!" Mrs. Freisberg smiled as Rebeka approached. The silver-haired woman squinted at the tree line through cracked glasses. "I haven't heard that sound in over twenty-five years!"

"I saw!" Rebeka waved back the way she'd come, then leaned on her knees, gasping. "They—" She took a deep breath, gulped, then continued. "They ran into a grolar bear at the logging road crossing."

"Whoa! Really?" Kile and his friends leaped up from the stoop of the old Thrift Store. "How long is it?"

"Those things could stretch kilometres!" Liz added. "Long chains of cars, carrying ore, grain, wood! Did you count them?"

"Just three, I'm afraid." Rebeka ruffled Liz's hair to the girl's annoyance. She turned to the others. "Three self-propelled passenger cars, bringing people." To Doctor Elijah King, standing in the doorway to his pharmacy, she added, "Dad, they got rifles."

In the distance, the train whistled twice. The rush of motors and clank of wheels started up again.

King stepped onto the street, as did Brody from the door of the hardware store and Karen from her coffee shop. She hadn't served coffee since the Manhattan Sea Wall failed, but she did serve a legendary bone broth. Karen handed Rebeka a steaming mug.

King glared up the line. "Southerners," he growled.

Brody chuckled softly and patted King's shoulder. "Of course, they're Southerners. Who else could they be? Californians would also be southerners to us."

"And the guns are not a surprise," Karen added. "You'd be an idiot to step into the wilderness without them."

"Still," King grumbled.

"Do you think they'll have news?" Ahead of them, Mrs. Freisberg stared at the train line. Her voice was eager, upbeat, but her hands twisted the strap of her purse. "Do you think they'll know about John?"

Brody, King, and Karen glanced at each other. The towns-folk stayed silent. Rebeka bit her lip.

"Maybe," said Karen at last.

King coughed. "I'm sure they have a few stories to tell."

"No harm in asking," Brody added. He glanced at Karen, who nodded and gestured at Kile. Kile nodded and ran into the coffee shop. He came out a moment later with a tray of steaming mugs and handed one to Mrs. Freisberg. She accepted it, not taking her eyes off the line.

The street filled up, more people hurrying in from the outskirts. Some carried whatever they'd been holding when they'd heard the train horn, mugs most often, but sometimes tools or a battered book. The younger kids joined up with Liz, chattering, while Kile hurried back into the coffee shop to deliver more bone broth. Some of the kids started playing train, running around in conga lines, while the bigger kids leaned on walls and pretended to be unimpressed. Old people frowned while parents leaned together and whispered.

Rebeka slung off her rifle, handing it to Brody. He checked the magazine. "You fired a shot?"

"A miss," she replied.

"You geotagged the spot?"

She rolled her eyes. "Of course, Other Dad."

"Hey," King chided. "Be kind."

"I *am* being kind, Dad," said Rebeka. "How long has it been since I lost a shell? Years? You two won't let me forget about that."

"Well, 'Beka," King began. "Bullets—"

"Bullets don't grow on trees." Rebeka rolled her eyes again. "If I had a shell casing for every time I heard that, we wouldn't have to worry about recycling our supply."

"How did you miss?" Brody cut in.

Rebeka shrugged. "The train horn disturbed the grolar bear."

"The same bear that got hit by that train?"

She nodded. "Geotagged that as well. Should still be a lot of usable flesh left."

"Good job." Brody gave Rebeka a smile and a wink. "You think the liver's okay?"

King sighed. "Don't you start, you two."

Rebeka grinned. "Yeah. Should be plenty of Vitamin A there! Don't want to run out of that." She looked up at King. "Right, Dad?"

He rolled his eyes.

The train horn sounded, closer this time. The town kids joined in, making whistle sounds in response. Conversations buzzed. Brody and King drew closer with the crowd, Rebeka a step behind.

"How could they be here?" asked Brody.

"They must have figured out a way around Otter Rapids," King replied.

Brody let out a chuff of disbelief. "They'd need to build a new bridge for that, past the ruined dam and overtop the old town. How could they have done that without us noticing?"

Karen paused between handing out mugs. "Well, it is a hundred and forty kilometres away."

Brody turned to her. "I saw the rail end this past spring. It's a dead drop into the canyon, and there's nothing there but rocks and trees and water. They'd have to have moved in supplies and built a bridge in less than six months. We should have noticed something."

"Could they have used the New Government Road?" asked Rebeka.

"It's in even worse shape," Brody replied. "It's washed out pretty much everywhere north of Iroquois Falls."

"Well, however they did it, they did it," said King, as headlights broke out from the treeline. He raised his voice over the shouts and cheers of the other townsfolk. "And now we're going to meet them." He nodded at the former station. "Appropriately, at the Meeting Hall."

As THEY WALKED toward the train station/Meeting Hall, Rebeka's vision flared. She staggered, then stepped to one side, leaning against a wall. She kept her implant eye closed as she massaged her temple.

Shadows fell over her. King and Brody looked down. They didn't say anything. They didn't need to.

"It's okay," she said through gritted teeth. She turned away, forced her eye open, then blinked rapidly. "Just a glitch."

Brody's voice pitched up. "Clearly, it's not."

"Other Dad—"

"Bex!" He waved his arms. "These are coming almost daily now! You can't keep living like this. We need to take you up the coast."

She glared at him. "Did the hospital in Attawapiskat take delivery of a new batch of implants?" She gestured at her implant. "Because otherwise, they're just going to remove this."

Brody started to shout, caught himself, and then lowered his voice. "Better that than pain."

"Easy for you to say," she snapped. "You're not looking at blindness."

"Brody?" King's voice was calm, quiet. "Go on to the Meeting Hall. Save us a spot."

Brody drew in his breath, looked at King, frowned at Rebeka, and then stalked off, shaking his head.

Rebeka pulled a necklace of metal beads from her pocket. She ran the rosary through her fingers and breathed deep against the memory of pain.

King pulled a match from his pocket. It flared to life as he crouched low to get a good look at her eye. Rebeka huffed but opened her eye wide. "The thing's still working, Dad! I would have had the bear if the train hadn't startled it."

"It's not about that, and you know it." King waved the match out and stuffed it back in his pocket. "Brody doesn't like to see you in pain. Neither do I. I'm not seeing any physical damage yet, but if this gets any worse, you're going to the hospital in Attawapiskat."

Rebeka looked away. The rosary beads clicked between her fingers. "Dad, I can't put food on the table with just one eye, and a normal one at that."

King gave her a tight smile. "You'll adjust. And it doesn't have to be just you who puts food on the table, you know."

"I'm the best shot in town thanks to this implant," she snapped. "If I don't put food on the table, what good am I?"

"You're my daughter; that's what good you are." He gripped her shoulder and gave it a squeeze. "And that's plenty good enough."

She pushed his hand away. "I don't want to talk about this right now." She pocketed her rosary and shoved past him. "Come on. We don't want to miss this meeting."

THE BRAKES SQUEALED as the train descended the line into town. Its horn blared, and kids who'd stepped too close clamped their hands over their ears. The train slowed as it reached the platform, which was now full of people.

Finally, the engines cut out and, brakes squealing, the train eased to a stop. Metal shutters pulled away from the windows, revealing soldiers in camo gear, faces obscured by netting and goggles. Rifles were slung over their shoulders. They stared out at the people on the platform and the people stared back. The kids and some of the older folks started to edge away.

At the head of the train, the cab door opened, and a man stepped to the edge. Rebeka recognized his long coat, netting, and hat from the logging road crossing. He looked out at the audience, then pulled off his hat and goggles, unwinding his kaffiyah netting, revealing the face of a clean-shaven man with short, brown-blond hair and dark eyes. "Hello!" His smile showed brilliant white teeth.

He raised his hat high, and his voice. "Hello, Moosonee! I'm so glad to see you all here! How long has it been? Twenty-six years? But you're still here! Wonderful! Wonderful!" He clapped, loud and hard, and the soldiers at the train windows started clapping as well.

At the back of the crowd, Rebeka watched the townsfolk look around, many confused. But as the applause continued, some straightened their shoulders, looking proud. She found herself nodding, thinking, *Damn straight. We're still here.*

The man continued, "My name is Drew McMurtry, and I work for the Toronto District Government."

He tossed his hat, goggles, and kaffiyah inside the cab, clambered down onto the platform, then gestured to the soldiers on the train. "Take the nets off, all of you! The blackflies aren't bad around here. Let everybody see your faces!" He turned back to the crowd. "Let everybody see everybody. This is . . ." He stopped, sighed, and, when he looked up, seemed almost in tears. "This is a great reunion after all this time. We're so glad to see you all there."

He clapped again as the soldiers removed their nets and goggles, revealing men and women. Some men had beards, some not. Some soldiers had close-cropped hair; others wore their hair longer. Without the keffiyehs and goggles, all looked . . . young. Nervous. Shy. They smiled and applauded, and, this time, the townsfolk clapped with them.

As the applause ebbed, McMurtry raised his hands. "I'd like to speak to your council. We have a lot of catching up to do." He gestured as two soldiers pulled open a loading door in the middle of the first car. Each held a cardboard box in their hands. "First things first, though: to the people of Moosonee, we're from Toronto, and we bring . . . chocolate!"

Two soldiers jumped onto the platform, opening the boxes to reveal rows of foil-wrapped bars. Everyone stared. Then the kids rushed forward en masse before being held back, barely, by their parents. After brief chaos, the crowd organized the children into lines. Each kid received one bar and thanked the soldier handing them out before going immediately to the back of the line for a second offering.

Rebeka looked at the boxes in the soldiers' hands and noted similar ones in the train car behind them. *There's probably enough in there to give every child quite a sugar high.*

King glanced at Rebeka. He and Brody shared a look. Then he nudged Karen, who nodded. She stepped forward to McMurtry and stuck out her hand. "Mr. McMurtry, welcome to Moosonee." Smiling, he shook her hand. "My name is Karen Quachegan," she continued. "I'm the . . . mayor of this town." She gestured at the station behind her. "Why don't we go into the Meeting Hall? We have bone broth."

Rebecca watched as Karen, Brody, and King led McMurtry into the station. Two soldiers followed close behind. On the train, four soldiers wrestled a waist-high crate to the edge of the train's loading doors and called for help. Townsfolk rushed forward to assist. As everyone worked, Rebecca counted the soldiers in her head.

Two dozen, she thought. *And all of them with guns.*

❋

AFTER THE SOLDIERS and townsfolk volunteers loaded the large crate onto a cart, Rebeka followed them as the soldiers guided the cart into the Meeting Hall. McMurtry, flanked by his two soldiers, sat at one side of the head table while Karen sat at the other, Brody and King beside her. Everybody clasped steaming mugs of bone broth. Townsfolk pulled up seats around them.

McMurtry gestured to the crate as it entered. "More gifts from the Toronto District Government. Chocolate is a nice treat, but probably not all that you need, am I right?"

"That's very generous, Mr. McMurtry." Karen smiled, looking almost embarrassed by all of these gifts. "We have been doing all right here since things stabilized. Some of the older ways helped, including hunting, but new supplies are always appreciated. We have to geotag our bullets so we can rescue and recycle them before they go extinct. The component parts of our rifles can be fixed up only so many times."

"That's why we're here," said McMurtry. "I think this will help provide all of the supplies you need."

King coughed. "We appreciate all of these gifts from the south, Mr. McMurtry, but we are all wondering how you came to be here."

McMurtry tilted his head. "Well . . . what was the last thing you heard from . . . us?"

"We heard the Manhattan Sea Wall failed," said Brody. "We heard there were riots. Then the electricity cut out and we lost the Internet. We had to rely on ham radios to get any sort of news after that. The last thing we heard from the south was the warning from Otter Rapids that the dam at the Abitibi Generating Station had collapsed and that we had to get to higher ground, fast. Since then, all our news has come from the north."

McMurtry nodded solemnly. "That . . . that must have been

really hard." He smiled, still solemn. "There were hard years for us, too, but we managed to restore order in the city and save the farms around it. We kept Holland Marsh from flooding, and that stabilized our food supply. We moved City Hall into Queen's Park, and since then, we've been bringing the surrounding settlements under our protection as we can manage it. Hamilton. Waterloo. Belleville. Ottawa's a big mess. And as for the Dominion of Montreal . . ." His lip curled a moment. "Well, we've banged heads with them, but I think we've come to an understanding. The peace has held."

He leaned back. "Since then, we've been reaching out, seeing who we can help, making things safe for everybody, bringing things back to some level of normalcy. There are jobs to be done—paying jobs—and we need people to fill them. We're trading with Michigan, the Boston Free State, the Montrealers, even. The world is starting to come back together, and we want to help that process along. And that's why we're here, with supplies and . . . more." He gestured to the soldier on his right.

The soldier, a woman, stood up. She had close-cropped blonde hair and wore a white armband on her sleeve emblazoned with a red cross. "Hello, everybody. My name is Sergeant Mireille Baker, and I'm a medic. With your permission, I'd like to talk to all of you and hear about any medical issues you might have. We've brought medicines, and we have access to more back south. Does anybody have any issues they'd like to go over with with me?"

Silence settled on the room as, without making it obvious, the townsfolk focused on King. He leaned back in his seat and gave a barely perceptible nod to Karen. She gave that nod back and shifted in her seat. "I'm sure many of us wouldn't mind being seen to by a southern medic."

The townsfolk relaxed. Hands rose. If McMurtry or any soldiers noticed the silence and communication, they didn't indicate it. Conversations swelled, people talking to Baker, people talking to each other. Karen turned to McMurtry and beckoned others toward them to talk business. Rebeka stepped closer.

"Things are happening in the Arctic," said McMurtry. "Nations are trading all the way to Siberia. There's mineral exploration. There's a lot of opportunity up there. You could be a part of that, and we could help." He smiled and nodded as though expecting thanks. "We can offer protection; stop those Greenlander pirates if they ever show their faces—"

The door opened, and soldiers and townsfolk entered, carrying boxes and heading for the storeroom. They jostled past Rebeka, who stepped back to let them pass, only to hear Kile shout.

"They're not pirates!" he blurted. People turned to see the boy standing to one side, holding an empty tray. McMurtry frowned, but Kile didn't stop. "And they're not called Greenlanders. Their nation is Kalaallit Nunaat! They show up every spring, trading seal meat and fruits from Europe for medicines and lumber!"

Kile's mother hurried forward and whispered to him. He glared at her. "Well, they're not!" he grumbled as she led him away.

McMurtry coughed. "Well, I'm glad to hear you've had good dealings with the people of the Arctic. Things can be different in different parts of the world. I know the Newfoundlanders aren't too happy with them." He laughed. "Anyway—"

"Excuse me?" Sergeant Baker was suddenly at Rebeka's side, staring at her. "Are you using an ocular implant?"

Rebeka blinked, then nodded. Baker took out what looked to Rebeka like a metal wand with an eyepiece on it. A light flashed on inside it. "May I?" Baker asked.

Rebeka nodded again, and Baker stepped her back, leaned close, and gently pressed Rebeka's eye open wider. She shone the light into Rebeka's pupil. Rebeka grunted as her implant flashed and flared.

"Sorry," Baker breathed. "How long have you had this?"

"I got it when I was four," Rebeka replied. "About a year before the Sea Wall fell."

"Huh." Baker shut off the light and leaned back. "Well, that explains it. Those things are not designed to last more than twenty years without regular maintenance, and you've made it last more than twenty-five!"

"Tell me about it," Rebeka grumbled. "My dads want me to go to the hospital in Attawapiskat, but what can they do about it?"

"Probably nothing except remove it," Baker replied. "But we can replace it in Toronto."

"What?" Rebeka stared at Baker. "You're telling me these things aren't extinct? Some of them survived the EMPs?"

Baker shrugged. "Not a lot of the old technology did, but some. We've stockpiled what we've found to use as spare parts." She looked Rebeka in her implanted eye. "Spare parts to fix exactly your problem."

For a moment, Rebeka stood speechless. Then, she whispered, "Wh-what would I have to do? Where would I have to go?"

Baker pulled a card from her pocket. "Take this. It's the address of Toronto General Hospital. Come to the city and make an appointment. We could see you within the day. It's as easy as that." She patted Rebeka's arm.

Then she moved on to her next patient, leaving Rebeka staring after her.

McMurtry and his soldiers stayed in town for two hours. Karen and others led groups down to the estuary, where the

Torontonians stared at the docks where rowboats floated and gulls cried above them. Finally, McMurtry thanked everyone, announced that he had to return south, and gave a speech about reconnection and hope. The townsfolk cheered as, with two loud whistles, the government train departed.

The townsfolk watched it go, then turned to the crate McMurtry's people had delivered.

In the Meeting Hall, Brody brought a hammer and a crowbar. Soon, they had the lid off and were tossing aside paper packing fluff. People crowded in until Rebeka waved her arms. "Hey! Give us room!" The people backed up.

"Everything we needed to help with your lives here, they said," King muttered. "If they'd given us some notice, I'd have given them a list."

"I'm sure there's plenty of things we can use," said Brody.

"I didn't like what they said about the Kalaallit," Kile grumbled. "It's the Scandinavians who are pirates; them and that European Federation they're forming. The Kalaalit Nunaat have to deal with them all the time."

"It's politics, Kile," said his Mom.

"Politics can kill, Mom!"

Brody pulled aside a sheet. "Here we are!"

Townsfolk surged forward again before backing up from Rebeka's baleful glare.

However, everyone liked what they saw. Murmurs of appreciation rose at the metal cans, glass jars, and packages wrapped in wax paper. Brody sniffed the paper packages. "Beef jerky."

"Beef!" Liz exclaimed.

Karen gathered some of the packages into her arms. "That's going on the menu tonight. It will make a nice change from moose."

Brody sniffed another package. "Coffee!"

Karen dropped the jerky. "Back, everybody! Back!" She grabbed the packages. "I'll serve this up tomorrow morning.

Bottomless cups all around, but only if you don't stampede!" This brought a cheer and some laughter from the townsfolk.

King looked deeper. "I'm seeing cabbages, zucchini, fruit preserves." Around him, people buzzed. Winter did not seem so cold now.

Rebeka pointed. "Dad, look at those jars. Are those medicines?"

King peered closer. "Yes! Antibiotics. Minerals. Multivitamins, and . . ." He pushed some jars aside, stopped, and then started laughing.

"What?" said Brody, as did others in the crowd.

"Elijah, what?" asked Karen.

"Dad?" said Rebeka.

He pulled something from the box and struggled to get his laughter under control. He held up a bottle. "They gave us Vitamin A!"

He started laughing again. This time, everyone joined in.

Karen and Brody passed packages to townsfolk, who hurried to the storeroom while King and Rebeka sorted through the rest of the crate. King removed the last item and swept his hand along the bottom of the crate. "That's all of it."

"Meat, vegetables, medicines, even candy and linens," said Brody. "Not a bad haul."

King looked up. "True. Not a *bad* haul." But he frowned.

Brody peered at him. "What's wrong?"

King said nothing. But for Rebeka, it clicked. "Everything we need to help us with our lives here," she echoed. "Any air canisters?"

King shook his head.

"Any rifle parts?" she asked.

"No," said King.

Karen halted. Brody raised his chin, realization dawning. "Any bullets?"

King looked grim. "No."

Silence descended on the Meeting Hall.

REBEKA CRESTED a hill and hit a blessed downslope as the rail line eased into the canyon of the Abitibi River. The dynamos of her railbike whined as the regenerative braking kicked in. Blackflies smacked against her visor and snagged in the netting of her kaffiyah. She looked ahead at the bend that would reveal the old community of Otter Rapids and the ruins of the generating station there.

Ahead, she heard the whistle of the government train blowing around a distant curve.

"EVERYTHING WE NEEDED, THEY SAID," Brody said. "Didn't they know we're hunters?"

"Who isn't this far north?" Rebeka muttered in reply. She ran her rosary beads over her fingers.

King sucked his teeth. "No. Not everything we needed. Everything they thought we needed. Everything they thought it was safe to give us. So we would welcome them the next time. The chocolate and candy were a nice touch. I'm surprised they didn't offer roses."

ON HER RAILBIKE, Rebeca rounded a bend, and the ruins of Otter Rapids spread out before her, denuded hillsides, old foundations and broken dam abutments showing where the community had been. She pulled to a stop where the rails used to end and stared ahead.

More trees had been stripped from the hills above the high water line to build a long, winding, makeshift trestle snaking along the canyon wall, skirting the townsite. It was at least a kilometre long—one point two kilometres, her implant told her —before it passed the remains of the generating station, and the rails gripped the ground again.

At the other end of the long trestle, the government train slowed to a stop.

MRS. FREISBURG HAD LEANED *back against the crate. "Why wouldn't they give us any bullets?" The townsfolk didn't answer. She didn't blink; the answer was obvious. So she moved on. "What would they want that they're worried we'd say 'no' to?"*

Karen stared at the ceiling. Brody fretted. King stared into the crate. Others shifted on their feet, nervous or disconsolate.

Rebeka's fingers stopped clicking. She looked up. "They want the Arctic." Everybody looked at her. "You heard them: there's resources up there. They'll need a port to access that, and we're the closest one they can get."

"How big a port?" Brody asked.

They stared out the station window at the battered, patched-up town, their homes, and the docks on the estuary a few blocks away.

"They'll need something that can handle a lot of goods," said King. "Something they can defend. You heard their cracks about 'Greenlanders.' They're not expecting the other players up north to play nice."

"They're not going to ask us for permission, are they?" said Brody.

"They may ask," said King. "But I don't think they're going to take 'no' for an answer."

REBEKA HOPPED OFF HER RAILBIKE. Keeping low, she crept along the railbed to the start of the trestle and zoomed in on the government train.

Her implant flickered. She grunted, frustrated, and tapped her temple. Then she focused closer.

KILE YELLED AS, at the station, he pumped the pedals of the railbike. "Come on and help, Liz! It's been a half hour, and the battery's just at fifty percent!"

Liz hurried over to help.

Rebeka set down her box on the trailer behind the railbike. Behind her, King continued. "Follow them as far as you can. Don't let them see you. Your implant should allow you to spy on them from far enough back. Find out what they're not telling us. You need to see how they act when their guard is down."

She nodded, then, after a brief hesitation, gripped King's hand and Brody's and pulled them closer. "Dad? Other Dad? The medic, Sergeant Baker . . . She said they could fix my implant in Toronto."

Silence fell between them. Brody looked at King. "Elijah, if there's a chance—"

King looked at Rebeka. "Do you think there's a chance?"

Rebeka sucked in her breath. "I don't know. If they could fix it, I'd get it fixed, but . . . What if they want to hurt us—"

King straightened up. "You have to make the call." He looked grim. "I'm sorry, but you have to decide whether we can work with them or . . ." He looked at Brody.

"Or?" Rebeka prompted.

"Or . . ." Brody sighed. "If we need more time to prepare for them."

Rebeka bit her lip and looked at King, then at Brody. She took a deep breath. "All right."

AROUND THE GOVERNMENT TRAIN, soldiers fanned into the bushes, stamping around, some taking bathroom breaks. Others gathered around—what were those things? Mounds? Mounds on pallets, covered in tarps.

They'd cleared the land and stashed these items before going into town, she realized. As she watched, soldiers pulled aside one of the tarpaulins, and Rebeka tuned her zoom higher.

"That... is a big gun," she whispered.

Her implant pulled up information from before the fall of the Manhattan Sea Wall. *Identification: Gomm Cogne 47, crowd-control configuration. Capable of sixty rounds per second, rubber buckshot.*

The soldiers moved it toward the train, looking north as they did so.

She returned to the railbike, unhooked it from its trailer, and pulled it from the tracks. She set it in the ditch, then faced the trailer.

AT THE STATION, Rebeka grunted as she, King, and six other townsfolk hauled the trailer onto the tracks and hooked it to the railbike. "Does this have to be so heavy? It'll be agony getting this to Otter Rapids."

Mrs. Friesburg and Liz rolled up with a cart. "This is the last bit of blasting material we salvaged from Victor Mine."

"If they've rebuilt the line the way I think they have," said Brody, "We need to direct the force of the blast down at the tracks. This thing has to be as heavy as possible so it doesn't become an upward projectile."

"It will still become an upward projectile," said King. "Just not a good one. Either way, make sure you're not nearby when it goes."

Rebeka nodded. She and Karen and other townsfolk began moving the explosives onto the trailer.

Mrs. Freisburg faced south, took off her cracked glasses, and closed her eyes. "John."

AT TRACKSIDE, Rebeka pulled the trigger over to prime it, only to have it flash and spark in her hands. She yanked it free lest it set off the explosives beside her. "God dammit!" She looked at the connection, but the box got hot and started smoking in her hands. She tossed it into the ditch. She took a deep breath, let it out slowly, and looked at where the trigger used to connect with the fuse.

"Percussion fuse," she muttered. "I can work with that."

She braced her hands against the trailer, braced her feet against the ties, and pushed. The trailer moved, slowly at first. She took one step, then another. The trailer picked up speed on the incline. She pushed harder, stepped faster, then stumbled and fell face-first onto the ties.

The trailer kept rolling, rounding the curve, accelerating down the incline onto the long trestle.

Rebeka staggered to her feet, legs bleeding. She unslung her rifle and sighted down the barrel at the fuse. Her implant calculated distance, windspeed, trajectory.

She glanced at the soldiers and the government train. She saw McMurtry shaking his head at the crowd-control weapon.

"Sorry, government man," she muttered. "You may have offered us the carrot, but you still brought the stick." She counted down the seconds to her shot.

Then, her implant flashed white.

She yelled and clenched her eyes shut against the pain. It was worse than staring into the sun. She tried opening her unaltered eye, but it was no good. She couldn't focus.

She smacked her temple twice, then once more, and her

implant switched off, leaving only darkness in her right eye, but thankfully, no more pain.

Growling, she switched her grip on her gun and sighted down the barrel with her left eye. The fuse blurred in her vision. *Focus*, she thought. *Focus!* She counted down.

At the other end of the trestle, someone shouted. She pulled the trigger.

The gun chuffed and shoved against her shoulder. A blink later, the trailer exploded. The blast pitched Rebeka onto the ballast.

For a moment, she stared at the sky with half her vision, listening as wood crackled and debris fell. Gradually, the buzz of blackflies and the chitter of birds returned, along with the rustle of pines.

She sat up.

The trestle, with its wood piled on wood, stood shaken and out of alignment, a huge chunk missing from its centre. Pieces burned. As she watched, piles broke away, knocking into other supports. Finally, with a groan and a rumble, the bridge came apart, tree trunks snapping like twigs as they avalanched into the canyon below.

Through the smoke and flames, Rebeka saw the government train on the other side of the gap. She saw McMurtry standing at the cab door. His shoulders sagged. Behind him, the train let out a long, mournful whistle that echoed off the hills.

And, across the hills, other whistles answered.

They weren't echoes. They varied in pitch. Rebeka counted them under her breath. "Three . . . four . . ." Some were faint with distance. "Seven . . . eight . . ." Others . . . others were close. "Eleven . . . twelve . . ."

Only then did the whistles stop, their howls fading to echoes, then silence.

McMurtry turned away. The soldiers climbed aboard.

Slowly at first, then picking up speed, the government train vanished into the woods.

FOR THOSE ABOUT TO ROCK

BY JEFF SZPIRGLAS

The latitude town known as the Viritrilbia
Mercury Colonies, July 19, 2184

JAMES ASSUMES THE STANCE: LEGS SPLAYED, SHOULDERS hunched, arms tensed. As his eyes survey the fifty thousand admiring faces, his ears sop up the rest of the anticipation.

"I LOVE YOU, JAMES!"

"NO, I LOVE YOU, JAMES!"

"I LOVE YOU MORE THAN THE TWO OF THEM PUT TOGETHER!"

James's eyes narrow to slivers of moonlight. He nods to himself and thinks, *Damn right, you do.*

But James is already spoken for. He's clutching his love as he speaks and softly strokes her neck for all to see. It is not the neck of Michelle Asbury, the most luxuriant weave of DNA ever spun and the only girl to have eluded him thus far. This neck of hardwood and lacquer lacks the warmth of soft flesh. Any pulse the Gibson Flying V gives comes from the electricity flowing between it and a sound system capable of shredding the hundred thousand eardrums before him into confetti.

He had considered naming his beloved guitar after Michelle Asbury. As he slowly pulls his fingers along the frets, he imagines they are the vertebrae of the neck he yearns to caress.

Just as the lights above him shift from blistering amber to sultry purple, James sneaks a quick peek at the setlist at his feet and then throws a glance at the band behind him. The rhythm guitarist nods at this signal, then strums the first few blissful chords of their latest make-out masterpiece, "Backseat Romeo." Back in the audience, cheers swell through the stadium. The onlookers sway their lighters to and fro, illuminating the darkness.

It's time, James thinks.

He takes one step forward and is hit with a blast of stage light so intense it's a wonder his eyeballs don't boil into foam. An amateur would flinch under the glare, but James has spent the last six months touring enough cities to fill up a passport the size of *War and Peace*. He can take the heat, both literally and figuratively. He peels back his lips, revealing a toothy grin that, when hit by the spotlight, shines like a beacon onto the spectators.

"GIVE IT TO US!"

James obliges by plucking golden notes from his guitar. The mystics in the crowd watch in disbelief as the notes wriggle up from between the strings, pair up in the air before them, and dance waltzes before being pumped through miles of cables, where they are amplified and sprayed over the audience.

James observes the sweaty faces in the front rows. He pays no heed to the fanboys, who have squeezed every last drop of his music into their minds so that little room has been left for anything else. His attention is taken by a couple fondling each other in the wandering spotlight, and he suddenly wishes he were down there with the one girl worth abandoning all of rock and roll for.

And then, as fate would have it—and fate always has it—there she is!

Michelle is stuck back in the fourth row, trying to push her way to the front of the crowd, so all James spots at first is a wisp of her hair, but it's enough. He recognizes her slightly upturned nose, the soft flush of her cheeks, the glistening sheen of those lips, and those eyes. Oh, those eyes. They're enough to make him want to stop mid-song to write one just for her.

Although he's way up on the stage and she's tucked back in the fourth row, James finds he can stretch his arm just enough for the tips of his fingers to brush against hers. That's all he needs.

He teases her out of the crowd, past the wall of beefy security guards, and pulls her onstage with him. She is wrapped snuggly in his arms, which is appropriate since this song—correction: this Power Ballad—is all for her. James knows he's going to break the hearts of all the babes who cleaned out their bank accounts for the privilege of front-row seats, but he can't help himself.

The band keeps playing, and the notes flutter onto the couple like rose petals. These are the kind of notes that could make an atheist a believer. These are the notes that James is going to kiss Michelle Asbury to.

The air between them crackles so much you can smell the ozone burning. James leans forward, closes his eyes, and then . . .

. . . and then the song gets bludgeoned to death by a pair of wooden clubs.

Someone is playing the drums. Badly.

James whips around and is faced with an adolescent male seated at the drums. He is brutal, he is relentless, and, as James soon notices, he is suddenly the only other person on stage.

The crowds have vanished, and the cavernous stadium has been reduced to four cramped, dirty walls and assorted pieces of furniture in ill-repair. The amplifiers and mixing board have vaporized. James no longer holds the sleek electric guitar in his hands; what he now clutches is, by his own admission, an antiquated piece of crap that can no longer be heard over the deafening din.

The incessant drumming has battered the dream into submission, and most importantly, it has taken Michelle Asbury with it. Now, she is lost amongst the twirling clouds of dust that the drumming has stirred up.

James's heart feels as if it has plunged into his intestines and taken up skateboarding there. He is not a rock god. His guitar strains to make the right notes. He does not even have a proper band. And most crushing of all, he does not have Michelle Asbury in his arms, and he's pretty damn sure he never will.

All he has is a mountain of math homework due first thing Monday morning, a mean case of acne, and now, thanks to his best friend on the drums, a splitting headache.

This, dear friends, is James's reality, and it sucks.

"Stop drumming on the wall!"

"Whaaaaat?"

"Stop drumming on the wall!"

"I can't hear you!"

"Stop drumming so you can!"

"Whaaaaat?"

"I said," James began, this time yanking the sticks from Dan's hands before they could punch holes in the wall, "stop the snarblin' drumming."

"You've got to learn some better swear words, man. Dude, we're going to rock so hard it'll put that student council back into the Earth Age!"

James blinked at the remark. "What are you talking about?"

Dan yanked the drumsticks back. "Damned if I know." He twirled them in his hands. "You gotta be careful with these things. They're breakable."

James didn't even bother responding. Now he was just too damned nervous.

For starters, their band, Foul Grammar, had never performed. Not publicly.

Oh, sure, they'd played plenty. Every Saturday after lunch, James would traipse over to the little cubicle that Dan called his "special place," which was the extra storage allotment that Dan's family had been given to keep their corn-harvesting gear. Dan had realized that if one were creative, one could haphazardly stack the gear in such a way that there was a reasonably sound-proof practice space.

The pair didn't need much rehearsal room. Dan's sticks were of Earth make, from an era when percussion tech allowed one to augment the sound of the rapping and banging of the sticks. Dan just had to alter a few pitches on his visi-screen and have them sound like whatever-sized drum kit he could imagine, cowbells and all. James, meanwhile, had to pair his guitar (also Earth-made, a family heirloom) with the visi-screen for largely the same effect.

So, with Dan brandishing his sticks like daggers and James raking his fingers across the strings, the boys did their best to approximate the 4/4 lurch of that ancient form of minstreldom known as Glam Metal.

But no matter how hard James played, the band's sound remained constant: an echoing, non-rhythmic pounding that masked all but the slightest traces of a tune.

If there was one thing the boys needed, it was to get amped up someplace with way better acoustics than the rumbling rail city of *Viritrilbia*.

There was always a tinny timbre to any of the music

produced in the rail cities that no amount of digital manipulation could disguise; good old-fashioned wood was the best material for bouncing sounds around a room in pleasing ways, but wood came from Earth, and Earth had long since gone silent.

Mercurian cities always had a low rumble that apparently drove people crazy when they first colonized the planet, but James didn't know any better. To his ears, the low rumble was just another sound he'd become accustomed to. He could feel it when he pressed his hands against the floors or any of the walls near the lower decks.

A better place to practise would help.

Of course, playing music that their peers actually liked would be another advantage.

Most music was assembled on visi-screens for school projects or the few dancing spaces where kids of their age and above could meet and mingle and groove to whatever fermented beverage was available for one's age bracket.

And most of it, according to Dan, sucked monkey balls.

Neither Dan nor James had seen an actual monkey to properly assess the quality of its balls, but there was certainly something missing in the sampled mixture of beats and tones that was considered popular music.

The boys had been able to access older channels and broadcasts to learn of the array of acoustic instruments their Earthbound forebearers had developed over the centuries. But nothing could beat the classical form of tinnitus-inducing music known by scholars as Classic Rock and Heavy Metal.

It was this antiquated form of artistry that Foul Grammar attempted to emulate. And today was the big reveal. They'd spent the last several months attempting to perfect the music, hoping that it would land them a spot at their school's formal dance.

More importantly, they'd hoped it would get them attention from the girls.

"I'm not saying we need to be perfect," Dan admitted, "but we have to be memorable."

James sighed. He knew what Dan was getting at and would have no part in this insanity.

"No way. Not that song!"

"Bruh, we're up against Hal Sethler. You know how popular he is, right?"

James shoved a desperate finger at Dan. "You do this, you're going to embarrass us more than I ever could with 'Backseat Romeo.'"

"You're not embarrassing yourself if you embrace the power and submit to the gods of rock."

"One of these days," James spat, "you're going to make sense. But today is not it."

"Too late, buddy. We're on."

BETTY REED WAS slender in figure and perfect in posture. She was president of the student council and somehow managed to squeeze in track meets thrice a week, all the while maintaining a grade point average that assured her an apprenticeship of her choice on any one of the seventeen cities or two polar statics.

James watched her examine the sign-up sheet on her personal visi-screen before proceeding to wrinkle her brow. There was no doubt she had already made up her mind about which band would have the privilege of performing at the school's formal.

"Great," James said sarcastically. "Betty Reed is in charge of things."

"You say that like it's a bad thing," Dan returned. His eyes were also locked on the president of the school council.

"Stop drooling."

Betty's attention remained on the list. "Right. Our next candidate is . . . Foul Grammar?" She turned to a colleague for confirmation. Michelle Asbury, at her side, nodded and smiled.

All eyes turned to the stage. James and Dan emerged from the wings, shuffling self-consciously.

Betty waited for others to follow. "Excuse me. Where's the rest of the band?"

"This is the rest of the band," James said.

"There are only two of you?"

"Well observed, Miss Reed. We're a rock duo."

Betty narrowed her eyes.

"Do the words 'White Stripes' mean nothing to you?"

"They do not."

Dan took this to be his cue. "Ancient Earth band: drums, guitar. That's all one needs to rock, and that's what we're going to do at the senior prom this year!" Dan closed his eyes and threw his fist into the air and waited for the applause that did not follow.

Betty cleared her throat. "It says here you're going to play something called 'Backseat Romeo'?"

"Would that we could, but the song is not ready for human consumption yet; instead, we are going to perform a little number I penned for this very occasion."

James looked up at Michelle once more. Oh, hell, she was definitely staring in his direction. Not only that but when James studied her lips, he noticed they were mouthing words that surprised him: "Hi, James." She had acknowledged his existence. How could this be? James was suddenly filled with so many questions that he completely failed to stop Dan from leading into the song that would be their undoing.

Dan clicked his drumsticks together. "One, two, three, four . . ."

Too late! He opened his mouth and began to scream out his carefully constructed lyrics:

You're buttering me up, and I'm dripping with juice
I'm stuffed with desire, and it's gonna burst loose
You're the one who makes life worth living
I want to be inside you when it's Thanksgiving
I'm your Lust Turkey! I'm your Lust Turkey!
Be careful where you carve me; don't turn me to jerky
Lust Turkey! Lust Turkey!

This was, of course, the student-friendly version of the song, still very much in development. Dan had lost sleep penning the lyrics to his magnum opus. The final "EEEEAAARRGH!" was the perfect touch, a climactic howl patterned after Roger Daltrey's banshee wail from the Olden Times. In rehearsal, it had led into one of James's blistering guitar solos, but today, it led into the standing-up-of-Betty-Reed-and-turning-on-of-her-megaphone.

"That's great, thank you," she said firmly, with the volume set just high enough to effectively kill the song and cause the rest of the student council to jam their fingers in their ears.

"But I never played my guitar solo," James pleaded, searching for sympathy. Only Michelle Asbury gave him a sad shrug.

"Can't hear the guitar over the drumming," Betty snapped. "In fact, I can't hear anything over the drumming."

Dan beamed, either not seeing where this was going or not caring. "Thanks, Betty. You are by far the most attractive student council president I ever voted for."

"WELL, *that* didn't go the way I was hoping," Dan moped, digging his hand into the box of bat crackers and crunching them into a paste.

James sighed. "You played 'Lust Turkey.' What did you expect?"

"It's our biggest hit."

"We don't have hits, Dan."

Dan shrugged. "Not yet, we don't."

James pushed away from the dirty metal wall separating their rehearsal space from the rest of Dan's set of home cubicles. "We're never going to have hits, Dan." He kicked at the pile of farming poles, only succeeding in stubbing his toe. "Snarbles!"

"Whoa, whoah. Language, James."

There were others their age who toyed with music, but they wanted no part of Foul Grammar. It would not do them well to associate with a band whose hastily assembled repertoire included such non-hits as "Kiss Your Gonads Goodbye," "Septic Tank Blues in A-flat," and "Your Love Is Like An Appendectomy."

James sighed. "I think this might be it, Dan."

"Don't tell me you're gonna quit the band."

"I think I'm going to quit the band."

"I said *not* to tell me that!"

"Dan, did we or did we not agree to form this band to meet girls?" James asked.

"We did."

"And how is that working out for us?"

"I think I may be getting somewhere with Betty Reed . . ."

"You're just getting us further and further away from *anything*," James huffed. He wanted to kick something else, but he was already in enough pain for one afternoon.

Dan looked like he was going to come up with some half-assed rebuttal, but instead, his attention was steered to the visi-screen in his hands. It was buzzing.

Dan looked down and saw the message in all caps, taking up the full width of the screen.

INCOMING TRANSMISSION, it read in angry red letters.

Red letters meant an unknown sender, and Dan shook his head. "I thought I'd set this thing to filter out all of the garbage."

He waited for the inevitable spamming of his screen with whatever advertisement some tool from a neighbouring rail city managed to sneak past the firewall or bullying put-down his peers had in store for him. What he got instead was a set of numbers.

Dan's first instinct was to smack his visi-screen against his knee, which sometimes did the job to get rid of bugs such as these. But the numbers remained, and Dan's confusion grew. He handed the screen to James. "What do you make of this?"

"Dude, those are coordinates," James said matter-of-factly.

Dan yanked the screen back from James and stared at it. "Oh," he said. Then, another thought. "Whereabouts?"

James took his own visi-screen, punched a few numbers into it, flipped through a few screens, and held up the answer. "Right there."

FIVE DAYS LATER, the meteorite struck.

The meteorite had been observed two days prior to impact and determined by science to be not worth the effort of exploding before it hit the planet's surface. There was no atmosphere on Mercury, and by all calculations, pulverizing it just meant that hundreds of fragments would still rain down on the surface. The cities would be spared, and the rails they travelled on would not be at risk.

There was one unfortunate casualty; the meteor wiped out James's favourite message scrawled in rover tracks along the surface of the planet, the great whopping "SUCK IT, VENUS" that could be read by their planetary neighbours and which had been inscribed in the planet's surface by Baelon Grackenhust a century ago when the planet had first been colonized.

The Signature Sands was something of hallowed ground; it was long considered a rite of passage to steal a rover and carve some kind of lewd slang into the rugged Mercurian landscape. Often the graffiti was relegated to initials of young lovers or jabs from one rail-bound city to another, but at least everyone could agree that Venus could, in fact, suck it and suck it hard. As hard as monkey balls, even.

Little of this really mattered, except for one thing: the location of the meteorite perfectly matched the one Dan had been sent on his visi-screen five days earlier, long before the Mercurian scientists picked up on it.

Nobody else on Viritrilbia had received such a transmission, as far as James and Dan could tell. James and Dan had discussed doing something rational, like telling their parents about it, but their adolescent minds determined that they had some kind of scoop, and scoops were worth keeping to themselves.

This was solidified with yet another glowing red INCOMING TRANSMISSION—only this time, the unknown sender's transmission bore a simple message. "Bring instruments and vacu-seals." Then another number. This was no location but a date.

Two weeks in the future, it turned out to be: precisely the amount of time that would pass before the impact crater of the meteorite would close enough for James and Dan to be able to reach the location with a stolen (er, borrowed) rover and get back in a couple of hours.

"You know this is a bad idea," James said, staring at the crater through the rover's scanner screen.

"They asked us to bring our instruments," Dan said as if this perplexing request somehow made everything cool.

"Our parents don't know we're here. Nobody knows we're here."

"Not until they start tracking the rover."

"By then, we could be dead."

But death eluded the boys as they exited the rover in their life-support suits, instruments and vacu-seals in hand, and trudged over to the crater.

Only it wasn't just a crater.

Whatever had caused the crater had punched a hole in the side of the planet, revealing some kind of cavern below. It was just big enough for the boys and their gear to fit inside, which might have scared them off had they not been so consumed with curiosity about the whole "bring your instruments" business.

Once inside, and once their gear was safely put down, James and Dan surveyed the cavern with their helmet lanterns.

The cave did not look like it had been made by the meteor impact. James knew meteor impact craters. They were messy; they threw debris everywhere. This was different. The walls were smoothed down, almost polished. The cavern was at least six metres high, its ceiling rounded almost into a hemisphere.

No, not almost.

"This cave doesn't look like a cave," Dan said.

"I'm beginning to get that feeling."

"We should report it."

James turned to Dan. "We report it, the authorities close it up, and then we can't use it."

"What do you mean, use it?"

"Don't you get it? We were asked to bring vacu-seals and our instruments. I mean, look at this place. Think of what the acoustics are gonna be like once we seal off the entrance and pump this place full of breathable air."

THE ACOUSTICS WERE, in a word, awesome. In two words, they were snarblin' awesome.

It was a far cry from playing in the tin box otherwise known as Every Room on Viritrilbia. The high-domed ceiling let the sounds bounce around, allowing overtones and undertones to mingle and reverberate in ways that were beyond pleasing to the ears. James strummed chord after chord and felt the hairs on his neck stand up. Goosebumps swelled on his arms.

"Do you think it matters that we don't really know how to play these instruments well?" Dan asked.

James shrugged. "You just keep hitting the drums; something good is bound to come out of them."

Dan nodded, smashing the two sticks against each other and letting the sound pump out of the portable speaker and fill the cavern.

They went through half their warm-up before James noticed that there was another voice in the cavern.

At first, he thought it was an acoustic phenomenon particular to the cavern, possibly even his own echo bouncing around. But no, there was another word mixed into the cacophony. Two, in fact.

"'Lust Turkey' . . ."

James and Dan stopped. They stared at each other. "Did you . . .?" James asked Dan.

Dan shook his head.

"But I didn't . . ." James said, only now beginning to realize that someone or something had led them here, away from their parents, in secret, to an as-yet-undiscovered cavern. And they had them take their helmets off.

"Oh, snarbles," Dan groaned.

"You've arrived at last."

It was hard to make much of the voice at first; there was too much distortion, like it was coming from a speaker or something electronic. But the only electronics in the cavern were the ones James and Dan had brought with them, and this was not coming from their gear.

No, the sound was emanating from the walls of the cavern itself.

James stopped, searching the cavern. "Who are you?"

"We have been waiting for you for some time."

"Oh, crap," Dan said. "Not good. Let's get outta here."

"No, don't go," the voice said. It was coming into focus now. The layers of distortion were peeling back so that the voice became singular. And female. "Please."

Again, James called out to the nothingness around him. "Who are you, and what do you want?"

There was no response at first.

Then, James saw it. Out of the corner of his eye, a rippling motion on the walls of the cavern. Reflected light, he imagined. But from what? Again, not his gear. Maybe from whatever had opened up this cavern in the first place.

Dan saw it, too. He pointed at the smooth walls as they began to shimmer, light playing off of them but from no apparent source.

"You must stay," the voice continued.

Dan was shaking his head. "I remember wanting to buy drugs from Hal Sethler, but I don't remember actually taking them."

The light—shades of greens and blues and amorphous—coalesced into something that James could now recognize. Something that seemed to have arms and legs and a face.

Yes, James realized as the image came into focus. A face.

A girl's face: wide-eyed and beautiful and projected on the wall before him.

She beckoned. "Stay," she urged, and James suddenly had no intention of going.

Again, the question: "Who are you?"

"Cavewomen!" Dan returned. "Or some kind of shared psychedelic experience. They'll eat us alive!" He thought about this. "Well, better than fried like eggs in the sun."

James shook his head, approaching the image. He held his hand out, noticing that the girl was doing the same. His fingers should have brushed hers, making contact, but instead, they passed right through hers. "It's just an image," he said, still not understanding.

"Play for us."

"What do you mean, us?" James said.

"What do you mean, play?" Dan said. It took him a second to remember that they'd brought their instruments.

More images began to swirl along the edges of the cavern. Colours that James had not previously encountered filled his field of vision, pulling and pushing against one another until they formed into limbs and bodies and . .. oh, they were all girls. All beautiful. All staring in his direction, all smiling and pointing, and now their voices came into focus, bouncing off the cavern walls, chanting together, "Play for us. Play for us. Play for us! 'LUST TURKEY!'"

"Did we just die, and now angels want us to play?" Dan said. "Because I am *in*."

"We're not angels," the first girl said. "Anything but."

Dan thought about this. "You look human," he mused.

"All Venusians are human," she said.

James and Dan stared at one another. "You're from Venus?"

"The enemy," Dan said under his breath. "No wonder they wiped out the graffiti."

"How did you get here?"

"We're still on Venus. Searching for more sounds. This cavern was designed to project and amplify."

"Did you make this place?" James wondered.

"Not us."

"But it was made." James had intended it to be a question, but it came out as a statement.

"To amplify," Dan added.

Once again, James and Dan stared at one another, a collective idea now swirling in their minds. They both smiled. "These girls are crazy hot," Dan said.

James nodded. "And they want us to play for them."

"Play for us," said the girl.

James strapped on his guitar, and Dan picked up the sticks, clicking them together. The room filled with the reverberations of the instruments and the increased excitement of their audience.

"You know, we're never going to actually meet these girls in real life," James noted.

"Well, that's rock and roll for you," Dan said. "Are you thinking what I'm thinking?"

James sighed. He never felt like he was destined to play this song, and yet, here he was.

And thus did Foul Grammar rock the universe.

COLD PAYLOAD
BY KATE ORMAN

Parker-Lee City
Mars, April 4, 2185

THE UPPERMOST LEVEL OF PARKER-LEE CITY HOUSED ITS LOWEST citizens, the miners and factory workers who processed Martian soil into rare earths for export. Closest to the surface, they were the most likely to be exposed to radiation and vacuum, industrial waste, industrial accidents. The middle level, where the technicians lived and worked, was a tight maze of metal buildings on either side of Central Street, cradled deep in the rock.

Up from the deepest level of all, the great palace of the Parker-Lee family, came Paynow the equerry, his royal uniform spangled with brilliant lights. His staff of state was a glowing white tube. He ran at a steady jog, crying out, "The Prince! His Royal Highness the Prince is on his way!"

Jung Michelle knew the prince was no prince. The Parker-Lees loved to play at being royalty, but like every great family, they lived under the law of Mons, such as it was. Still, here Jung was, in the carnival crowd with everyone else.

Behind Paynow, the prince's great float emerged from the underworld on a platform lift, a kaleidoscope of lights and mirrors and artificial jewels pulled by a team of robot dogs. The Central Street was wide enough for the float, plus a crowd two deep on either side. The float shot out streamers and confetti as it came, ostentatiously wasting paper. The prince, clothes so brilliant you could barely see him, reached into a great bag and tossed gifts into the cheering crowd.

Underneath, the float was just an ordinary surface vehicle. The prince was just David Parker-Lee, the heir. And a new book-tape player or a jar of Venusian jam wouldn't make any difference to Jung Michelle's life. The ones who would really benefit from the prince's largesse would be the troglodytes on the upper level when he distributed packages of food and medical supplies.

Jung's tablet buzzed. A customer was asking to meet her at her office. Jung's eyes widened at the ID. She responded that she'd be there in ten minutes. There was no hope of walking there along Central Street; she squeezed her way back home through the warren.

Her tiny apartment was on the second floor, its flat roof pushing against the roof of the cavern that the middle level was built into. The back wall displayed pleasant footage of a field of alpine flowers. The apartment doubled as her office; there was just enough room for a second chair for her clients.

This would be Jung's first client from the palace. Slightly panicked, she took a moment to comb sparkling confetti out of her fine, straight black hair.

Then the client was at her door: Royal Advisor Lee Idris, golden-haired, impressively tall even for a Martian. He wore white gloves, and his cuffs were edged with dish-grown fur. His uniform bore glittering carnival decorations. He had brought a garland of real flowers. Jung took it with both hands, bowing. She remembered not to offer anything she had, middle-level water, coffee, alcohol—not to a palace official.

"The matter is this," said Lee directly, handing over a small envelope. Jung opened it to find a black ceramic key chip edged with gold connectors. "Can you decrypt the data it contains?"

"Of course I can," said Jung, then remembered who she was talking to. "Advisor, the code—unless there's something unusual about it, I'll decrypt it for you in a day or so."

"There may be something unusual about it," warned Lee.

"Can you tell me something about what it contains?"

"No." He glanced around Jung's apartment. "Someone with your talents ought to have better quarters than these. A private bathroom, at least."

It was quite the promise. "I have to ask this, Royal Advisor," said Jung. "This code. Why bring it to me? The palace must have better cryptanalysts."

"The palace also has too many eyes and ears," said Lee, with a smile full of dazzling teeth. "And people are so much easier to break than ciphers. My contact ID is in the envelope. Good sol, then." He shook Jung's hand and was gone.

THIRTY-SIX HOURS LATER, Jung knew that she wasn't going to be able to decipher the contents of the chip, no matter how much time she was given.

In her time, she had dealt with countless encoded files of varying legality, including a stolen Anastas design file and a *billet-doux* sent to a minor Parker-Lee cousin. She knew every Martian code, including the rotating asymmetric ones the smugglers used when they skimmed off the palace's Venusian imports. But this? It was just an anonymous blob of bits. The Advisor had been right; there was some secret spice in this one that made it unique.

Letting the Advisor down could have more serious consequences than having to keep using the public baths, but there was nothing else she could do.

There was half a mug of cold and bitter coffee left. She drank it and called Michaela. "A Binary Large Object. I've got one I can't decrypt," she said.

Michaela laughed. "It must be something special."

"It's confidential," Jung said. "I'll have to hand it over in person."

"My schedule—there's a gap in it. Come right over."

Jung came right over.

Michaela, Jung Michelle's work-clone, was markedly better at cryptography than Michelle. She took a steady paycheck from the Parker-Lees while Jung relied on freelance security work.

"If you can break it," said Jung grudgingly, "the remuneration belongs to you." Michaela's apartment/office was already larger than Jung's, with a small rug and a painting, even a pet, but every Martian needed more space. Even clever Michaela didn't have a private bathroom.

Michaela plugged the key into her workstation and took a quick glance at the contents. "Where did you get this?"

Jung put a finger to her lips. "Hush-hush."

Michaela raised her eyebrows, amused, and mimicked the gesture. "Sleep. You need some," she said. "Go home."

JUNG SHUFFLED through the entertainment set up in the streets —gambling tables, sideshow games, acrobats, stalls with sweet rice cakes and moon cakes and beer. Everywhere, strings of dazzling lights. Everywhere, cleaner-bots sucking up confetti and trash.

She slept for fourteen hours. She woke out of a dream of a

pair of hungry baby birds that swallowed endless crawling black insects, stuffed into each egg-eyed nude face by a shining father.

She called Michaela. Her clone-sister didn't answer.

No sleep-message, no busy-message; just no answer. Uneasy, Jung told the tablet to locate her sister. All it produced was a dormitory address on the upper level.

Jung felt herself go cold from her toes to her scalp. "This has to be a mistake," she murmured, but she knew it wasn't.

The door to Michaela's apartment let her in. The place was cold and empty. There was no sign of the chip key.

Michaela hadn't checked in with the system for eight hours; she could be anywhere. Jung had her tablet bring up a map to the dormitory.

MIDDLE-LEVEL PEOPLE DIDN'T GO to the upper level. The only thing Jung could think of was to use one of the platform elevators that travelled between the strata of the city. The nearest one was on the north side, in a loading bay roughly cut out of the rock, full of fresh-made metal goods and bagged textiles. The place smelled of chemicals and rusty dust.

A couple of women in grey overalls were lounging in front of the doors to the platform. "The elevator. When does it go up next?" she asked them.

"When it's fully loaded," said one of the women. They both had that dried-out, prematurely aged look of upper-levellers.

"We can't let you on it," said the other guard.

"A special fee," said Jung quickly. "Do I need to pay one?"

The guards looked at one another. The first one said, "It's . . . twenty credits?"

Jung tapped her ID card against the guard's.

The platform was slightly larger than her apartment. She

was alone amongst cartons of electronics and pharmaceuticals. Almost all the manufacturing work was done on the upper level and exported downwards, but the risk of radiation meant fine work had to be done mid-level. There were also frozen boxes from the palace; the upper level would soon be feasting on its yearly ration of meat.

It wasn't long before the platform lifted on its quiet motors. Jung travelled through a tall, unlit tunnel, seeing by the light of her tablet. After a few minutes, the lift bounced to a stop at the top; Jung blinked in the light of a warehouse. She paid another special fee to the surprised workers at the top and slipped quickly into the network of rough-cut tunnels, following the tablet's map.

It was dark here, lit dully by lamps dangling from the low ceiling. Her ears kept popping, which meant that somewhere, there was an airlock that needed a technician. It smelled intensely of the fine dust that glittered in the air and clung to her shoes. There were no cameras.

Michaela's assigned dorm was near the surface, just below the water tanks that provided extra insurance against radiation. Jung climbed ladders, surprised by how many levels there were. She passed dorm rooms with their doors open, six or eight bunks littered with personal possessions; public baths that smelled of chlorine and sewage; a cafeteria where a handful of workers on break played cards, eyeing her business suit curiously. One of them stood and called "You lost?" but she didn't stop.

Her tablet buzzed. Michaela had checked in with the system—or someone had checked her in. She was in a clinic near the surface. Jung changed direction, breaking into a run, kicking up dust.

She arrived panting at the tiny room—big enough for one patient, no more. Michaela lay on a trolley, breathing through an oxygen mask, showing classic signs of vacuum exposure: bruised face, trails of blood from her nose and ears.

"Get out of here," said the technician before she looked up. "Oh. You're the next of kin."

"What happened?"

"There was a spacesuit accident," said the technician. "It happens when they're new."

"A proper hospital. She needs one," said Jung. "She's got insurance. She's a direct family employee."

"Not anymore," said the technician.

WORK-CLONES WERE an ancient idea made real. If you're going to make a genetically modified embryo with the kind of brain that will excel at mathematics, why use it to create just one worker? Much more efficient to split that embryo into a quartet of workers with standardized abilities.

Work-clones were Martian citizens with the same rights and responsibilities as anyone— and an advantage for the Parker-Lee family over the other families, who said they found the whole business distasteful.

Jung Michelle and her clone-sisters had been raised and educated together until their different capabilities became obvious. The problem was that brain development is contingent; even identical twins don't have quite the same neural structures. Jung was second-best, not quite good enough to work for the palace, but clever, able to run her own freelance business. Miki taught cryptography theory at the college. The fourth sister had died before birth.

The clones had not been close, not since they became adults and work filled their lives. But sometimes, Jung and Michaela met to discuss the latest in cryptography, and once Michaela had invited her to assist in cracking one of the Tanskas' codes. That was when Jung realized just how sharp her envy was of her smarter, more talented double: the woman she was supposed to have been.

MICHAELA DIED while Jung waited in the corridor outside the clinic. They cleared the corpse out quickly for an incoming cancer case. It went to reclamation, like anyone's.

Jung clutched the key in her hand, ignoring everyone as she travelled the elevator platform back down, stumbling through the streets, through bright music and the overwhelming smell of barbecued meat. The level's ventilation systems would carry that smell for a week.

Free food, free games—how could anyone complain?

Her tablet buzzed. There was a physical package waiting for her at the deliveries office. The key! But when she tore the tiny bundle open, there was just a scrap of paper that said *Roland*.

Jung called the reclaimers and let them know to clean up Michaela's apartment and re-home her pet. She asked for an hour to collect any items of value. There was only one thing she was interested in: the tarantula's tank. The bottom was filled with Martian dirt, and there were a couple of miniature plants and a ceramic log, for Roland to sit on, she supposed. She couldn't see the spider.

Had Michaela really expected Jung to put her fingers in and rummage around in that soil? Even the censors had probably left Roland alone.

Carefully, she lifted the tank. The chip key was taped to the bottom.

Once home, she fell into her chair and plugged the key into her workstation. At once, a text message from Michaela opened up using their private cipher. Jung decrypted it in her head.

It's not a Martian code. It's one of the Horus series. They haven't been used since before Earth went silent.

An Earth code, thought Jung.

That's why I couldn't break it. The Royal Censor's people: when I tried to look up the Horus codes on my tablet, fifteen minutes later, they were knocking on the door. They left, but I'm not sure what's going to happen next. Keep your head down.

The Censor had terminated Michaela's family employment and catapulted her into the upper levels, all while Jung had been asleep. And perhaps arranged a little accident, as well. All while leaving the key in Michaela's possession so that Jung could retrieve it.

Jung had been threatened in her time as a freelance coder; but offended royalty moved with a swiftness and with a finality that she had never imagined.

She drank a beer and tried to make sense of it.

It made no sense.

Technically, Michaela should not have been working on the cipher. But she was doing a job the palace wanted done, something they'd authorized. There might have been legal implications, but not this . . . summary execution.

Jung imagined being rushed through the same process, plucked from her apartment, dropped into a work gang upstairs, finding herself pulling on a spacesuit before she knew what was happening. No. She'd know what was happening. If she played this wrong, it could still happen.

To get the specs on the Horus algorithm without setting off the same alarms as her sister, Jung set up a series of relays that reached a database in the Joseph Greene HAVOC. It was quick; this year, Mars and Venus were on the same side of the sun.

Horus turned out to be a collection of codes from forty years ago, still in use sometime before the Earth lost its voice. Adequate for civilian-grade encryption, nothing top-of-the-line. They'd long since been retired because of a vulnerability in the elliptic-curve family they used: a simple Shor attack could break the keys without falling below the noise threshold.

Jung began to weep. The codes were not particularly powerful. Whatever was encoded on the key, its owners hadn't thought it was worth someone's life.

Cold, thought Jung Michelle and froze her tears. *To survive this I need to be cool as the surface, cold as the poles.*

SHE WENT OUT, found an electronics store, and bought a second workstation. She left the new machine on the desk in her quarters and took her own workstation to a locker in the public baths. It would keep working on decrypting the files on the key. The Horus code itself could be cracked in twenty minutes with modern machines. The real work would be breaking the key used inside. When it succeeded, it would buzz her.

When she got back to her apartment, there was a giant standing in the doorway.

He was simply the biggest human being Jung had ever encountered. His reddish hair brushed the ceiling. He had a pointy nose and pale skin and wore dark pants, a white shirt, and a red tie. "Jung Michelle? My name is West," he said. He put a huge hand on her shoulder. "Inside. Shall we go?"

Smiling at his grammar, Jung led the way into her apartment. The chair was too small for him; he was obliged to sit on the bed, shoulders hunched. "I'm out of coffee," Jung admitted, "but there's some beer if you'd care for it."

"No, thank you," he said. "I'm here because I think you

might be able to help me recover something that was stolen from me."

"I'm a cryptanalyst, not the Lost Property Office," she said. "What makes you think I can help you?"

"Maybe I should help myself," said West. "You just sit there, nicely and quietly."

Cool, girl. Space-cold. She sat with her hands in her lap while the giant pulled her apartment apart. He even smashed the back wall screen in case there was something hidden behind it. It didn't take him long to finish.

She said, "Whatever you're looking for, I obviously don't have it."

"Who does, then?" He crouched down, peering at her.

Jung shrugged. "I can try to find out."

He put his hands on his knees. They really were enormous. "How would you like a hundred thousand credits?"

Jung whistled. "Leave your ID," she said. "I'll let you know."

West considered. He sent his ID to her tablet. Then he picked up her new workstation and walked out with it. She wondered if the keyboard would be too small for his fingers.

She wished she could simply hand the key back to Lee Idris and say she'd failed, but it was far too late for that now.

JUNG CALLED Miki and told her the news about Michaela. "I know you two haven't seen each other for a couple of years," said Jung.

"We had a fight," said Miki. Tears rolled down her face, but she kept her composure. "A stupid fight about palace politics. After that, we just sort of fell out of touch." She blew her nose. "The upper level. What on Mars was she doing there?"

"I have no idea," Jung lied. "She was reassigned there, but I don't know why. Yet."

"I can help you," said Miki. "A lot of people in the palace worked with Michaela, knew her. I can ask around about her reassignment."

"Don't."

Miki stared.

"Palace politics," Jung added quietly. "Leave it with me, Miki. I've suddenly got a lot of attention."

Miki said, "Contact me if you find anything out," and rang off.

As soon as Jung put down the tablet, it buzzed. She didn't recognize the ID. "Hello?"

"Is this Jung Michelle?"

"Yes, it is."

"I'm calling on behalf of my employer, Zhang Nikodem," said the man on the other end. She'd heard of Zhang; he was the young heir to a small monazite mine south of the city. "He'd like to speak to you—right away, if it's convenient."

"It's convenient," she said.

"Then would you come to the Armed Aphrodite Hotel, Room 12?"

"I'll be there in fifteen minutes."

Jung had never been to the Armed Aphrodite before, though she'd seen video of the interior. In the foyer stood a silver-plated statue of the Greek goddess, holding a spear. The floor was polished red stone; everything else was black or white or mirrored. There were rugs everywhere. As far as Jung could tell, the door to Zhang's room was actual woodwork.

A servant let her in. Zhang sat beside a hologram of a fire

that emitted real heat. He was Martian, tall and thin as a cable. He looked like he was only just out of his teens but had the confidence and poise that came with money—or he was good at faking it. She seemed to remember something about that mine not delivering what it had promised.

Zhang shook Jung's hand and guided her to a pair of plush white chairs. When he asked if she wanted anything to drink, she shook her head.

"You must want to get the key off your hands," the boy began. "Your clone-sister . . ." He trailed off delicately. "But you had it first. The palace won't hesitate to do the same to you if they think they must in order to keep their secret. You'll need seed money to start a new life somewhere else. I'm keen to invest in you."

"This key that everyone keeps talking about," said Jung. "What is it?"

Zhang said, "Mr. West didn't tell you?"

He knew West? Were they allies? Rivals? "He offered me a hundred thousand credits for it."

Zhang let out a long whistle. "Mr. West was too stingy!" he said. "I'd be happy to pay you two hundred thousand credits."

Never mind a private bathroom; wealth like that could buy you a position in the palace. What could possibly be worth that kind of money? "I can't help you locate it unless I know what I'm dealing with."

"The story—I'll tell you it." Zhang steepled his hands. "Two decades before the fall of Earth, there was launched an artificially intelligent spacecraft on a mission to Ariel, one of the moons of Uranus. Ariel contains a liquid ocean beneath its surface, which it was thought might contain life.

"Ariel Lander successfully reached the moon and drilled down into its ocean but found nothing living. However, its AI pilot thought to look for life where no one had expected it: on the moon's icy surface."

The boy sat forward. "It seems the hot extremophiles of Mercury have their counterpart in the cold extremophiles of Ariel. I'm sure you can see the ramifications, Ms. Jung. Extremophiles to make fuel and even food in the cold areas of Mercury. Food and fuel in the frozen Martian night.

"The lander collected a good sample of the life forms and set out for Earth. That was about forty years ago. The craft has crossed the orbit of Mars, and its AI has begun to broadcast requests for landing instructions."

Jung saw it. "The key identifies the bearer as the legitimate mission control."

"With that key, it would be possible to program the craft to go into orbit around Mars. A laboratory could be constructed in space to examine and manipulate the alien organisms." Zhang had credit signs in his eyes. He had it all planned out. "It's the most extraordinary legacy from our sadly missed sister world. And why shouldn't you have a part of the profits it will generate?"

Cold. "Be serious," said Jung. "Two hundred thousand credits? Make it five hundred thousand, and I'll let you know when I get my hands on the thing."

Zhang smiled lazily. "Time. I'll need it."

"So will I," said Jung.

WEST SHADOWED HER CLUMSILY, always visible out of the corner of her eye. Clearly, she was meant to understand there was no point in her trying to get away from them. She went back to her apartment, bounced a data request off a Venusian satellite to the repository on Deimos, showered, and ate.

The Ariel Lander was real, said the repository. Its mission to look for alien life was real. She had only half-believed Zhang's story, but at least this part of it was true.

Lee Idris didn't seem as impressive on his second visit, despite the fur cuffs and the teeth. This time, he didn't bring her flowers. "How is it coming along?" he asked.

"It's coming along," she said. "A question—may I ask you it, Advisor?"

He graciously assented.

"Why do the Parker-Lees play at being royalty?"

"What would you do," he said, "if you had enough money to do anything you wanted to?" He smiled. "Half a million credits, for example. Or more?"

He'd come to buy the answer out from under Zhang's nose. Pity it wasn't quite cooked.

She said, "My question—you didn't answer it. The other families live in luxury, but they don't play dress-up. Is it a challenge to Mons's authority? Or have they all quietly gone mad?"

She knew Lee had no way to answer either of those questions or even acknowledge them. There's no formal etiquette for talking about treason. He didn't even stop smiling, though she could see the alarm in his eyes. He raised an appalled eyebrow.

"I think it's so there's a ready supply of rewards for the mid-level," she went on, rather enjoying herself. "Prestige. You yourself have it—Zhang Nikodem can only crave it. What were you before you became an Advisor? A surveyor? A clerk? What favour did you do the palace that earned that uniform?"

"Girl," he said, "I rather think you're losing your marbles."

She grinned back at him. "You could be right."

"You'd best take more care." He came out and said it. "Think of your sister."

Cool. Cold. "What would your associates think if they knew you'd come here to see me by yourself?"

"Oh, I only wanted to see if there was anything you needed," he said with the last of his sangfroid and left.

Her tablet buzzed. The hidden workstation had completed its work more quickly than she'd expected.

So, now she had what that motley crew wanted. A Martian entrepreneur, a royal official, a brute. She didn't believe for a moment that West was somehow Zhang's competitor with a hundred thousand credits up his sleeve. Zhang had bankrolled him to make the starting bid—assuming any of that money really existed. They had all obviously made a deal with each other. She'd bet that any one of them would betray the others, given the slightest opportunity.

She sent an encrypted message to Miki. Then she went to fetch her workstation.

SHE WAS SITTING IN A CAFÉ, going over the decryption, when West sat down in the chair opposite her. He didn't have to do anything else, didn't have to touch her. She was in his grip as surely as if he'd grabbed her by the shoulders.

"At least let me finish my coffee first," she said.

He shrugged with one shoulder.

"You're a Venusian, aren't you?" She didn't bother to keep her voice down; people were staring anyway. Good; what could he do to her, here in public? "Did you Sam Dekker on your way over here?"

The corners of West's mouth twitched. He said nothing.

The only trouble West had had getting into the chair was that it was two sizes too small. He walked comfortably, even if all the ceilings were too low for him. "You've been here for a while," Jung guessed.

West slowly moved his massive head from side to side. "Lotta practice."

"How did you get mixed up in this, Mr. West?"

He shrugged one-shouldered. "Mr. Zhang needed muscle."

Under his breath, he grumbled, "Because they're littler than me. They think I'm just muscle."

"Why—what was your last job?"

He fixed her with his squint. "I'm a percussionist."

Jung wasn't sure how to take that. She glanced around the café, making sure they weren't alone.

She couldn't help feeling a little sorry for West. Except for his criminal pals, he was alone, alone and painfully conspicuous. She wondered who'd convinced him that Mars was his best bet, who'd taken his money to stuff him into a bottle and throw him across space.

She didn't want to know what he'd done on Venus. But Zhang knew.

Drumroll, please, she thought. "They're protecting you."

West opened his eyes. She had him, she thought. She had him by the shoulders.

He pushed himself up out of his chair. This time, Jung saw the moment of hesitation, the need to do consciously what ought to be unconscious.

He was so obvious. He wouldn't last half a Martian year.

He stuck his huge face right next to hers and muttered, "I didn't kill your sister."

"I know you didn't," she whispered back.

"Now, why don't you come this way?"

"I've finished my coffee anyway."

WEST LED OR, rather, followed Jung to the hotel and up the black-carpeted stairs to Zhang Nikodem's room. Lee Idris was there, holding a firearm in one hand and a glass of Venusian schnapps in the other. He smiled that dazzling smile, full of the arrogant power of the palace, and Jung hated him.

"Have you had any success?" said Zhang. "I'm prepared to offer a down payment."

"I don't want your money," said Jung. "I want justice. Do you think you can give me that?" She looked at the threesome. "Which of you had my sister thrown out of her family job and reassigned to the upper level? Which one of you put her into an airlock with a malfunctioning spacesuit?"

The three of them looked at one another.

"The answer is none of you. The palace didn't know the key had been stolen. They were shocked when Michaela searched for the Horus codes. They treated her like any palace spy. If I'd been the one who brought up the Horus files, it would have been me in that airlock.

"Therefore, if you want the code," Jung went on, "you'll hand Advisor Lee over to the royal authorities."

They were staring at her with no pretense now, with faces like famished animals. They glanced at Lee with the same look.

Zhang said, "We couldn't do that to our friend!"

West said, "He'd tell them everything."

"Lee brought me the key," said Jung. "The rest of you can walk away from this, but stealing royal property is treason."

Zhang said lightly, "Ms. Jung, surely you see that, at this moment, you're not in a position to dictate terms."

"I've got what you want," said Jung. She proffered the workstation, the key still inserted in its side.

"And we've got you," said West.

"Anyway, we can all walk away," said Lee, "with what that key's worth. Or fly away. I'm going to relocate to a HAVOC and grow raspberries."

"The Ariel Lander isn't anyone's property," Zhang pointed out evenly. "We're engaged in salvage, not theft."

"The key belongs to the King."

"Parker-Lee is no king," snorted Lee. "However much he likes to cosplay one."

"Someone pays for my sister," reiterated Jung.

"If we have to hand someone over, hand over West," said Lee. "With his record, he'll make a beautiful foreign spy."

West, surprisingly, ignored him. "Why Lee?" He was looking at Jung with those open eyes again.

"Because they'll know it was someone in the palace," Jung explained patiently. "They don't have to know who else was involved."

"I'm afraid that is true," said Zhang. "Lee has left more than one set of guilty fingerprints at the palace."

He turned to West. West glanced at Jung, then turned to look at Lee meaningfully.

"Now see here," said Lee, brandishing his gun.

West slapped it out of Lee's hands. Zhang plucked the gun up from the carpet gingerly and pointed it at Lee, who looked as though he was going to cry.

Zhang told Jung, "My tablet has access to an aerial on Mons. The incoming transmissions from Ariel Lander—take a look, you can see them."

She spun the tablet around and looked. What Zhang said checked out. "All right. I'll copy over the identification code."

Lee made a break for the door. West smacked him across the back of the head so hard he went face-first into the carpet and stayed there.

"Very well," said Zhang. "The first command we send is a simple 'Do you hear me?'" He tapped at his tablet. "Of course, there'll be a delay in transmission of several minutes. Once we've established contact, we'll be able to reprogram Ariel Lander to change its course. Then we must be patient—it will take some years to arrive. By then, our space laboratory will be ready and waiting."

Several minutes stretched out into too many minutes. Zhang tried resending the signal. Another quarter of an hour passed. Zhang slammed the tablet down. "It's not working!" he growled.

Stooping over the desk, West said, "Are you sure she got it right?"

"That was the first thing I checked," said Zhang.

"It's a fake," laughed Lee groggily from the carpet. "All this for a fake code."

"I don't think it's a fake code," said Zhang. "I think it's the identification code for some other spacecraft. Good enough to fool someone who knows what they're doing."

"Good enough to fool you," said Lee.

"Good enough," said a new voice, "to find out the pilferer in the Royal Observatory."

Jung looked up, then jumped to her feet. It was the prince's equerry, Paynow, in his normal uniform now. He stood inside the doorway while a remarkable number of constables flooded into the room. Blue and red lights flashed on their helmets, filling the room with bewildering light and coloured shadows. One quickly picked up the gun from Zhang's desk while half a dozen surrounded West, forcing him to his knees. He was still as tall as any of them.

"They followed you?" gulped Zhang.

"I told them where they could find me," said Jung.

"But it gets worse!" said the equerry, clapping his gloved hands. "Not only was the code fake, the extremophiles were fake as well. Ariel Lander is real enough, but its AI realized early on that Earth had fallen silent, and its only hope of survival was to convince someone, somewhere, that it had a precious cargo on board."

Lee said, "You decoded the key yourselves."

Paynow inclined his head. "It wasn't hard to get the truth out of it. Ariel the moon is, tragically, as sterile as space."

"The lander. What happens to it?" asked Zhang.

"I suppose it will circle Earth until, eventually, its orbit degrades," said the equerry.

"Never mind the lander," said West, "what happens to us?"

"Be happy, Mr. West—you're going home. Mr. Zhang and Advisor Lee will be . . . having difficult conversations in the Department of Justice."

Jung's coldness melted. "And what about me?" she blurted.

"You thought you were acting on legitimate palace business," said Paynow dismissively. "You'll be compensated."

"Compensated!" cried Jung. "What about Michaela? She died because of this royal trap! She never had any idea of what was happening!"

"Oh, well, my dear," said Paynow, flashing perfect teeth. "That's the sort of thing that happens during carnival!"

BIG FISH, LITTLE FISH

BY JAMES BOW

Moosonee, James Bay Shore, November 30, 2177

WHEN MCMURTRY RETURNED TO MOOSONEE, HE FOUND IT empty.

He jumped off the train onto the platform. Soldiers followed, rifles drawn, sweeping the Meeting Hall and the Main Street before a party headed toward the community centre, but he could tell what their report would be. All the stores were closed. The coffee shop had a sign on its window saying, "Thank you for your patronage." Above the sound of soldiers' shouts and footfalls, he heard only the gulls above the estuary and the rustle of distant dry leaves.

He tightened the collar of his cloak. The first flakes of snow fell around him.

A sergeant ran up from the train station. He saluted. "Mr. McMurtry? Telegram, Senior."

McMurtry took the slip of paper, unfolded it, read it, and folded it again. He sighed.

"Senior?" said the soldier.

"It's okay," McMurtry replied. He headed for the train. "I have to go and make a report."

McMurtry sat in silence as his train headed south. He stared out at verdant forests, rutted roads, and ruined towns rebuilding into villages. The further he went, the better repaired the buildings were and the more activity around the stations.

What did I do wrong? he thought. *Why did they run away from me?*

He thought back to the explosion, the chasm opening up in the trestle, the young woman standing at the other end, rifle in hand, a distant figure of defiance.

And he saw that woman again at Washago Station, just before Lake Simcoe.

He caught it out of the corner of his eye, the figure, her arms by her sides, rifle in hand, the dark, whole-body stare. He blinked and peered out his window at the people on the platform. But he couldn't see the woman now. The train lurched and started forward. McMurtry settled back in his seat and stared ahead.

"What did you say to them?"

McMurtry stood before Minister Dinsdale, hands clasped in front of him. "Nothing that I shouldn't have, Minister."

Dinsdale peered at McMurtry over his glasses. "You must have said something that alarmed them. That alerted them."

The crowd-control guns were probably what alerted them. I said we shouldn't bring them, but you overruled me. He swallowed these words. "I said I was with the government and that we were here to help."

Dinsdale grunted. "Well, we have the port lands, at least. That's not nothing. We'll start shipping supplies and personnel ahead of the winter. We'll have a functioning and defendable port by the spring. But if we spooked the locals, we don't know what they're saying to other locals. We don't know what reception we'll get in Attawapiskat or up the Ungava. The Greenlanders could take advantage of this dissension."

Not Greenlanders, Kalaallit Nunat, McMurtry thought, but he kept his head down and said nothing.

Dinsdale tapped at his tablet a moment, then looked up. "What are you still doing here?"

"Um . . ." McMurtry swallowed. "I just wanted to know, Minister . . . I was grateful to be sent into the field. I just . . . When will my next assignment be?"

Dinsdale frowned. "We'll tell you. In the meantime, go to your desk. I'm sure there's paperwork to do."

McMurtry stepped back, fidgeting. "Yes, Minister." He turned away.

"McMurtry?"

He turned, hope rising.

"See your office manager. We've reassigned the desks."

McMurtry nodded and left.

"THIS WAY, SENIOR." A young woman holding a clipboard led McMurtry, holding a box of personal effects, between rows of crates, battered chairs, and sheets on ropes, separating desks. At least the light was natural, from windows propped open with sticks, though the air remained musty. McMurtry shuddered. *This place will be an oven come summer.*

The Whitney Block had been built almost two hundred fifty

years before beside Queen's Park, the seat of the old Ontario government that now held Toronto's District Council. Its upper floors had spent most of their life abandoned, unable to be modernized, before being pressed into service as one of the few structurally sound office buildings left in the city. McMurtry stepped around electricians taping wires to the walls and ceiling while the woman led him past others setting up and personalizing their desks.

"We've just opened this floor," the woman continued. "Cleaned out a lot of pigeon droppings, I'm told. Sent them to the farms in Niagara."

"Ah." He dodged a worker hurrying from his desk, report tablets under his arm. He looked at the woman, at her close-cropped dark hair, red lips, and bright blue eyes. "Um . . . Listen, what's your name?"

"Nelissa, Senior." She gave him a bright smile. "Nelissa Stronach, general administrative assistant. I just came aboard."

"Ah." McMurtry smiled back. "Well . . . welcome aboard, Nelissa. I'm Drew McMurtry." He wasn't sure of his current title. "You can call me Drew."

She nodded. "Certainly, Senior." They'd reached the last desk in the row. She gestured at it. "This, I believe, is yours." She stood, hands clasped in front of her, waiting.

McMurtry stared at his box of possessions, then at her. He set the box down. "Um . . . thank you."

She nodded and left.

McMurtry sat at his desk. A young man strode up, dumped a pile of folders in his inbox, and stalked off.

McMurtry looked around a moment, at the room that took up most of the floor, at his office colleagues. He fished inside his box of possessions and pulled out his new nameplate. Apparently, he was a Deputy Adviser, Accounts Administration, whatever that meant.

He thought back to Moosonee. *Where had the residents all*

gone? That girl . . . Baker told me that she'd had an ocular implant that needed replacing. What happened to her? Did she get help? Did she lose the eye?

What could I have done differently?

I could have done something.

Couldn't I?

His gaze fell on the wall beside him. A framed picture was mounted on it, showing a line of fish swimming in the ocean. Well, the smallest, on the left, was swimming. The one behind it had its mouth open to eat it. The one behind the second also had its jaws wide, as did the last one, the biggest of all.

Beneath the picture, in white serif capital letters against a black border, was the word "CONTINUITY." He wondered if it was supposed to be inspirational.

A silly thing. McMurtry stood up. *I should be able to find a decent replacement.* He grabbed the picture, only to have his fingers slip off. He gripped the frame again, but it refused to move. He couldn't even get his finger behind it. He stepped back, staring at the picture.

The picture let itself be stared at.

Around him, the office buzzed with hushed conversations and the scrabble of pencils.

McMurtry returned to his desk, grabbed the first folder from his tray—*Form I-121989, Authorizing the intake of produce from newly acquired lands in the Grey-Bruce District*—picked up a pencil, put his head down, and began to work.

Form W-583145: Authorization to transfer 10,000 pounds of non-perishable food into the ration pool for distribution among the population.

Form T-68223: Authorization to commit forty tractors and related support equipment to the farms of Haliburton and to coordinate their use by local farmers.

Report C-618: On normalizing relations with the Dominion of Montreal; benefits and points of contention.

December 15, 2178

IT MAY NOT HAVE BEEN a corner office—though McMurtry had never aspired to one—but at least he could see the See-En Tower through the nearest window. The broken spire rose over the city as it had done for two centuries. Some downtown towers remained abandoned, south windows blown in, north windows blown out, their upper floors useless until elevators could be rebuilt, and there was plenty of rebuilding still to be done. This hadn't stopped people from taking up residence in the lower floors. McMurtry wasn't sure if they should do that, but it wasn't his problem, nor his department.

On the sidewalks of Queen's Park Circle, men and women strode to work, cloaks flapping behind them. McMurtry smiled to see them, then frowned as he saw one woman not walking. She stood, people flowing around her, and as McMurtry watched, she looked up.

He couldn't see her face, but he felt their gaze connect. In her silhouette, he thought of the woman standing on the other side of the broken bridge a year ago.

"Catch!" Nelissa shouted.

He looked up as a roll of red-and-green streamer sailed at his head. "Wha—hey!" He batted it out of the air, then caught it. "What was that for?"

"It's time to redecorate your desk, Senior," Nelissa called.

"Don't be a fuddy-duddy! You don't want us decorating your desk for you."

"You really don't," said Brian from somewhere beneath a mass of tinsel. Beside him, Agatha pulled tape from its dispenser like a sword from its sheath.

McMurtry sighed. "Fine! Toss me the blue streamer." He caught the bundle Nelissa tossed him. He looked out his window again, but whoever had been standing below, if they had been there, had gone.

The door to the Minister's office opened. Dinsdale poked his head out. "McMurtry? With me, please."

Everybody in the office gave McMurtry a look of sympathy and support, combined with a shrapnel-avoiding half-step back.

"I'm sure it's fine," he muttered. He handed the streamers back to Nelissa. "Keep decorating." He walked to Dinsdale's office.

He closed the door behind him. Dinsdale stood beside his desk, flipping through McMurtry's report. "Good work on the Montrealer report. A lot of valuable insights here. It will be put to good use in the District Governor's office."

McMurtry quietly let out the breath he was holding. "Thank you, Minister."

Dinsdale set down the report and looked directly at McMurtry. "I thought you'd appreciate knowing this: we've repaired the Coast Road up James Bay. Our people have occupied Attawapiskat."

McMurtry blinked. "Minister?" he said at last.

"Port Moosonee is secure," Dinsdale replied. "Our shipments start in earnest this spring, and I expect we'll have our first contact with ports in Siberia this summer. Happy Hollymass."

"Oh." McMurtry caught a smell of salt air and heard the sound of gulls and the rustle of barren trees.

"I thought you'd be pleased that our James Bay initiative was a success." Dinsdale gave McMurtry a stern look. "In spite of whatever caused our initial misunderstanding last year."

"Yes, Minister."

Dinsdale picked up a tablet and began sorting through the notes. McMurtry turned to go.

He hesitated at Dinsdale's door. "Minister . . .? Were there people in Attawapiskat when we got there?"

Dinsdale looked up. "Hmm?" He glanced at his tablet. "Apparently. This time, they chose not to run."

McMurtry stayed with his hand on the doorknob. "Was there . . . resistance?"

Dinsdale shrugged and set the tablet aside. "Nothing we couldn't handle."

McMurtry opened his mouth to say something but stopped.

"Don't worry about them," said Dinsdale. "They're under our protection, now. They should be grateful." He gave McMurtry a cool smile. "Go back to the party. I hear the Secret Santa's about to start."

Outside, Nasser, sitting at the desk closest to Dinsdale's door, looked up. "Bad news?"

McMurtry jerked back to the present. "What? Oh! Uh . . . no. Not bad news. Good news . . . I guess."

He walked through the Holly-mass preparations to his desk. He thought about looking out the window but decided not to in case the silhouette was there. As he reached his chair, he found himself staring at the motivational picture. "Wait." It was as he'd seen it, every working day of his life this past year, but with a difference. The line of fish with jaws open to eat each other remained, but the smallest fish wasn't there anymore. "Where did the little fish go?" he muttered.

"What little fish?"

He jumped as Nelissa stepped beside him. Before he could think of anything different to say, he blurted, "In the picture?"

"What picture?"

McMurtry's mouth hung open.

But Nelissa gave him a smile and shoved a foil-wrapped box in his hands. "Happy Holly-mass."

He blinked at her. "Isn't it supposed to be a *Secret* Santa?"

She patted his arm and gave him a chaste kiss on his cheek. "I think we have enough secrets, don't you?" She turned away. "Come on. We don't want to miss out on the cocoa."

He gave the picture one more look before he followed her.

Form M-81834: An authorization to send crowd-control equipment and military personnel vehicles to the James Bay shores.

Form M-82337: An authorization to send additional ammunition, fuel, and military rations to the James Bay shores.

Report C-723: The benefits and drawbacks of opening trade with the California-Cascade Federation.

McMURTRY HESITATED after he filed the report in his outbox. He pulled some of the forms from before and looked them over. Behind him, the city disappeared in snow.

We were supposed to help. Why do I feel like we're not helping?

And, from some deeper part of his brain: *What did the little fish do to anybody?*

What can I do about this? I should do something about this. But what can I do?

What did Sergeant Baker tell me?

He opened his file drawer, sorted through requisition forms, and pulled one free. He grabbed a pencil from its holder.

Form W-338219: Authorization for the transfer of medical supplies, including implants, to the James Bay shores.

July 21, 2183

"Oh!" Nelissa covered her face. "This is so embarrassing!"

McMurtry let out a short laugh. "And yet, you agreed to it."

"My patriotic duty," Nelissa shot back. She covered her face in her hands again. "Still embarrassing!"

"It'll be fine," said Brian. There were murmurs of agreement from the rest of the office staff.

Nasser cleared their throat. "It will be fine . . . Senior."

Brian flushed. "Oh, right. Sorry. I'll remember next time." He paused, then added, "Senior."

Nelissa glanced at McMurtry. *That's also embarrassing,* she mouthed.

He smiled and shrugged.

They stood at the windows, looking down from the Whitney Block at the restored Hepburn Block, an eight-storey-tall glass-and-concrete box. *Just forty years younger than this building and so much more work to be done,* McMurtry thought. *They built things quickly in the 1960s and built things to last in the 1920s.*

Across part of the face of the Hepburn Block, tarps came off, sliding to the ground. Behind them, against a blue background with a red maple leaf in the top corner, was a stylized image of Nelissa, cloak billowing, facing the future with determination. Level with her feet in block letters half a storey tall were the words "FORWARD TOGETHER."

Beside him, Nelissa's face was as red as the maple leaf, but as her colleagues clapped and cheered, she smiled.

"The first of a dozen across the government buildings of this city," said Brian. "Senior, you promise you'll remember us when you're off being rich and famous?"

She huffed. "I'm still working here, you know." She gestured out the window. "That's a side job for public morale." She glared and pointed at one of her guffawing colleagues. "Shut up, you!" Then she laughed and went on. "I'm still just a Deputy Adviser, like Drew here. That's what I'll stay for now."

Somewhere in the crowd, McMurtry thought he heard someone mutter, "Not for as long as Drew's been Deputy Adviser, surely."

"Shush," said someone else.

Drew ignored them.

At the next desk, Nathan picked up his tablet. He frowned. "Hey, do you folks think we should be worried about this Federation business?"

McMurtry looked over. "Which one?"

Nathan looked confused. "You mean, 'which business'?"

"No, I mean which Federation," McMurtry replied. "There are five."

"Five?"

"Yeah." Nelissa counted them off on her fingers. "The Federation of Oceana and Micronesia, the Federation of African Nations, the European Federation—which is really getting up everybody's nose in the Arctic—, *la Federation des las Americas*, and the California-Cascade Federation."

"So," Brian drawled, "FOAM, FAM, EFF, FAS and, er . . . KIFF?"

"It's not really our business," said McMurtry. "We're the Ministry of *Northern* Affairs, remember? Unless it's the Europeans messing around in the Arctic, the rest are just someone else's department."

"You sure?" Nathan held up his tablet. "It looks like the FAS and the Californians are about to get into it. They've had a naval encounter off the tip of the Baja."

"Which is on the other side of this continent," said McMurtry. "Diagonally."

Nelissa sighed. "Still, you'd think we'd have learned to work together better with everything that's happened since the Manhattan Sea Wall."

In the Minister's office, they heard Dinsdale say, "Thank you, District Governor. I'll check."

Everyone headed for their desks to look busy. Dinsdale emerged, looking preoccupied, and headed for Nasser's desk, whispering to them. Nasser nodded and pulled some folders from their inbox. McMurtry found himself standing by the window with Nelissa. He saw her glance at her eight-storey-tall likeness and smile.

"Congratulations," he said and held out a hand. "On this and the promotion."

She clasped his hand and smiled at him warmly. "Thanks, Drew."

The moment stretched, the two staring at each other. Nelissa raised an eyebrow. McMurtry opened his mouth to form a question about coffee and a place to drink it. If only he could figure out the words.

Behind them, Dinsdale straightened up. "Thank you, Nasser."

McMurtry stepped back. Nelissa's smile turned sad. "We should get back to work," she said.

"Work." He coughed. "Yeah. Uh—" But she was already heading for her desk.

Dinsdale beamed at her as he approached. "There's our face of hope!" Nelissa blushed anew.

McMurtry tucked his head, grabbed a folder from his inbox, and got back to work.

Report C-768: The challenges of trading with the European Federation; best approaches for access.

Report C-850: Reforming the United Nations of Earth, Assessment of Possible Initiatives.

Report C-903: The potential threat of the Kalaallit Nation on Toronto and Montreal interests. Is a reassessment in order?

September 14, 2188

NELISSA TAPPED her fingers on McMurtry's desk. He leaned back, frowning at the metal band on her ring finger. *Well*, he thought. *You had your chance.*

"What are we looking at?" Nelissa asked.

He snapped back to attention. Beside Nelissa, Minister Dinsdale zoomed the tablet in on a photograph. He sucked his teeth. "I think McMurtry's assessment is accurate. This is Lake Champlain, and these appear to be a massing of amphibious forces. We know Montreal doesn't have this amount of equipment. Besides, these are facing north."

"So, the Free State of Boston," said McMurtry. "And the numbers suggest they're planning an attack."

Dinsdale darkened the tablet. "A fair assessment, McMurtry."

"Why did this end up in my inbox?" Nelissa asked. "And where could Boston have got so much equipment or soldiers?"

"I can only speculate on the first question," Dinsdale replied. "This wouldn't be the first piece of misaddressed mail this or any government has seen. As for the soldiers and equipment . . ." He lowered his voice. "We've been monitoring military buildup along the Atlantic coast, likely supported by the Federation."

"Which one," Nelissa began automatically. "There are five—"

"Four, actually," Dinsdale cut in.

"Four?" McMurtry echoed.

"*La Federation des las Americas* and the California-Cascade Federation announced a merger yesterday," Dinsdale replied. "By mutual agreement, or so they claim. Troops moved across the Colorado River a couple of hours later."

McMurtry and Nelissa straightened up.

"It may be three shortly," Dinsdale continued. "Reports suggest the Europeans and the Africans may be close to an agreement, and this one might actually *be* an agreement." He slipped the tablet into a folder. "Good work, you two. I'll get this to the people responsible." He turned away.

"Minister!" McMurtry jumped to his feet, then froze as Dinsdale turned back, eyebrows raised. McMurtry stammered but continued, "What are we going to do about this? Aren't we going to warn the Montrealers?"

Dinsdale pursed his lips. "They probably already know. If not, well, worse for them."

Nelissa gasped. "Shouldn't we do *something?*"

"Not our department," Dinsdale replied. "Ministry of *Northern* Affairs, remember? Others in this government are already paying attention, and they may be saying that it does us no good to tie ourselves up in a war the Dominion of Montreal will likely lose." A smile flickered on his lips. "And it's not without its silver lining. This may be a good opportunity to bolster our Arctic defences without interference from the Ungava Peninsula." He raised the folder in a salute. "Thank you again, you two. Keep up the good work."

He walked away, leaving Nelissa and McMurtry staring.

They looked at each other, Nelissa's expression a plea. In the end, McMurtry could only shrug.

Nelissa turned away with a huff of disappointment.

McMurtry watched her go, shame rising. He pushed himself out of his seat. But before he could follow, something caught him out of the corner of his eye, and he found himself staring at the CONTINUITY inspirational picture on the wall.

The line of fish eating fish wasn't a line anymore. Instead, the fish formed a circle, chasing each other, jaws wide.

He ran a finger over the top of the frame. It came away grey with dust.

He looked closer at the picture. He could see the texture of the paper behind the glass.

And reflected in the glass...

For a moment, he stared into the reflection of the woman at the bridge. She was right beside his desk, glaring. But when he turned around, the space was empty. The office ticked along like Tuesday.

He glanced once more at the picture, wiped the dust from his finger, then grabbed his cloak and headed for the stairs. He needed to walk.

Report C-1577, The obligations and benefits of military cooperation with the Free State of Boston.

Report C-1855, Military assessment of the activities of Appalachian piracy on Lake Eerie.

Report C-1900, Military assessment of the cessation of acts of Appalachian piracy on Lake Eerie.

Report C-2072, An assessment of the state of the Appalachian government, given the attacks on its southern borders.

March 7, 2190

McMURTRY HUMMED as he hopped over the slush at the curb. The sun warmed his face, though the wind chilled his back. He nodded good morning to familiar strangers in the street. He nodded to the eight-storey image of Nelissa on the Hepburn Block. It had been a good weekend: just himself at home curled up with a good book.

He grabbed the morning order of coffee from the espresso stand in the lobby and hurried up the steps. He stepped into the office and staggered back from the volley of raised voices.

"Listen to yourselves," Nelissa shouted. "You make it sound like they're pontooning across Lake Eerie right now! The Appalachians haven't signalled surrender!"

McMurtry's brow furrowed. "What's going—"

"The Appalachians haven't signalled a thing for a whole day now," said Brian, grim. "Not since—who are they, again? The *Federales* or the Californians?"

"I don't know!" Nathan moaned. "They've changed their name again! I think they're calling themselves the Federation of Earth Nations." He waved his arms. "Whatever! They're playing this world like a godsdamn game of *Risk!*"

McMurtry set the coffee down and raised his hands. "What are you—"

"Whoever these people are, they're grouping together and moving in," said Brian. "The rumours I've heard suggest they've got ten thousand troops garrisoned in the ruins of Cleveland, ready to roll."

"They wouldn't!" Nelissa gasped. "They wouldn't dare!"

"Okay, enough!" McMurtry yelled. In the silence that followed, he continued more quietly. "First thing's first: where's Minister Dinsdale?"

"Across the street," said Nasser from their desk. They nodded out the window at Queen's Park. "Meeting with the District Governor."

"That's good," said McMurtry. "Because if he was here, he might have a few choice words about us panicking about—" He frowned. "What are we panicking about?"

"Haven't you seen the news?" Agnes handed over a tablet. "The Appalachian government went silent thirty-six hours ago."

McMurtry flipped through the news headlines.

UNKNOWN INCIDENT AT
MISSISSIPPI-OHIO CONFLUENCE

FEDERATION INVOLVEMENT
FROM TEXARKANA BASES?

NO ANSWERS FROM GOVERNMENT OFFICIALS!

McMurtry checked the site address. "These are private media, not official government reports." He handed the tablet back. "If something was on its way, we'd know. You're panicking over a lack of information, over rumours. We need facts."

"Drew's right," said Nelissa. "I'm sure the Minister is being briefed on this right now. We'll ask him when he gets back."

"Um . . . everybody?" Nassar stood, staring out their window at Queen's Park. They beckoned everyone over. "Something's happening at the legislature."

Vehicles were lined up in front of the legislature building. People were running out of the building in them. As soon as each one was full, it peeled off, screeching as it turned a corner, heading north.

"That—" Brian began. But his drawl died in his throat. There was no joke to make of this. No assurance, either.

McMurtry drew a deep breath. "I'm sure that there's a reasonable explanation—"

The stairwell door creaked open. Everybody turned. Minister Dinsdale walked in, hands in his pockets, eyes on the carpet, shoulders slouched. Questions died on everyone's lips. Everyone stared as Dinsdale shuffled past them to his office door.

At his door, he hesitated, then turned and gave them all a tight smile. "I'm proud of you all."

Everybody stared as if they were under a spell.

He nodded. "Now, go home, all of you. Right now. That's the safest place to be."

He stepped back and shut the door.

"What?" The spell broke. They started forward, but Nelissa shouted, "Wait!" They looked at her, and as they did, they became aware of a new sound rising: a rumble to the south. Everybody stepped to the windows and looked out at the city.

People stood on the sidewalks below, staring south. The few vehicles on the street had stopped, people getting out to stare as the rumble rose. It was a clatter, with a whine of motors and gears, backed by a steadily rising buzz.

"Are those tank treads?" Brian whispered.

"No, they're plane engines," said Nelissa.

The answer came to McMurtry. "They're both."

Specks appeared in the southern sky, behind the See-En Tower and the renewing skyscrapers, growing bigger, flattening out to wings with propellers.

Then, triangular specks rushed in above the propeller planes. They burst past in the sky above with a roar.

Everybody staggered back. Brian knocked into McMurtry.

He caught his foot on a desk leg and fell to the floor, knocking his head on the edge. Around him, everybody shouted.

"We got to get out of here!"

"Wait!" That was Nelissa.

"They're going to start bombing!"

"We can't stay here!"

"Run!"

McMurtry blinked through the pain in his temple, then rolled to one side to avoid the stampede. "Wait," he gasped. "Nelissa!" He blinked tears. "Everybody!"

The door slammed. The voices faded. The rumble and roar of tank treads and planes did not. McMurtry rolled onto his hands and knees, used the desk to haul himself up, and touched his forehead. It stung, but no blood came away on his fingers. That was a good sign, wasn't it?

He looked around at the empty office, made messy by everybody's hasty departure. For a moment, he didn't know what to do. Then he looked out at the south window again, at the propeller planes. *Those are bombers.*

He turned for the exit.

And found himself staring at the woman from the rail bridge, standing between him and the exit. She had an eyepatch where her implant had been and a rifle in her hand.

McMurtry blinked at the pain in his head. He struggled to focus. The woman spoke with grim calm. "You pushed us aside. Then you stood aside as your neighbours got overrun. Now, it's just you." She folded her arms. "You are going to learn what it's like to be overrun. You are going to understand what it's like to have no one in your corner. You are going to know how it feels when there's no one to help you now."

McMurtry took a shuddering breath. "Please—"

She stepped aside, clearing the way to the stairwell door. "Run!"

Terror took him, and he ran, clattering down the stairs, staggering at the bottom landing, crashing through the door into reception. The lobby was empty, but it vibrated with the rumble of approaching war machines. He shoved through the revolving door into the front courtyard.

The traffic was gone. The people were gone, fled to their nearest hiding spaces. Only the determined stare of Nelissa on the eight-story face of the Hepburn Block greeted him. The sounds of tank treads pressed closer, and he ran, past government buildings, broken subway entrances, hospitals under repair. At the ancient memorial *The Surrender of Saint Gumby*, he staggered to a stop, seeing the woman from the bridge standing at its base, arms folded, head tilted, unpatched eyebrow raised. Then, the line of armoured vehicles swung into view at the south end of University Avenue.

He ran again. The slam of his footfalls echoed off glass and concrete. Every street had emptied, every store closed. Every house had its shutters drawn. He ran past more building-sized images of Nelissa looking calm and carrying on. He heard no gunfire, no explosions, but still, the rumble-clank of tank treads continued. The buzz of propellers became background. The roar of jets punctured his fog of pain and fear and made him run faster. He tripped on streetcar tracks and rolled, swinging back to his feet to run again, barely breaking step.

On the face of an apartment block, Nelissa blew him a kiss.

Finally, he reached his own street, ran to his own house, dashed up his own walkway. He fumbled with the keys at the front door and staggered inside. The sounds of invasion continued. He locked and bolted the door, dragged a bookshelf in front of it, then backed away, down the hallway, down the stairs to his basement.

The sounds followed him into the musty darkness. He looked for something to hide under. In the end, he could only press himself into a corner, hugging his knees to his chest, wishing his friends were here to help. Wishing for Nelissa. Plane propellers and jet engines continued to roar, tank treads to rumble. He put his hands on his ears, buried his face in his knees. *Please go away! Just make it go away!*

Please!

MCMURTRY COULD NOT REMEMBER SLEEPING, but one moment, he blinked, and there was light filtering in through the small windows near the ceiling, and it was silent.

He lifted his head, then stood up unsteadily. No roar. No rumble. For a moment, he wondered if he was deaf, but he heard the scuff of his shoe against the concrete floor and, as he listened harder, the faint sounds of birdsong outside.

He let out his breath and leaned his forehead against a wall. *Knock! Knock! Knock! Knock!*

He stumbled back, his heart pounding.

The knocking came again. He looked up at the ceiling. It came a third time as he climbed the stairs and a fourth time as he shouldered the bookcase aside and opened the front door.

A soldier stepped back, wearing camo gear and a rifle slung over his shoulder. His armband didn't show Toronto's colours, but a green flag with a gold four-pointed star McMurtry hadn't seen before. A second soldier stood two steps to the first soldier's left. A man with a clipboard stood between them, clean-shaven and wearing a hat, grey pants, and a long, beige cloak.

The man looked up from his clipboard. "Mr. McMurtry?"

McMurtry tried to stare past the man and the soldiers up and down the street. The houses still stood, as did the trees. None of his neighbours were outside. No vehicles rolled. But he did see pairs of soldiers walking up walkways and people with clipboards walking between them.

The man in front of him cleared his throat. "Mr. *Drew* McMurtry?"

McMurtry jerked to attention. He nodded.

"Mr. Drew McMurtry, Deputy Adviser, Accounts Administration at the Ministry of Northern Affairs in the Whitney Block?"

McMurtry nodded again.

The man flipped the pages of his clipboard, circled something, then nodded. "That's still standing." He looked up at McMurtry again. "Report to your desk for an all-staff meeting, nine o'clock tomorrow."

He nodded at McMurtry, then turned on his heel. The soldiers followed the man down the walkway, then up the street to the next house.

SOLDIERS SWEPT the streets as McMurtry left for work. Guns slung over shoulders, they pushed brooms and carried garbage bags, corralling what remained of the litter. The soldiers didn't look at McMurtry, and McMurtry didn't look at them. None of the people who were suddenly back on the streets, heading to work, looked at the soldiers. They hurried along, their heads down, and so did he.

On the face of the Hepburn Block, soldiers were repainting the inspirational art piece, changing the blue background to green and painting over the maple leaf with the four-pointed star. They seemed to be painting a band on Nelissa's arm.

McMurtry hesitated at the revolving door but entered anyway. He shared a look with Ms. Stacey at reception, but neither said a word. He went upstairs.

He entered his floor and let out a breath of relief to see all his colleagues at their desks. "Thank—" he began, then stopped. Nelissa was jerking her head, gesturing to his seat. The Minister's office door was closed.

That's when he noticed the soldiers standing in the corners of the room. McMurtry took his seat. Silence stretched. The air felt as oppressive as summer.

Finally, the Minister's door jerked open, and a young man stepped out, holding a clipboard. At first, McMurtry thought it was the same man who was at his door the day before, but this man's hair was a little longer and darker, and his clothes were more ornate.

The man beamed at them. "Good morning! I'm delighted to see you've all turned up. I realize these past few hours have been stressful for you all, but that's in the past now. I'm your new supervisor. You may call me Mr. Scranton."

Scranton stepped to the middle of the floor and turned slowly, addressing everyone. "I want to assure you all that, while I may be new to this job, nothing is going to change about your work. Your hours will remain the same, your pay will remain the same, and your duties will remain the same. I expect nothing from you that you haven't already provided in the past. I know you all do exemplary, important work. Where would our governments be without the knowledge and institutional memory of the workers at their desks? We believe in the future, and we believe in moving toward that future. I'm delighted to have you all with me as we embark on that journey."

He nodded at everyone, his smile as bright as the dawn. "I'd like to say that I have an open-door policy. My door may be closed right now, but you're always welcome to knock. As your supervisor, think of me as a resource to help you be the best you can be at your job. So, ask me anything! Anything at all!"

"Where is Minister Dinsdale?" said McMurtry.

Around him, his colleagues tensed, but McMurtry stayed where he was, hands clasped on his desk. Scranton stared at him.

Then Scranton looked down and flipped through his clipboard. He ran a finger down a page, nodded, and then looked up. "That's irrelevant. Any other questions?"

Silence reigned.

"Good!" Scranton beamed. "So, before we return to work, I'd like to invite all of you to come to the meeting room to learn and take the oath of allegiance to the Federation of Earth Nations. This is entirely voluntary. Those who wish to take the oath, please stand up now."

For a moment, no one moved. Everyone glanced at each other, at Scranton, at the soldiers in the corners, at the soldiers' guns. Brian stood up.

He was followed by Agatha, who was followed by Nathan, and then by Nasser. McMurtry felt himself rise to his feet, though he wasn't sure if his brain had given the order. Soon, everyone in the office was standing.

Everyone except Nelissa.

She sat in her chair, back straight, hands clasped across her lap, staring straight ahead.

Behind her, McMurtry saw the woman from the bridge glaring at him.

Brian shifted as if to sit back down, but a soldier reached up and touched the butt of his gun. Brian halted, then slowly stood straight again.

Scranton nodded. "Fair enough. Everybody, let's go."

Scranton led the way. A soldier followed, nudging people forward. McMurtry stood, staring at Nelissa. She looked up at him, her eyes wide, her cheeks pale. For a moment, McMurtry could only stare back.

Then, a soldier was beside McMurtry. "Senior," the young man said, his voice low.

Nelissa's lips tightened. She focused ahead. Beside McMurtry, the soldier waited.

McMurtry looked down. He turned away. He followed the others to the meeting room, feeling the glare of the woman from the bridge on his back. The door closed behind him.

Scranton stood beside a whiteboard at the front of the room. On it, the Federation of Earth Nations's pledge of allegiance was written out in full.

"Everyone . . ." Scranton faced the whiteboard. "Place your right hand over your heart and recite the words before you as we say—"

Voices filled the room. "I, hereby accepting citizenship of the Federation of Earth Nations, voluntarily and consciously swear an oath to observe the Constitution and laws of the Federation of Earth Nations, the rights and freedoms of its citizens; to fulfill the duties of a Federation citizen for the benefit of the state and society; to protect the integrity of the Federation of Earth Nations; to be faithful to its leadership, and to respect its cultures, its history, and traditions."

NELISSA WAS NOT at her desk when they returned. McMurtry filed in with the others, silent.

At his desk, he stared a moment out his window. They were almost done repainting the eight-storey-tall poster to have a green background. They'd kept Nelissa's face, placed a Federation armband on her, and even kept the "FORWARD TOGETHER" message at her feet. Vehicles drifted along the streets below. People walked carefully. Soldiers swept litter from the sidewalks.

He turned away and found himself staring at the inspirational picture of CONTINUITY.

The line of fish was gone. It was just one fish, now facing the viewer, its mouth open wide.

McMurtry sat down. He pulled a folder from his inbox and grabbed a pencil.

He looked once at Nelissa's empty desk.

Then he put his head down and got back to work.

FAMOUS LOST WORDS

BY IRA NAYMAN

Katherine Goble Johnson HAVOC
Venus, May 13, 2195

THE PROBLEM WITH WATER IS THAT IT DOESN'T PURIFY ITSELF.

You're probably thinking, *Well, sure, but why would water mined from below the surface of Mars need purifying?* Bless your naïveté! We barely know each other, and you're already asking me silly questions!

As everybody knows, water is made up of "H" and "O." But frozen water can contain all manner of impurities: "C," for instance, or "N" or even "Li." Yes, "Li!" Yuck! Sometimes, there are even heavier elements, some of which can be very unpleasant to encounter when all you want is a cool drink of "H" and "O." So, in an ideal world, you would like to purify your water before drinking it.

There is a second reason for purifying water: moving it from Mars to one of the High-Altitude Venusian Operating Cities floating in that planet's atmosphere is expensive and not entirely certain. Once in a while, one of the ice transports will think to itself, *Hey! That asteroid looks interesting! I wonder what's going on on its surface* . . . Then, it will veer off course to investigate, usually with explosive consequences. Nobody knows why. The programming for the transports is simple by Venusian standards, but it's still more complex than any single human being can comprehend.

Or, it could be caused by solar flares. Yeah. Sure. That could be it. In space, solar flares cover a multitude of sins.

For this reason, the HAVOCs of Venus recycle their liquid waste. Much of this is done at the major recycling plant on the *Katherine Goble Johnson* HAVOC, which also maintains a vast tank full of purified water for emergencies. When another HAVOC comes within handshake distance of *Katherine Goble Johnson*, they exchange fluids. In case of—that sounded bad, didn't it? I meant the other HAVOC gives *Katherine Goble Johnson* its waste water in exchange for fresh. (I accept no responsibility for whatever meaning your mind may have attributed to my original statement.) In case of emergency, the *Katherine Goble Johnson* HAVOC has a specially outfitted ship that can be used to transport fresh water to any point around Venus.

Anoush Ramaswamy, a small man whose fastidious outward appearance masked a chaotic frame of mind, thought water recycling was the most boring thing in the world. So, naturally, he was the Chief Engineer responsible for the smooth running of the *Katherine Goble Johnson* Filtration Plant. The universe has a . . . *precious* sense of humour.

In his spare time, Ramaswamy built an antenna out of spare parts, outdated parts, broken parts that he fixed as best he could, and purchased parts. Then, he wrote a program that would search the sky for a signal and alert him if one was received. The process took more than seven years to complete, but it was with a great deal of satisfaction that he fixed the antenna to the outer shell of the HAVOC and aimed it in the direction of Earth (the program was designed to move the antenna so that it would remain pointed at Earth even as the HAVOC moved around the Earth-facing part of Venus).

That was five months ago. Typically, Ramaswamy spent his day monitoring the flow of H_2O through the filtration system, then came home to see if the antenna had picked up anything. And he was disappointed when the system responded, "You have no new messages."

Ramaswamy spent the next day monitoring the flow of H_2O through the filtration system, then came home to see if the antenna had picked up anything. And again, he was disappointed when the system responded, "You have no new messages."

Ramaswamy spent the *next* day monitoring the flow of H_2O through the filtration system, then came home to see if the antenna had picked up anything. And yet *again*, he was disappointed when the system responded, "You have no new messages."

Ramaswamy spent the next day monitoring the flow of H_2O through the filtration system, then came home to see if the antenna had picked up anything. And he was ready to be disappointed when the system responded, "You have no new messages," but he was ecstatic to discover that the system responded, "You have one new message." Excited, he commanded his tablet to play the message. This is what he heard:

". . . no curiosity, no enjoyment of the process of life. All competing pleasures will be destroyed. But always—do not forget this, Winston—always there will be the intoxication of power, constantly increasing and constantly growing subtler. Always, at every moment, there will be the thrill of victory, the sensation of trampling on an enemy who is helpless. If you want a picture of the future, imagine a boot stamping on a . . ." the recording began. This was followed by three seconds of a baby cooing joyously. This was followed by sixteen seconds of a band singing, "Love is all you need," over and over again.

What the hell was that? Ramaswamy thought to himself the first time he listened to the transmission.

That . . . doesn't really make sense . . . Ramaswamy thought the second time he listened to the transmission.

*The first transmission from Earth in years, and **this** is the best they can come up with?* Ramaswamy thought the third time he listened to the transmission.

This is the first transmission from Earth in years, and I'm the first person to hear it. How galactic is that? Ramaswamy thought the fourth time he listened to the transmission.

I wish Arthur was here. He would know what to do, Ramaswamy thought the final time he listened to the transmission.

Arthur Windswept was Ramaswamy's husband. He lived up to his name: no matter how he styled it, his sandy brown hair always looked like it had just been blown by air currents on a moor. Not that the native Venusian had ever been on a moor, but his hair didn't know that. Windswept was the practical one in the relationship. When the first iteration of Ramaswamy's program created a feedback loop of sound that threatened to deafen people within a ten-block radius of their home, Windswept took one look at the program and fixed it. (Although their neighbours gave Ramaswamy the cold shoulder, Windswept didn't have to pay for a drink for seventy rotations.)

Unfortunately, Windswept was working on the *Pamela Sargent* HAVOC, investigating why its water system had backed up and sprung leaks in fourteen places. Eventually, he would determine that chewing gum had somehow managed to get into the system; once all of the offending material had been removed and the leaks plugged, Windswept would recommend that the HAVOC suspend Take Your Kids to Work Day for the foreseeable future. But that was three days in the future, and Ramaswamy had to do something now.

Fortunately, Ramaswamy knew what it was: he had to inform the group he thought of as Big Mother (but that everybody else knew as the Venusian Council) of the message.

THE POLITICAL RESPONSE

"A quorum having been reached, I call this meeting to order," said Councillor Ernesto Flapdoodle, who had a streak of gold glitter on his cheek, a streak that crossed his prominent jawbone and clashed with his grey hair. This tended to undermine his authority as chair of the meeting, but he appeared to be unaware of the substance, and none of the attending Councillors felt comfortable enough to point it out.

To be fair, Councillor Flapdoodle's day job was teaching grade school; stray streaks of glitter came with the territory. And it wasn't like he was the only one who had been unprepared for the meeting. Councillor Madeleine Zapdos, an engineer who had worked a double shift on the new, as yet unnamed, as yet unfinished HAVOC, appeared in pink jammies, her eyes puffy, her rat's nest of blonde hair rezoned as a rat's condo. "I continue to object," she said in a voice so husky it could have pulled a sled across the Arctic. "This is too important to be dealt with by a mere quorum—the full Council needs to meet to deal with it."

"Your objection has been noted," Councillor Flapdoodle responded, trying to keep the irritation out of his voice and almost succeeding. "However, not all of the Councillors could be pulled away from their other duties. Or sleep. Good luck trying to pull them away from their beds. We have managed to get a quorum. The meeting shall begin."

"Suck it up, Madeleine," Councillor Fiona Wong chastised. Her security uniform was perfect because of course it was. "The sooner we get this meeting started, the sooner it will be over, and we can get back to . . . whatever important things we were doing before it was called." Councillor Wang never wasted an opportunity to let everybody know she felt politics was beneath her, despite the fact that everybody knew. Boy, oh, boy, did they know.

"Can we get on with the meeting, please?" asked Councillor Richard Hebrides, the only Councillor who actually lived on the *Perelandra* HAVOC. "We open for breakfast in ninety minutes, and the eggs don't scramble themselves!" He was big and broad and had a face borrowed from a twelve-year-old even though he was sixty-four, a look which made people uncertain about whether they should respond to him with respect or laughter.

"Umm, yes, certainly. Of course," Councillor Flapdoodle responded (without, the record should note, respect or laughter). The Councillor turned his attention to his left for a couple of seconds and listened intently; eventually, he hissed, "She's already had one glass of juice. If she has another, she'll be in the bathroom for the rest of the day! No, she cannot have one for at least another . . . two hours." Then, he returned his attention to the meeting, a smile returning to his face almost as if it had been CGIed over his real mouth. "Sorry about that," Councillor Flapdoodle apologized. "Children."

The other Councillors muttered agreement with varying degrees of vehemence.

Because they were scattered across multiple HAVOCs, the Venusian Council had to meet virtually, each looking at a screen filled with the faces of the others in a ritual that had been established over a century ago. Ordinarily, this would not be a problem: meetings were scheduled at regular intervals around the other duties of the Councillors. However, in order to deal with this emergency, the Councillors had to . . . improvise.

Councillor Flapdoodle took a moment to centre himself. Then, he said, "Okay, we've all heard the transmission that came from Earth. What—"

"It couldn't have come from Earth," Councillor Zapdos croaked. She took a healthy swig of a dark, steaming liquid in a glass that quickly appeared in and just as quickly disappeared from her image.

Councillor Flapdoodle, who was eminently flappable, blinked a couple of times. "I don't—do you—hunh?"

"Our scientists are very clear on this point," Councillor Zapdos croaked. The liquid hadn't helped. "Nothing survived on the planet's surface. The message couldn't have come from Earth."

"That may be true, Madeleine," Councillor Hebrides, who couldn't have been more than twenty-three, with a tattoo on his right shoulder that could have been a blazing comet or an abstract collection of lines and shapes (art being in the eye of the beholder), began. "But we have to—*bzzt*—if there is a possi —*bzzt click bzz*t—ave to deal with the—*bzzzzzzzzzzzzzzzzzz* . . ."

"Richard?" Councillor Flapdoodle asked. "*Richard?*" After a couple of seconds of buzzing, he added, "We seem to have lost Richard."

"We have lost our quorum, then," Councillor Zapdos gloated. Croakingly.

"The hell we have!" Councillor Wong roared. "Quorum isn't lost until somebody actually calls the question. *And you will not dare call the question!* Perelandra has probably just moved behind another HAVOC. It will either relay his messages, or he will emerge and be able to resume communications. Either way, I don't want to waste the next five minutes, so let's continue. He was going to say that we have to take into account the possibility that some people on Earth survived and deal with the political ramifications of that if it turns out to be true."

"Yes, let's, umm, push through and keep the meeting going," Councillor Flapdoodle suggested. "I agree that—"

". . . zzzzzzzzzz—lo?" Councillor Hebrides could be heard again. "Can anybody he—*bzzt click*—orry. Have I regained contact? Ernesto? Hello, Ernesto?"

"We are receiving you loud and clear, Richard," Councillor Flapdoodle responded. "Before you cut out, you started saying something . . .?"

"What? Oh, right," Councillor Hebrides sighed. "I was saying that we should treat the message as real on the off chance that it is. Because if it is, there will be real consequences for all of us who live off-Earth."

Councillor Wong grinned. On her already severe face, it looked like a threat.

"But . . . but . . . but," Councillor Zapdos sputtered. "What does it mean? The message makes absolutely no sense! Are you suggesting that the survivors on Earth are all demented?"

"It would explain a lot." Councillor Wong's grin turned into a smirk.

Councillor Hebrides shook his bald head. "It doesn't matter," he insisted. "What is important is that a message would indicate that there are still people on Earth. If true, that would mean, among other things, that we would have to prepare some sort of diplomatic response to their existence."

"If that's the case, what sort of diplomatic response should we be considering?" Councillor Flapdoodle asked.

Councillor Hebrides shmushed his lips together and moved them around, indicating that he was thinking. Eventually, he said, "The way I see it, there would be two options open to us. On the one hand, there is a lot of anger among Venusians toward the people of Earth. They had—"

"So much anger," Councillor Zapdos muttered agreeingly. Or agreed mutteringly. Some combination of agreement and muttering.

"It's a lot," Councillor Hebrides repeated. "I have no doubt that many Venusians would be happy to ignore the message and let the Earthers stew in whatever hell they have made of our home planet."

"Sounds good to me," Councillor Zapdos concurred. "If that's our recommended course of action, we can end the mee—"

"On the other hand," Councillor Hebrides continued, his high voice threatening to squeak, "I think it's fair to say that nobody wants a repeat of the debacle with the miners from the Asteroid Belt."

There were several moments of sombre silence. Nobody disputed that it was the right decision at the time, but most Venusians had the grace to acknowledge, however deeply, that it still sucked.

"Are you suggesting that we send a ship to Earth to see if we can make contact with survivors?" Councillor Wong asked, working her incredulousness muscle hard.

"We wouldn't want to go to the expense unless we were absolutely certain there were survivors," Councillor Zapdos croaked.

"Just so." Councillor Hebrides nodded. "I would suggest that we try to make radio contact with Earth. If we connect to Earthers, we can learn what condition they are in and why they decided to contact us now. Only then—"

"And why their communication was so cryptic," Councillor Zapdos interrupted.

"I don't know," Councillor Flapdoodle mused. "I find there is poetry in a child's cooing."

There was a moment of embarrassed silence. "Aaaaaaany-way," Councillor Hebrides finally continued, "once we have made contact with the Earthers and satisfied ourselves that they do not have a hostile intent toward us, then we can decide if we want to send a ship to make face-to-face contact with them.”

“Assuming that there are places on Earth that haven't been so environmentally degraded that we could even survive on the surface,” said Councillor Wong, doing her best to kill the buzz. Killing buzzes was her thing. She was a definite buzzkill.

“That's a long—*bzzzt*,” Councillor Hebrides tried to say. “We shouldn't wor—*bzzt click bzzt*—y that time, we will know if—*bzzzzzzzzzzzzt!*”

“Aaaaaand, we've lost Richard again,” Councillor Flapdoodle announced.

“Probably a solar flare,” Councillor Wong stated. The *Perelandra* HAVOC was the only one in the chain that was currently on the sun side of Venus, which made its communications vulnerable to disruption due to solar flares (remember the whole “multitude of sins” thing?). The HAVOCs were shielded from solar radiation, of course, but if human technology was perfect, well, Earth would still be alive, wouldn't it?

“Okay, then,” Councillor Zapdos brusquely said. “We will attempt to contact any survivors on Earth, and if we are able to establish communications with them, we will decide how to deal with them based on what they tell us about their conditions and intent. If there is no other business—”

“Oh, there is always other business,” Councillor Flapdoodle, to her dismay, argued. “What, if anything, should we tell Venusians about the message? How long should we wait until we tell them? How should we prepare for their response? And I feel certain that, in the course of our discussion, we will have other thoughts . . .”

The groans of the committee members could have been heard on Earth.

THE SCIENTIFIC RESPONSE

"It goes down smooth," Dan "Doc" Terwilliger warned the others, "but it has a kick. I would recommend sipping your beakers slowly. Sip. Very. Slowly." It's not that the researchers couldn't have drunk the alcoholic homebrew out of glasses, but what would be the science in that? And if the beaker hadn't been properly cleaned and happened, therefore, to be laced with the residue of substances from experiments it had previously been used for, that just made it all the more sciencey.

Carlotta Frump fearlessly chugged the contents of her beaker. "Mmm . . . not bad," she commented. "Throaty, with an aftertaste of elderberry and formaldehyde. But I don't see where the—WHOA!" Frump grabbed the edge of the desk she was sitting at to keep from falling out of her chair.

Harindur Noonian-Tepperman sipped at his beaker. "A negative example is still an example," he said to himself, loud enough for the others to hear.

The three scientists had been running simulations of plant growth in a lab on the Sarah Zettel Farming Platform to determine how they might increase crop yields in Venus's nurseries when news of the message from Earth was sent to them by the Council for analysis. Terwilliger, an androgynous figure with deep blue seas—er, eyes—and short, spiky white hair, had been saving the homebrew for . . . they didn't know why, really, but this seemed like as good a time as any to break it out.

Frump, a plump, middle-aged woman with kindly eyes that hid a manic imagination, tapped the edge of her beaker and roared, "Barkeep, another!"

Noonian-Tepperman, his face made up of sharp lines under dark skin, his brown eyes trained to give away nothing, sipped at his beaker daintily; he wasn't a big drinker, but he didn't want to ruin the moment for the other scientists who, to his complete surprise, he considered friends.

Weird friends with whom he frequently disagreed, but who is to say what constitutes a successful friendship?

The three were sitting at the end of a long room filled with tables featuring a riot of state-of-the-art computers, microscopes, centrifuges, 3D printers and, for some reason, an ancient hotplate and pot for coffee. Whether they were willing to admit it or not (and Noonian-Tepperman was adamant on the issue), if an ocelot overloaded the 3D printer with demands for food pellets, causing a fire that destroyed the lab (which wouldn't happen—there were no ocelots on any of the HAVOCs over Venus—but as a scientist, you get used to conducting thought experiments like this), the hotplate and the pot for coffee would be what they missed the most.

Terwilliger played the message for the third time. "So, what do we make of this forty-six-second message, mmm?" they asked over their silver-rimmed glasses.

"It didn't come from Earth," Noonian-Tepperman said with such finality you could be forgiven for thinking that it was the last thing anybody said before the heat death of the universe.

"Obvo!" Frump enthusiastically agreed, taking a big gulp from her beaker. Which was empty. She turned the beaker over and moued as a single drop fell out of it onto her free hand. She licked her hand and, turning the beaker right side up again, banged it on the desk three times to indicate to the barkeep that she was getting impatient with the service.

"We're agreed, then," Terwilliger summed up. "The message couldn't have come from Earth. The question then becomes: where did it come from?"

"A prank by somebody on Mars?" Noonian-Tepperman suggested. You could tell it was a mere suggestion by the way it only contained the finality of the sun going nova and wiping out most of the solar system.

"Pfft!" Frump waved the suggestion away. "Boring!"

"What would your explanation be?" Noonian-Tepperman, his voice as cold as interstellar space, demanded.

"A black hole," she stated, the beaker in her hand forgotten for the moment.

"A black hole?" Terwilliger asked, just beating out Noonian-Tepperman by a fraction of a second.

"Mm-hmm." Frump nodded seriously. "We know that Earth sent signals out into the cosmos, first in the form of radio, then film and television, and finally computers, for maybe three hundred years. Some of them could have fallen into a black hole. Now, if, as some theorize, a black hole is actually a worm-hole, and if, as some conjecture, information is not destroyed and actually leaks out of black holes, it could be hypothesized that the message was spat out by a second black hole and directed back at us. Voila!" Frump twirled her hands in the air in what she hoped was a visual metaphor for magic; the effect was somewhat dampened by the fact that her free hand knocked into the hand that held the beaker, both ultimately falling onto her lap.

"Hmm . . ." Terwilliger hmmed. "But Carlotta, the message contains three distinct elements, not one."

Frump loudly pffted. "Who knows what goes on inside a black hole? Maybe information gets all . . . jumbly-wumbly. I'm too sober for this kind of speculation!" She rose and walked over to the jug that contained the alcohol. Terwilliger, who was sitting next to the table on which the jug sat, moved his hand in the direction of the jug. Frump gave him a look that stated in no uncertain terms that if they were intent on keeping the jug from her, she would be quite happy to find out what a black hole would do to the information contained in their body. They delicately removed their hand.

"Perhaps a theory containing fewer . . . hypotheticals would be better," Noonian-Tepperman commented. Frump, intent on pouring liquid into her beaker, didn't take in his words.

Terwilliger took a sip from their beaker and shuddered. "Did you have one in mind?" they asked.

"As a matter of fact . . ." Noonian-Tepperman put the beaker to his lips, thought better of it, and put it down on the desk near him. "Earth's civilization collapsed, but that didn't mean the end of its technology. There were, for instance, thousands of satellites circling the planet. Perhaps one of them had been programmed to send a message into the cosmos containing a cross-section of the sounds of human experience—Earthers used to love doing shit like that. That could be what Ramaswamy picked up."

Terwilliger frowned. "It would be a hell of a—Carlotta, what are you doing?"

Next to her chair, she was bent over, trying to put her flask on the desk and . . . missing. "Almost there," she assured them as she stuck her tongue out of the side of her mouth.

"It might be easier for you to just hold the beaker in your hand," Noonian-Tepperman gently suggested. He sounded like the wrath of God, but for him, that was gentle.

"Good point," Frump agreed. After several seconds of trying unsuccessfully to sit down, Noonian-Tepperman suggested, "Standing is good for you. Good for your heart."

Frump nodded.

"It would be one hell of a coincidence," Terwilliger continued, "for Anoush to have aimed his antenna in just the right direction to capture the signal when it was sent."

Noonian-Tepperman shook his head. "For all we know, the satellite could have been transmitting the message at periodic intervals since the twenty-first century. In such a case, it would be only a matter of time before somebody on Venus noticed it."

"Perhaps." Terwilliger pursed their lips, unconvinced. "But if that were the case, why haven't we heard it again? We're now using the best antennae at our disposal, aimed directly at the spot where Anoush said his antenna's program told him the signal had originated from. Yet, we have heard nothing."

Noonian-Tepperman shrugged. "It would depend upon the interval, wouldn't it?"

Terwilliger nodded. They picked up the tablet that lay on the table next to them. Venusians tended not to personalize their work spaces, since any *tchotchke* they could imagine wanting would take resources to make, and resources were always scarce. However, there was no end to the personalization of their electronic devices they could accomplish: Terwilliger's tablet featured a screensaver of a cat in a dashiki clinging to a bar, under which could be found the words, "Hang in there, baby." They had no idea what the image meant, but they found it soothing for some reason. They tapped the screen and, when it came to life, opened a word-processing program and typed in notes of the discussion so far. A couple of minutes later, they put the tablet down and asked, "Other thoughts?"

THE MILITARY RESPONSE

First Officer Roland Smedley looked like he was made out of bricks: square torso, square head, rectangular limbs. Even his salt-and-pepper buzzcut and thick moustache exuded solidity (in addition to world-weariness). In a career that spanned more than thirty years, he had seen a lot of hairy security situations and mastered them all. But if there was one thing that unnerved him, it was the screaming of children that dully came through the wall of his office on the *Chris Jones* HAVOC.

"Have you heard the message?" he asked through gritted teeth.

"I have," First Officer Wilhelmina Fijit answered. Fijit, a small woman with big red hair who spoke with the authority of a Viking warrior, sat across the desk from Smedley in his small office. Belying her name, she was the most-still human being on the HAVOC; it was as if she were posing for a photograph that was never taken. Fijit appeared to be completely unfazed by the screaming of the children (although, owing to an incident with a security whistle when she was three years old, she had lost much of the hearing in her right ear, her dominant ear, so the screaming of the children might have been no more to her than a slight background hum).

"What was your first impression?" Smedley followed up.

"It couldn't have come from Earth," Fijit confidently asserted.

"It did not come from Earth," Smedley almost as confidently agreed.

"May I ask a question?"

"Of course."

"Why are we wasting our time discussing it, then?"

Smedley sucked on the edge of his moustache, a habit he was unaware of that would have made him a terrible poker player if he had ever indulged in gambling. Eventually, he stated, "The *Perelandra* panjandrums have decreed that we need to determine a threat assessment if the message came from Earth."

"There is no threat. The message did not come from Earth," Fijit averred. "If I could get back to my station, now . . ."

"Unfortunately," Smedley suggested a sigh but was too much a military man to make one, "they will not be satisfied if our report is less than fifty pages long."

Fijit allowed herself the luxury of shaking her head. Twice. "Politicians!" she muttered.

"I know," Smedley sympathetically agreed, "but what can we do? The system only works when all of the different parts work in tand—excuse me a moment, will you?"

Smedley opened the tablet on his desk and buzzed his aide. "Senior?" a young man's voice said.

"Come in here, will you?" Smedley commanded.

"Right away, Senior."

As Smedley closed his tablet, the door opened, and Isaiah Jackson, a bright young thing who was a little too beanpoley for most people's taste but who wore his security uniform rather smartly, walked into the room. For the brief time the door was open, the screaming of the children was louder, more coherent; one boy in particular petulantly shouted, "It's not fair! It's not fair! It's not fair!" over and over and over again.

The moment the office door was closed, Smedley demanded, "Isaiah, is there any way we can shoot those children and put them out of my misery?"

"I would have to check regulations," the aide replied, "but I'm pretty sure the answer would be no."

"Right, then. Get me some aspirin and a pair of earplugs," Smedley ordered.

"Yes, Senior. Right away, Senior." The aide was already halfway through the door by the time he finished talking. For a brief moment, another boy could be heard shouting something about "peace" or possibly "a piece," and then the screaming of the children became background noise once again.

"That doesn't worry me," Smedley admitted once the door had been firmly shut. "We'll get some private to write the threat assessment the Council wants. No, what worries me is where this message came from and what it might represent."

Fijit blinked. "Do you think it could have come from Mars?"

"We have to consider that a real possibility," Smedley told her. "We could be looking at a situation where people on Mars are working with people on Venus to smuggle medicines or some other precious commodity to them, and some poor schmo of a sanitation worker intercepts their communications without knowing what he has heard."

"That's hard to see in the message," Fijit stated, so much dubiousness dripping from her voice that somebody would have to mop it off the floor when the meeting was over.

"We cannot rule out the possibility that the first part of the message is in code." Smedley sucked at the other half of his moustache, indicating deep thought. "You have to admit, there are dark overtones to that part of the message. I suppose we will need to explore the possibility that there is a subversive group on Venus looking to overthrow the government."

"What about the last part of the message, the cooing infant and the jaunty song?" Fijit reminded him. "Neither of those elements seem threatening in any way."

"There could be messages embedded in those sound clips," Smedley spit-balled. This was turning into a very wet meeting. "Or they could have been included in the message to throw us off the scent. We'll have a better idea of what we're dealing with after the message has been thoroughly analyzed." Before Fijit could respond, Smedley held up a finger and said, "Give me one more second . . ."

The First Officer buzzed his aide again. "Senior?" Jackson answered.

"Isaiah, how much longer is the birthday party next door going to last?"

"Let me see . . . approximately twenty minutes, Senior," Jackson told him.

Smedley growled. Putting his office next to the largest room in the HAVOC seemed like a good idea at the time, inasmuch as it gave him immediate access to meetings important to the security of Venus. He hadn't considered the possibility that other groups might have their own uses for the space when it was free. Other groups that could be very loud. And annoying.

Smedley cut off the connection with a stab of his finger that fell just shy of having enough force to crack the glass screen. He had lost enough tablets to know exactly where that line was.

"With all due respect, Roland," Fijit said, "this doesn't seem all that promising. For all we know, that sanitation schmo put together this message himself to get some attention."

Smedley's moustache shrugged. "I know. But we have to look into it anyway. Unless you have other thoughts?"

"I GOT YOU A PRESENT," Windswept said, holding out his hand. He held a small figure, made out of repurposed cellulose, of a dolphin that had half-emerged from the side of a pyramid.

"Oh, you didn't have to do that," Ramaswamy off-handedly responded. What he meant, of course, was: *why did you do that when I didn't get anything for you?*

"I know," Windswept grinned. "I wanted to." What he meant, of course, was: *I wanted to.* Some characters are easier to read than others.

As you might imagine, resources in a series of closed environments like the HAVOCs are limited. (And if you can't imagine, you really should read more science fiction.) Resources are generally used for the most immediate needs, such as maintaining life-support systems. But on the seventh day of the strawberry festival, surplus resources are divided among the adults in each HAVOC to create whatever they see fit. Ramaswamy used his to create a spare piece for the antenna. He . . . would probably be upset if you knew that, especially in light of the gift Windswept had made for him, so pretend that you don't know.

"What is it?" Ramaswamy asked, taking the object from his husband and turning it this way and that in his hand to look at it from a variety of angles.

"What does it look like?" Windswept asked.

Ramaswamy thought for several seconds. "It looks like . . . a fish," he tentatively stated, "emerging from out of a triangle."

"That's exactly what it is!" Windswept said with a grin. What he meant, of course, was: *I love you too much to let your silliness spoil this moment.* Sometimes, subtext can be generous.

Ramaswamy set the dolphin/fish thing on the table at which he was sitting, next to his tablet. Then, taking Windswept's hands in his and looking into his partner's eyes, he said, "I have some exciting news."

"Oh?" Windswept ohed. "Did something happen while I was gone?"

Ramaswamy nodded vigorously. "Yes! There was a message from Earth!"

"A message?" Windswept tried to sound enthusiastic, but it was a hard slog—like knee-deep in swamp water hard.

"That's right," Ramaswamy enthused. "A message!"

"From Earth?" Windswept was really losing the battle for enthusiasm.

"I know." Ramaswamy refused to notice. "Isn't that amazing?"

Not breaking eye contact, Windswept suggested that he hear the message.

"I thought you'd never ask!" Ramaswamy told him. Recovering his hands, he turned to the tablet, opened the recording software, and played it for his husband. When it was over, he asked, "So, what do you think?"

"It's a bit . . . obscure." Enthusiasm had lost, and there was nothing left to do but to clean the dead bodies off the battlefield.

"I know!" Ramaswamy responded. "It will take some of Venus's best minds to –"

"Did you check the antenna array's concurrent input data log?" Windswept interrupted.

"Umm . . ." Ramaswamy answered.

"You know, to confirm the direction from which the signal came?" Windswept followed up.

"Err . . ." Ramaswamy replied.

Windswept kissed him on the head, being sure to avoid the beginning of Ramaswamy's bald spot because that's what people in love do when they know their partner is sensitive about a subject. "You're such a goof," Windswept said with a grin that could disarm a Cossack.

Windswept brought himself a chair and told Ramaswamy to "shove over." When his partner was sufficiently over, Windswept sat down, faced the tablet, and started typing. In less than a minute, he said, "Well, isn't that interesting ..."

"Interesting?" Ramaswamy croaked. "Like, like, like that's a fact that could change the way we look at the universe interesting? Or like a mob with torches and pitchforks should be arriving at our door any second now to have a little conversation with me interesting?"

Windswept smiled at him. "Like you're-such-a-goof interesting," he answered.

Ramaswamy pouted. "I'm not familiar with that kind of interesting."

Sweeping a hand toward the screen and rolling his chair back a little, Windswept said, "See for yourself."

Ramaswamy rolled toward the desk and looked at the screen. "There's nothing there," he commented.

"That's right," Windswept agreed.

"But if the antenna received a message from Earth, there would have been a time and source coordinates," Ramaswamy reasoned, turning toward his husband.

"That's right," Windswept agreed, looking into the eyes of his beloved.

"There can only be one conclusion ..."

"That's right."

"The message arrived with hidden code that erased the concurrent input data log!"

"That's wrong."

"That's wrong?"

"That's wrong. Although I suppose I was wrong when I

agreed that there could only be one conclusion, so let's call it even."

"But if a signal came from somewhere, whether it was Earth or any other point, it would show up in the log. The only way the log would be empty is if the message didn't come from space at all." Windswept nodded in encouragement. "But if the message didn't come from space, where did it come from?" Windswept looked as meaningfully as a dictionary in the direction of the antenna. "No!" Ramaswamy exclaimed. "It was a hallucination?"

Windswept nodded. "It was a hallucination."

"Hallucination" is a technical term for what happens when a computer goes a little . . . funny in the head. You know. Funny. It makes something up that sounds reasonable but is, in fact, completely untrue (sort of like a global climate change denier).

"I was so sure it was a message from Earth!" Ramaswamy muttered, disappointed. "The program told me it had come from Earth—even told me where it originated from. Some place called Tarana!"

"You wanted to believe that somehow, somebody on our home planet had survived. That's totally understandable—we'd all like to believe it," Windswept magnanimously said. "But it just isn't true."

Ramaswamy sighed and looked at the floor. Windswept put a comforting hand on his shoulder. "As long as nobody knows about the message," he assured his husband, "no harm done."

"Erm," Ramaswamy replied, "Yeah. About that . . ."

GROWING UP ON MERCURY
BY JOANNA KARAPLIS

The latitude town known as the **Leigh Brackett**
Mercury Colonies

NEW KID
April-June 21251

Leigh Brackett
April 16, 2152

DEAR STELLA,

I miss you so much already! I'm only a few latitudes away, but it feels like I'm on another planet entirely. I knew the *Leigh Brackett* was smaller than the *Messenger,* but I didn't know they also lost some of their sections when the *Apollo* attacked. I can walk from one end to the other in less than twenty minutes. I'm seriously getting claustrophobic already.

Our quarters are way smaller than on the *Messenger*. My room is just a bed and a dresser, that's it. If I want a desk, I have to use the kitchen table—which is also small. Mom says I should be grateful because there are families of four and five sharing quarters the same size as ours. So, I should be happy I don't have a dad or brothers and sisters?

They don't have any more food than back on the *Messenger*, either. And it tastes worse here. I didn't think that was possible.

The only thing that's the same is the Robinson Rails and that smooth feeling as the *Leigh Brackett* travels along them. Sometimes, I go to the front of the town and just stare at them, wishing that they were leading me to the *Messenger* instead of just around and around the planet, always escaping the Sun.

If you can't already tell, it's depressing here. Everyone lost someone in the attacks. Some people lost everyone. Being all the way over here, I feel like I've lost everyone, too—you and Lukas and Hiroshi, and everyone else—but at least I can write to you. And I know I'll see you again someday.

As soon as I can, I'm coming back to the *Messenger*. Don't you dare forget me!

Miss you,
Isla

The *Messenger*
April 17, 2152

Dear Isla,

We all miss you, too. It's so unfair! Sorry that the food there sucks. It's mostly the same here, but Dad says our rations will get increased soon because of the iron cornrows. Plus, we don't have as many people to feed now that so many have gone to the *Leigh Brackett* and other latitude towns. At least you didn't have to go to the *Baxter-Nordley* . . . that place is definitely haunted. Just thinking about it makes me want to puke.

Lukas and Hiroshi say hi. I told them they can write to you too, but you know how they are. Anyway, hang in there!

Miss you too,
Stella

April 18, 2152

Dear Stella,

Tell Lukas and Hiroshi I said hi back.

It's so boring here. I'm in school, but the classes are way smaller than on the *Messenger*. I don't even know what I'm going to pick as my vocation now. I always wanted to be a teacher, but it would be so boring with so few students. Are you still going to be a journalist?

My mom has been busy setting up a council. There are a few *Leigh Brackett* people on it, but mostly, it's people from the *Messenger*, like us. The *Messenger* people are there to lead, and the *Leigh Brackett* people are there to advise since they know their people better.

Speaking of the *Leigh Brackett* people . . . it's hard to make friends with them. They call themselves "LBs" for *Leigh Brackett* —at first, I thought they were saying "elby," and I was so confused! So, I've mostly been hanging out with other kids from *Messenger* families, although there aren't many of us. My mom says I'll make new friends, but she doesn't get it. I don't want *new* friends. I want my *old* friends!

Everyone keeps saying they're happy that we've come to help, but they don't look happy when they think we're not look-ing. Even though we brought rations, I think they feel like we're a burden. It's always on the news how we can't waste a single scrap now that the Earth won't be bringing us supplies any time soon. Do you think anyone is even still alive down there?

I never thought I'd say it, but I even miss Lindsay and Qin and all the stupid drama. We didn't get along, but at least we were honest about it. I can't figure out which LB kids in my class actually like me and which are just being polite. It sounds weird, but I'd be kind of relieved to find out someone hated my guts because then I'd at least be making an impression.

As soon as I can, I'm coming back to the *Messenger*. With or without my mom. I'll be a teenager next month, and then before you know it, I'll be eighteen and *freeee*!

Miss you,
Isla

April 25, 2152

Dear Isla,

Your mom being in government is actually kind of cool. I was going to be a journalist, but now that we have Stadtholder Adelheid leading the *Messenger*, she's inspired me to think about a career in politics. Like, now that the *Messenger* has colonies, we have to keep good relationships with them and take care of them. We're learning about it now in civics class, different kinds of governments and diplomacy. Diplomat Stella . . . I can almost picture it! Maybe I'd get to come to the *Leigh Brackett* on a mission and see you! Wouldn't that be cool?

Stella

April 26, 2152

Dear Stella,

You'd make a great diplomat. But don't worry about visiting the *Leigh Brackett*—by the time you're a diplomat, I'll already be back on the *Messenger*. Maybe I'll be a cook because no one should have to eat food this bad. There must be a way to make protein loaf taste good without Earth supplies . . . I know Venus is really far away, but maybe there's a way to get some of their honey to Mercury?

Speaking of trading . . . I really miss meeting up at Terminal. I always looked forward to docking there and having a big party with everyone from the *Hermes* and the *Apollo*. I never thought about the other latitude towns and how they could only send a few people in land speeders to trade and catch up.

Since my mom is mayor, she's leading the *Leigh Brackett* delegation to Terminal next week. I begged her to take me along, but she says they've only got fuel for one land speeder, and all the seats are taken by council members. It's so unfair! I haven't seen you in ages, and it's not like I take up much room!

Oh, and some of my LB classmates have started calling me Your Grace because my mom is mayor, ha ha, so funny. Did I mention how much I hate it here?

Miss you,
Isla

May 17, 2152

Dear Isla,

I'm sorry you missed Terminal! I think I saw your mom meeting with Stadtholder Adelheid. Lukas, Hiroshi, Qin, and I snuck into one of the receptions and stayed up until past midnight! There was hellfire to pay when our parents finally found us, but it was so much fun. Wish you could have been there!

Stella

May 18, 2152

Dear Stella,

How are things going? How are Lukas and Hiroshi? And Qin
—you went to Terminal with her, are you friends now?

I can't believe I've only been here for a month. It feels like a
year already. The longest, worst year of my life.

We finally have more food, but it's still gross, so I don't know
if that's a plus or not. I don't feel like celebrating my birthday
tomorrow, but I know my mom will try to make a big deal out
of it even though I won't be having a party. At least I'm finally
going to be a teenager, which means I'm even closer to coming
back to the *Messenger*!

Miss you,
Isla

May 21, 2152

Dear Stella,

My birthday wasn't actually that bad. I mean, it wasn't great
since you and Lukas and Hiroshi weren't there, but my mom
took me to work with her instead of sending me to school, and
everyone was really nice. I got to check out the new council
chambers and sit in the mayor's chair. I can't believe I'm finally
a teenager!

Hope to hear from you soon. What are you going to do for
your birthday? Are you having a party? I wish I could come.

Miss you,
Isla

June 10, 2152

Dear Stella,

Are you okay? I haven't heard any bad news about the *Messenger* or anything, but since I didn't hear from you on my birthday I got worried that maybe something had happened to you. Anyway, please let me know you're okay.

Miss you,
Isla

[No further messages]

REFERENDUM
September 2196

The latitude town known as the Leigh Brackett
Mercury Colonies, September 16, 2196

"I KNOW this is the last class of the day, but I have you for the next thirty minutes, so please focus . . . Aiden, that means you."

Aiden's head jerked up from his screen, where he'd been busy outlining his next article for the *Leigh Brackett High News*. Civics class might help him become a better journalist, but it was so dry. He had no idea why the teacher was calling on him —had she asked him a question?

He was saved by Mina, who tended to dominate the class discussions. "Ms. Yoshida, do you think the *Messenger* is going to accept the referendum results if the *Leigh Brackett* votes to be independent? Or is there going to be a war?" Mina was training to join the Security Guild. Did she *want* to see action? Hadn't she studied what happened the last time the *Leigh Brackett* was at war?

The upcoming referendum was the hottest topic on Mercury. The news screens were full of "Vote Yes" and "Vote No" ads and heated discussions, not just from *Leigh Brackett* pundits but from Journalists' Guild offices across Mercury. It had also become a frequent lunchtime topic at Aiden's school, where even kids like him from *Messenger* families were finding themselves unsure how—or whether—to defend the hometown they'd never even visited.

"Queen Beatrix will never let the *Leigh Brackett* separate," said Aiden's friend, Niall Rance. "It would be more expensive for the *Messenger*. And super embarrassing. Plus, it could start independence movements in the other colony towns."

"What if all the colonies petitioned for independence at once?" asked Petros. Like Niall, he was from a *Messenger* family. Unlike Niall, he was dating an LB classmate and openly pro-independence, even though, like the rest of the class, he was seventeen and therefore not eligible to vote. "The *Messenger* wouldn't be able to quell all those revolutions at once!"

"Quell revolutions? The *Messenger* isn't about to open fire on its own colony," said Niall. "After all, they saved the *Leigh Brackett* after the *Apollo* attacked us. And a lot of us are originally from the *Messenger* anyway."

"Speak for yourself," said Mina. "My grandparents were both born on the *Leigh Brackett*. That makes me third-generation. And I don't consider Beatrix my queen. I've never even seen her in person!"

"Who has?" said Niall. "And most of our parents were born here too. Just because my grandparents were born on the *Messenger* doesn't mean my family doesn't belong here."

"I'm not saying *Messenger* descendants don't belong here," replied Mina. "Just that they shouldn't be in charge of everything. They're only about a third of the population, but they make up two-thirds of our council. Mayor McGill wasn't even born on the *Messenger*."

"The only reason *Messenger* people are in charge is because *your* ancestors *begged* them to be. That's how the *Leigh Brackett* became a colony in the first place."

"If you love the *Messenger* so much, you're welcome to go back there."

"Believe me, I would if I could."

"Settle down," called Ms. Yoshida. "There's no need for a civil war in our own classroom. But it's a good question: what do you think might change if the *Leigh Brackett* becomes an independent town instead of a *Messenger* colony?"

Aiden tuned out again; the news screens were always on at his house and he was sick of hearing all the theories about what would and wouldn't change: mostly taxes, trade, and politics. Besides, whether the *Leigh Brackett* became independent or not, he intended to move to the *Messenger* for work after graduation, so it wouldn't affect him anyway.

FINALLY, civics class was over, and Aiden was free to head to the school's Journalists' Guild office. It looked like a standard classroom, with chairs and screens, but the chairs were arranged in a large circle and each screen was displaying a different news broadcast on mute. It looked chaotic if you weren't used to it, but by now, the busy screens faded into the background for him.

He took his usual seat in the circle of chairs next to Niall.

"Okay, folks," said Mr. Kerrigan, bringing the group to order. "I know you've all got pieces you're working on, but I've got some exciting news: the *Leigh Brackett Voice* is putting together a special edition about the upcoming referendum, and they've agreed to feature some student pieces."

Aiden felt an electric buzz go around the room. So far, their work had only appeared in their school newsfeed and was read mostly by other teenagers and, sometimes, their parents. Getting a story in the *Leigh Brackett Voice* was a chance to prove their skills and perhaps secure a junior reporter gig after graduation. It certainly wouldn't hurt if the *Voice*'s star broadcaster, Bobi Lum, knew your name. *It might also get the attention of the* Messenger's *Journalists' Guild Office*, thought Aiden.

"I have a few ideas," continued Mr. Kerrigan, "but let me hear your pitches."

This was Aiden's favourite part of journalism class: selling a story. Often, he would only have a spark of an idea when he raised his hand and would flesh it out as he pitched it, propelled by adrenaline. He searched his mind for something he could build on, cursing himself for not paying closer attention to the referendum news.

"I want to write about the history of the *Leigh Brackett*," said Halia. "My grandparents say that we used to learn a lot more about it in school before the *Messenger* took over. Now, our history classes are split equally among all nineteen latitude towns, even the ones that are dead, so we only learn a bit about our own home."

Aiden rolled his eyes. The LB kids were all alike; only they could think it was an issue to learn about different towns. That's why none of them ever talked about wanting to leave the *Leigh Brackett*.

"Great, Halia," said Mr. Kerrigan, typing it into the screen. "But let's keep it to highlights—perhaps a timeline? We need to keep the reader's attention. You can link to sources for more information."

Halia nodded. Aiden was sure she'd include more links than timeline points.

"I want to write about the *Messenger* and how they fought the *Apollo*," said Beckett. "Both my grandparents were part of that battle. They don't like to talk about it, but they're always saying how important it is to pass down family knowledge, so I bet they'll agree to it."

"A firsthand account—sounds great," said Mr. Kerrigan. He added it to the screen. "Symone, can you write a short piece on the difference between a colony and an independent town? Compare how government works, trading relationships ... does that make sense?"

"Sounds like homework," muttered Symone, but he didn't protest further.

Mr. Kerrigan stepped back to survey the screen. "The *Voice* may not have room for all of our stories, but this looks like a good list. Does anyone have any other ideas?"

Aiden still hadn't thought of a good angle. Feeling the opportunity slipping away, he panicked and blurted out the first thing that came to mind. "Maybe I could interview some *Messenger* families? See how they feel about the referendum?"

"Um, aren't we supposed to be impartial?" asked Halia. "Interviewing only *Messenger* folks sounds more like *propaganda* to me."

Aiden felt his face grow hot. He could feel the LB kids smirking at him and the other *Messenger* kids stiffening with anger on his behalf. As he tried to think of a retort, Mr. Kerrigan addressed him. "Aiden, I like the interview angle. We need some video content—why don't you interview a few citizens for their opinions? Halia's right: look for people with different backgrounds so that you can present multiple perspectives. The human-interest angle would make for very compelling storytelling."

"Okay." Aiden let go of a breath he hadn't realized he'd been holding. It wasn't going to be easy—especially finding LB people who would agree to be interviewed by him—but it would make a great portfolio piece. And he'd need it—he'd be going up against every journalism grad who wanted a spot on the *Messenger*, so competition would be as fierce as the Sun.

He left the guild office with a spring in his step, already picturing his byline in the *Voice*.

HE MADE it home just as his dad was putting the finishing touches on dinner. Aiden set the table, and his dad served up three plates of food and took his seat. "How was school?"

Aiden shared the news about his *Voice* assignment. "I have to interview some people about the referendum."

"What kind of people?"

"Like, regular people. People who were born here, people who came here from the *Messenger*. People who were here when the *Apollo* attacked. Different perspectives."

"Hmm. I can put you in touch with my friend Frank Furlong; he moved here from the *Messenger* years before I did."

"Thanks. I know a lot of people who were born here, but it's gonna be harder to find someone who lived through the *Apollo*'s attack." Aiden left the rest of his thought, *and who will agree to be interviewed by me*, unsaid.

The door opened, and Aiden's mom strode in, eyes glued to the screen in her hand. Her dark hair was pulled back in a bun, but it was falling out of place, strands escaping all over. As mayor of the *Leigh Brackett*, she was always stressed, but lately, she'd been working even longer hours. She washed her hands and joined them at the table, planting a kiss on Aiden's head and then her husband's. "Dinner looks great!"

Aiden filled her in on his assignment and wasn't surprised when she produced a name instantly. "Talk to Cynthia Niu. She was my age when I came here, and we were in the same class. I got to know her pretty well. We haven't spoken in a while, but I'm sure she'd be happy to help with your story."

Would she? wondered Aiden. She'd feel obligated to, of course. Aiden's mom had been part of the first wave of help from the *Messenger*; his dad hadn't come until years later. Aiden's mom liked to joke that that was why she got married and had him so late—she was waiting for the perfect *Messenger* man to arrive. Which was why Aiden's parents were so much older than his friends' parents, most of whom were born on the *Leigh Brackett*.

Aiden put his doubts aside and noted FRANK FURLONG and CYNTHIA NIU on his screen. "This piece could be good for my portfolio," he said. "Especially if I'm sending it to the *Messenger*'s Journalists' Guild office."

"Wonderful," said his mom. "I still know some folks there, so I can also put in a good word for you."

"I want to earn a job, Mom."

"You'd still be earning it! I just don't want you being from the *Leigh Brackett* to be a disadvantage, that's all."

"Okay." Aiden knew it was pointless to argue with his mom, but he was determined to get a position on his own merits. If his assignment went well, perhaps Bobi Lum would agree to be his mentor and put him in touch with some of her contacts.

Well, he could dream, anyway.

THE INTERVIEWS
Published in the *Leigh Brackett High News* and reposted in the
Leigh Brackett Voice
October 10, 2196

VIDEO INTERVIEW 1: CYNTHIA NIU

How old were you when the Earth went silent?

I was twelve. I lived with my younger brother and my parents in the second-to-last section of the *Leigh Brackett*. It had six sections back then. Not like now.

At first, I didn't know what it meant when I heard that Earth had cut off contact. I thought maybe they were mad at Mercury for something. There had been trade disputes before, but usually, the grownups would grumble for a few weeks, and then things would be back to normal. I'd never even seen someone from Earth—since the *Leigh Brackett* just sent land speeders to Terminal for trading, I never went to the big receptions hosted by the *Apollo*, the *Messenger*, and the *Hermes*. Sometimes, I would watch the broadcasts of the ceremonies, but they never really felt real.

It didn't take long for me to realize that this time was different. The adults weren't mad; they were scared. It was unnerving seeing all the people who were in charge look so worried and lost.

Even now, if I think about those days, my stomach aches. My family had always had enough to eat, even if we'd never had lavish feasts like I saw in the Terminal receptions. But within a week or so of the Earth going silent, I realized that our portions were getting smaller, and there were no more snacks. We had to conserve our supplies because we didn't know when —or if—the Earth would be bringing more.

Back then, I didn't know how my parents weren't hungry; they didn't eat with us at dinner and said they'd eat later. They acted like they were totally fine. It wasn't until I was much older that I realized they were giving us most of their rations. They were slowly starving to death.

What do you remember about the Apollo attacking?

I remember waking up to loud noises and my parents pulling me and my brother out of bed and rushing us out of our home. We were evacuating to the front of the *Leigh Brackett* because the back was under attack. I didn't have time to take anything.

There were so many people, so many families. You had to stay close, or you'd get swept away with the crowd and lost. My brother was crying because he was scared and tired, but he was too big to carry.

I remember everyone's faces because they all looked the same. Wide, unseeing eyes. Grim expressions.

When the blasts hit the tail of the *Leigh Brackett*, we all felt it. I was worried that our whole town was going to fall right off our Robinson Rails. We didn't know how bad the damage was but we kept running forward, forward, forward. Even my brother moved faster.

It smelled smoky, like down in the trackworks. And it was so noisy, with alarms going off and people screaming and crying. I was too shocked to scream, but I remember that my tears soaked my shirt, and I was damp and cold. I wanted to change my shirt, but all of my belongings were back in my room, and I didn't know if my home still existed.

We kept pushing forward, from one section of our town into the next. I was so tired, and I wanted to use one of the shuttles, but they were all full, and my parents didn't want to wait in line for an empty one. Suddenly, there was a blast that was bigger than the rest, and the *Leigh Brackett* lurched to one side. Everyone fell on top of each other in a huge pile. I couldn't breathe or see. I was sure that was it, that we were all going to die. I even remember giving up and accepting it as I lost consciousness.

What happened next?

When I woke up, most people were sitting huddled together on the floor. A few were standing. Everyone was talking, but it blended into a low murmur. I noticed a pile of clothes in a far corner. I remember wondering where they'd come from. Maybe there was a dry shirt there that would fit me.

Then, someone dragged a lifeless body over to the pile and added it to the others. And I realized that it was everyone who'd suffocated or been trampled or crushed to death. It wasn't a very big pile, thankfully, but it was still too many people. Too many neighbours, friends, family members. Children like me.

When I looked back the way we'd come, I realized that it looked different. Darker. It took me a long time to realize that we had become the tail section of the *Leigh Brackett* because the sections behind us were gone. And I knew not everyone had made it out. The last shuttle—the one my parents didn't let us get on—never arrived.

Why didn't the Apollo *finish you off?*

Honestly, I don't know. Maybe their land speeders were running out of fuel, or maybe they'd taken everything they could carry back to the *Apollo*. I assume they planned to come back for more, but thankfully, the *Messenger* got to them first.

How did you feel about becoming a colony of the Messenger?

It wasn't really a choice. We were a tiny, damaged town, and we needed someone bigger and more powerful to help us get back on our feet. We needed all the help and supplies we could get to survive and rebuild. And we needed protection in case something similar happened in the future.

We'd lost so many people, and everyone left was traumatized; we would have had trouble keeping order on our own. It felt like joining a family, in a way. We've developed closer relationships with the *Messenger* and its other colonies than we had before the Earth went silent. So, there have been a lot of benefits.

Will you be voting for the Leigh Brackett *to gain its independence?*

I don't want to seem ungrateful, I really don't. But . . . it's been almost forty-five years. We're stable now. We don't need any extra help from the *Messenger* and we haven't for a while. It doesn't make sense to have the *Messenger* running our council.

If becoming a colony was like joining the *Messenger* family, becoming independent is like moving out. We'll still always be family, but that doesn't mean we have to live together.

VIDEO INTERVIEW 2: FRANK FURLONG

Why did you choose to come to the Leigh Brackett?

AFTER THE *APOLLO* WAS DEFEATED, Stadtholder Adelheid asked for volunteers to go to the other latitude towns and help. Some of the towns had been completely destroyed—so if you volunteered to go to one of those, it was a scavenging mission, you understand? You'd go assess the damage, see if the town could be rebuilt. If not, you'd salvage whatever was still usable for the *Messenger* and the other colonies. Metal. Screws. Wires. Fabric. Scraps of food. Anything you could transport, really. We couldn't afford to waste a thing since we didn't know if the Earth would ever send more supplies. We didn't even know if anyone was still alive on Earth.

I guess that's not something you kids even think about now, right? You learn about Earth in your history classes but you were born into a world where it might well have never existed. You've never known what it was like to have supplies arrive from there, stuff that we don't have on Mercury. Stuff we've had to learn to live without.

Anyway, I thought about helping with the scavenging, but those kinds of missions sounded too depressing. And I didn't need more of that. Life on the *Messenger* was all I'd ever known, but it was also full of bad memories. So, starting over in a new place was appealing. My wife, daughter, and I arrived in June 2152. My son was born here two years later.

I knew your grandma. She was really influential back then, just like your mom is now. Like mother, like daughter. She helped a lot of people and sacrificed a lot. I'm sorry you never got to meet her.

How did the Leigh Brackett *people treat you?*

At first, they were really relieved to see us. They needed a lot of help. A *lot*. They'd lost their leadership, most of their military, and a fair number of their trackworkers. I'm an engineer, so I headed up their Trackworkers' Guild to get things functional again. It was dirty, dangerous work, but I'm used to that. It feels good to make a difference. Without working tracks, there wouldn't be a town, you know? The Sun never stops, and we can't afford to, either.

Anyway, mostly folks were nice. There was always a bit of distance. People don't like to feel like they're getting charity, like they're worse off. Sometimes, I think they resented us for not losing anyone in the attacks, even though we had our own tough times on the *Messenger*.

Will you be voting for the Leigh Brackett *to gain its independence?*

Maybe? To be honest, I don't know. The *Leigh Brackett* folks have a bigger stake in this than those of us who came from the

Messenger. I don't know how it would change things to be an independent town again. I just hope that people will keep their heads on both sides.

Will you return to the Messenger if the Leigh Brackett *becomes* independent?

I've lived here more than half my life. My son was born here, and my daughter doesn't remember her life back on the *Messenger.* They both have their own families now, and I don't think they'd go with me if I left. And my wife would never leave her grandkids, no way, no how! Besides, I'm too old to start over now. This is my home now, colony or not.

VIDEO INTERVIEW 3: STUART RANCE

You were born on the Leigh Brackett: *do you consider yourself a* Leigh Brackett *citizen?*

THE *LEIGH BRACKETT* is a colony of the *Messenger,* which is where my family is from. So, I'm a citizen of the *Messenger* who happens to live on the *Leigh Brackett.* That's how I see it, and I know a lot of people agree with me. Even if some of them are afraid to say it, it's just the truth.

Do you like living on the **Leigh Brackett?**

I haven't lived anywhere else, so I don't have much to compare it to, but yeah. It's a good town with good people. Apart from this referendum nonsense, there isn't a thing I'd change.

Have you considered moving to the **Messenger?**

I'd love to, but it's not that easy. Their town is much bigger than ours, but it's not like they have a bunch of extra space—they've got the largest population on Mercury. And it wouldn't just be me, it would be all my relatives. I couldn't just take my husband and kids and leave my parents, my brothers, and my nieces and nephews behind. Family is everything. We'd all have to find new jobs, new homes, new friends . . . it just doesn't feel fair that *Messenger* families like mine will feel like they're not welcome on the *Leigh Brackett* if it's no longer a colony.

What will you do if the **Leigh Brackett** *votes for independence?*

Listen, the *Leigh Brackett* is stable and successful now *because* of the *Messenger*. Why would we want to risk changing that? If the *Leigh Brackett* votes for independence, I hope the *Messenger* says no for the colony's own good. Or, at the very least, I hope they'll send land speeders to take back all their citizens who won't want to live here anymore. It won't be easy for us to start over, but it will be our only choice. This place is going to fall apart if it's not allied with the *Messenger*, and I don't want to be here to watch.

VIDEO INTERVIEW 4: FELICITY KERRIGAN

You were born on the **Leigh Brackett,** *right?*

YES, in 2176. My dad—your teacher—was born here in 2151. He was a baby when the *Apollo* attacked. He and his mom survived, but his dad and three of his grandparents didn't. He says the food shortage after the Earth went silent is the reason his generation is shorter than their children . . . not enough protein when they were growing up.

So, you and your father have never known the Leigh Brackett *as an independent town?*

My grandmother tells us lots of stories about what it was like before the *Leigh Brackett* became a colony of the *Messenger*, but no, we've never experienced it firsthand.

What do you think will change if the Leigh Brackett *is independent?*

Well, we'll have our own independent Security Guild again, which is important. It's great to have the *Messenger*'s protection, but I think every town also needs to be able to defend itself, just in case.

As an independent town, we'll be able to negotiate and build our own relationships with all latitude towns on Mercury, including the *Messenger*. We know quite a lot about the *Messenger*—I know more about Queen Beatrix and Queen Dowager Adelheid than I do about the *Leigh Brackett*'s past leaders. But I don't think they really know much about us. It would be nice to build a more equal partnership with them.

What do you think about people who say they'll return to the Messenger *if the* Leigh Brackett *becomes independent?*

I hope all the *Messenger* members of the council decide to go back or at least step down. It's about time that the *Leigh Brackett* was governed by people who answer to our town, not to the *Messenger* . . . no offence.

A VISIT FROM *THE MESSENGER*
October 2196

THE *LEIGH BRACKETT VOICE* did not publish all of the submissions from Aiden's class: they chose Halia's timeline, Beckett's article about the *Messenger*'s battle against the *Apollo*, and four of Aiden's eight video interviews. Within a day, Aiden's interviews went viral. He watched as they were reposted on newsfeeds from across Mercury, including the *Messenger*'s. By the day after that, the pundits were publishing their own responses.

Cynthia, Frank, Stuart, and Felicity were becoming mini-celebrities on the *Leigh Brackett*. Stuart found himself thrust into the role of pro-*Messenger* spokesperson, although he did not appear to be comfortable with public speaking. The other interviewees did their best to stay out of the spotlight.

Overnight, Aiden became the centre of attention at school. Kids he'd never spoken to, both LB and *Messenger*, wanted to know if he thought the *Leigh Brackett* would vote for independence and what side he was on. Niall also found himself in the same situation, as his uncle's interview had been the only pro-*Messenger* viewpoint that the *Voice* chose to publish. Aiden wondered if Niall was regretting volunteering his uncle as an interview subject; he wasn't used to being in the public eye.

Outside of school, Aiden was being bombarded with interview requests from all over Mercury, which his parents agreed he shouldn't respond to. He wasn't sure if they were more proud or annoyed—certainly, they hadn't expected his school project to gain planet-wide traction. But the October 17 referendum was the hottest news story on Mercury, and Aiden's name was now connected to it. He hoped that Bobi Lum knew who he was now, although no one from the *Voice* had reached out to him.

A few days after Aiden's videos went viral, the *Messenger*

announced that they were sending a delegation to the *Leigh Brackett* in advance of the referendum. This announcement unleashed a new wave of speculation: how many people would be in the delegation? Would Queen Beatrix be part of it? How long would they stay? Were they coming to observe, or did they intend to influence—or even stop—the referendum? The *Leigh Brackett Voice* was all over it; Bobi Lum assured their viewership —which was now planet-wide—that they would be covering it live on behalf of the Journalists' Guild.

October 16, 2196

THE *MESSENGER* DELEGATION was slated to arrive the day before the referendum, which the pundits generally agreed did not bode well for the vote proceeding as planned. There was a nervous energy in the air that Sunday morning as the arrival time drew nearer. The landing bays were blocked off with barricades and security, so people congregated in the main agora. Aiden noted that some of the men had weapons hanging from their belts. Surely they weren't expecting a fight with the *Messenger* visitors? Or each other? Ms. Yoshida's admonishment about not starting a civil war in the classroom came to mind.

Finally, the delegation arrived: five land speeders, a sizable amount. Surely that meant Queen Beatrix had come after all? Aiden found himself jostling the crowd for a better view, thankful for his recent growth spurt. He was hoping that the large screens around the agora would show a broadcast of the inside of the landing bays, but instead, they displayed a view of the balcony where his mom and the council members were waiting to receive their guests. The feed had a line of text scrolling along the bottom: "*Leigh Brackett* Voice—Live!" He searched the crowd until he spotted five people from the *Voice* set up a few metres to his right.

Aiden manoeuvred through the crowd until he reached the news crew. This was a perfect opportunity to watch live reporting firsthand and perhaps strike up a conversation with them once the broadcast was done. He'd let them know that he was the one who had done those viral interviews, and then everything would flow from there.

When the *Messenger* delegation filed out onto the balcony, all dressed in smart navy blue dress uniforms, Aiden noted that they were all quite tall and muscular. Were politicians on the *Messenger* so different from those on the *Leigh Brackett*? And wait ... were they armed? The *Voice* crew appeared to be having the same thoughts as he watched them zoom in on the delegation. Aiden had never seen a delegation from the *Messenger*, but he was also surprised to count two dozen members. They could have fit in two land speeders; why did five ships arrive? Perhaps they had brought supplies or gifts? Otherwise, it was a waste of precious fuel to travel with only four or five people per vehicle.

Flanked by several members of the delegation was a graceful woman whose outfit stood out from the others. She was wearing the same navy blue uniform, but it looked more ceremonial and included a bright orange sash draped over one shoulder. She looked regal, but not like any of the images of Queen Beatrix that Aiden had seen. She walked over to Aidan's mom and bowed her head slightly. "Mayor McGill. Isla. So good to see you again."

The camera zoomed in on Aidan's mom, who smiled tightly. "Ambassador Cooper. The *Leigh Brackett* welcomes you and your delegation. It is an honour to receive you."

"Please, call me Stella," the ambassador said with a smile. She looked out at the crowd. "Thank you for your warm welcome. I bring greetings on behalf of Queen Beatrix and the *Messenger*. We are eager to work together to strengthen the prosperous partnership between the *Leigh Brackett* and the *Messenger*."

Aidan's mom turned to face the crowd beneath her in the agora. "Ambassador Cooper and her delegation will now meet with the council of the *Leigh Brackett*."

There was a low murmur from the crowd; Aiden could hear snippets of the concerned whispers. He'd expected the loyalist *Messenger* families to be excited about the delegation—many of them had dressed in the traditional navy blue of the *Messenger* for the occasion—but everyone seemed unnerved by the size and distinctly military appearance of the delegation.

"I will have more to share with you all after these talks. And tonight we will honour our guests with a reception . . . I look forward to seeing many of you there." Aiden watched as his mom bowed, then turned and led the ambassador to the council chambers behind them.

"We'll have more for you once the *Leigh Brackett* council and the *Messenger* delegation return," promised the *Voice* newscaster, standing with the now-empty balcony as her backdrop. "Until then, let's hear some early analysis from Bobi Lum."

Aiden tried not to stare too obviously as Bobi entered the frame, brushed her asymmetrical black and red bangs away from her face, and began to speak.

THE COUNCIL CHAMBERS had high ceilings and a long table lined with chairs that were more utilitarian than comfortable. One of the walls featured a ceiling-to-floor portrait of Mercury, with all nineteen latitude towns labelled. The remaining three walls bore large screens set to a live feed of the stars outside, creating the impression that the council was floating in outer space.

Mayor McGill took the seat at the head of the table and offered

Ambassador Cooper the seat to her right. The rest of the council took their seats. There were several empty chairs, but the *Messenger* delegation chose to stand along the walls, silent and stony-faced.

"Would it not make sense to start with an initial meeting before taking up the time of the entire council?" asked Ambassador Cooper.

"The council values transparency and collaboration. I wouldn't feel right meeting with representatives of the *Messenger* without them present. But on that note, surely some of your delegation could remain outside of the chambers? We weren't expecting quite so many of you to attend, and we don't have enough chairs."

"Oh, they're fine standing. They're professionals. And if you're sure you'd like to have the council present, we can proceed. But I do hope this discussion will not be too awkward."

"And why would it be awkward?"

Ambassador Cooper paused, fiddling with the gold braiding on her sleeve before gathering her thoughts and fixing the mayor with her gaze. "You say your council values transparency, so I will speak plainly. The independence movement on the *Leigh Brackett* has caused the *Messenger* to doubt whether you are fit to continue leading."

If she was surprised, Mayor McGill's expression did not show it. "Why is that?"

"Surely, with the right leadership, the people of the *Leigh Brackett* would be honoured to be part of the *Messenger*'s family and would not feel that they had anything to gain by severing those ties. Are they not aware of the benefits of the *Messenger*'s protection?"

Before the mayor could answer, one of the council members spoke. "Excuse me, Ambassador. My name is Leslie Andrews, and I want to say that the *Leigh Brackett* has faith in Mayor

McGill. Her willingness to let the people have their say in a referendum is proof of her leadership."

"I was against it at first," added another council member. "Most of the council was. But we heard a number of compelling arguments from the public, and it was clear that there was widespread support for a referendum."

"It didn't happen overnight," said Andrews. "This issue has been brought to the council numerous times over the years."

"How interesting that I had not heard about it until now, then," said the ambassador.

"It was mentioned in my regular reports to Queen Beatrix," said Mayor McGill. "But this is the first time we reached the point of declaring a referendum."

Ambassador Cooper surveyed the council with heightened interest. "How many of you on this council are originally from the *Messenger*?"

Eight of the twelve council members slowly raised a hand, including the mayor.

"Eight to four. With that majority, surely *Messenger* members are able to veto any measures that the *Leigh Brackett* members propose?"

"Technically, yes," said Mayor McGill, "although we strive for consensus, so it rarely comes to that."

"And yet the council—including you, Mayor—did not veto the motion to hold a referendum on the *Leigh Brackett*'s independence?"

"As the council has stated, the people wanted a referendum. We are leaders, not dictators. We are charged with acting in the *Leigh Brackett*'s best interests."

"Even when those go against the *Messenger*'s best interests?"

"Is a referendum really against the *Messenger*'s best interests? I expect Queen Beatrix would want to know how the people in her colonies truly feel. This is her opportunity."

"Indeed." Ambassador Cooper rose. "Thank you all for sharing your perspectives. While I respect your council's values and protocols, I must insist on a private audience with Mayor McGill on behalf of the *Messenger*. Thank you for your understanding."

She smoothly swept one arm toward the chamber doors. The *Messenger* delegates nearest to the doors moved forward and opened them.

For a few tense moments, no one moved. Then, the mayor gave a slight nod, and the council members rose as one and slowly filed out, followed by the *Messenger* delegation.

The last two *Messenger* delegates paused and looked to the ambassador. "Go ahead," Stella said. "The two of you can stay just outside. I'll be fine." They nodded and left, closing the doors behind them.

THE COUNCIL CHAMBERS felt cavernous now that just the two women remained. After allowing the silence to settle, the mayor addressed her guest. "Ambassador Cooper, what private message does the *Messenger* have for me?"

The ambassador sighed. "Isla, please call me Stella. Why are you acting like you don't know me?"

"The last time I saw you, we were twelve. And then you stopped answering my letters. You haven't been a part of my life for almost forty-five years."

Stella looked down, hands in her lap. "You were my best friend. But I didn't know when I'd ever see you again, and I just . . . ran out of things to say." After a beat, she met Isla's gaze. "You said you'd come back to the *Messenger* as soon as you were an adult. I half expected you to show up at my door on your eighteenth birthday!"

Isla smiled, allowing herself to indulge in nostalgia for a moment. "That was always the plan. As soon as I could, I was going to find my way home."

"Well, you don't have to wait anymore." Stella's tone became official and practised. "On behalf of Queen Beatrix, I am hereby relieving you of your position as mayor and transferring you back to the *Messenger*."

"And what if I resign? I've been mayor for almost twenty-five years, after all. Perhaps the *Leigh Brackett* would benefit from some new blood."

Stella smiled. "In that case, I would be happy to accept your resignation."

"Then I resign . . . and will stay on the *Leigh Brackett*."

Stella's smile dropped. "But why?" Seeing Isla's expression, she quickly composed herself. "I'm afraid that's not an option. Queen Beatrix was quite clear on that point."

"You're sending me back in disgrace?" asked Isla.

"On the contrary, the *Messenger* thanks you for your service, and you and your family will be welcomed back warmly. There will be many opportunities waiting for you." Stella adjusted her sash. "Isla, I know you've built a life here, and people look up to you. But that's precisely why you can't stay. It would be unfair for a new mayor to compete with that . . . it will be a smoother transition for everyone this way."

"A new mayor . . .?"

"Well, now that you've resigned, the *Messenger* will need to select your successor. I will serve as interim mayor until then, and my delegation will remain with me to ensure a smooth transition."

"Do I even have to ask whether you plan to proceed with the referendum?"

"It will be postponed until the new mayor is established. And if any of the council members resign, we'll need to replace them as well. That may take some time."

Isla slipped back into the mantle of mayor. "The people will recognize your delegation for what they are: soldiers. Their presence here will only increase the popularity of the independence movement. I fear you are acting rashly. Is this Queen Beatrix's direction?"

"As ambassador, I represent both Queen Beatrix and the *Messenger*." Stella stood. "Can I trust you to share this development with the public without inciting violence, or would you prefer that I deliver the news? I would hate for anyone to get hurt."

Isla rose to her feet and straightened her shoulders. "The people will take it better coming from me."

INDEPENDENCE
October 16, 2196

THE CROWD in the agora was restless. Aiden felt like it had been ages since the council and the delegation retired to the chambers, and then everyone except his mom and the ambassador had filed out, expressions grim. Now, the council members were lined up on the left side of the balcony, and the *Messenger* delegation stood on the right, closest to the chamber doors.

The *Voice* had long since run out of commentary and was now just broadcasting the tense scene on the balcony. When Aiden flipped through his newsfeeds, he saw that newscasts across Mercury had picked up the *Voice*'s feed and were rebroadcasting along with their own commentary to fill the dead air. He wondered how many people on the *Messenger* were watching.

Finally, the chamber doors opened, and Aidan's mom strode out, the ambassador on her heels. His mom stopped at the front of the centre of the balcony, overlooking the people gathered below. Everyone fell silent in anticipation.

"I was only twelve when I came here with my mother, and I spent years waiting until I would be old enough to return to the *Messenger* on my own," said his mom. "But during that time, I watched my mother, Morna McGill, assemble the first post-*Apollo* council. I saw how hard she worked to earn the trust of the *Leigh Brackett* survivors.

"She governed for twenty years, from the time the Earth went silent until Mercury had finally found its bearing as an independent planet and not an Earth colony. She saw us through famine, shortages of all kinds, uncertainty, and fear. Then, just as things were finally returning to a new stability and she was considering retiring, her heart gave out . . ."

Aidan's mom and the crowd fell silent together, remembering. When she spoke again, there was a new resolve in her voice. "When she died, so did my plan of returning to the *Messenger*. I'd spent years putting my life on hold because I thought my time here would be temporary. But I finally realized that the *Leigh Brackett* was where I belonged. There was nowhere that felt more like home than the council chambers.

"You all know the rest. I became the *Leigh Brackett*'s second mayor, attempting to pick up where my mother had left off. I moved forward with my life: I married, I had a son. I heard the people's calls for independence grow with each passing year, and this year—with the unanimous support of the council—I proposed a referendum." She glanced to her left; the *Voice* camera followed her gaze and zoomed in on the ambassador, who looked uncomfortable.

"I'm proud of my forty-four years on the *Leigh Brackett*," continued Aidan's mom. "I'm proud of this town, and I'm honoured to have been a part of it. But it's time for me—and the *Leigh Brackett*—to start a new chapter. Today, I am stepping down as mayor."

The camera panned the crowd to capture reactions—an instinct that was rewarded with looks of shock and dismay, Aiden's among them. The view returned to the two women on the balcony.

Ambassador Cooper took a few steps forward to bring herself in line with Aidan's mom. "Mayor McGill, the *Messenger* owes you a great debt for your twenty-five years of loyal service. You are leaving a legacy that will be forever remembered in the history of the *Leigh Brackett*, the *Messenger*, and Mercury itself."

The ambassador turned and bowed her head to Aidan's mom, then faced the crowd once more. "Citizens of the *Leigh Brackett*, though change is ever constant, it is rarely easy. Mayor McGill has served you faithfully, and I know you will miss her. But she and her family will be warmly welcomed back to the *Messenger*, and I will do my best to live up to her legacy and humbly serve as your interim mayor until the *Messenger* selects a suitable replacement."

"No more *Messenger* mayors!" rang out a voice from the crowd. It came from Aiden's left, and he watched as the *Voice*'s camera panned to find the source. Was that . . . Mina? She was only a metre or so away; how had he not noticed her before? The crowd took up the chant: "No *Messenger* mayors! No *Messenger* mayors! No *Messenger* mayors!"

"Please remain calm," said Ambassador Cooper. Aiden noted that she didn't look concerned . . . and then he caught flashes of navy blue in his peripheral vision. Scanning the agora, he saw that the *Messenger* delegation—soldiers, more like—were lining the perimeter. There were some near every exit, and they were armed. How had he missed their departure from the balcony? He quickly looked back up to the stage . . . but the *Messenger* delegation had not moved.

Which meant . . .

That's why there had been five land speeders instead of two. The *Voice*'s cameras had noticed the *Messenger* forces, too—

but the discovery was mutual. As the cameras zoomed in and panned, a group of *Messenger* soldiers approached the news crew.

"The *Messenger* believes in the freedom of the independent press," said Ambassador Cooper, "but we request that the broadcast be temporarily paused to avoid distraction and miscommunication."

Aiden stumbled as someone backed into him, knocking him off balance. It was Mina, and she'd brought friends. The students linked arms and began to create a barrier around Bobi Lum and the news crew. Without pausing to think, Aiden found himself squeezing into the middle of the circle before it was closed off. As he watched, more people from the crowd joined in, standing shoulder-to-shoulder and linking arms to create a second circle to shield the inner circle. Soon, there was a third circle and a fourth.

The group of *Messenger* soldiers slowed their approach. Aiden assumed they were evaluating the situation, although he couldn't see their faces behind the dark visors of their helmets.

"Bobi Lum, reporting live from the *Leigh Brackett*, where Mayor McGill has stepped down, and a surprise military force from the *Messenger* is moving in to cut our broadcast . . ."

Aiden was now shoulder-to-shoulder with Bobi as the circles of protection tightened. Bobi dropped her on-air persona for a moment to hiss, "Who are you?"

"A-adien. Aiden McGill."

Bobi studied his face. "Wait . . . McGill? You're the mayor's son?"

Aiden nodded. Not exactly how he'd intended to get Bobi Lum's attention, but he certainly had it now.

Bobi smoothly turned back to the camera. "I'm here with Mayor McGi—*ex*-Mayor McGill's—son, Aiden McGill. Aiden, you're from a *Messenger* family who's done very well on the

Leigh Brackett. What do you think about your mom stepping down? Do you think she wanted to, or was she forced?"

Aiden tried to ignore the *Messenger* soldiers who were closing in on the *Voice* crew. Were they going to open fire? Mina was part of the innermost circle; something about seeing her straight back and braced stance gave him courage.

As he looked into the camera, his stomach felt queasy, but that feeling was replaced with a familiar jolt of adrenaline that he recognized from journalism class: he was pitching a story. Except this time, he was pitching it to the *Messenger*.

"I can't speak for my mom," said Aiden. "I don't know what she and the ambassador talked about." Bobi looked disappointed, but Aiden pressed on. "But I learned a lot about the *Leigh Brackett* and the *Messenger* through my interviews. Cynthia Niu is only alive today because of the *Messenger*. Frank Furlong and countless others like him helped to rebuild this town after the *Apollo* tried to destroy it. They didn't have to. They could have stayed on the *Messenger*. They could have left the *Leigh Brackett* with half a town, wounded citizens, no military or leaders, and supplies that were running out. But they didn't. Because no matter what town you were born in, we are all Mercurians."

The crowd's murmurs told him he was on the right track. He allowed himself a quick scan of the agora; the *Messenger* soldiers still surrounded them, but they didn't appear to be advancing anymore, and their weapons were pointed down. Bobi nodded, and Aiden continued: "In 2152, the *Leigh Brackett* asked for help. And the *Messenger* helped. A lot. But now it's 2196, and the people of the *Leigh Brackett* are asking to speak. The *Messenger* should listen."

Bobi Lum tapped a finger to her earpiece. "We're receiving a broadcast from the *Messenger*. Please wait as we patch it in."

Bobi touched Aiden's arm, indicating he should turn and

face the balcony. As Bobi and Aiden turned together in the tight circle, the news crew pivoted to stay in front of them, now with their backs to the balcony. With the balcony in view, Aiden could see that half of the large screens were broadcasting him and Bobi. The other half were blank except for an icon indicating that a feed was being connected. And then the icon was replaced with . . . was that Queen Beatrix?

"Thank you, Aiden," said the queen. "And thank you, Bobi Lum, for patching me in. I've been following your coverage closely."

"Thank you, Be—Your Grace?" Bobi actually appeared flustered for once.

"When my mother, Queen Dowager Adelheid, sent help to the *Leigh Brackett* and other latitude towns, she intended it to be a temporary solution," Queen Beatrix said. "Over the years, the colony relationship became . . . more permanent. We were under the impression that this arrangement continued to be mutually beneficial. But now I see that we should have been listening more closely to make sure it was still serving you.

"We are not dictators," the queen continued. "Another thing my mother did was establish the Journalists' Guild and ensure that it would be independent of any town on Mercury, including the *Messenger*. I would like to thank journalists like you, Bobi Lum, for fulfilling their function and holding the *Messenger* accountable."

Aiden could see Bobi's cheeks redden. "Thank you, Your Grace. Uh . . . your thoughts, Mayor?"

The *Voice*'s camera zoomed in on the balcony. Ambassador Cooper had stepped back to join the *Messenger* delegation, leaving Aidan's mom at the front of the balcony. She addressed Queen Beatrix on the screen. "Your Grace, I appreciate the offer Ambassador Cooper extended to return to the *Messenger*. And while I wasn't planning on retiring just yet, I do think it's time that the *Leigh Brackett* had a new mayor . . . one that's not from the *Messenger*."

"I don't disagree, but your timing presents an issue . . . don't you have a referendum scheduled for tomorrow?" asked the queen.

"I do. *We* do. Will the *Messenger* respect the results of the referendum, whatever they may be?"

"We will," said Queen Beatrix. "I won't pretend that it won't make me sad if the *Leigh Brackett* chooses independence. But I remain hopeful that even if you do, you will still think fondly of the *Messenger* and be willing to build a new relationship together."

"You have my word," said Aidan's mother. "If the people of the *Leigh Brackett* will have me, I will resume my duties as mayor, and the referendum will take place tomorrow as planned." The ensuing roar from the crowd left no doubt that the people would indeed have her.

"Thank you, Mayor," said Queen Beatrix. "And thank you, people of the *Leigh Brackett*, for your cooperation. We will await your decision. Farewell for now!" She bowed to the screen and ended her broadcast.

People watching from all over Mercury were left with the sight of Aiden McGill and Bobi Lum, staring speechless into the camera. The silence was pierced by Mina breaking formation and leaning over Aiden to shout into the camera, "We did it!"

EPILOGUE
November 2196

THE FIRST PRESIDENT of the *Leigh Brackett*, Athena Kasimidi, worked closely with former mayor Isla McGill on the transition from a *Messenger*-controlled council to an elected government. The *Leigh Brackett* did not, as some had feared, descend into chaos and economic ruin. On the contrary, its people embraced their newfound independence with pride, even the *Messenger* families. Stuart Rance did not move his family back to the *Messenger*.

Nor did anyone else.

ON THIS DAY IN 2199

On this day, the Federation of Earth Nations launched a rocket from an old U.N.E. spaceport on the coast of the former Republic of Guyana.

THE ROCKET SHUDDERED AS THE ENGINES ENGAGED. G-FORCES pressed Pendrick and Fenning into their seats. The helmets muted the cacophony into a roar felt more in their chests than in their ears.

The radio hissed and spat. "Launch is confirmed. Telemetry is good. Good luck, crew of the *Endymion*, returning us to the Moon."

"Confirmed, Ground Control," Fenning replied. "We'll do you proud."

The skies outside the viewing port turned from grey to blue, then deeper blue, then black. Fenning and Pendrick focused on their dials and gauges as, in their ears, communications sputtered.

Pendrick switched to a private channel as the g-forces

eased. "Are you sure this ship is capable of reaching the Moon?"

Fenning nodded.

"And back?"

Fenning shrugged.

Pendrick goggled at him. "What—"

"It's fine," said Fenning. "Federation scientists have been working on this for years, reverse engineering components, restoring systems. This ship is as new as the day it was born." He calculated in his head. "Sixty-two years ago."

"But . . ." Pendrick tapped the controls in frustration. "Communication's so spotty with interference!"

"That's deliberate," Fenning replied. "To keep things quiet. We don't want the other planets to overhear us."

Pendrick stared at him. Fenning touched his controls. "Prepare for lunar insertion burn."

On this day, Jacqueline Khan sat beside her sister's hospital bed. Elizabeth was surprisingly perky for someone who had just been through yet another bout of spinal surgery. She had already asked twice for a tablet. "The stories are bouncing around inside my head," she said. "I need to let them out. Plus, I'm bored."

"You're always bored," said Jacqueline as she set up their next game of Go. They'd been playing together since childhood. It had always helped, she thought, to have something to do that required concentration, that could distract her from the constant pain and the restrictive exoskeleton. But even now, as she slid her first piece onto the board, she felt the disappointment tingle through her fingers as it stayed in place, not floating free, as limited by gravity as she was.

"WHY DON'T we just tell them?" Pendrick asked. In the rear viewport, the Earth shrank until it was framed by the casing. "Surely they'd want to know?"

"They've done without our presence for nearly fifty years," Fenning replied. "We don't know how they'll react when they learn we're returning. We've got to do this right."

There was a long pause. Then Pendrick looked ahead. "Okay." He touched his controls and tapped a gauge. "I'm starting to pick up the automated beacon from Eagle Platform." He peered closer. "The base appears to be on minimal power and life support."

"Nearly fifty years," Fenning muttered. "We're lucky to have even that. Good news."

"Plotting course for approach and landing." Pendrick flipped switches. "Earth Control has been informed." He grimaced. "Assuming they can hear us."

On this day, Anoush Ramaswamy and Arthur Windswept sat on opposite sides of the couch in their living area. It was a very small living area. It was a very small couch. The distance between them was more conceptual than physical. Ramaswamy was reading an academic paper on the possibility of communicating with extraterrestrial life on his comm. Windswept was reading The Collected Works of Chuck Tingle *on his comm. Eventually, he looked up and gently said, "It could be true."*

Ramaswamy snorted. "Not going to get fooled again," he grumped.

Windswept nodded. The pair went back to reading.

ON THE MOON, dust shifted for the first time in decades as the rocket's exhaust touched the surface. The decelerating *Endymion* eased onto its landing pad. Contacts rose up and engaged in silence. Lights around the landing bay flicked on.

"Good work," said Fenning in the cockpit. "We have a green board. Air supply connection with base confirmed." He started to unbuckle his restraints.

The oxygen indicators flashed green, and Pendrick flipped the catches on his helmet and pulled it off. He took a deep breath and let it out slowly. "It seems weird not to tell them," he said.

Fenning looked over at him. "Who?"

"The colonies. We used to have . . ." He waved a hand, then hesitated. "Grandpa . . .Grandpa told me stories about the U.N.E., how we built an empire of humanity throughout the inner solar system. Reached as far as the Jupiter moons, farther still by robot. And then . . ." He swallowed. "And then things fell apart. We used to have so much—"

"Eight billion more mouths to feed." Fenning faced the controls. "Plenty of good tech that we no longer have, yes, but the U.N.E. still let the collapse happen."

Pendrick frowned at Fenning. Fenning didn't look up from the controls. Silence stretched.

"The collapse happened under their watch," Fenning said at last. "Everything we had, gone because they couldn't stop it. The signs were there; they had to know what was coming. It didn't just suddenly happen. There was no last good day that everyone had before it all went to hell. That's privilege talking. The U.N.E. was either complacent or in denial."

He turned and stared hard at Pendrick. "We are going to be neither."

On this day, James sat jamming on his guitar, looking through the protective domed windows of his Mercurian home and out at the cosmos. He and Dan had written seven albums, although Lust Turkey *had been the most profitable by far. He wondered if he had another hit in him. He stared into the vacuum of space and said aloud, "On this day," once, twice. It had a good ring to it. It would make for a great song. Then Dan elbowed him out of the way and told him he had an even better song title. It was called "Rock Your Balls Off."*

THEY CLIMBED down the access ladder within the Endymion, Pendrick leading the way. At the base, Pendrick hovered by the hatch while Fenning checked the controls.

"We've got a good seal," said Fenning. "Pressure is point-nine normal, optimal oxygen-nitrogen mix. The air scrubbers seem to be functional." He smiled. "Not bad for nearly fifty years." He tapped in a code, and the door slid open, revealing a narrow corridor leading down to another door.

Their breath fogged and crystalized as they stepped onto the ramp, falling out of the air. Lines in their pressure suits glowed orange.

"What's our temperature?" asked Fenning.

Pendrick tapped at the screen on his wrist. He shivered and coughed, releasing a cloud. "Minus sixty-one. Think the whole base is like this?"

"Probably." Fenning clanked down the ramp. "At least, at first. No reason to keep the heat or lights on."

On this day, Nic stared at a heap of wet trash. Nic's mother had made them memorize the exact spot on the map where the rumoured refuge of Amberston stood just days before she was dragged away by Federation thugs in the middle of the night. But all Nic saw here was a flooded landfill and mountains of garbage.

Nic walked to a fork in the path and stood a long time, wondering if they were being an idiot and if Amberston was a myth. Then they saw it: a flash of orange as a piece of buried glass in the second path caught the sun. Amber glass. A signpost.

Nic hurried down the path, came to a new fork, and found another glint of amber to point the way. They followed each marked fork, delight rising.

Finally, they stepped onto a wide plateau filled with wheat. Beyond were other cleared patches studded with ramshackle scavenged houses, smoke rising from a few chimneys.

Nick sifted their backpack and headed for the nearest one.

"Do we know what's out there?" Pendrick asked as he followed Fenning down the ramp.

"I can't think there'd be much," Fenning replied. "Our reports indicate the lunar personnel cleared up everything when they evacuated." He looked back at Pendrick with a grin. "No monstrous science experiments left behind to eat us."

"Thank you," said Pendrick sourly. "But I wasn't talking about here," he added. He waved at the outside around them, beyond the corridor walls and its curved ceiling, indicating the space outside. "There. Who's out there to hear us?"

Fenning tapped in another code at the second door. The screen flashed green, and the door slid open, revealing a wider, taller corridor with a level floor. Lights in the ceiling flickered on. Vents coughed, then breathed chill air that warmed slowly.

Fenning led the way inside. "There was a long while where we couldn't even listen. We can only guess what happened over the first twenty years and extrapolate from what we know now. The Asteroid Belt is silent. The Jupiter moons are silent. No surprise there; they're surely empty. But Venus is alive, and so is Mars. Even Mercury, which shocked our scientists. They're very interested in how they pulled it off."

Pendrick's brow furrowed. "How are they going to find out?"

Fenning smiled at him. "We have our ways."

Pendrick followed him down the corridor.

On this day, Jung Michelle squeezed into an airlock with Gerald Parker-Lee. She had a gun, but all Gerald could see was her crazy grin. "Now then, Your Royal Highness," said Jung, "me and my leukemia are hoping that your family will do the right thing. Otherwise, you and I are going for a little walk."

Gerald gulped. "But we're not wearing spacesuits!"

"That's the thing," growled Jung. "The spacesuits you've been issuing for decades are so useless that a quarter of the workforce has one cancer or another."

"Well, what's it got to do with me?"

"Sometimes, Highness, you just have to pick up your bed and hit the nearest example of royalty with it. And when I hit you, I hit the jackpot!"

FENNING and Pendrick walked through corridors where people eight abreast could pass. They entered and left a lounge area with faded but comfortable-looking plush chairs. They passed through a corridor of staff quarters, doors all closed, before entering an open office area with rows of desks, empty now save for blotters, blank monitors and keyboards.

Something caught Pendrick's eye, and he picked it up, turning it over in his hands: a square frame around a blank screen and no ports to plug anything into. He pressed the power button, but it wouldn't turn on. It was supposed to hold a picture, but of what, he couldn't tell.

He started as Fenning was suddenly in front of him, gently but firmly pulling the blank frame away. "Best not to touch anything we didn't come here to touch." He gave Pendrick a bright smile. "Best not to dally."

They walked through a corridor where the lights flickered. Pendrick frowned at them. But he could breathe without releasing a cloud of fog now. Their footfalls continued to echo.

On this day, Marcus raised a hand to hide the setting Martian sun as he looked beyond the pollinator drones to his equals working the fields. He believed he could feel the ground hum from the factories beneath his feet.

Now, the machines live in the dark instead of us.

Paradise Dome had no central spiral. Marcus stood where it would have been, bent precariously over a cane, one hand held against the sun. He felt pride as an exuberant youth with steadfast hands wrestled a long tuber from the earth.

That is the only earth that matters.

"Your grandfather . . ." Fenning said suddenly. "I know he worked for Earth Space Command."

Pendrick kept his eyes on the shadows as they walked. "You read my file."

"I always read the files," Fenning replied. "But that's not what I wanted to ask. Your grandfather was there, wasn't he? On that day? In Houston? He was the one who begged the colonies to forgive us."

Their footsteps beat and repeated against the clicks, hisses, and groans of expansion joints. Finally, Pendrick said, "Yeah."

"Did he turn out the lights before he left?"

Pendrick stopped. Fenning turned and stared at him. Silence stretched, relatively speaking.

Fenning smirked. "Well, not that it matters much." He waved at the corridor around them. "They turned out the lights here. Shut everything down to standby, a gift they weren't sure anybody else would receive. So, perhaps he or maybe somebody else did the same. It seems the U.N.E way. If you can't stop the downfall, exit as gracefully as you can. Mind how you go."

He turned and walked away. "Don't think we aren't grateful," he added over his shoulder.

After a moment's hesitation, Pendrick followed.

On this day, Capella Scott watched with pride as the skow Flying Squirrel eased into low Venus orbit, loaded with refined treasures from the ' Ayló ' chaxnims. Her apprentices' fingerprints were all over it. Sure, Venusians would never be as good at keeping the ships flying as the miners were, but they were as skillful as it was possible for a bunch of acid skysailors to be. These days, that was enough.

IN THE DISTANCE came a bang as reheating corridors expanded. Pendrick flinched, but Fenning kept walking.

Pendrick picked up the pace, falling into step with Fenning. "Are you worried about what the colonies think of us? Are you worried about what they remember?"

Fenning raised an eyebrow but kept walking. "Me? No. Others? Maybe."

"Why?"

"Well . . ." Fenning sighed. He waved at the walls around them. "Look at this place: empty. The Jupiter moons: empty. The Asteroid Belt: empty. At least this place could evacuate to the Earth, such as it was."

"So?"

"Think of what it was like for the others," Fenning went on. "One moment, we were there. Next moment, we weren't. We couldn't help. We couldn't even advise. How do you think that felt?"

Pendrick looked down. "They must have felt . . . utterly abandoned."

"Now you know why we're keeping silent."

"It's not right!" Pendrick's voice echoed back from the corridors. He flinched and continued more quietly. "We were partners—"

"Colonizers," said Fenning. "There's a difference. There's a big difference. Some of them weren't happy to have us around in the last few years. Some of them were making noises about independence. Especially the ones that depended on us the most for their supplies. But even then, as their colonial power, they had expectations of us. We were the ones who were supposed to fix things if things went bad. Except that didn't happen. We ghosted them. We shirked our responsibilities and left. We as much as told them that they were on their own, whether they were ready for that or not. Some may cheer to see us back, but we can't expect a universally joyous response when we re-emerge."

For a long moment, there was only the sound of footfalls.

On this day, salvaged personnel carriers rolled through the old border at Chelela Pass. The guardhouses sat derelict, the prayer flags long ago blown away.

PENDRICK WALKED BESIDE FENNING, thinking long about what he'd just said.

He cleared his throat. "That . . . surely that depends on what we ask of them when we re-emerge, right?"

"Yes," said Fenning. "It does."

On this day, Aiden interviewed his former classmate, Mina, about the life of a new cadet on the Leigh Brackett. *They found themselves having dinner together that night . . . followed by breakfast the next morning.*

"WE'VE TALKED about what the colonies lost," said Fenning. "You ever think about what *we* lost?"

Pendrick jerked up and looked at him.

"I thought you would have," Fenning added. "Given the stories your grandfather told you."

Pendrick narrowed his eyes at him. "More than the eight billion mouths to feed, you mean?"

Fenning chuckled. "Touché." He turned, and they walked. "But the truth is, losing eight billion is no small thing. The math alone blows the mind: dropping eight billion in forty-eight years means nearly 167 million more deaths than births each year, and that's assuming a steady rate, which it wasn't. Think of the damage those people do fighting not to be one of the eight billion to go. And even when there are eight billion fewer mouths to feed, there are far fewer hands to grow the food for the remaining mouths to feed. Far fewer hands to maintain, run or rebuild the machinery."

He sighed. "Even asking two billion people to bury the remaining eight takes so much out of you. Out of your time and out of your spirit. Maybe our planet couldn't handle ten billion people back in the U.N.E's day, but cutting us back to just two billion almost cut us back to zero."

Pendrick said nothing. Fenning looked at him a long moment, then looked ahead. He continued. "Still, we've ignited an industrial revolution with less, but there's expertise to consider. You stand a four out of five chance of losing the one mechanic who knows how a system works—more if you consider how much knowledge fails to pass through the generations. You have to hope that the one out of five remaining is either really lucky or a quick learner. It's why the School of Reverse Engineering is so big at the University of Rabat."

Fenning stopped. Pendrick almost bumped into him. The two stared at each other.

"It's why *you're* so valuable," said Fenning.

On this day, Rebeka tucked a photo of her son into her coat pocket. Leaning against the barrier, she lined up her sight and zoomed in on her quarry through her ocular implant.

THE CONTROL ROOM DOORS PARTED, and Fenning and Pendrick entered. More desks sat empty. More control panels sat dark. Outside, seen through wide windows of perspex and transparent aluminum, Eagle Platform stretched out. The *Endymion* was the only ship occupying the landing pads. Above the horizon, the blue-grey sphere of Earth hovered in the black.

Pendrick frowned at one of the desks. Unlike the others, a single tablet sat askew. The chair behind it had been pushed back, but both were covered with dust.

He picked up the tablet. It flashed to life.

"Let me see that." Fenning snatched the tablet. He scrolled through the text.

> *That's it, then. The sun is out. The Moon is grey, but it's shining grey. The Earth is waiting.*
>
> *I'm not a good person, but I'm not a bad person either. This is me. Jericho Cavender. The last man on the Moon. Signing off.*
>
> *Remember me.*

Pendrick looked over his shoulder. "Anything useful?"

Fenning shook his head. "Nothing relevant." He hit delete and tossed the tablet back on the desk.

Pendrick snatched the tablet and turned it on, but the screen remained blank. He glared at Fenning's back.

"What did I say about dallying?" Fenning didn't look back. He walked along the line of controls, tapping each one before he spotted one in particular. He pointed at it. "There you are."

He grabbed the seat and sat down.

On this day, Stella leaned back in her comfortable office chair and took another look at the latest reports from R2R Co-op. They'd had a good quarter; some engineers in Perelandra had sent in a new seed-sorter design proposal, and their Martian office was actually making a little progress in that market, despite fierce opposition from the Families, of course. *And there was a personal letter from her son, Marco, letting her know that the farm on Britomart was doing great and there was another baby on the way.*

"Hey, Dad," she said to the air, feeling contented but a little sad as well. "Wish you could see this."

"Code, please," said Fenning.

"Huh?" Pendrick looked up, blinking.

Fenning raised an eyebrow. "The reason we're here? The reason *you're* here? Your grandfather's code, handed down over two generations after the U.N.E turned out the lights and turned on password protection."

"Oh." Pendrick looked down.

After a moment, Fenning cleared his throat. "Let's not forget, Pendrick, what you—what we—have to lose."

Pendrick sighed. He took a deep breath. "Bravo. Echo. Zigma. Thebes. Forty-two. Seven. Nine. Three."

Fenning dutifully typed the words and numbers in. The screen flashed green, and menu items opened. He leaned back in his chair, smiling. "We're in business."

On this day, Drew McMurtry lay in his grave, seven years after taking his own life.

A shadow fell over it, and someone laid a white rose on the stone.

As FENNING SAT and worked the controls, Pendrick took a step away, then another, then another. Hands shoved into his pockets, he slowly wandered around the control room, stopping at panels and casually reading the descriptions of the controls. Finally, he reached a display marked "Communications." The screen was on but blank, with a portion showing a red square with the words "NO SIGNAL."

Pendrick glanced back at Fenning, who sat engrossed in his work.

Pendrick scanned the switches and controls. He skipped the keyboard and focused on a red button marked "FULL BROADCAST."

He pulled a hand from his pockets. He reached out . . .

"Don't."

Pendrick turned and flinched to see the gun. Fenning held it steady in one hand, aimed at his chest, while he kept staring at the controls and typing with one hand.

He stopped typing and eyed Pendrick over his gun. He gave him a sad smile. "Don't."

Pendrick looked back at the communications board, then slowly backed away.

Fenning nodded and pocketed his gun. He jerked his head. "Come over here. Somebody deserves to see this, and it might as well be you."

On this day, Ganymede lived.

PENDRICK STOOD BEHIND and to one side of Fenning, arms folded across his chest, while Fenning worked the controls. "Just a few more inputs," he muttered.

On the screen, a window opened up, flashing yellow, then green. *Signal received. Security code accepted.*

Fenning leaned back. "There." He stood up and gestured at the windows. "Come on. I think we might be able to see it from here."

Pendrick stayed where he was, eyes on the floor. Fenning rolled his eyes and grabbed his arm. "Come *on!*"

They went over, Fenning keeping Pendrick in front of him. They stopped at the windows overlooking the lunar surface. Earth hung just over the horizon.

And in the blackness above the Moon, new stars flickered to life.

Pendrick swallowed.

Deck by deck, section by section, the pinpricks drew out the rough shape of a dozen metal objects in orbit around the Moon —the U.N.E's interplanetary ion ships, capable of constant acceleration across interplanetary space, able to cross orbits in weeks instead of months, slumbering since the Earth fell silent.

Fenning let out a chuff of a laugh. "There we go. Now we get back to where we used to be."

On this day, the Earth woke up.

THE FALL OF MCMURDO
BY JAMES BOW

Town of Shackleton's Coat
McMurdo Republic of Antarctica, April 15, 2200

ON HER LAST GOOD DAY, JOAN'S BOYFRIEND PROPOSED TO HER ON the gun range of Shackleton's Coat as the sun set for the last time before August.

It was Prospectors' Day, mid-April, with the sun halfway gone beneath the horizon on the Gulf of Filchner in the Southern Ocean, sending the normally grey mountains aglow. As adults laughed and children played, she and Anders teased and tagged each other as they helped everyone stack up piles for the bonfires. When the musicians launched into a reel, Anders tossed a plank aside, caught Joan's hand, and twirled her into a dance. Jed, her husky dog, loped and barked. Joan laughed and turned with him once around the bonfire pile before she shook him off. "You'll make me dizzy—I haven't eaten!"

"Well, you've got to keep your strength up," Anders chided.

"But I don't want to spoil my appetite!" She nodded at the food area, where men and women worked the outside grills and ovens. The smell was already enticing and aggravating. *Why can't they be ready* now?

Anders laughed. "They won't serve for another half-hour yet. And, shouldn't you wait thirty minutes after a meal before strenuous activity? You're telling me I have to wait a whole hour or more before we can dance again?"

Joan raised an eyebrow. "How fast do you intend to spin me?" She patted his arm. "Come on, there are other things we can do besides dancing."

They set off toward the fairy lights twinkling against the twilight. The winds from the south blew chill. Joan's breath fogged, and she consented to Anders clasping her close for warmth as they meandered to the gun range, Jed trotting beside them.

"Who will show off their skills on the range?" called the barker, a bearded man standing behind a table with rifles neatly laid out. "What about you two— oh!" He smiled as Joan and Anders approached. "You two! I thought you'd never come. Care to put on a show?"

Joan rolled her eyes. "Maarten, I'm not some circus act!"

But Maarten half-turned to the crowd on the sidelines. "So far, nobody has hit the far target in our challenge, and here are the best sharpshooters this side of the equator." He turned to Joan. "You won't believe how many people bet they'd beat your distance record."

"Anybody do it?" asked Anders.

"Not even close."

Anders picked up a rifle, checked the chamber to make sure it was empty, then sighted down the barrel. "How many targets?"

"Five," Maarten replied. "At five-hundred-metre intervals to 2.5 kilometres."

Anders grinned at Joan. "If I down all five in five shots, you give me a kiss."

Joan rolled her eyes, then let out a quick laugh. "All right. Try it."

Anders stepped to the firing line. Maarten pulled the warning siren, and everyone nearby grew quiet. Anders took aim, then pulled the trigger. The gun chuffed. A second later, the first target, a small red disk on a pole in the snow, shattered. Another chuff and the second target shattered: a kilometre away, then one-point-five kilometres, then two, then two-and-a-half. The monitors in the distance waved their flags. Around them, people whooped and cheered. Anders turned to Joan, smug.

"Ah, well," she said. "To the victor go the spoils." He grunted as she grabbed him by his coat flaps and pulled him in for a kiss. This time, the people around them let out a "woooo!" She pulled back, looking smug, while he blinked dreamily.

She took his gun and reloaded it. "My turn. Will you kiss me if I shoot all the targets?"

Anders blinked some more. "Sorry, what?"

The crowd laughed.

He shook clarity into his head. "Right, right!" He laughed, then said, "*Two* kisses if you can take out all the targets."

Someone in the audience chortled. "Anders betting against our own Long Watchman to take out five targets? He just wants to be kissed."

Joan wrinkled her nose at the mention of the Federation's legendary sniper, but she smiled to see Anders blush at the comment about wanting to be kissed. But then, Anders tilted his head. "Joan, if you can shoot just the last target without hitting any of the others beforehand, I'll marry you."

She stared at him.

He smiled at her, daring.

She raised an eyebrow. Then she turned and sighted down the barrel. "All set up?" she called.

"All targets ready," Maarten replied. He sounded the warning siren.

Behind her, someone muttered to their friend, "That's an impossible shot! Those targets are lined up in trajectory. You *have* to shoot them in sequence; otherwise, you're shooting blind. There's no way she can do this!"

Joan wiped her cheek on her shoulder, then sighted down the barrel again. She held her breath. When Anders leaned toward the spot just behind her ear, she didn't move as she growled, "Don't even think about it."

Jed also growled a warning. Anders backed away fast.

Joan breathed deep, focused, then tilted the barrel up a fraction of an inch.

The gun chuffed. A second later, the two-point-five kilometre target shattered.

The audience let out a gasp of delighted disbelief. "The Long Watchman couldn't shoot like that!"

Joan pulled the trigger again and again, and the targets shattered in reverse order: two kilometres, one-point-five, one kilometre, five hundred metres. She lowered the gun, straightening up as everyone cheered.

Anders stared at the range, mouth agape. He turned that gape to Joan. Then he closed his mouth. A grin dawned, and he took her hand and got down on one knee.

Joan blinked. "Anders! You weren't serious—"

"I am," he replied. "I've been in love with you since we first met, and now I know: you are the one I want to spend the rest of my life with. Please do me the honour of becoming my partner, now and forever."

Joan's heart stuttered, but as the words sank in, so did the certainty. "Yes," she gasped. She pulled him to his feet and embraced him. "Yes, Anders, I will!"

The crowd around them clapped. "Awww!"

She barely remembered handing back the guns and walking close with Anders as the sky deepened. People gathered, engaging in old conversations she'd hardly listened to the first time.

"Are we still on for Defence Drill?" asked Ingrid.

"Of course not," said Anders. "Not the day after Prospectors' Day."

"Yeah," Ingrid replied. "I doubt you'd get a good performance after all that celebrating."

"Well, it's not like the Feds are going to attack us," Anders chimed in. "I'd like to see them get across the Screaming Sixties. After a few hours on the Southern Ocean, we could hold them off hungover."

"Yeah, and what about those pirates?" said Maarten, laughing.

Everybody chuckled at this. Maarten squinted one eye shut and growled, "Arr! It be cold down here! This buccaneer be a-buckling!" This brought a new burst of laughter.

"Then who's attacking their ships?" asked Ingrid.

"No one." Joan rolled her eyes. "I'm sure they're making it up."

"We've shown there's no way any of our ships can be up there," Anders added.

"That's a lot of evidence to just fake, though," said Ingrid. "If they're blaming us, making us scapegoats—"

"Well, the president is on it," said Elnar. "He's talking to the Fed's Director General as we speak."

Joan tuned out the others as they reached the buffet tables. Her stomach growled. She pulled away from Anders and gestured toward the plates. "Come on! I'm famished." He smiled as he joined her, looking over the devilled eggs, waffles, lefse, and rakfisk, and the latest vegetables harvested from the hydroponic greenhouses. Nothing could destroy this perfect moment.

"Everybody!" shouted someone near the projection screens. "Breaking news! The president is on the vid!"

Joan looked up. People approached a large video screen, showing a grey-bearded man on the steps of a solar plane, speaking to a line of microphones. He held up a tablet.

"Turn it up! Turn it up!" people shouted. The volume indicator edged upward.

"To the people of Antarctica, I have here . . ." The President intoned, waving his tablet. ". . . a document signed by myself and the Director-General of the Federation of Earth Nations. This document enshrines the peaceful coexistence of our nations, now and forever."

Cheers rose—on screen and in the crowd. People hugged. Joan gripped Anders's hand and pulled him close.

Then someone else shouted, "Hey! The sun's almost set! Light the bonfires!"

The crowd faced the sun. The bonfire piles stood in silhouette against the bluing dusk. Cheers rose as a man and a woman stepped into view from either side, holding flaming torches aloft. They faced each other and, with a nod, turned and touched their torches to two small piles.

Flames leaped up, then fanned out, running along channels toward the large piles in silhouette. The flames reached each pil, then raced over the surface. Soon, their light blinded everyone watching, just as the last of the sun slipped below the ocean.

Joan hollered with the crowd, a wordless cheer of patriotism and celebration.

Then, with a harsh whistle, a rocket slammed in and exploded in the first bonfire.

Joan barely had time to duck as flaming debris rained all around them. People shouted, screamed, ran, while Joan struggled to peer between people, scanning the horizon. *Where did that come from? Who fired at us?*

A second rocket exploded.

"Joan!" Anders screamed.

She shoved her way through the melee. *Where are they shooting from? Where—*

Jed ducked and weaved between people's legs, barking furiously.

A flicker in the distance. A black dot against the blue. The wail of a distant siren. A flash of a light that winked out, like someone covering it up in a hurry.

Then she heard the sound, echoing off the surrounding mountains, the roar of engines, the rattle of rotors. She counted at least a dozen dots advancing from the sunset. Then, more flashes—red and yellow. *You can't cover up the flare of rockets launching.*

"Quadrocopters!" she yelled. "It's an invasion!"

She couldn't think anybody could have heard her in all the chaos, but as she turned, she saw Maarten and others of the defence team rushing for the gun emplacements. She started after them.

She stumbled when Anders caught her arm. "Joan! Wait!"

She pulled out of his grip. "We've got to get to the gun batteries!" she yelled.

Anders shook his head. He dodged a mother cradling her child. "Get the children and their parents to the shelters! Go!"

She staggered to a stop. They shared a look. Beside them, Jed whined. Joan swallowed, then nodded. Anders did, too, and ran. Joan turned to the crowd. "Come on!" she shouted, waving. "This way! This way to the shelters!"

The stampeding crowd kept running, but more and more people followed Joan's voice as she hurried and gestured toward the bunker gates in the nearby hillsides. She reached the first gate while others took stations beside other door controls and started waving parents and children through. "Hurry!" She lost count of the people who passed her and hoped this was a good thing. "Hurry!" Fire lit the sky, and a shockwave knocked her ears as the gun emplacements lit up, shooting back at the dots that were now silhouettes. Joan could see the quadrocopters' four rotors, their blimp-like bulk. *Troop carriers. At least a thousand soldiers bearing down!*

Rockets rained down, striking toward the gun emplacements but away from the civilians. Joan swallowed but grabbed someone who stumbled, pulled them to their feet, and shoved them forward. She felt heavy wheels rumble as the first doors slid shut. The last stragglers scrambled past. The second door closed.

Joan placed a hand on her door's controls and looked across the common. As the gun batteries blasted in the distance, she saw one more person, a man, clutching a young girl, running hard. "Come on!" she yelled.

With a whistling roar, a rocket appeared out of the sky. She glimpsed it over the man's shoulder. Before she could even scream, the explosion sent a gout of rock skyward. Spitting dust, Joan darted forward, looking for the man and his newborn child, but saw nothing but a crater.

She drew a shaky breath and backed up to the shelter door. She slapped the emergency button. As the shutters closed, she ran for the gun batteries that were blasting away.

The lead quadrocopter let out a bellow.

Joan clamped her hands over her ears and hollered. Her feet gave out, and she fell hard on the snow and lichen. Jed whimpered beside her, but she couldn't move to comfort him. Ahead, her town's gun batteries slowed.

The bellow stopped, and Joan lay gasping a moment before she struggled to her feet. She ran, trying to get as much distance as she could before they fired the sonic weapon again. Anti-aircraft fire picked up.

Then, with a whistle of rocketry, the nearest gun emplacement exploded. The blast flung Joan on her back. She stared at the sky, dazed, as Jed leaped around and barked at her, frantic.

She sat up. The gun emplacement stood, roof exposed, silent, but the gun still pointed at the invaders. Grunting, Joan clambered up and clawed across the lichen, up the stairs, through the broken door.

She gagged. Bodies and parts of bodies littered the floor. She was too shocked to register the smell. She focused on the gunner's seat, stumbled over, grabbed the man lying limp at the controls—

—grabbed Anders, who slumped in her arms. He was still warm, but the way he slumped, like a bag of bones, told her all she needed to know. As did the large piece of shrapnel lodged in his eye. A strangled, keening cry escaped her lips.

The quadrocopters were close now, crossing from sea to land. They turned, firing, their aluminum fabric skins rippling in the kickback. The last of the gun emplacements exploded. More ships sauntered in.

Joan put her arms around her fiancé and twisted him out of the seat, casting him to the floor with the rest of the bodies. She struggled into the chair and took hold of the gun. There was no computer to help her, but she didn't need to aim. The lead ship filled her sight, presenting its flank, its rotors blurring.

These things are designed to stay aloft after tremendous damage, but they are piloted. The pilots are at the front of the personnel pod. Aim there. Three shots to get through the shielding. The fourth to take out the pilots.

She flipped the switch to manual firing, felt the round fall into the clip, and pulled the trigger.

The blast, too loud to hear, kicked her in the chest. The chair rocked. She caught sight of the round rocketing at the lead ship. A fireball consumed the nearest rotor and blasted open the aluminum fabric of the balloon, but she didn't stop.

Another round fell into place. She fired it. A third round fell. Fire. Then, one more.

She couldn't see the personnel pod amid the flames, but she could see the quadrocopter jerk, then list to one side, knocking into its neighbour. Fire consumed them both as they descended to the ground with a roar. Joan yelled, a wordless holler of triumph and anger. Then, as the fireball cleared, the next quadrocopter appeared, its guns aimed right at her.

In that second, flight overruled fight. As she heard the whistle of the rocket rise, Joan twisted out of her chair and staggered for the stairs. The blast threw her through walls that were no longer there, and she fell a full storey, landing hard on the lichen-covered stone. Her vision flickered to black. She heard a jumble of noises she could hardly identify. Quadrocopter motors easing down. The crunch of landing gear. The fact that there were no more gunshots. A whine. Something licking her face. Wait, that was something she felt, not heard. Something tugged at her shoulder. A bark. Jed.

She groaned. *Just let me lie here*, she thought. *Just let me be.*

She heard a clatter of something hitting stone. Then footfalls. Voices.

She blinked her eyes open, then pushed herself on her hands and knees. There she stayed, halfway between moving and collapsing, with a choice to make. *Stay? Surrender? Die?* As footfalls approached, the fog cleared. *No.*

She shoved herself upright and almost fell over. She caught herself on Jed, who braced for her. She pushed again and got her feet under her. Footsteps, voices, closer still.

"Come on, Jed," she breathed, staggering away from the gun emplacement, away from the shore and her home. "Let's go."

With her dog, she ran for the wilderness.

JOAN FOLLOWED the New Glomma River, keeping her head down in the twilight. At the first bend, she looked back at Shackleton's Coat. She saw familiar homes but with windows dark. The backs of a dozen quadrocopters sat in silhouette behind them. Smoke still rose from the one she'd shot down and the one it had taken down with it. Then lights played across the surface of the aluminum fabric of the quadrocopters. Headlights started rolling between the houses, which stayed dark.

Joan put her head down and followed the river upstream. Jed followed. Her thoughts roiled.

Our bonfires! We set their signal fires for them.

She stumbled on the stony ground but pushed on.

That must have been why they sounded so interested in peace. It wasn't just to surprise us; they wanted us relaxed enough to celebrate. They wanted us complacent enough to light our fires!

She ignored the ringing in her ears, the chill that sent her shoulders shivering. The symptoms of shock. She put one foot ahead of the other, occupying her thoughts with civil defence procedures.

The first line of defence: the gun emplacements and shelters. At the first sign of attack, send the civilians to the shelters and staff the gun emplacements. Target the invaders and fire.

Should that fail, activate the second line of defence: retreat to the armouries. Replenish supplies and ammunition. Fall back to the mountains.

The armouries were ten kilometres back from the coast, up the rivers. *Retreat and regroup. Fight back. You can do this.*

One foot, then another. Step. Step.

The long twilight deepened. The wind howled from the interior, blowing cold and promising snow.

How did they get their troop carriers across the Southern Ocean? Quadrocopters can't cross that distance on their own. They need support ships. Places to stop and refuel.

Then, as she stumbled, something clicked.

The pirate attacks. It wasn't us, so maybe it's them — a distraction? A cover? A false flag!

We thought they were faking evidence. Maybe they used the attacks as a way to sneak the quadrocopters through.

She slipped and caught herself on rough rocks, scraping her palms raw. The scream that came out was mostly anger. She swallowed it and scrambled into the dark.

Habit kept her moving forward. A narrow path slipped between outcroppings, then opened into a flat place that was cupped in the rocks like a meadow in a forest. Jed darted from behind her, sniffling the bare rock.

On the other side of the clearing was a door, grey metal set in stone.

I made it, thought Joan. *The armoury. I'm here. Why am I here?*

Oh, right. How could I forget?

The wind picked up. Snow blew in, stinging her tear-streaked cheeks. Joan stumbled over to a grey metal door in an alcove carved into a mound of bedrock. She touched the doorknob, and a keyboard display lit up faintly in red. She tapped in her code.

She barely heard the lock click in the howling wind. She pushed open the door and fell through. Jed loped in after her. Joan picked herself up and shoved the door closed. The lock beeped and clicked. She turned, fumbled for the light switch, but stopped when she felt it.

For a long moment, she just stood there, hand brushing the light switch. But she didn't turn it on.

She slid down the face of the door and curled her knees to her chest. Jed whimpered and nuzzled up to her. She didn't push him away.

Sobs filled the dark room.

FOR THE FIRST WHILE, Joan slept. When she didn't sleep, she cried. There was nothing else to do but feel Jed press up against her, his breath on her cheek. She was grateful for that.

After hours of this, she thought, *No sun is going to wake me. I can't sleep forever.*

Much as I would like to.

Jed's toenails scraped as he skittered back while Joan shoved herself onto her knees. She felt up the wall for the light switch and flicked it on.

She'd had the sense to close her eyes. The back of her eyelids shone red. Jed barked once.

"Sorry," she muttered. She looked around at the armoury.

She was in the mud room. Cold weather gear and equipment hung on the walls. Ahead of her was another narrow door. This was by design, she remembered: a choke point. The main equipment rooms and the command centre would be deeper, protected from aerial and ground attack, ready to counterattack if . . .

If we'd been at all prepared for this.

We weren't. We drilled, but it's become less about civil defence and more about team building. We never thought invaders could cross the Screaming Sixties. We never thought they'd bother with us. Until they did.

But the control room would have communications equipment. There'd be connections to other armouries. There'd be news.

"Come on, Jed." She strode for the inner door. It swung open with her code. She followed the hallway past storage rooms, munition rooms, and larders she knew would be full of cans. She passed open rooms lined with empty bunks.

She kept going to the farthest room. It opened to her code.

As she entered, lights flickered on to reveal desks and whiteboards.

She looked around. *How long will it be before the FEN find this place? They knew exactly how hard to hit us and when —Prospectors' Day, when our guard was down. They knew how to attack our defences; they must know where our defences are. They'll be hunting them down to eliminate any resistance.*

She tapped the main computer, looking for updates.

No locations were given for the other armouries because of course not. But she could still see whether they were active or not.

Half had winked out without ceremony. *FEN takeover or destruction?* she wondered. *Whatever. It makes no difference.* She confirmed the signals. Only half of McMurdo's armouries remained.

She leaned back in her chair.

Orders. Orders. What are my orders?

She cast her mind back to the defence drills. *Should the first line of defence fail, retreat and regroup. Gather at the armouries, rearm, and strike back.*

She looked around the empty control room. *Regroup here. I need to make this place ready for that.*

She went room to room, Jed jogging behind her. She checked the gear room, making sure the winter gear was sorted and ready to hand out: hooded coats, pants, gloves, and boots, all in lichen-grey camo. Googles and masks, all ready.

She checked the expiry dates on the food cans, moving the ones that needed eating first to their own section. She sorted the water purification tablets and made sure the first aid kits were stocked, though the best medicine in the wilderness of Antarctica was not getting hurt in the first place.

In the ammo room, she sorted the guns and the air canisters and made sure the replenishers were ready. And bullets. Boxes and boxes of bullets.

This took a couple of days. Joan slept on the first bunk she could clamber onto. As she worked, she kept an eye on the door, making sure a loaded rifle sat close at hand. She hoped she could tell friend from foe the moment she had to make that decision.

But nobody approached the door.

In the control room, another five armouries blinked out. Communications stayed blank until . . .

A broadcast came up on the control room's main screen from the capital. Joan pulled a chair up to the screen, sat down, then stood up. She leaned against the back of the chair, then finally straightened up, her hands clasped in front of her, fingers fidgeting. Jed sat down beside her.

The STAND BY screen flickered, and Joan saw the stairs to the capital building at New Nuuk. A crowd stood under floodlights, staring silently, a sea of wool hats facing a podium set up in front of the capital steps.

They were surrounded by FEN soldiers, standing casually, guns holstered but present. A quadrocopter floated above the capital, the roar of its rotors the only sound above the wind.

The capital doors opened, and a man strode out, making a beeline for the podium, easily outpacing his FEN escorts. He gripped the sides of the lectern, beaming.

Joan frowned. *Who is that? That's not our president. He looks familiar, though.*

The man waved to the silent crowd as if they were cheering masses. "To the people of Antarctica! I have great things to tell you!"

The new president's name came up at the bottom of the screen. Joan's eyebrows shot up. "Samling?" *The leader of that wacky opposition party. What the hell is he doing there?*

Samling went on. "For the last several weeks, there has been an ill wind rising across this continent. Disquiet overtaking minds, doubt hampering spirits. Today, I tell you, alongside our

Federation friends, that this is at an end! Today, we take our place among our friends in the Federation of Earth Nations to guide our future together. Together, we will work for the benefit of all humanity . . ."

Joan's jaw clenched. "That little . . ." she sputtered for the right word. "That little . . . Quisling!" *If Samling was this ready to take over, he could have helped lay the path. His people could have corrupted our government, our security forces. No wonder we fell so quickly!*

She stabbed the monitor's power button, wishing she could punch the screen black instead. She turned away, leaning against the console. Jed looked up at her and whined.

She turned back and called up the report on the other armouries. Two more had blinked out and . . .

She frowned. So had hers.

She looked behind her. She was alone. She checked the cameras. No movement outside. She checked the systems— everything was functioning, but her armoury was no longer showing as active.

She cocked her head. *Is someone trying to hide me? That's encouraging.*

She listened to the hiss of the ventilators. She looked again at the perimeter cameras, but they still showed nothing different from what they'd shown the past week.

Still, no one has come. Not even FEN soldiers. I'm on my own here while my country falls apart around me.

She looked at the rifle leaning within reach.

I'm all alone here, with all this gear.

She looked ahead.

But what do I do? I'm alone. What on Earth can I do on my own?

She stared at the blank screen. Certainty rose with the slow inevitability of an Antarctic sunrise.

Resist.

She picked up her rifle and turned it over in her hands. She peered down its sight.

One wasp can do incredible damage to a much larger animal or person.

Motioning for Jed to follow, she headed for the gear room.

You just need to know where to sting.

THE MAYOR'S house in Shackleton's Coat had been taken over by the leader of the local occupation force. From two kilometres away, Joan looked in through the window.

The local commander had passed through her sight several times as though pacing, though not regularly enough that she could time him, dammit. Earlier in the day, all houses had been searched, all weapons confiscated. A quarter of the people had been sent in trucks to a "processing facility" down the coast. Trucks were returning with some of them but at a trickle. Joan was certain at least a few would not be coming home anytime soon.

The commander had given the orders, standing to one side as FEN soldiers conducted the searches and herded people into the trucks with batons. Meanwhile, a handful of soldiers delivered sacks of food to the remaining households. Carrots, literally.

She sighted through the window again and saw the commander standing off to one side, still for the first time she'd seen him. She took aim and wrapped her finger around the trigger.

And another person entered the window frame. A woman. Joan didn't recognize her. But the woman was in uniform. A FEN uniform. Why was she standing so close to him?

The woman reached up and kissed the commander.

Joan stayed where she was for a long moment. *What am I*

doing? Am I really going to kill this man in front of someone he loves? Am I really going to kill this man?

At the back of her mind, she heard the howl of the quadro-copters' sonic weapons. She saw the inrush of rockets and the man with his newborn baby who suddenly wasn't there anymore.

She pulled the trigger. The gun chuffed. Seconds later, glass shattered. She saw a mist of red.

By the time FEN soldiers found her position, she was long gone.

SHACKLETON COAT'S next district governor died at his press conference. FEN soldiers had scoured the surrounding area for hours but missed a critical outcrop.

The district governor after that died in a darkened room when he turned on his stove for his tea and stepped in front of the pilot light.

A week later, in the next town, the new FEN-assigned Chief of Police was found dead in his office. FEN investigating officers determined the shot either came from two hundred metres in the air or had been fired blind on the ground from five times the distance. They searched for drone copters and found none.

Then, the residents joined the resistance.

Joan never met any of them, but when the third district governor blew up in her home, she knew somebody had mucked with his gas main. In other towns, equipment stopped working, quietly or spectacularly. The mineral extraction plants shut down, and Joan made sure that anybody who tried to punish the strikers was shot.

When the second FEN-assigned Chief of Police ordered arrests, local officers took people into custody, then departed, leaving the Chief alone with the incarcerated townsfolk. When they returned, the Chief was dead in a cell. The townsfolk were gone. The local officers disappeared with them.

The strikers were forcibly removed from the mineral extraction plants, though they were sent home instead of incarcerated. FEN soldiers took over the jobs, and high and thick security walls went up around the plants. A moral victory, if not a complete one.

Posters went up, condemning terrorism, threatening arrests, and putting a bounty on the Grey Bullet.

Joan raised an eyebrow above her scope. *Grey Bullet? That's what they're calling me?*

She shrugged a shoulder. *I'll take it.*

When FEN soldiers came to take a town into custody for one too many acts of sabotage, Joan shot the officer in charge and the second in command from completely different vantage points. The soldiers panicked and shot at the hills randomly while the townsfolk escaped. Then, the soldiers ran. Later, when the townsfolk returned, new FEN soldiers stayed in camps at the edge of town and made no move to take any townsfolk in custody.

Joan watched them through her scope. Then, on the opposite side of town, her eyes alighted on a message stamped into the snow.

Thank you, Grey Bullet.

She smiled. Then she moved on to the next town. Jed loped after her.

JOAN CIRCLED HER REGION, going from town to town, helping where she could from a distance. She headed for the coast as the sky started to fitfully lighten toward the mid-August dawn. Eventually, she made camp at a plateau overlooking the Port of Endurance. Her scope moved along the blinking lights and the impounded fishing boats bobbing in the water. Federation quadrocopters sat berthed in the distance. She saw troop carriers and supply boats painted in Federation green.

She smiled. *If I can catch them while they're moving troops through here, think of the damage I could do.*

Then she heard a distant bellow—not a sonic weapon blast, but similar enough that the hairs rose on the back of her neck. She shifted her scope along the horizon and caught it.

A quadrocopter was approaching from the sea.

Joan followed it on her scope as it pulled up to a dock and lowered itself into place. A gangway extended. Soldiers emerged. Her finger tightened on the trigger.

I should wait. See who else arrives. Why give away my position for a foot soldier?

But as she watched, the soldiers took station, guarding access points and eying sight lines (except not hers). She raised an eyebrow at this and kept watching.

A figure in white strode down the gangplank. Joan watched the newcomer through her scope. The figure was dressed as a sniper, as if sniper was a costume. He was covered head to toe in white, goggles and hood hiding his face, a long-range rifle with scope slung across his back. Joan's frown deepened.

This has to be the Long Watchman—the way he's dressed, the way the others stand back like they're afraid.

He looks like he's come here from Siberia, or as if he expected Antarctica to be as it stopped being over a century ago.

She let out a short, angry laugh.

Do they think we're still snowbound? The ice sheets haven't been a thing for decades. But now the Long Watchman is in my sights, and I can stop this fight before it starts.

Joan focused on the white figure, calibrated the distance, zoomed in, touched the trigger . . .

And her scope went blinding white. Joan yelled, and her gun chuffed. She staggered back, clutching her eye. "What the hell!" She tried blinking the spots from her eye, but they persisted.

As she stood, she remembered: she'd fired a shot after her aim had been disrupted.

Which meant she probably hadn't hit what she was aiming at.

But I did give away my position, and a good sniper could line up a return shot in—

She dived for the ground just as a bullet shattered the rock face where her head had been.

Whoa! Not that fast!

She almost made the mistake of lifting her head up before two more shots zipped by way too close. *He sighted me in seconds. He has me pinned down!*

She rolled across the plateau, keeping her head down. She managed to grab her pack along the way. The rocks clicked and sprayed as bullets followed her, but she finally got behind an outcrop where she could raise her head. She judged the run to the path that led to her escape, put her head down, and bolted for it. One more shot clicked in the rocks above her head, and she was through, down the path, and into the Antarctic wilderness.

THEY SENT the Long Watchman after me!

She clutched her gun closer and puffed up the slope. Jed dashed along beside her.

He holds the world record for the longest kill. He assassinated the President of Cascadia. He put down the rebellion in Australia by taking out its leadership one by one. He doesn't miss unless he's bracketing, and, in the end, he doesn't miss.

"Come on, Jed," she puffed. "Faster. We got to be faster!"

She stumbled over the summit of a mountain pass. Below, a

remnant ice field glowed green in the light of the Southern Aurora. The wind blew colder. Joan and Jed ran on.

FOR THE NEXT FORTY-EIGHT HOURS, Joan ran. Each time she and Jed settled behind an outcrop, they had less than thirty minutes before a bullet cracked against stone. She tried to sight back on her pursuer but saw nothing among the rocks and shale.

The temperature dropped. The wind picked up. The lights of the Southern Aurora faded as clouds pulled in. And as the light faded, so did the visibility of the path behind her.

Antarctica is working against me! she thought as exhaustion and hunger scrambled her senses. Then, as she stumbled and fell onto Jed, the warmth of his fur, the nuzzle of his snout, shook some sense back into her.

He's not bracketing. He's herding me, driving me forward. I can't outrun him. I should stand and fight.

She shoved herself to her knees and looked around at the darkening path. *I need to find a place with good cover to get my sight in.*

The shale lands offered no outcrops to hide behind. Her eyes fell on the foot of the glacier and tracked up its slope. Her camo gear was grey, but so, too, was the ice at the glacier's face. There was high ground up there. It was a place she could dig herself into, bury herself, and wait until the Long Watchman came close enough for a possible ambush.

Keeping low, she and Jed ran for the glacier, splashed across the proglacial lake, and climbed up the rock-strewn ice slope.

She reached the top and staggered in the face of a hurricane wind like the blast from a freezer. Ice crystals sandblasted her face. She bent double and pressed on a few hundred metres before choosing a patch of ice and digging in with her rifle. She made a hollow in the dusty snow, called Jed to her, and lay on her stomach, sighting back through her scope the way she'd come.

The wind rose. Snow descended like a curtain until she could hardly tell where the ground ended and the air began. For the next half-hour, she struggled to keep her eyes open against fatigue and the biting wind. The path she'd come in on remained empty. Joan's spirits flagged.

He can wait me out. Dying from exposure or dying by his gun— there's not much difference to him, is there?

Then, movement caught her eye. She focused on the white-on-white of the path. It still looked empty. She focused through the scope, then saw it again: snow shifting, a rock suddenly skittering to one side.

No way.

She pulled back the focus, aiming for the air above and slightly ahead of the small rockfall. She pulled back further before she made it out: a ghostly gap in the driving snow, body-shaped.

A cloaking device? They gave him a cloaking device?

She smiled as she aimed. *Not that it's going to help you now.*

Suddenly, the figure flashed into existence, his white suit shining, overloading Joan's scope. She clenched her eye shut and let out a strangled yell. She clenched the trigger. Her gun kicked and chuffed, but she knew not to trust it. She staggered to her feet, hand over her blinded eye, as she glared at the path behind her. She brought her gun to bear. "Come on! Let's finish this!"

She was speaking to the wind and snow. She couldn't see anything or anybody. Jed growled low, then barked. Joan swung around as a figure in white stepped into view, gun raised. Joan's aim was ninety degrees off.

For a moment, the two stared at each other. *One move,* thought Jone. *That's all it would take to finish him.*

And for him to finish me as well.

The Long Watchman cleared his throat. "We need—"

Suddenly, a groan echoed around them, rising above the wind. The Long Watchman straightened up. Joan's brow furrowed. *What was that?*

The ice shuddered beneath their feet.

Joan and the Long Watchman looked at their feet, then at each other. The ice groaned and shuddered again.

The Long Watchman drew a deep breath. "Uh . . . we should—"

The ice collapsed beneath them, and Joan, Jed, and the Long Watchman fell into a crevasse.

Dark ice rushed past Joan's face. She smacked an outcrop and felt her arm crack, but it happened so fast she couldn't register any pain before she struck water so cold it shoved the breath from her body. She struggled for the surface—now her arm blazed and gasped for any hint of air, barely aware of the ice tunnel walls rushing around her. *Underground river*, she thought. *I can't—*

She banged into something soft. Was it Jed or the Long Watchman? She kicked, but when she tried to punch, her arm blazed with new fire. She grabbed with the hand on her uninjured arm, trying to fight off her assailant and hold on at the same time.

She gagged as they went under.

Then, just as suddenly as they'd fallen, she felt the ice vanish. She was flying, then falling. The roar of water had a distant echo.

She hit the lake with a splash and struggled for the surface. She one-arm swam in a random direction until she felt ground beneath her feet. She scrambled up a gravel bank.

She heard Jed whine and, further away, someone throwing up water.

She reached for her gun, reared up, tried to bring it to bear, but her other arm wouldn't work. And before she could do anything, the figure tackled her. Joan screamed and kicked, but the figure rolled Joan on her back and straddled her, shoving her down and grabbing her throat. Then the Long Watchman yelled as Jed clamped his jaws down on the man's arm, pulling back.

"Stop!" the Long Watchman yelled. "Stop fighting me!"

"Go to hell or Mount Erebus!" Joan shouted back.

"Listen to me!" the Long Watchman yelled. "Your arm is broken! We're going to die out here!"

"I hope so!" Joan grunted.

"We're going to freeze to death!"

Even as she struggled, Joan frowned. *What's wrong with his voice?*

"You're not going to be able to do anything unless we mend your arm," the Long Watchman shouted. "We need shelter, now! We need to get out of this blizzard!"

Joan blinked up at the Watchman. What was he proposing?

The sniper pulled his hand away from Joan's neck and pointed. "There's a cave two hundred metres downstream. We can shelter there, and I can fix your arm, but you need to call off your dog!"

Jed's growls intensified as he yanked at the Watchman's gloved hand.

Call off Jed so you can strangle me properly? I don't think so!

But even with Jed, he could have killed me already. Why hasn't he?

The Long Watchman scooched back a bit and raised his free hand. "Truce! Truce! Or else we're both going to die!"

His voice was almost lost to the wind. Joan realized she was shivering, and she couldn't stop. She sat up. "Jed!" she yelled. "Let go!"

Jed looked at her, then let go, backing up. But he focused on the Long Watchman and growled low.

"Good," the Watchman yelled. He reached into his pack. "Now give me your broken arm."

"What?"

He pulled a tube from his pack. "Do it!"

She held up her arm, and the Long Watchman slipped the tube over her wrist. He tapped it, and the tube compressed immediately, taking the shape of Joan's arm and clipping the broken bones together with a sharp jab of pain. But the pain immediately subsided, leaving Joan gasping mid-yell. Instead, the splint gave off a gentle, soothing heat.

The Long Watchman stood up and held out a hand. "Cave!" He pointed. "That way! Now!"

Joan looked around, but she might as well have been in a void. "How can you see anything in this?"

"I've got technology!" The Watchman leaned into the wind. Joan rolled over and struggled after him. Feet slipping on icy gravel, Joan walked blind until darkness loomed in front of her, the ground dipped, and the sound of the blizzard cut out so abruptly that Joan wondered if her eardrums had burst. They stumbled down a slope, unable to stop, before they fell to their knees in a cold cavern. Joan's broken arm twinged, but the splint stayed firm. Her arm didn't flex.

"Light," gasped the Long Watchman.

Joan pulled off her pack and grabbed the portable lantern. She could use both arms almost equally well. She wound up the battery and tapped the switch. Pale light pushed back the gloom.

"Heat," she breathed.

"I've got Sterno." The Long Watchman pulled the tab off the lid of a can. "Matches wet. Got anything to light it?"

Joan pulled the flint lighter from her pocket, grabbed the can, and set it alight. "We need more. Got more?"

The Long Watchman wheezed. "Yeah." Two more cans clanked on the stones between them. Joan lit them both.

They crouched closer on either side of the flames, Jed placing himself between them, glaring at the Long Watchman. Joan looked him up and down, then focused on his white hood and the goggles over his eyes.

The Watchman stared back. "You don't have an implant."

"I'm sorry?"

"An ocular implant," the Watchman replied. "The FEN were certain you had one to make the shots you made."

Joan shook her head, bewildered. "I don't see why. It's just mathematics."

"Huh," said the Watchman. He pulled off his goggles, pulled back his hood—

—to reveal long brown hair going white, tied back in a ponytail. One eye's metal surface reflected the flames. The Watchman had a lined, cynical face . . .

A woman's face.

Joan stared at her. "You're the Long Watchman."

The woman raised an eyebrow. "Yeah."

"You. The Long Watchman."

The woman rolled her eyes—human and ocular implant— and unzipped her jacket and shrugged it off. "Pleased to make your acquaintance."

Joan narrowed her eyes. "The Long Watch*man*."

The woman sighed. "If it's any consolation, they refer to you, the Grey Bullet, with he/him pronouns as well."

Joan stared, then let out a chuff of a laugh. "Two hundred and sixty years since the Siege of Sevastopol, and they still can't think of women as snipers."

The Long Watchman chuckled and shook her head. "Yeah. Nothing changes."

Joan breathed heavily. "Well." Another breath. "What the hell are we going to do now?" Even with the heat from the Sterno, she still couldn't stop shivering. Her clothes felt like ice packs.

"This heat will be useless unless we get into dry clothes." The Long Watchman nodded at the Stereo. "Do you have dry things?"

"I—" Joan flinched as the Long Watchman opened up her pack and tossed her a shirt. She quelled an impulse to toss it back. "Why are you helping me?" She held up the wrist in its splint. "Why did you fix my broken arm? Aren't you planning to kill me?"

The Long Watchman gave her a rueful look. "Those are my orders."

"And?"

"They sent me here to kill you, not let you die from hypothermia."

Joan stared a moment, bewildered. Then she shrugged off her coat.

As they changed, Joan watched the Long Watchman out of the corner of her eye and saw her pull a laminated photo from her wet shirt pocket. The woman breathed a sigh of relief to see it. She looked it over a moment before tucking it into her dry shirt.

Moments later, they sat on either side of the fire, wearing clothes they'd borrowed from each other while their gear dried on the stones. As she rubbed her splint and flexed her fingers, Joan glared across the flames at the Long Watchman. The woman reached up and popped the ocular implant out of her eye into her palm. Joan flinched.

"I'm off the clock," the Long Watchman replied as she tugged an eyepatch into place. "And if you're thinking about grabbing it and destroying it, well, one: that will just piss me off, and two, the Feds will simply give me another one. Unlike my hometown's hospital, they have a stockpile that survived the fall of the Sea Wall."

Joan just stared. The Long Watchman pocketed the

implant, then reached into her pack and tossed Joan a protein bar. "Here."

Despite herself, Joan's stomach growled. She unwrapped the bar, brought it to her mouth, and then stopped. After a moment's thought, she broke the bar in two and tossed one half back to the Long Watchman, who caught it.

The Long Watchman chuckled, took a bite, and swallowed. Joan watched her, then took a bite of her own. After swallowing, she broke the remaining piece in half, fed some to Jed, and ate the rest herself. She repeated this when the Long Watchman fished out another bar and broke it in half, taking a bite.

"So, what do we do now?" asked Joan when they'd finished eating.

The Long Watchman pulled a beaded necklace over her head and ran it through her fingers. A rosary. She looked at the snow-veiled entrance to the cave. "Rest. Wait until the weather changes. Decide then."

"Okay," said Joan. "Are we just supposed to sit here?" Jed sidled closer and pressed up against her side. Joan leaned into his warmth.

The Watchman didn't look at her. "What part of 'rest' did you not understand?"

"Okay," said Joan again. She leaned against the cave wall while the Long Watchman's rosary beads clicked. The woman muttered under her breath.

Joan glared. "Do you have to pray so loud?"

The clicking paused. "I'm not praying," the Long Watchman replied.

For a moment, the only sound was the howling wind outside. Then, the clicking and muttering resumed.

JOAN SLEPT LONGER than she'd intended. When she woke, the light outside had barely changed. Her body ached like it had been in a washing machine filled with stones. Her arm ached, too, but the splint was still doing its work. She stared at it a moment before looking around.

The Long Watchman still sat across the Sterno fire from her. Jed looked up at Joan from his forepaws, then resumed his glare at the woman.

"According to my watch, it's morning," said the Long Watchman.

"Oh," said Joan. *I'm not going to ask how you slept.*

"How do you feel?"

"Fine." *I'm not going to make small talk with you.*

The Long Watchman reached into her pack and pulled out a ration bar. "Hungry?"

Joan's stomach growled. "No."

Silence stretched.

"So, how old are you?" the Long Watchman asked suddenly.

Joan thought about answering,*"What business is that of yours?"* but she was too weary to fight on that ground. "Twenty-nine," she snapped. "Why?"

"Huh," said the Long Watchman. "I wondered."

"What did you wonder?"

The Long Watchman shrugged. "I was twenty-nine, once."

Joan's eyes narrowed. "What's that supposed to mean?"

The woman looked away. "Nothing much." A pause. "I mean . . . I don't think we're that much different."

Joan stiffened. "Do not go there."

The Long Watchman just stared back.

"Do *not* go there," Joan yelled. "We are nothing alike! You are a stone-cold killer! Do you think we have anything in common because you used to be my age? You're an assassin! You're a murderer! You fight for murderers! I could never be anything like you!"

The Long Watchman tilted her head. "I see that you don't notch your gun. That's good. And yet you have thirty-four confirmed kills over the past three months."

Joan said nothing.

"Yeah, the FEN have been counting." The Long Watchman leaned forward. "You've taken shots that I'd be hard-pressed to make, so I think there are things in common there."

"Really?" Joan let out a short, sharp laugh. "How many notches would be on your gun if *you* kept score?"

The Long Watchman looked Joan in the eye. "Three hundred and ten."

Facing that one-eyed stare, Joan could not help but shudder.

The Long Watchman looked away, then leaned back. "When did you become a sniper?"

Joan glared. "Take a wild guess."

The woman chuckled. "Yeah. I know. But how long have you been a sharpshooter? When did you realize you had the talent?"

Memories hit Joan, though she tried to shut them out. Walking with her father on the shale lands, the Weddell Sea and the Southern Ocean in the distance. Viewing through the scope, catching a glimpse of a tail and twitching whiskers. Staring into the middle distance, she said, "My dad took me out hunting for spinifex and plains mice. Sometimes, kiwis." Despite herself, she smiled. "He taught me everything about the gun: how to assemble it, respect it, and use it safely." She heard the click of parts connecting and smelled the tang of polish. "Then I hit the first target I shot at. I hit shots he couldn't. He was astounded, then proud."

"So, they put you on hunting detail?" asked the Long Watchman.

Joan nodded. "I also signed up for the defence militia."

"So, you've been a sniper since you could hold a gun."

"No." Joan faced the Watchman. "I didn't have to be. Not until you FEN attacked us!"

"But it started with the hunting," said the woman. "The moment they realized you were good at killing animals from a distance, somebody thought about putting you to work killing people."

"Nobody put me to work!" Joan's voice rose. "I volunteered! And only for hunting!"

The Long Watchman gave her a baleful glance. "But people suggested that you volunteer, correct? Same here. Though they made that suggestion more forcefully."

"That's different," Joan snapped. "I'm defending myself, my country. You're the invader here. You shot first!"

The woman smirked. "I'm pretty sure you took the first shot at me."

"You know what I mean!"

"I do."

Silence descended. After a moment, the Long Watchman fished through her pack and brought out another ration bar. Joan's stomach growled, but she maintained her glare as the woman broke the bar in half, took a bite out of one, and tossed the other to Joan. Joan fed a bite to Jed and ate the rest.

"Why are you trying to be nice?" Joan asked. "Do you think that makes up for . . . for everything?"

"I'm not trying to be anything," the woman replied. "You're hungry. I have food. I give you some of mine. That's the way things should be."

"And yet," said Joan. "Do you expect me to be grateful?"

"No."

"Do you expect us to fall in line with these little shows of compassion?" Joan snapped. "I saw the FEN delivering carrots; is that supposed to make up for the killings, taking over our homes, our lives?"

The Long Watchman stared at Joan evenly. "Would you rather that the FEN let you starve?"

"I would rather you left us alone!"

"That's not up to me."

"Then why the hell are you here?" Joan yelled. "What did we ever do to you? We were trading with each other! We were coexisting! Why did you have to—" She shuddered as the memory of the rocket blast struck her thoughts. The vanishing father and child. The red mist in the window. She focused on the Long Watchman and bared her teeth. "Why?"

The woman's mouth quirked up into a sad smile. "I can't speak for the Federation."

"You just kill for them."

The moment froze. The woman's eyes narrowed. She fished her ocular implant from her pocket and clicked it in place beneath her eyepatch.

Joan stared with grim satisfaction. "Back on the clock?"

Jed let out a low growl.

The woman took out another ration bar and unwrapped it. She didn't split it and share it this time. "Coexistence is not enough for them; it never has been. Tolerance terrifies them. They want control. Maybe because of the chaos of the past fifty years, I don't know, but that's what they want."

"They, they, they," Joan parroted. She jabbed a finger across the fire. She winced as she jostled her broken wrist. "*You* pull the trigger for them. If you are not they, what are you doing, doing their dirty work?"

"I have a son."

Joan glanced at the woman's shirt pocket and the photograph inside, but the Long Watchman didn't pull it out.

The woman leaned forward, rubbing her forehead. "I haven't seen him for seven years. Not since they drafted him. But they send me postcards that he's signed."

Silence descended. The wind howled outside the cave mouth.

"So, that's how they hold you," said Joan.

"That's one way," the Long Watchman replied. "They have many others, not the least of which is that they have more than enough people to follow orders and stop you if you try to defy them."

Joan stared at the woman for a long moment. Finally, she looked away, saying nothing. Jed sidled up next to her.

"No comment?" said the Long Watchman.

"What is there to say?" Joan replied. "I have quislings at home. I have cowards around the world, and that's why we're here."

The Long Watchman stiffened. "I'm not a coward."

Joan's mouth quirked up. "I didn't specifically say you were."

"I had no choice."

"Just following orders."

The Long Watchman leaned forward. "Why do you resist? You're a hell of a sniper, but you're one woman against an invading army. Against the world. The FEN has everything. They've re-established the World Government. They have their spies; they have their police. They have me and people like me. All that you have left is you. It's over. You lost. Why do you keep fighting?"

Joan looked the Long Watchman in the eye. "Why did you stop?"

The Long Watchman glared at Joan. Joan glared back. But neither said anything. Joan's gaze drooped away as her arm twinged, and fatigue and boredom set in. The howling wind filled her mind and senses.

Then suddenly, through the wind, the Long Watchman spoke up. "Every month, they send me postcards."

Joan looked up.

The Long Watchman continued. "Just blank cards that my

son has signed—not even pictures of where he's serving. Not even drawings. They've done it once a month since they drafted us both, me to the sharpshooters, him to the infantry. Every month, he signs them and nothing more."

Joan said nothing, but she listened. The Long Watchman sat hunched, eye unfocused, staring at the cave floor. The silence stretched. Finally, Joan could stand it no longer. "What happened?"

The Long Watchman looked up at Joan. "This time, he wrote to me." She pulled a card from her pocket—not the laminated photograph. She tossed it over the fire, where it landed in Joan's lap.

Joan picked it up. The Long Watchman took a shuddering breath. "He said he was proud of me."

Joan glanced over the card, the youthful but neat strokes of the pencil, the name signed with a flourish. *You bring glory to the Federation. You bring glory to Mother Earth.*

Joan stared at the card, then at the Long Watchman. Then she got up and held it out to the woman over the fire.

"They threatened to take him from me if I didn't do their bidding." The Long Watchman snatched the postcard. "They threatened to kill him." She swung her hand up, and Joan was sure she'd fling the postcard in the fire, but instead, she sat frozen. Finally, she tucked the postcard into her pocket. "They didn't kill him, but they still took him from me."

Silence descended again and stayed. Outside, the wind howled and the snow swirled.

JOAN STARTED awake to see light entering the cave. It was eerily quiet. It took her a minute to realize that the wind had stopped. She sat up and blinked as the splint fell away from her wrist, leaving a pale patch of skin. She blinked and pushed up her sleeve. She flexed her wrist and fingers. No pain. Her fingers worked as well as before.

She looked across the campfire, which was now out, the cans of Sterno packed away. She looked to the cave mouth and saw the Long Watchman standing with her back to Joan, staring out, silhouetted against a sky that was turning blue, edging towards orange.

The Long Watchman turned and faced her. "Hey."

Beside Joan, Jed growled low, but the Long Watchman ignored him. She nodded over her shoulder. "The weather's changed, and the sun's coming up."

"I can see that," said Joan.

The woman had her gun in her hand. It just hung there, but it was still in her hand. Joan eyed it.

"I need you to understand something," said the Long Watchman. "I chased you across this wilderness for what? Days? I took many shots at you. Not one of them hit. Did you ever wonder about that?"

Joan's brow furrowed. "I thought you were bracketing."

"I don't bracket." The Long Watchman gestured at her implant. "I just hit."

"You were herding me," said Joan.

"Yes."

"Why?"

"I needed to have this conversation," the Long Watchman replied. "The thing is . . . reinforcements are coming. Listen."

Joan listened. The air was so still, she thought she'd gone deaf until she heard the distant creak of the remnant glacier retreating, a stone slipping into the glacial lake, and beyond that . . .

She felt it in her chest before hearing it: a distant, steady drumbeat, rising like dread—the sound of quadrocopters.

Then, with a bellow, one rose over the mountain pass, just ahead of the Sun.

The Long Watchman stepped to the rocks where they'd left their clothes to dry and picked up Joan's grey camo. She looked at her. "It's time to get dressed."

TWO QUADROCOPTERS DESCENDED the shale lands alongside the remnant glacier. One landed, and a dozen soldiers strode out. Guns ready, they made for the cave.

The one in the lead stepped forward, hands tightening on the gun, while his colleagues followed, casually stepping behind him.

"Grey Bullet!" he shouted. "We have you surrounded! Come out! Now!"

For a moment, nothing happened.

"Grey Bullet!" the soldier yelled. "This is your last warning!" Over his shoulder, he added, "Get a grenade ready."

They froze as they heard a scrabble of stones. A grey figure emerged from the darkness of the cave mouth, dressed head to toe in camo gear, arms out, rifle in hand, pointing down. The soldiers backed up, guns ready.

The Grey Bullet stepped down from the cave mouth.

There came the sound of a compressor firing. A red spout erupted from the Grey Bullet's chest. She let out a strangled scream and sank to her knees. She struggled for breath, let out another gurgled yell, and fell to her side, staring up at the sky. Her gun slipped from her fingers and rattled down the shale.

A white figure emerged from the cave, rifle in hand. "The bounty is mine," rasped the Long Watchman. He slipped an implant into his coat pocket and slipped on an eyepatch beneath his cowl.

The soldiers looked from the dead body to the sniper and back, then lowered their guns and approached.

A flurry of hair, paws, and teeth leaped from the cave

mouth and charged at the soldiers, barking furiously. It straddled the prone body and bared its teeth, snapping at anybody
who came close. The soldiers staggered back, momentarily
startled, before bringing up their guns.

The Long Watchman swung up her gun at the dog. "Back!
Get back!"

The dog raised his hackles, brought his head low to the
ground, and snarled.

The Long Watchman took a quick step forward, stabbing
the air with the muzzle of his gun. "I said get back!"

For a moment, everyone stood poised. Then, slowly at first,
the dog backed up. It looked at the body, whined once, and
then bounded away.

The Long Watchman watched him go. Then he faced the
soldiers. "What's next?"

A LAND SPEEDER arrived to take them back to the Port of
Endurance. The Long Watchman sat in the middle, in his own
row, as the soldiers talked quietly among themselves. No one
looked at him. The driver glanced back, but the sergeant in the
passenger seat nudged her and glared meaningfully, and the
driver kept her eyes forward.

The Long Watchman said nothing, gloved fingers fussing
over rosary beads.

As they reached the harbour, a quadrocopter loomed
ahead. It let out a hoot as it approached. The Long Watchman
stiffened a moment, then relaxed. It wasn't a sonic blast. The
quadrocopter lowered, a gangway opened, and dock workers
began to connect it to the dock. A man in a well-fitted suit
climbed down and walked up the deck toward them. He shook
the Long Watchman's hand. "Well done."

"Is this it?" the Long Watchman asked. "Am I done here?"

The well-dressed man shrugged and nodded. "With the Grey Bullet dead, the Politburo believes the remaining resistance in McMurdo will crumble. We won more through demoralization than bullets by taking this place so quickly. Shock and awe, they called it in the before days. It's why we had to act fast on the Bullet. He was becoming quite a symbol."

"And now he becomes a martyr," said the Long Watchman.

The man laughed. "Martyrs don't aim nearly so well." The soldiers laughed as well. The Long Watchman stayed silent, and the laughter faded. The silence lengthened awkwardly.

"So, where do I go next?" asked the Long Watchman.

The well-dressed man coughed. "I'm not sure. My orders are to get you back to Ushuaia, where you'll be flown to Rio for a debrief. I've heard there's been unrest in old Amazonia. Maybe you'll be sent there."

"So, back to the Federation," the Long Watchman muttered. "Good."

"Definitely good," said the well-dressed man. He stepped aside and waved the Long Watchman forward. "Get on board. I have some paperwork to complete, and we'll leave soon after that."

The Long Watchman nodded and watched as the well-dressed man went off with the soldiers to the port offices. He walked toward the dock, stopping at the edge of the water and looking up at the quadrocopter that would take him home.

Then he lifted his eyepatch, glanced around to make sure he was alone, and whistled.

Jed bounded out from behind crates and ran up to the white-clad figure. She bent down and scratched his ears as he nuzzled her.

Joan stood up.

"I'm done," the Long Watchman had said. "All I can ever be is a weapon to them. They know that because of what they have to hold

over me. But I'm done being their weapon. I'm taking it out of their hands."

Joan pulled a photograph from her pocket. It showed a mother hugging her young son, both smiling at the camera.

"Find him," the Long Watchman had said. "He's in their army, being fed their propaganda bullshit. Get him out if he's willing to go. Stop him from hurting anyone if he's not. Either way, make sure he's no longer an asset to the FEN."

Joan had looked up from the photo. "What do I get in return?"

The Long Watchman had looked hard at her. "Whatever you can take. Whatever it is, I hope it's a lot and that you rip it out of them painfully."

Joan looked up at the quadrocopter. "I just have to know where to sting."

She replaced the eyepatch, pulled up her hood, and patted Jed. Together, they hurried up the steps into the quadrocopter.

An hour later, the quadrocopter sailed toward the Southern Ocean, carrying the Grey Bullet into the heart of the Federation.

ABOUT THE AUTHORS

Phoebe Barton is a queer trans science fiction writer. Her short fiction has appeared in *Analog* and *Lightspeed*, and her story "The Mathematics of Fairyland" won the Aurora Award for Best Short Story in 2022. She lives with her family, a robot, and multiple typewriters in Hamilton, Ontario, Canada. Find her online at www.phoebebartonsf.com.

Kate Blair is a British-Canadian author. Her first YA adult novel, *Transferral*, was optioned for television and nominated for the MYRCA, Snow Willow, and Sunburst Awards. Her second, *Tangled Planet*, was optioned for film and longlisted for a Sunburst Award. Her middle-grade fantasy, *The Magpie's Library*, was an OLA Best Bet and was nominated for a Northern Lights Award. Her latest YA, *A Mist Of Memories*, came out in May 2023.

James Bow is the author of six novels, from the YA fantasy Unwritten Books trilogy to the urban fantasy *The Night Girl* to the Prix Aurora Award-winning YA SF novel *Icarus Down* to his most recent book (and first novel of the Silent Earth Sequence), *The Sun Runners*. He is a science fiction and fantasy fan in general and a *Doctor Who* fan in particular, having written and edited fan fiction, which is how he got into editing this anthology in the first place. By day, he is a communications officer for the *rare* **Charitable Research Reserve**. He is also the husband, writing partner, and great big cheerleader of Erin Bow, whom he lives with along with their two children, Wayfinder and Eleanor, in Waterloo Region. Learn more at www.bowjamesbow.ca.

Cameron Dixon lives in Toronto and works in media accessibility, providing closed captions and described video for television programs. He wrote this story shortly before seeing a once-in-a-lifetime total solar eclipse. He'd like to think that was the Moon saying thanks. It wasn't, but come on, give him this.

Mark Richard Francis started life on this pale blue dot in the mid-1960s. As a child, he vastly preferred Mr. Spock over Sesame Street and was engrossed in the works of Asimov, Bradbury, Clarke, and Heinlein before he was ten. After completing community college, he started an unfortunately short writing career in the public relations department of a major Toronto teaching hospital. Economic necessity grappled him into an IT position for twenty years, which led to a managerial position in a massive automated warehouse complex. Leaving behind that job and three grown-up children, he left the GTA during the pandemic to settle in a rural home adjacent to Fredericton, NB, with his spouse, Bonnie. Tired of technology, he is back in school, studying accounting. He prefers writing. "The Musk-hole King" is his first published work of fiction.

Joanna Karaplis is the author of *Fractured: Happily Never After?* and *Timbertown Tales: Chester Gets a Pet*. She began her career in the Canadian book publishing industry, working at publishing houses in her hometown of Vancouver and then in Toronto. She now works in communications and lives in Toronto with her family. Her non-book hobbies include swing dancing and practising other languages (Japanese and Spanish).

Kari Maaren is a Canadian writer, cartoonist, musician, and academic whose first novel, *Weave a Circle Round*, won the Copper Cylinder Award and was a finalist for the Andre Norton Nebula Award and the Sunburst Award. She has a completed webcomic, *West of Bathurst*, and an active one, the award-winning *It Never Rains*. She is fond of bewildering stories full of time loops, references to nineteenth-century poetry, and a cavalier defiance of the laws of physics.

Fiona Moore is a BSFA and World Fantasy Award finalist, writer, and academic whose work has appeared in *Clarkesworld*, *Asimov*, *Interzone*, and five consecutive editions of *The Best of British SF*. Her most recent non-fiction is the book *Management Lessons from* Game of Thrones. Her publications include one novel; numerous articles in journals such as *Foundation*; guidebooks to *Blake's Seven*, *The Prisoner*, *Battlestar Galactica* and *Doctor Who*; three stage plays, and four audio plays. When not writing, she is a Professor of Business Anthropology at Royal Holloway, University of London. She lives in Southwest England with a tortoiseshell cat that is bent on world domination. More details, and free content, can be found at www.fiona-moore.com, and she is @drfionamoore on all social media.

Ira Nayman is a humour writer who combines his preferred genre with a healthy dose of speculative fiction. He is the author of eight published novels, and thirty published short stories. For three years, Ira was the editor of *Amazing Stories* magazine. His first post-*Amazing* editing gig, an anthology called *The Dance*, was published in early 2024.

Kate Orman is best known for her *Doctor Who* TV tie-in novels, but is also proud of her original science fiction, published in *Realms of Fantasy*, *Cosmos*, and *IZ Digital*. Her goal is to publish an original SF novel. Her hobbies include ancient Egypt and the search for exoplanets and exomoons. She lives in Sydney, Australia, with her husband and co-author, Jonathan Blum.

Jeff Szpirglas is the author of more than thirty books, mostly for young readers and ranging in subject matter from vomit and bodily functions to scary stories. He has worked at CTV Television, and was an editor at *Chirp*, *chickaDEE*, and *Owl* magazines, and is a regular contributor to *Rue Morgue Magazine*. He is married to (and sometimes writes books with) Danielle Saint-Onge when he's not busy being a dad to kids and pets or teaching grade school. He lives in Kitchener, Ontario, but his heart lies in the caverns of Mercury.

KICKSTARTER THANK-YOUS

We are grateful for the contributions of our Kickstarter supporters, without whom this anthology would not be possible. Thanks go out to:

Jolene Armstrong
Paul Bristow (UK)
Eric Bow
Edward Brain
Elaine Chen
Sean Corcoran
Karl Cyr
Colleen Feeney
Clive Francis
Mark Richard Francis
Robert Fraser
Amy Heidman
Colleen Hillerup
Andrew W.H. House
Cathy Green
Marguerite Kenner and Alasdair Stuart
Owin Lambeck
Brian Lindsay
Donna Lyons
Kari Maaren
Neil Marsh
Melanie Marttila

Charles & Heather Martin
Greg McElhatton
James Davis Nicoll
Darwin O'Connor
Ruth Ann Orlansky
Ed Orman
Natalie Peck
D.K. Perlmutter
K. Pocock
Linda Ponting
Mary Jo Rabe
Terry Rudden
Matt Spoon
Jeff Szpirglas
The Tonjes Family
Candace Waldron

. . . and two other individuals who wished to remain anonymous.

Thank you!

BOOKS

Founded by award-winning author Edward Willett, Endless Sky Books assists authors with publishing all kinds of books, from children's books to poetry to novels to nonfiction. Select titles, like this one, are released under the Endless Sky Books imprint.

Find out more about Endless Sky Books on our website, endless-sky-books.com, and visit our sister publisher, Shadowpaw Press, at shadowpawpress.com.